THE PRINCESS
WILL SAVE YOU

THE
PRINCESS
WILL SAVE
YOU

SARAH HENNING

TOR

THE PRINCESS WILL SAVE YOU

Copyright © 2020 by Sarah Henning

A Tor Teen Book
Published by Tom Doherty Associates
120 Broadway
New York, NY 10271

www.tor-forge.com

Tor® is a registered trademark of Macmillan Publishing Group, LLC.

The Library of Congress Cataloging-in-Publication Data
is available upon request.

ISBN 978-1-250-23742-2 (hardcover)
ISBN 978-1-250-23741-5 (ebook)

Our books may be purchased in bulk for promotional, educational, or
business use. Please contact your local bookseller or the Macmillan Corporate
and Premium Sales Department at 1-800-221-7945, extension 5442,
or by email at MacmillanSpecialMarkets@macmillan.com.

First Edition: 2020

Printed in the United States of America

0 9 8 7 6 5 4 3 2 1

To Justin—
I'll be after you in a heartbeat if you're ever
stolen away by pirates.

And to Nate and Amalia—
yes, this is a kissing book. Again. Sorry.

They met as most friends do.

Right place, right age, right interests in common.

Picking up sticks in the dirt, calling them swords. Bumps and bruises and shared smiles.

And then when it came time to separate, suddenly it felt impossible. The newness dissolved over the shared hours into the seed of something more.

Something shaped in a way that forever stretched where the newness ended.

Something that, later, felt very much like love.

THE PRINCESS
WILL SAVE YOU

CHAPTER
1

❧

THE whisper and clang of steel rang out over the foothills of Ardenia, a princess and a pauper meeting swords.

Left. Right. Cross. High cut. Mid-cross. Hanging parry. Stab.

"You've been practicing," the princess accused the boy with a laugh that played across the little meadow they called theirs. The palace grounds of the Itspi had plenty of rolling land but not much that provided privacy. But this patch of mostly flat earth surrounded on three sides by fragrant juniper trees was one they'd claimed long ago as children.

It was an open secret within the castle that Princess Amarande of Ardenia spent far too much of her time here and with this boy. Luca. It hadn't been anything to worry about until recently.

"Simply trying to avoid a devastating injury."

"Come, Luca, I think you want to do more than avoid injury." She tilted her head as their swords met at chest height, their faces and flushed cheeks inches apart. They were dressed alike—training breeches, tunic, chest and wrist armor, but their heads bare. The princess's auburn hair had already begun to abandon her hasty braid, swirling in curled wisps about her face. "I think you want to win."

At this, Luca only grinned, dimples flashing as he lunged forward. His sword—blunt for practice but still hard-as-nails Basilican steel—tapped Amarande against the waist, right under the protection of her chest plate. A warning of what could be done for real.

"Always, Princess."

"Then let's make things more exciting, shall we?"

She'd phrased it as a question, but Luca knew better. Better than anyone. Luca, who ran her father's stable. Who had as much a right to call the palace home as Amarande herself. He drew his sword back, high guard stance and ready to block—just as General Koldo had shown him in a moment of pity for the boy who dared tussle with the Warrior King's daughter.

Still, he wasn't quick enough.

Before his sword was in place, Amarande had bent to her boot and in a lightning strike launched a small knife straight for his face. It wasn't a dull practice blade. It was real—the one she'd carried since before she'd learned her letters. Lessons from King Sendoa's soldiers had always been just as important as anything her tutors managed to teach her. Blunt swords could bruise and hack, but this knife could split, slice, cut.

Luca moved just in time, sword useless and weak hand up, fingers quick enough to catch the last inch of the knife's hilt. This he'd practiced, too.

In the space of a blink, he had the blade flipped in his palm and shot it right back at her. He aimed to miss, of course, but it was a left-handed throw and not as accurate. Thus, it came far too close, snagging the leather of her shoulder guard and sending her flat on her back in the grass.

"Ama," he whispered, dropping his sword. Taking a tentative step toward her.

Again, a mistake.

From the ground, Amarande swung a leg hard, kicking his feet out from under him. Luca flew up and then back, landing in a heap, the wind and her name knocked out of him. Before he could even attempt to right himself, the princess was sitting atop his stomach, her knees locking his arms against his heaving ribs. One arm ran stiff across his chest plate, right under his collarbone, further pinning him in place; the other held the knife at striking distance.

Before his next breath, he could be dead.

"You *have* been practicing."

She said it with admiration, but a tight-lipped type of triumph crossed the princess's face. She examined her prey, trapped as he was—it was amazing what small but mighty could do to a boy even as strong as this one.

A smear of dirt streaked across Luca's forehead and up into his short black hair. Sweat ran in a single rivulet from one temple, snaking around his long lashes and down his cheek, pausing only briefly to dip into the shadow of a dimple as he gritted his teeth in a smile. His eyes regarded the knife in the princess's hand, an inch from his throat.

And then those eyes, the golden color of sun on snow at dawn, lifted to hers and Amarande felt her heart melt like wax near a flame. The fighting tension of her body fled until the knife was still an inch from his throat but not a threat. Luca's fingers brushed her cheek, sweeping a lock of windblown hair behind her ear.

Growing up, the privacy of the meadow had given room for her to share lemon cake stolen from the kitchens and for him to calm her when the king went off on another journey with his regiments and beloved Koldo, keeping the kingdoms of the Sand and Sky safe by answering every ally's call. But for the last year, there'd been *this*.

Something almost tangible sat between them—responsibility, expectations, rules. The same inescapable things that had rendered the amusement in their earlier words heavy and misshapen.

Amarande straightened, removing her arm from his chest. Luca raised himself onto his elbows. Their eyes remained locked as his lips parted, and Amarande wondered if he'd actually say it. That he felt it, too, and that she wasn't the only one carrying an unspeakable hope thick in her gut.

Instead, he said, "Of course I practice—I fight *you*."

As she found the words to answer him, a shout went up from well beyond their meadow, the call of welcome bells clanging across the grounds. Clearly Amarande's father had returned from his solstice charity, empty-handed after delivering fruit and bread to mining families along the Ardenian border with the Torrent up to where it joined with Pyrenee. She would have to go soon—wash up for dinner by his side, listening to stories of sweet-faced mountain children running down dirt tracks after his horse, songs trailing. Someday, when the Warlord no longer reigned, maybe he'd let her go with him.

But for now, for this moment, she wanted to be nowhere other than with Luca.

Yet they were interrupted again—a rider coming over the hill. Amarande's training came back to her in a rush, her father having engrained it in her since the day he put a tiny wooden sword in her hand and began to share the things all living warriors knew.

Beware or be dead.

Make the first mark.

A warrior made is a warrior alive.

The first tenet whispered in her ear, and the princess shot to her feet, the abandoned knife now clutched in her fingertips. The castle grounds weren't dangerous, but preparation paid off.

The rider scrambled down the steepest part of the hill, a tough grade before hitting the flat of their meadow. Not armored—in riding gear only—he flew toward them on a dappled mare with wild legs. It was then that Amarande recognized that it wasn't a he, it was a *she*—General Koldo, the king's best friend and second. She was the leader of his army as much as she was Amarande's surrogate mother, and the princess had never seen her with a note of fear on her sun-mottled face. And yet there it was as she came closer, braid flying out behind her as the horse's hooves kicked up plumes of rust-dirt dust.

"Ama!" The dam broke on the panic rising within Amarande.

Koldo called her Ama in private, alone, but never in front of anyone else, even Luca, who used the nickname in the same way. With the general, she was always "Princess" in a space such as this.

The fact that Koldo broke her own protocol was just as terrifying as the fear that rode her tone.

Luca felt it, too, tensing at Amarande's side. His fingers brushed hers as if he wanted to grab them, to give her an anchor for the blow that they both could see coming.

Koldo reached them and before she even dismounted, the princess registered tear tracks on her dusty cheeks. Amarande's heart began to fail before the words were even out, breath seeping out of her lungs, until all of her had evaporated into the mountain air. She watched the words fall from Koldo's lips outside of herself, above, shattered.

"The king is dead."

CHAPTER
2

❧❦❧

IN a single breath, everything had changed.

One moment King Sendoa was sipping from his ancient water-skin, the next a gruff cough, and death. The whole of it so quick, he fell from his horse's saddle in a royal heap, no one fast enough to realize he needed saving, let alone catch him.

It was the king's heart, some said, drumming to a stop. Maybe his blood, gone haywire in his brain. Or his lungs, an old illness creeping up in the altitude.

Amarande didn't believe any of it.

When the dust and chaos of that day settled and the next came, General Koldo stood in the too-bright light of midafternoon in the sitting room of the princess's chambers. Amarande was curled up, barefoot on the golden cushions of a long divan, still in the clothing she was wearing when it all crumbled. Only her chest plate and boots were missing, ripped off the second she'd thrown herself into her quarters.

She'd begged Luca to stay, and he did, with her at every moment, only leaving to tend to the horses. He greeted Koldo with a nod from his spot on the other end of the divan.

"The Royal Council requests your presence, Ama." Koldo's voice wasn't what one would call soft or gentle. It was battle tested and measured. But just the drop of her nickname at the end of the sentence made the princess want to run into Koldo's arms and stain her full garnet-and-gold regalia with tears. The word "Ama" on the general's lips would forever sound different, no matter how many times she'd said it before. "If you do not feel well enough, I can propose a time tomorrow."

The princess swallowed, willing her parched tongue to work. She wasn't accustomed to the way so many tears could leave a person with nothing left.

"No, no, I'll go."

Koldo had met with the council only an hour after returning to the castle with the news of Sendoa's death on her lips. In many ways she was closer to the king than even Amarande herself—if she could discuss castle business after such a shock, so could Amarande.

It was what leaders did.

Though Amarande wanted Luca to come with them, it was not allowed, and so he departed to ready the stable for the hordes of equine funeral guests. When he was gone, the maids appeared, and the princess shrugged on a clean dress: shiny black with a lace bodice and long sleeves, as was the style. Rather than dainty slippers, she strapped on her boots, the knife she kept there pressed into her skin in a way that grounded her. The scuffed toes of each boot peeked out from the dress's hem, but comfort and preparation trumped fashion.

The Royal Council of Ardenia met in the North Tower of the Itspi, the whole northern wing set aside for matters of state. The glittering sandstone walls of her home pressed in on Amarande as she walked shoulder to shoulder with Koldo. The familiar corners and edges felt like both too much and not enough. She could relish the Itspi's embrace or be crushed under the weight of the walls— either was possible. Nothing felt right without her father here.

The great garnet-studded doors of the council room were thrown open. As the princess and the general entered, they were greeted by Councilor Satordi, de facto leader of the council and the Warrior King's top advisor.

"Princess Amarande, General Koldo, welcome," Satordi said from his seat. Amarande had always seen all members of the council stand when her father entered the room. Yet Satordi and the other two councilors, silver-haired Garbine and rosy-cheeked Joseba, stayed seated at the table that dominated the room. The three of them were the image of melted candle tapers at the great table, with their gold-and-white silken robes weeping from their shoulders. Behind them, tapestries of kings past covered the walls in dark-woven judgment. The only illumination was backlight from windows, ringing the council in the halo of late afternoon.

The councilor gestured before him. "Please, sit, and we shall begin."

There were chairs carved with the thick tracing of a tiger's head—Ardenia's sigil—meant for guests, but they were apart from the table, not pulled up as for equals to the council. Amarande's stomach dropped at the implications. Still, she didn't make a statement by pulling a chair close to the table, nor did she stride over to the chair reserved for her father, on the north curve of the oval.

In her estimation, no man would ever be worthy of sitting there.

Though deprived of sleep and sustenance, Amarande willed herself to stand before them, rather than sit apart as a guest. Koldo stayed pin straight by her side but slightly behind, much like she did when accompanying Sendoa into any lion's den.

When Satordi realized they weren't going to sit, he folded his fingers and continued. "We have much to discuss."

Yes, they did.

First and foremost: succession.

The laws had it that in the Kingdom of Ardenia, succession fell along the male line, but that possibility had ended with her father. There was no male heir of which to speak—no uncles, cousins, nephews. Only the sixteen-year-old girl King Sendoa had raised in his image in the years since Amarande's mother gained the nickname the Runaway Queen.

Because of it, with Sendoa's last breath, Amarande had not only lost her father; she'd also lost her independence.

The laws were clear: To rule, she must be wed.

Meaning her title and Ardenia itself were now items to be bought, bartered, stolen.

For the good of her people.

For the gain of valuable pastures and stunning mountains, for diamonds mined for trade and gold pieces, for armored men and women whose only peer was death itself.

And no king in the Sand and Sky could let such a prize go to another.

On the great table that sat between the council and its princess lay a scroll, its wax seal crumbling, freshly opened but as recognizable as it was predictable. A marriage contract, likely from their closest neighbor, Pyrenee.

Soon there would be three, the other kingdoms of the union—Basilica and Myrcell—sending riders ahead of their royal funeral processions, jockeying to gain the council's attention. *Stars*, she nearly expected a contract from the mysterious Warlord who ran the Torrent, because the windfall was too delicious—no kingdom on the continent of the Sand and Sky had left a sole female heir in a thousand years.

The king had not invited her to the council room for much of her childhood, but he'd made it a point to bring her along in the past year, extending her leadership training beyond the sparring arena and weapons armory and into the political landscape. Therefore, the council knew her better now than ever, and she them. Still, Satordi's demeanor, though respectful, had the quality of a mentor who wished for his student to listen, not participate. That, combined with the certitude that the council had purposefully not stood or placed a chair at the table for her, set a particular tone.

And so, despite her exhaustion, Princess Amarande decided to set her own.

The princess's eyes swept from the marriage contract to Satordi's face. "Before we discuss matters of succession, I believe we first must address the formation of an investigation into King Sendoa's murder."

The shoulders under each of the councilors' robes stiffened. As usual, Satordi spoke for the group. In Amarande's time in this room with her father, it had become clear to her that proximity to power had made this man believe he had more of it than he truly did.

"Princess Amarande," Satordi began, that tone of his sharpening. "You are well aware that the exalted Medikua Aritza has examined the king's body and has found no evidence of foul play, as seconded by General Koldo, who was by his side the entire day and did not witness anything untoward."

Amarande didn't bother to spare a glance toward the general. Yes, she knew that a natural death was Koldo's official estimation, and that she had been the one who watched the king's life leave him in real time. The councilor was using Koldo here, dangling their love for each other in front of the princess and hoping she'd bite.

He should've known better.

"Medikua Aritza is a gifted healer and indeed exalted, but she is not aware of all the possible methods of attack." This was true—the highest medicine woman in the land made it a point not to know about political intrigue purely for the sake of wanting to be completely unbiased when someone threw gold pieces at her for a potion. "General Koldo is a gifted warrior, but that doesn't mean she's always correct. Even to her experienced eye, the stoppage of a heart from poison would appear the same as the stoppage of a heart from natural causes."

Koldo nodded, her long brunette braid slithering across her garnet cloak broach. "Council, that is an accurate assessment. I have never witnessed a man die from natural causes. I agree with the princess on this matter."

The general took a slight step forward so that she and the princess stood precisely shoulder to shoulder before the table, a front.

"I realize that both of you were closer to the king than I." Councilor Garbine stood, the fire within her a low, ever-present boil. "And therefore I realize it may be as difficult as his death itself to admit to yourselves that sometimes devastating moments happen in unspectacular ways."

Amarande and Koldo said nothing.

The gray-haired woman smiled at the princess, all the heat in her eyes, her hands brought in front almost as if in prayer to the stars. "Your Highness, did you want your father to come home with a sword run through his back? Relieved of his head? Or not at all, turned to ashes in a Torrent fire pit?"

Amarande swallowed. "No, but I find any of those scenarios easier to believe than that the strongest man in the Sand and Sky keeled over in his saddle from nothing at all."

Garbine's lips parted in reply, but Satordi held out a hand to stop her, standing himself with an impatient sigh. "We cannot afford to upset every kingdom on the continent chasing down something we cannot prove. It will disturb our allies."

Garbine and Joseba nodded, the long game playing out in their minds. The contract on the table seemed to catch all the windows' light.

"Are we to simply accept what happened?" Amarande's voice was still calm and polite, but something was lit from the ashes of who she'd been since the news, and it burned beneath.

"Yes, Princess," Satordi answered, clipped. "At this moment in time we will accept it because we have much more pressing matters to discuss."

Amarande hadn't thought her request a difficult one—in fact, she'd believed it would be the natural course—and therefore hadn't planned for a fight. But her body was suddenly ready for one. The princess drove her heels into the marble tile, strong legs grounding her further, all muscles rigid from her calves—the right one tense against the knife in her boot—to the curve of her jaw. "I see nothing more important."

Satordi rapped a knuckle on the table and blinked at Amarande.

"Because *you* refuse to see. There is much more to ruling than what is right in front of your face." He threw his arms wide, dark brows pulled tight. "Your father's death is in the past. The future of Ardenia needs your focus now. I implore you. You want to be a ruler? Act like it. Hear me."

Amarande's jaw clenched. She said nothing. Koldo stood silent at her side.

After a pause long enough to ensure he'd regained control, Satordi continued, immediately addressing the matters he thought more pressing. "We have received a generous proposal for your hand from Pyrenee. It is simply a preliminary offer and more will likely come. The real negotiations will begin once each royal party arrives for King Sendoa's funeral."

The princess took a thin breath through her nose before delivering her stony reply. "I'm not marrying."

"Why resist marriage, Princess?" Garbine asked. "That is your responsibility as princess of the Sand and Sky—it must happen eventually. Why not now, when your kingdom needs you?"

Easy for Garbine to say, when she'd chosen those robes over the ability to wed. Purposely giving up one's freedom to love was completely different from being born with it already stolen away. Even worse—what if acceptance of an offer meant not only no chance at love but also aligning herself with the nobility who had killed her father?

"Yes, my kingdom needs *me*. Not some usurper king, who may have had a hand in the death of his predecessor, all the while forcing his queen into a relationship that benefits only him. How is that good for Ardenia? How can a man chosen via contract and council have the best interests of Ardenia closer to his heart than myself? Surely my father worked with you to account for that—he wouldn't have allowed it."

Now Joseba stood—thick eyebrows knitted together, fingers twisted in a calm knot. He was barely older than the princess herself, and he'd only been a councilor since the death of his great-uncle two years hence. He was baby-faced and his innate kindness still intact, yet to be completely dismantled by Satordi. "Your father did not . . . object to the process, Princess."

"Because he didn't expect *to be murdered*," Amarande spat. Satordi gave an exasperated sigh, but the princess ignored it and continued. "I want time. I want what is best for my people. Change the law and allow me to rule outright, not rush into some marriage that will hand my father's beloved land and his daughter over to someone who only wants it for personal gain. Diamonds and soldiers and location—we all know what is so attractive to outsiders about our home."

Joseba pursed his lips before continuing, measured. "Time is a pleasant notion, Your Highness, but it doesn't shield Ardenia from its current vulnerability. Without a contract in place soon, Ardenia will be seen as headless—"

"'Seen' being the operative word, Councilor. Others' lack of vision is not our problem," the princess said, and then turned to the rest of the group. "We all know the Itspi's foundation consists of laws, decrees, and directives mixed with mortar and stone. Surely there's precedent for who rules after a king's death and before the marriage of his daughter? If not his own blood, then whom? If there's not precedence for that in enough statutes to swallow a millennium, surely my father had a plan. He always had a plan."

She looked each one of them in the eye. "What is his plan?"

After a long pause, Joseba's tongue stumbled over the words, though he knew the answer. "It's designated in the king's will that General Koldo be the regent."

The eye contact the three councilors made with Koldo told the princess that this was not a surprise to the general. It was, however, a surprise to her. This must have been discussed in the meeting they'd had in those hours after the news, while she was a wreck of shock, haunting her chambers with Luca by her side.

And no one, not even Koldo, had thought to tell her.

Amarande swallowed, face placid, not daring to give herself away with a sideways glance to the general. Still, she angled herself toward Koldo and reached up to give her a hearty pat on the back. "See there? We're far from headless. And with a female in charge of the throne. Was that so hard?"

She said it with all the confidence she could muster, thick with irony, though a tiny voice in her head wondered why her father hadn't simply assigned her regency and circumvented the whole succession problem. There had to be a reason, but at that moment Amarande was too relieved by Koldo's new reality to care.

The princess addressed the general. "General Koldo, as regent, you must agree that an investigation into King Sendoa's death is warranted before we rush into a marriage contract with possible suspects?"

"Of course. I will see to it at once."

"Thank you, General Koldo. You display such loyalty and leadership. The Kingdom of Ardenia is in debt of your service."

Three thin sighs came from behind the great table.

"Your Highness, we're still vulnerable," Joseba continued in his soft way, cheeks a ripe red. "Regency is meant to be a temporary solution. Not to mention outsiders will see this as martial law—unstable."

Amarande nearly laughed. "Was my father not called the Warrior King—the ruler of the most powerful army on the continent? Was that martial law?"

Satordi ignored the princess, continuing Joseba's argument. "Not to mention primitive. Reckless. Weak."

"*Weak,*" Amarande echoed, no longer able to hide her anger and disappointment. Every spark within her had become a flame, the haze of the past day burned off, her grief reinforcing her words, her stance, the directness of her tone. "The law is what makes us vulnerable, Councilor. Change the law. Allow a queen to rule in her own right."

Satordi couldn't allow that statement to stand. "Princess, you must marry. This is not up for discussion."

"My mother married for position and *left*. Left my father and *me* and never returned." All three faces behind the table closed up—the Runaway Queen was never spoken of. The king hadn't allowed it. Amarande speaking of her in front of them trotted a piece of King Sendoa into the room that his advisors never saw. To her surprise, Koldo tensed, too, though she knew all of this and more.

"Though he'd learned to love her, she'd never learned to love him. And it broke his soul to know that she couldn't bear life with him. He was not enough. *I* was not enough." Amarande's voice had become too loud in her own ears. She swallowed and reset, her tone quieter yet still fierce. Sharp. Splitting. "Never mind what her absence did to my childhood, because she taught me something. I will not give anyone my hand without love on both sides of the contract. I refuse to be broken for status or prodded by duty. *I* deserve that—*Ardenia* deserves that."

She took a step forward and wiped the contract off the polished table, letting it flutter to the marble tile. "If my father's *fine* choice of a regent is seen as weak, then change the law and let me lead. Marriage can wait."

Joseba scuttled around the table and lunged for the fallen contract, as if it would lose its validity if it sat discarded too long. Satordi spoke again as soon as the parchment was safe in the councilor's soft palms. "Your Highness, to amend the law, we must have the approval of the entire union of the Sand and Sky. It can't simply be changed on a whim."

"*Stars*, Satordi! You've had *fifteen years* of a ruler without a wife. *Fifteen years* of knowing a male heir wasn't in Ardenia's future. *Fifteen years* to get the union votes and rewrite the laws. Yet you didn't."

Yet my father didn't.

A new tendril of anger snaked up from the pit of Amarande's stomach, cold water on her flame. She took a deep breath.

"My father's blood flows in my veins—that's what is so precious to this kingdom. To this line. To these contracts. I have that blood—what does it matter if I'm a girl? What's more important? The blood or the law?"

Satordi stuttered, standard answer not getting the strongest start. "The laws of the paternal line were written centuries ago to fortify—"

"'Fortify' means to strengthen, does it not? How does this law strengthen the Ardenian position by handing our throne to someone who may have had a hand in murdering our king, rather than delivering it to a ruler of his own blood?"

Amarande let that sit for a moment, watching the council fumble for an answer that didn't come. "My father commanded the largest army in the Sand and Sky, and you're saying that, though I am his child, I can't do so because of my sex? Never mind the fact that my father installed *a woman* as my regent."

"Well—"

"Men do not have a monopoly on strength. My father believed that—Koldo was his second-in-command for a reason. And he made sure I knew that—or have you forgotten that my father trained me from the time I could walk to hold a sword, throw a knife, track prey?"

Satordi stiffened. "No one has forgotten that, Princess."

"Good. Then you know what you're up against if you want me to agree to this contract or any of the others you're awaiting. I will always fight for the future of Ardenia. And I expect this council and its regent to fight, too."

And with that, Princess Amarande turned on her boot heel— meeting adjourned. She nodded at Koldo, who tipped her chin back, and took for the now-closed doors while leaving the regent and the council with the only words she truly wanted them to remember.

"Change the law."

CHAPTER
3

❧

THEY did not change the law.

The contract did not disappear. It gained company. One from each kingdom, as Amarande expected.

Worse, within days the leaders of the other kingdoms of the Sand and Sky arrived, one by one.

Bear, Shark, Mountain Lion—Basilica, Myrcell, Pyrenee.

Each of them owed their crowns to King Sendoa, their sworn protector of the realm. The man who lent his army to quell the Warlord's raids from deep within the Torrent, to hunt down the pirates who haunted trade routes through the Divide that separated Pyrenee from Eritri, to clear mountain passes clogged with boulders after a hard snow.

All these people who got far more out of their alliance than Sendoa himself, coming to take more—his crown, his land, his legacy.

At least, that was Amarande's opinion.

She didn't want to see these people. These brutal, horrible, hungry people.

Not a one was good.

Domingu—the blue-eyed, craggy-faced king of iron-veined Basilica who'd lodged a blade in the back of his own brother fifty years ago for his crown. Amarande had no doubt that he'd kill the mother of his most recent children for a marriage that might buy him half of the Sand and Sky. His contract promised as much without saying so—that woman was his fifth wife, after all.

Akil—the boy king of Myrcell, with its lowland beaches snaking across the southern belt of the continent. Twenty and newly married, he'd traveled to the funeral alone, his wife conspicuously absent as her groom angled for a more enticing prospect. Akil had a nice smile and it made Amarande sick that he could wield it along with such cruelty. Did his queen mean nothing to him?

Renard, the first son of Ardenia's mountain neighbor, a year older and everything a prince should be—clean, respectful, teeth-achingly traditional. He was like a painting come to life and as uninteresting as a blank canvas. Still, he wasn't yet a king, his mother standing in as his regent until he turned eighteen. Amarande was bitter that Pyrenee—with approval from the Sand and Sky—had obviously changed its succession rules to accommodate his father's death four years ago, but Ardenia had no such plans.

No, she didn't want to see any of them, and they apparently didn't want to see her either, hiding away in the guest quarters of the Itspi. But she knew the Royal Council was meeting with each party, shuttling from room to room, ahead of the funeral. Forging ahead with new contracts, her future—Ardenia's future—parsed out in lines of looping text. Despite, or possibly because of, her reasonable requests.

It made her livid.

Which meant the princess required two things to mend her frustrations: Luca and cold, hard, deadly steel.

Whenever she came to him this way at the stable, Luca's answer was the same: "Always, Princess."

And so, on the morning of her father's funeral, Princess Amarande stood at the edge of their meadow with a knife in her hand. Before her, Luca set his feet in the shade of a great juniper tree with a peculiar bald spot about six feet up from the ground.

For the twentieth time that morning, he held a sprig of the tree's berries in his hand and, giving a shout, tossed it over his head—up and up to the branches. The princess tracked it up and then down, drawing back before, in a blink, a knife shot out of her hand. The tip caught the berries through their arterial stem, impaling it in the tree at the same height as the boy's head, dead center of the bald patch.

Her best one yet.

Luca flashed a smile as warm as the sun before yanking the knife and cluster down with it, berries shaking free and tumbling off the stem and onto the ground below. He tossed the knife back at her, a friendly hilt-facing lob, not a sharp sling.

As she caught it, a slow clap came from behind, the beat of it drumming off the mountains that peered down upon them. Princess Amarande turned, joy wilting.

Prince Taillefer.

Renard's younger brother by eleven months, blond and fox eyed. Freshly picked sprigs of white flowers were twisted into a vine around his neck. It was no secret that Taillefer had an interest in the natural arts of botany and anatomy—second sons always needed a hobby.

"Well, after that display, I'll venture to say that if you marry my brother, I'll be king within the year."

Not only brutal but also bold, this one. No introduction. No condolences. Simply a grotesque prediction and a sly grin.

Amarande blinked at him, her grip on the knife suddenly mean enough to etch her knuckles in stark white.

"I'm not marrying your brother."

"Surely we can make a deal," the prince said, arms going wide. His voice lilted like a market vendor with a far better pitch than wares. "You marry him, bleed him dry, and make me king, and I'll install you in your Itspi with your stableboy and a firm promise that I'll never touch you."

Luca looked away, blush crawling across his high cheekbones.

Taillefer smirked. Amarande's icy façade wavered slightly, her blood suddenly too warm for her body. It was impossible to tell by his fox-like smile if he was kidding, but serious or not, the second son of Pyrenee had hit his mark.

"Much of that deal requires my pain and your promises," the princess said. "That's not a balance that can end well for me, Your Highness."

This only made Taillefer grin more and cock a brow. "You're suggesting I should take the Domingu route, are you not?"

She wiped the knife blade against her pants. "How you steal the crown is none of my business, but I don't plan to help you."

"Fair enough." The prince took a step toward the castle with its red-stone turrets scraping the clouds. Then Taillefer stopped. "As a point of reference, my brother is two inches shorter than this strapping young lad. Aim low, Princess, or you'll miss your opportunity altogether."

And with that, Prince Taillefer dared to turn his back to the Warrior King's daughter and her knife.

When the second son of Pyrenee had made it up the hill and through the gate to the yard, Luca appeared at Amarande's side. "Are they all like that?"

The princess's eyes didn't waver from the red spires of the Itspi. Her home had become an asp's nest.

"Greedy? Backstabbing? Opportunistic? Every last one of them. And yet behind closed doors the council bathes them in sagardoa and compliments while negotiating the theft of Ardenia."

Luca considered that. She'd told him much about the laws of succession that had left the kingdom in such a position. "And they don't include you?"

"They know I won't consent—I've made that much clear." Amarande ripped her eyes away from the Itspi and turned to Luca, frustration pinking her cheeks. They hadn't even involved Koldo, though she was regent. Amarande had seen her around the grounds, working with the soldiers far too much for her to be in those sagardoa-splashed meetings. "And the last thing they want is me making the thieves uncomfortable with my demands."

Luca paused, snatching Amarande's hand to make a point. Her blush rose further. "If they won't hear you in private, you'll just have to bring your concerns into the open."

As he spoke, his eyes skipped briefly to the arena, nestled below the castle yard on the other side of the grounds. The site of the day's funeral. Where royalty and commoners alike would come together to bid King Sendoa farewell.

Yes, that was exactly what she needed to do.

CHAPTER
4

❧

THIS was not his death to die.

Nothing like any of the blows King Sendoa delivered in life had taken his own. There wasn't a jagged stitch across his throat, thread straining to hold his head flush to his neck. Both arms were there, too, crossed primly about his barrel chest, and no gaping hole underneath his palms from a heart taken as a prize for killing the Sun and Sky's greatest warrior.

No, as expected, as described by General Koldo and the soldiers who'd been with him that awful day, there wasn't a scratch on him.

Sunburn sat uncomfortably across his paled cheeks, copper hair ablaze in the late afternoon of the mountains. Gold pieces pressed down on closed eyes—in Amarande's mind they were still a brilliant green, though he'd taken his last breath five days before.

This was the body of the warrior Sendoa, king of Ardenia.

Lying in state upon a raised dais, in pristine condition, a man who led the most powerful army in the world from the front lines, serving as protector to the realm of the Sand and Sky.

He'd survived it all—blood loss, frostbite, starvation.

Heartbreak.

And now Princess Amarande stood before her father on the dais, head bowed, clasping her hands tightly against the stiff black lace of her bodice, trying for once to look the part of a storybook princess.

Respectful. Feminine. Lovely.

There for the world to see, throat and wrists heavy with the best diamonds of the Ardenian mines. A mourning veil draped across her face, black as night but unable to defeat the sun, as strong as it was this close to the heavens. The ice-and-night display was at the request—*demand*—of the council.

Because, even now, even saying good-bye, she was upon the auction block.

Behind where she stood on the dais, the royal leaders of Pyrenee, Basilica, and Myrcell all bowed their heads with one eye open, appraising their target from the arena floor. A performance of mourning for Amarande as much as for the citizens of Ardenia who packed the stadium seating. Strategic. Brutal.

Bile crested in Amarande's throat as she cataloged her father's features for the final time. Soon his loyal soldiers would close the coffin lid, and Sendoa's face would only live on in castle paintings that never got it quite right. Dulling the fire in his hair. Straightening the nose he'd broken at least six times. Blurring the gash on his cheek given to him by the Warlord of the Torrent—a forever memory for one of the few outsiders to see the man's face and live to tell.

But she'd stood there too long.

The crowd's feelings were starting to show. The masses were embarrassed to watch this sad girl bent before the only parent she'd ever known. Wooden seats sighed under the shifting weight of Sand and Sky nobility, murmurs growing loud enough that the commoners and low-level soldiers seated in the stands could clearly hear the shape of royal whispers.

It was time for more closed doors, more whispers, more sagardoa—Ardenia's high-hill orchards produced the best cider in all the world.

The moment passed, General Koldo rose to her feet, ready to

guide her princess offstage—to stop her from making things any more uncomfortable with her open grieving. Standing, too, was Prince Renard of Pyrenee—his mother, Dowager Queen Inés, must have urged him forward, an effort to show Myrcell, Basilica, and all commoners of Ardenia that the winning contract had already been arranged.

The princess was surprised when Koldo sat back down, allowing Renard to step up onto the dais and press his hand to the lace at her spine, patting, ready to steer her away.

Very well then—now people were *really* paying attention.

She sweetened the pot by reaching for her veil, lifting it off her face, letting her anguish out into the sun. Between the sight of Renard "consoling" her and the opportunity to witness tears, snot, or something else painful, this was a development to write home about.

They wouldn't be disappointed.

"Guardians of the Sand and Sky and loyal people of the Kingdom of Ardenia," the princess began, the very first sounds from her lips killing off every murmur within the arena and maybe all of the Ardenian countryside. She continued to the heavy silence of a thousand people holding their breath. "Your remembrance of my father is heartening and very much appreciated during this difficult time."

That was when someone began to clap. It seemed to start with King Domingu and his ilk, who were surely eager to get back to angling for the diamonds at her throat and in Ardenia's mines. The noise was enough to prompt Renard to add further pressure to her back as if to help her down from the dais.

"Thank you, but I'm not yet finished," Amarande said, her gaze finding the Basilican king—her barely known-to-her great-grandfather by way of her mother's side—watching him intently until the silence was renewed. Her father had taught her more than how to use a long sword.

When the quiet returned, she set a tight-lipped smile upon her face and found Luca in the crowd. He was seated with the other servants of the Itspi, in the very first row of the stadium seating, sandwiched between Abene and Maialen, the tough-bird, Torrent-born sisters who raised him after his mother passed of illness. Luca returned her gaze, chin tipped—*go on.*

"I have something I would like all of you to hear, yet I will only say it once."

That was another of her father's sayings.

If people are tired by the sound of your voice, they no longer hear you.

These people had barely ever heard her speak a word. The commoners and court alike had only ever seen their princess in her father's mountainous shadow, playing a part—they'd never heard her speak without cause. They hadn't heard her father's advice, meant for her ears alone.

She was going to make these words count and do everything in her power to make them listen. Giving them a single chance to hear what she had to say only made it more enticing.

The silence sat heavy in the mountain breeze. The entire mood of the arena had changed from sad but bored to the perfect posture of interest.

"As you know, the laws of the monarchy require the marriage of a female heir to secure the ruling powers of the Kingdom of Ardenia, as directed by the Sand and Sky. All that is required is for the Royal Council to reach an agreement with the most ideal suitor. A wedding, a new alliance, someone else to call king. It is an archaic law—one that must change. But, as every person in a position to vote for such a change would benefit by marrying me"—her eyes settled on the three royal families before her—"it will not."

There wasn't a pin drop in the pause. Every ear was trained to Amarande and the dais. The princess lifted her eyes to the faces of her citizens, leaning forward from the stadium seating.

"Therefore, as your rightful ruler and the last remaining blood of King Sendoa, I have a requirement as well: my consent." At this, she paused again, testing the silence. "Hear me now: I will not allow the Royal Council to make this choice for me. Any marriage contract will require my signature to be valid."

Her words ringed around the arena, repeated on shocked lips. Beside her, Renard's hand dropped.

"You can't be serious," he whispered, incredulous smirk pinned to one corner of his lips—a speck of humanity coming to the manicured surface. It was a whisper, but the crowd was on high alert now and nearly everyone heard it, the murmurs stopping midsentence.

When Renard realized he'd been caught, the prince turned on the manufactured charm, smirk slipping into a grin, blue eyes glinting in the full sun.

"We are very serious in the Kingdom of Ardenia, Your Highness." Amarande gave him a smile that was as sharp as an aragonite cave flower—cutting, hard, and beautiful. "My father did not raise me to settle; he raised me to rule. And if I must have a man for that, I demand a partner who cares as much for the Kingdom of Ardenia and its people as I do. I won't approve of less. No signature—no consent, no contract, no wedding." She looked out to the crowd in the stands—her people, not the sycophants closest to the dais. "Each one of you is my witness and we must make it so."

"Don't be ridiculous, Princess," the prince said with an exasperated little laugh. The kind men give women as a way of closing doors that were only very narrowly open in the first place.

And that was his mistake.

In a flash, the princess unsheathed Renard's sword and had the tip pressed to his sternum before he could even react, that dumb little laugh still puffing its way out into the arena air.

The crowd gasped, the royal guard of Pyrenee half-rising in their seats, reflexes steering their hands to their scabbards. Dowager

Queen Inés was completely out of her seat, a gold-bangled arm thrust to the side to bar their attack, ordering their stillness.

These people had most likely never heard Amarande speak, and they had certainly never seen the girl Sendoa crafted with hours in the yard, covered in dust and bruises and blood. But today they would see exactly who she was.

Renard kept his cool, looking amused, but Amarande was close enough to witness the blood draining from his face. The miscalculation in the cut of his shoulders. She'd embarrassed him by stealing his weapon as easily as he hoped to steal Ardenia's throne. Amarande bared her teeth into something that would look like a smile to everyone but him.

"I am not ridiculous; I am discerning. I will not settle and neither will my people."

Silence broke as a clamor arose from the commoners in the stands, the applause drowning out the thunking of the princess's heart as she stood there, eyes locked upon Renard. The Ardenian royal party on the arena floor—the council, Koldo and her men and women—were forced to applaud as well, though Satordi in particular looked like a marionette, forced into action.

Amarande lowered the sword and again addressed the crowd. "My requirement stands as my contract to the good, strong people of Ardenia. I will not sell you to the highest bidder. I will not allow a usurper to ruin this land with a gold band and some words for the sake of *tradition*. My father had many chances to join his kingdom with another while he was alive and he didn't, for the best of Ardenia." She looked Dowager Queen Inés dead in the eye as she spoke—made sure the older woman knew the princess was aware of the marriage proposals she'd lobbed at her father before her husband's body was even cold. "And I pledge to my people that I will do the same."

With this, she presented the long sword back to Renard—gilded handle first, emeralds glinting a deep green in the cutting sun. He reached out slowly to grab it, as if it were a trick, as if he'd lose his arm as easily as he'd lost the weapon in the first place. Amarande had serious doubts he'd know how to use that sword if he managed to keep it in his possession.

The princess's eyes flashed to the ruthless old Domingu, whose expression had settled into one of calculation.

"Now I am finished."

CHAPTER
5

❧

IN the moments after the funeral, Amarande was whisked away by the Royal Council, her plea heard, conversations to be had. In Luca's estimation, she'd been perfect—confident, fierce, lovely.

Stealing Renard's sword had been a nice touch. Words were worth much, but pressing a man's own blade to his chest?

A point made indeed.

The smallest of smiles touched Luca's lips as he trod the path from the arena to the stable. With a little laugh he whispered to himself, "She's going to kill him."

It wasn't funny. Not really. But if the Sand and Sky didn't change that blasted law, Renard or any other poor bastard who tried to marry Amarande without her approval couldn't say she didn't warn him.

And if she did manage to change the law without blood on her hands and became free to rule and marry as she pleased . . . well, Luca kept the hope in that thought locked far away where it couldn't annihilate every fiber of his being.

Luca stepped into his stable still dressed in his finest clothes—a hand-me-down cloak, tunic, and trousers from King Sendoa himself, about twenty years and fifty pounds of muscle between himself and the original owner. He strode through the workshop and into his quarters, built off the back of the barn.

Just hours after her father's death, Amarande had begged, nagged, and ordered him to move into the castle. He'd wanted to say yes. Of course he had. But then who would tend to things here? The horses still needed water, food, shoes, care. And if he didn't do those things, who would? Luca felt as loyal to the hours he spent here as he did to Amarande, much preferring to earn his keep with hard work rather than with favor.

And so, carefully, he removed the silken clothing and folded it away onto the open shelves and pulled on plain rough-spun work clothes. He had plenty to do before dinner, tending not only to the Itspi's horses but also to the horses of the men who'd shown up to steal Amarande away.

Her great-grandfather (yes, truly)—King Domingu. The neighbor boy—Prince Renard. The newlywed—King Akil.

Bear. Mountain Lion. Shark.

Again, a smile touched Luca's lips, because none of them had a chance.

Still, he wouldn't let their horses suffer. It wasn't their fault they'd been dragged hundreds of miles into this mess.

He'd start with the purple-and-gold-clad horses of Pyrenee. The soldiers kept theirs close, near the military quarters, but the royal family's carriage horses made their beds here, in his stable's guest wing. There were five in all, each of them the color of fresh snow—Pyrenee preferred white horses for official business, and they'd arrived with their undercarriages a ruddy brown from hard travel through the mountains dividing the two kingdoms. Luca had already spent much of the day returning the horses' coats to their original state.

Usually, all of Luca's horses received hay, but he'd learned quickly that the high horses of other kingdoms were accustomed to finer things. Horse bread, fresh-cut pasture grass, and, in the case of Pyrenee, oats.

As he finished, Luca realized the cord on the oat bag had gone bald and would need to be replaced—slick rope never knotted tightly. Oats weren't the price of gold, but they weren't as easy to find in Ardenia as hay, and he didn't want to waste them. These horses could be his guests for days before their riders rushed away in failure.

He stepped out of the stable wing meant for guests, fingers still fiddling with the drawstring, the promise of his own dinner on his mind.

His mistake.

He'd only been trained to fight a girl who didn't want to hurt him.

Luca heard the blow before he felt it, the thick side of his own practice sword cracking him in a wide smack across his back. Tall as he was, the shot sent him off-balance, stumbling forward, one boot dragging a divot in the packed sod. Luca's hands flew forward, bag of oats and all, but only the bag grazed the dirt, his legs doing enough to keep him from sprawling, face first, on the floor. He immediately tried to rise but was cut down again, this time with a boot to his exposed gut. He fell to the side, rolling onto his back, free hand up in weak defense.

A crush of blood hit all Luca's senses at once—the sound of it pumping through his hearing, the tang of it on his throat, clinging to any air his bruising lungs were able to capture. Garnet spots slinked across his sight as he opened his eyes to blurry vision.

It was then that Luca felt a sword to his throat—the swooped kind they preferred in the Torrent. Even without full sight he knew what sat across his windpipe, pressing in a curve as deep as the coming crescent moon.

Luca blinked again, and his vision cleared to faces staring down at him. A tall boy, a short boy, and a girl. The tall boy had the tawny brown skin of Myrcell, and sweat-slicked curls hugged the smooth angles of his face. The shorter one had to be from across the Divide: Eritri, most likely, given his features— blunt, broad, and blanched. His hair was so blond it was almost white, eyes a saltwater blue, forehead wide as the sky. The girl, though, she had the burnished skin and honeyed eyes of the Torrent. Like him.

It was the girl who held the blade to his throat, as fierce as anything he'd ever seen, and he couldn't help but think Amarande would appreciate her if her blade were pointed elsewhere.

The tall boy rapped Luca's ear with the thin edge of the practice sword. It stung almost more than the pulsing misery of his midsection, front and back. "This can't be right; he's of Torrent."

"Watch your tongue," the girl snapped, eyes cutting dangerously to the Myrcellian boy. After a nice, hard glance, she turned her attention back to Luca, her lips pulling up at one corner of her mouth. "I'd say general suspicion is correct—look at those cheekbones. What princess is going to turn them down?"

The short boy nodded. "He's the one. Haul him up. Let's go."

The tall one wrapped a mammoth hand around the neck of Luca's work tunic and used it as a handle to right him to his knees, ripping the fabric in the process. He then bound Luca's wrists in a length of rope as the shorter boy yanked away the oats—spilling them everywhere as he slung the bag to the girl. She caught the drawstring with a single hand and no comment, stuffing it in a pack slung over her shoulder. Then the girl moved her sword tip to hover directly in line with Luca's eyes as his equilibrium changed, rotated, reset.

It was then that Luca finally felt he could speak, blood spotting his words, though he couldn't tell if its place of origin was his chest or his gut.

"Who are you? Where are you taking me?"

"We're pirates for hire, and you, stableboy, are blackmail," the short one said. From this perspective he wasn't actually very short;

he just looked that way next to his tall companion. It was clear he was in charge of whatever this was, though Luca was sure the girl could eat him for supper.

"Blackmail?"

The leader boy held up a piece of parchment. The outside was marked in a blunt scrawl: *AMARANDE*. "Here's the mail. Now we disappear you away into the black night until your princess takes the hint and marries our guy."

The sun was still mostly up, but Luca didn't argue. "And if she doesn't?"

At this, all three of them smiled, something hard in it. It was the girl who spoke, twisting the tip of her blade into Luca's sternum as she said the words. "Then I guess you'll find out what the letter says will be done to you."

Luca swallowed the blood in his mouth and looked right into the girl's eyes. So much like his. It was like staring into a pond. "My princess won't bow to your demands. But what she will do is come for me, which means she's coming for you, whether I'm alive or not."

And though he'd addressed the girl with the blade, it was the leader who answered this time, because he seemed like the type who couldn't help himself.

"The princess will save you. Yes, yes, that's right. That's how all the storybooks go." Laughing, the boy turned his back to Luca, dismissal in everything from his tone to his body language. For someone who let others do his fighting, he seemed to have a dangerous misunderstanding of motivation.

Luca's eyes narrowed on the back of his neck, which was peeling from days in the open—Eritrians weren't cut out for direct sunlight. "You don't know my princess."

The boy scoffed. "Oh yes, I'm sure she's different."

Another dismissal—this one punctuated by the wave of his ringed hand over his white-blond head.

And maybe that wave was more than a dismissal—maybe it was an order, too, because with that the hilt of the stolen practice blade came crashing down on Luca's temple. Another rebuttal died on his lips, and the world faded to a deep, fuzzy black.

CHAPTER
6

❧

"**Your** Highness, are you mad?" These were the first words out of Satordi's mouth once they'd reached the north tower.

Princess Amarande had been cushioned by councilors and guards herding her away from the prying eyes of the arena and into the council room. The moment the door was shut, Satordi had turned on her. He didn't take a seat behind his great table—he was angry enough to stand in front of it, a livid font of static energy beneath his white-and-gold robes. Garbine and Joseba flanked him, jaws working.

"Furious, actually, that you'd trust me to be your queen but not to be present for any of the necessary deliberations, which shouldn't be necessary in the first place. You refuse to investigate an avenue to change our patriarchal system for the good of Ardenia. You've only spent time bartering this country's future—my future—behind my back." Amarande stood her ground, Koldo hanging close enough that her broad shoulder armor brushed the princess's black lace sleeves. "I took my chance and said my piece. And I could have said so much more. It is more than likely one of those people killed my father or placed the order. What they stand to gain is too great for them not to be suspects in the investigation our regent has organized."

The princess turned to the general, a request for an investigation update ready on her tongue, when Satordi held up a hand.

"Do not change the subject, Your Highness. I realize that you have much to learn, Princess, but make no mistake, your *piece* was a threat—out in the open, where the stars and every being from here to Indu could hear it. If you'd said such a thing behind closed doors the result would have been more diplomatic."

"I can't have a discussion if I'm not invited."

Satordi's mouth flattened. "Don't be a child."

"I am a child, which is exactly why you believe you can ignore my requests and demands for consent, and simply sell me—*and our kingdom*—off to the highest bidder."

"Councilor Satordi," Koldo started, voice as hard and steady as the Basilican steel in her scabbard. "As regent, I request you include Princess Amarande in the betrothal process. It is a necessary education for our future queen."

Amarande wondered why Koldo hadn't inserted herself into the process as well, but perhaps she felt it not her place. They would have to discuss the fault in that logic immediately after the conclusion of Satordi's current diatribe.

Satordi squeezed his eyes closed. "Very well. Princess, if you'd like to be part of the process, dinner tonight at eight in the red hall." Satordi nodded to the left of Koldo. "Captain Serville, arrange it that Prince Renard is there at that time."

That wasn't what she'd meant at all, and surely that was not what Koldo had in mind, but to push back now really would be a child's move. She didn't say no, but she wouldn't lose an opportunity to force the underlying point.

"That will give me an excellent chance to interrogate him on my father's death." Amarande smiled something bloody. "Shall I move on to dessert with King Akil? Myrcell is known to have the highest concentration of hemlock in the Sand and Sky."

"Princess, your father's death has nothing to do with whom you wed." The councilor pinched the bridge of his nose. "We do not have time for this. We simply do not. We have much bigger things to worry about."

"It has *everything* to do with it. I do not understand why you keep imploring me to see the bigger picture when this *is* the picture. He was murdered—what is bigger than the murder of your king? What?"

Satordi's eyes flew open. "War."

Amarande's mouth went dry. "What?"

"Along with the funeral procession, each kingdom brought regiments of thousands to line our borders. Pyrenee, Basilica, Myrcell—all three are ready to strike. Sign the wrong contract and it will not matter how you or your people will live under a new king, but rather how many of them will die."

"That can't be true." This time, Amarande looked to Koldo for confirmation.

The general's dark eyes held her gaze. "It is true. I've seen it myself. Ardenia's army is the greatest on earth and the chosen protector of the realm. But even our army will be stretched by multiple fronts."

Stars War. At the doorstep of Ardenia. Again, no one had told her. Not even Koldo.

War was what her father had worked so hard to prevent—he had built every Ardenian into a warrior not for the purpose of war but for the maintenance of peace.

That moment of ultimatum on the funeral dias, once so sweet, faded to ash upon her tongue. Her mouth was so dry she could barely get the next words out, her heart thrumming against the bodice of her mourning gown.

"And if I play the part? Make each of them happy, with enough promises to the losers to send them home with diamonds spilling out of their pockets?"

Satordi shrugged his thin shoulders—the movement was a heavy thing. "It may not be enough to prevent war. Diamonds and a throne under pressure are too great an opportunity for greed to ignore."

CHAPTER
7

WAR.

The word rang in Amarande's ears, down her throat, and into the pit of her stomach. Scorching it all.

The threat was great enough that at that very moment Koldo and her regiments were headed out, fanning across the borders, each with an ear to the ground and an eye on the line.

A single arrow and it could begin.

Rather than turning for her chambers to prepare for dinner, the princess rushed down the stairs of the north tower and out into the yard, making a beeline for the arena.

The crowd was gone, the stone stands now quiet. The only sound was the echoing in her ears of that small word that meant so much. *War.*

On the arena floor, the funeral benches were gone, dusty divots in their absence. Now all that remained were decaying flower petals from bouquets of mourning and, on the dais, her father's body lying in its ornate coffin, the tiger of Ardenia a bejeweled mosaic across the closed lid, its garnet eyes burning toward the stars above. Sendoa's famed swords, Egia and Maite—truth and love—crossed over the gold scrolling at the tiger's breast as they'd been crossed over King Sendoa's back in battle.

Egia and Maite weren't fancy, not like Renard's gold-and-emerald sword. The hilts were plain as the ones carried by the

king's guard, yet they held their own special music, thrumming
deep within the ridges of Basilican steel. There were songs at court
about Egia and Maite containing magic welded impenetrably into
their depths. Amarande wasn't sure about that, but they had kept
her father safe until the very end. Until the enemy couldn't be met
with steel.

Amarande ran through the arena, steps never hesitating until
the toes of her boots brushed the dais. She stepped onto the platform and pressed both hands onto the casket, the gold inlay warm
and glowing despite the dusky light. She wasn't one to cry, not really,
but these days were unlike any others in her life, and tears came
easily as she sighed over the swords.

"Father, I'm sorry. So, so sorry."

She wasn't sorry for resisting—he'd taught her how, after all.
No, Amarande was sorry that the people of Ardenia would suffer
no matter what came next.

She placed her hands on his coffin, pressed them hard enough
she hoped he could feel the warmth of her fingertips. The need
there. The princess squeezed her eyes closed, letting the breeze
shuffle her veil in the falling night.

Her father had made it clear very early in her childhood that
though he was known as the Warrior King, he preferred to save
lives without lifting his sword. He spent much of his time in the
council room or officers' tent, sifting through the options so that
each one touched the light.

Examining all the angles.

Positives. Negatives. Consequences.

Take something at face value and you miss at least half of it, Ama,
he would say. Then he would wave a big, freckled hand toward the
mountains. *When diamonds are first found, what do we see? Just a
spark. Just a piece. But when it's fully revealed, is all that's there that
little piece? No. The facets are endless. And that first sparkling piece? It
might not be the most beautiful part.*

The facets here were endless as well, and likely just as sparkling in a deadly sort of way.

The kings before Sendoa hadn't made Ardenia a military power—her father had been the one to build his great army, drafting any man or woman who offered themselves. Thousands upon thousands did, and Ardenia's military grew into the enforcers of the realm, maintaining a perilous peace for kings who, in Amarande's current estimation, didn't deserve the aid.

His only failure was the Torrent. That kingdom—Torrence—fell before she'd even been born. The ruling family, the Otxoa, had been driven out in what the conquering Warlord deemed "the Eradication of the Wolf." A king, queen, heirs, and everyone they loved. The end of the line—extinct after a thousand years. Rebels had even murdered every black wolf within the Torrent's borders. The symbolism was lost on no one: the ancient sigil stamped out, too.

Her father hadn't been able to save it. Hadn't even tried to reinstate it in all the years since. He'd guarded against raids, but he'd never seriously tried to remove the Warlord, even when they came face-to-face.

Why have the greatest army in all the world if there were no war in which to use it? Why maintain it? Why continue the narrative of greatness? Teach his daughter to fight as if she were one of the soldiers herself?

Protection, yes, but there must be more.

Protection not simply from the plagues of the realm but from something *within* it.

For fifteen years, he had avoided marriage, even when the possibility was handed to him on a silver platter by Pyrenee.

Amarande knew a lack of love kept him from joining hearts—he would not suffer again or force another to suffer.

But what if it was more than that?

And, why—*why*—did he not use his influence to change the

law and allow her to rule in her own right? Instead of setting up a situation where mostly grown men fought over her like a pack of wolves over carrion?

Her father was so careful. Thoughtful. Strategic.

Wasn't he?

He had a plan. He always had a plan.

Didn't he?

Amarande's eyes flew open. She'd come here for her father's guidance and received nothing but more unanswerable questions, swirling before her mind's eye, the facets in all their shine blinding.

CHAPTER
8

WITH Koldo already winding her way south with a full regiment, there was only one person alive Amarande could talk to about any of this. The one person who knew her well enough to see the facets through her eyes and listen well enough to help pull her through.

The princess ran through the grass, the knife in her boot thunking soft enough that only she could hear it under the hiss of wind through the juniper trees in the failing light. She paused at the stable's edge.

"Luca."

Usually, one time was all it took.

But nothing.

"Luca," she tried again, louder this time, as she stepped inside, breathing in lavender oil and new hay. The only answer was the stamp and snort of horses, rustling themselves into comfort.

Amarande wondered if he'd gone to dinner. If she'd missed him, and if he was lounging in the kitchens with Abene, Maialen, and maybe old Zuzen and his nightly pipe.

Dinner. Like she was to have with Renard far sooner than she preferred. A meal that could save war on one front but spark one on another, the southern kingdoms joining forces against the two northern kingdoms.

She needed to talk to Luca. Badly. To see his face. The understanding in his eyes as she explained. The flash of a dimple as he bit his lip to think. The tone of his voice as he nudged her toward the type of revelation that always hit her all at once—a dive into an icy lake.

Amarande called his name a third time and knocked on his quarters. The little wooden door opened in answer and she immediately knew she must press again for him to live within the castle. She may not be allowed to rule on her own, but surely she could make that much happen.

The room was empty and she gently shut his door. After she returned to the stable entry, she worked through the wisdom of hunting down Luca and his thoughts while gambling her chance to be on time for dinner with a boy whose army slept at her border.

And that's when her eye caught it: a scrap of white parchment, folded neatly atop a mess of horseshoes and nails upon the workbench.

AMARANDE.

Luca knew his letters—Sendoa had made sure of that, as he had for all the palace's children—but that handwriting wasn't Luca's.

The tremble returned to her fingers and this time her fear was there, firing up as it should have the second she saw Koldo sprint-stumbling down the hill from the castle the day her father died. It was a new fear—an anticipation of something shocking and awful.

Amarande's heart rate spiked and her face burned as her fingers fumbled, cold, and she forced them through their tremble to work. She nearly dropped the parchment as it yawned open.

The words flashed before her eyes almost as if she already knew them. As if that new fear had scrawled them on the page itself, dragging the ink through the services of a left-handed scribe.

Marry Renard or you will never see your love again.

CHAPTER
9

LOVE.

The letter had named him right, though she'd never used that word with him. With Luca. With her love.

But that's what he was. That was what they'd danced around. What they didn't dare speak into the atmosphere. It was there—at least for her.

Hanging there between them during their time together, as tangible as their class, titles, and all the other things that gave that word a dangerous weight.

Luca was her love.

The reason—beyond her future and her hopes for Ardenia— that Amarande had spoken out at the funeral. Her feelings for him certainly weren't a secret. She felt as if they flashed, bare, each and every time she spoke his name. But she'd never acted upon what bloomed in her heart, and somehow she'd felt that would keep him safe from the agendas and desires of everyone else.

Clearly not.

Renard had made a move. Possibly spurred on by his brother, with one well-placed comment in a desperate ear ahead of the funeral. Each had his own desire, threaded through the same path.

Her heart and Luca.

She read the words again. Over and over. Crumbling the parchment more with each pass.

Marry Renard or you will never see your love again.

Marry Renard or you will never see your love again.

Marry Renard or you will never see your love again.

Finally, her fingers failed, the paper drifting to the hay-pocked dirt. It didn't seem right that the thing was featherlight. Not with all it meant.

Her first instinct was to run after Luca.

To find where he'd gone, who'd taken him, and retrieve him.

To make him safe again with her own hands and skills.

Someone had stolen her father away from this world, and now Luca was stolen, too.

But then she thought of Satordi. Of both the look on his face little more than an hour ago when he said, *Don't be a child,* and the sting of his words days ago—*You want to be a ruler? Act like it.*

The princess Satordi wanted would stay, not follow her impulses into the near dark.

Wouldn't be impetuous.

That princess would keep a cool head, using her words and diplomacy to avoid war on all sides and ensure no harm to Luca.

But the princess her father taught her to be, while strategic, wouldn't sit and wait. Wouldn't suffer through dinner with the boy who stole away her love—would she?

Make the first mark.

Holding Luca for the ransom of Ardenia's future—her future—was quite the mark to make.

What had King Sendoa done when he found her mother gone? Had he run after her? Or had he retreated to his war room to run it over in his mind? When the Runaway Queen had left, he'd been at the front, ironically protecting Renard's father from an invasion across the Divide by Eritri. But if he'd been home, he would've done something—wouldn't he? When he returned home, he *had* done something, hadn't he?

Just as at his grave, with each new question another appeared.

"Stars."

With all her father taught her, how was it that Amarande suddenly felt as if she didn't know anything at all?

Now, standing before the great roaring-tiger doors of the red hall, the princess pressed shaking fingers to the sides of the garnet ball gown upon which her maids had insisted—another dress of mourning black would have been her first choice. Diamonds bled from her throat across the lace pulled tight over her bodice. The dress flared from the waist, silk in the same color, draped to her boot toes but not farther—trains and the princess did not mix well. Her hair, a fire-roasted chestnut in the dim light of the castle as the sun disappeared into twilight over the mountains, was down with the exception of a small braid pulling the hair off her temples—a crown, a maid had called it.

As she had that afternoon in the arena, Amarande looked the part.

But more than that, she knew she could be the princess she needed to be in that moment.

She could be diplomatic.

She could sit across from Renard and not rip Luca's location from his throat.

She could mirror him—be as reserved as her official portrait, her temper tightly contained deep below the proper surface.

Yet what she could be wasn't all she was. It never would be.

And so, folded over her heart was the scrap of parchment that claimed Luca, rescued from the stable dirt. A reminder. A promise.

And pressed tight against her ankle was her boot knife.

Amarande squeezed her eyes shut, touched her palms to the doors' smooth paint, and stretched a warm smile across her face. It felt all wrong—wicked, misshapen—but it was what needed to be done.

Save Luca.

Avoid war.

Get the damned law changed before the reading of marriage vows.

Beyond the doors, a surprise: The Royal Council was not there. The entire dining hall was empty save for a single table set for two. At one end stood Renard—still with his fancy sword—flanked by four barrel-chested men in the deep purple of Pyrenee, the growling muzzles of gold-thread mountain lions winking in the torchlight from their right breasts.

At her end, a single place setting. No babysitters. No parchment. She'd pictured his contract as a centerpiece, sitting between them as they ate. But no, nothing lay between them but yards of lush velvet, the golden tablecloth bare. On each side, the red-clay walls of the Itspi glittered—garnets sparkling within the stones like bloody stars, pulsing like a heart.

The crown prince of Pyrenee smiled in greeting, those impeccable manners on display. His flaxen hair was combed and neat, parted nicely; his clothing, a regal pairing of Pyrenee aubergine, crisp white, and gold touches. Though shorter than Luca, the boy was still tall, almost as tall as her father had been. But where Sendoa was all muscle, excess sagardoa, and scar tissue, Renard was still growing into his frame, no more dangerous than the suits of armor she'd passed in the hall. Again, she thought he looked as if he'd stepped straight out of a painting, clean as he was. Bland as he was. At least his brother, Taillefer, seemed to be the owner of independent thoughts.

"Princess Amarande, it is lovely to see you—I wasn't convinced you'd come."

In truth, Amarande hadn't been sure that she would either until she was standing before the red hall herself, but she hated that he could see it, too.

Yet in stealing Luca, he'd ensured she would be there.

Keeping his eyes on her, Renard addressed his escort. "Gentlemen, you are relieved."

The men hesitated and the princess didn't blame them—they'd been sitting with the Dowager Queen when Amarande had stolen their prince's sword.

Renard was either stupid or completely underestimated her. Or possibly, he overestimated what he could do with that sword. Which was literally nothing; she was sure of it.

Still, the guards left, shutting the door on the way out. Leaving them completely alone. Amarande decided not to accept her natural place setting, moving away from the seat directly in front of her—which put her back to the door and likely the guards, who would most definitely stay within a command's reach. She made a show of crossing the room to the chair closest to Renard.

The prince took the hint, palace-trained manners baked in with his charming appearance, and he pulled the chair out for Amarande, allowing her to sit down before helping her scoot it in.

Through the motion, his sword hung between them. Amarande placed a napkin in her lap, knuckles fading to white as she gripped the cloth, struggling not to snatch away the glittering Basilican steel yet again. Not to press the tip of the weapon to the soft flesh under his jaw and demand Luca in exchange for his sorry, bland life.

But the princess held her impulses long enough for Renard to slither away, crossing the room and seating himself at the other end of the table.

The menu was simple—lamb and carrots and a crusty hunk of sweet sheepherder's bread, washed down with sagardoa. Her father didn't take kindly to a big show of things, preferring to eat the food of his people, rather than spend his resources attempting to eat as a king. And the kitchens would abide by that rule until they were ordered otherwise.

But this meal wasn't completely normal—the lamb was precut.

Rather than a large slice, they'd each been given a plate of pieces no larger than her thumbnail. Renard took one look at his plate, smirked, and grabbed his single utensil—a spoon. Satordi and the council knew she could do much with a knife and fork.

They could've at least hidden their plan by pretending to make lamb stew. This was just *overt*.

"Odd cuisine you have here, Princess. I have no doubt I will learn to like it in time."

It was almost funny, how he'd said it, if not for the tinge of entitlement in his voice. But what Renard wasn't clever enough to recognize was that this meal wasn't just an indictment of her temper; it was commentary on the fact that he couldn't protect himself.

Again, her father's voice clanged in her ears. *If you underestimate an opponent, you overestimate yourself.* Clearly King Louis-David hadn't shared the same wisdom with his elder son before failing lungs buried him.

And though she was playing polite, she would let him know he'd misjudged.

She was her father's daughter, after all.

Coolly, pleasantly, as Satordi would demand, she renewed her smile. "That is assuming much, Your Highness."

Renard grinned quickly in return, but when he spoke his voice had settled into something cold. "You've agreed to dinner with me, and that leads me to assume you've read my contract and are considering it."

Amarande dropped her own forced smile and focused on not diving across the table, tackling him to the floor, and bashing his head against the snow-white marble.

"I've read it."

"And?"

"If you think I'm signing that contract, you don't know a thing about me."

Renard settled his eyes fully upon her now. They were the color of a ruined glacier—snowy edges, the deep blue ice exposed and unstable. "Piercing" would be one way to describe them, but Amarande had little belief he had the spine to wield anything with the will to puncture—a sword, a fork, eyes that were stunning, yes.

"Oh, I know plenty about you, Princess. And I admire you. Today you saw your opportunity and you took it—admittedly at my own expense." He arched a brow. "And now all of the Sand and Sky knows what you want."

Amarande's heart thudded against Luca's ransom note.

"What do you think I want?"

Renard raised his cup and took a long pull of sagardoa. He didn't wince, though the tart cider was known to peel paint. The prince placed the cup back on the table with steady fingers and dried his lips politely with his napkin.

"The same thing I want—to rule."

The princess bared her teeth. *Oh no.* This boy had taken Luca. She wasn't about to let him draw her in with false equivalence. "You and I are not the same. If we were, there'd be no need for us to be at this table."

"Oh, but we are, Princess." His fingers fiddled with his spoon. When his eyes shot up, Amarande felt as if she were peeking behind the curtain, if only for a moment. "The laws do say I shall be king when I turn eighteen—eleven months, sixteen days, and four hours from this moment. That is an eternity as the son of Dowager Queen Inés."

His voice sliced through the syllables of her name in a way that wasn't loving.

"My father had an inkling that he would pass early. And so he petitioned the Sand and Sky to allow him to set up a clause allowing my mother to care for the Crown as regent until my eighteenth birthday." Though she already knew it, Amarande's heart soured at this—Pyrenee had planned. Why hadn't Ardenia, who had greater need? "A fine arrangement indeed, except he never knew the depths of my mother's ambitions."

Ambitions. Inés certainly had them, sending her first proposal of marriage to Sendoa before the party from Ardenia had even arrived for King Louis-David's funeral. Amarande's father had never considered that one or any of the dozens that followed. He wasn't willing to remarry, his shattered heart not in it, even with the promise of power that could come along with vows.

Again, Renard took a long pull of sagardoa. His cup would be empty soon.

When the prince spoke again, his voice was low—matter-of-fact. "It's not a stretch to imagine my mother in the chambers of Domingu or Akil right this moment, drawing up plans for a marriage that would give either man two kingdoms, and her a chance to steal mine with another heir. A year is long enough to rewrite laws and bear a child."

Stars, he was right. Surely Inés had pursued Akil before he'd wed his new bride, and now with the chess pieces shifting further on the continent, new paths to greater power had been revealed. And there was nothing Domingu wouldn't do for a crown—the whole world had known that for fifty years.

"She would circumvent her own son?"

He nodded simply, hair spun gold in the torchlight. "Our arrival in Ardenia has only proved it—she hasn't met once with your council. She's too busy making her own arrangements."

His eyes met hers.

"But our laws also say something else. I may take the crown before my eighteenth birthday if I complete a single task—marry."

And there it was.

Renard faced her directly now, cheeks reddening as he made his case. His matter-of-fact attitude was gone, passion coloring his features. "You must marry to rule. I must marry to rule. We are alike, you and I. Join me and we shall start a new era—one that weds our countries and keeps our people safe."

Presentation finished, the boy sat back and drained his cup, eyes pinned on the princess's face throughout the whole indulgent length of it.

It would be so easy, of course.

To say yes.

To align herself with Renard.

To use their compact to force the southern kingdoms to decide if war would truly win them more power or just cause them to lose a huge swath of population and gold in trade.

To do as the paper folded against her heart required and get her Luca back to her.

But.

This boy owned more of the black that infected his mother's heart than he knew—or liked to show.

The princess tipped her cup to her lips and took a swallow . . . and nearly coughed with surprise. It wasn't sagardoa, after all. No, it was unfermented—juiced apples augmented with a hint of spice. Renard didn't have the constitution for drink; he had a sweet tooth. Perhaps he thought he was drinking actual sagardoa and impressing her. She nearly laughed before flashing the first smile she didn't have to work for in the past hour. The prince had drawn his weapon and set his stance, attack chosen. And now she'd tease apart the weak side.

"If we are truly equal, then we must discuss the terms of Pyrenee's contract, because the text simply doesn't support your argument."

The passion leeched from Renard's face, the painting-perfect exterior back in place. "How so? I believe it does nothing but establish full unity."

If his mother truly did not want to see him wed, then she didn't have anything to do with the contract Pyrenee sent over ahead of the funeral—meaning Renard was the one who'd approved every entitled stipulation. Worse, too, he knew what had been written and still seemed to believe what he'd said—that they were equals. But even in the mildest sense of his contract, they were not.

Renard's blind privilege set something loose in her gut, hot and unsettled. Amarande forced her fingers to do something other than reach into her boot; she picked up her spoon and took a piece of lamb.

"'Full unity'—yes, I know all about your request for military occupation of Ardenia until I 'give' you an heir."

"Princess, that clause is simply to avoid having Pyrenee's own Runaway Queen." Across the table, Renard's smile broadened—it was a slippery, snakebit thing, and Amarande knew he meant every inch of what he didn't say outright.

Renard didn't want his own heir born of a missing bride. But also left unspoken was what so many had whispered since her mother's disappearance—that Queen Geneva hadn't run away at all. That she'd been murdered by Sendoa, his tracks covered by a story and his own army vouching for his location a hundred miles away. Renard was suggesting he was "protecting" Amarande from the same fate—at least until an heir was in the picture.

She'd been wrong when she'd thought him to be as boring as blank canvas. There was some color to him, after all. Each one of them dark.

Amarande clutched the fabric of her skirt, the blood under her skin throbbing like a second pulse against the boot knife. "And so you would keep my people hostage like you keep Luca."

Renard didn't react to Luca's name. "Are they not under martial rule already? General Koldo is the designated regent, is she not? A general in charge—martial rule by definition." He smiled. "They would have it so much better under us."

Satordi's prediction of the situation parroted back on this boy's lips.

The feverish thing in her gut clawed past her heart.

She had to leave now or he was a dead man. Which meant war. Which meant something black for Luca.

Amarande stood. "There is no *us*. There will never be an heir sharing our blood. You will never touch me. You will never have Ardenia."

Or Luca.

With that, she lunged for the doors. Renard shot to his feet, cutting her off as she passed him with a hand on her wrist. Squeezing, tight, enough to bruise. "Princess, you won't get a better arrangement. Your people won't get a better arrangement."

"Let go." Her eyes slid to the sword at his hip, threat clear.

"As you wish." He dropped her wrist but not eye contact. "But you're making your path more difficult, my princess."

Yet it was her path to choose. She would do it her own way.

This conniving boy had stolen her Luca away, and she would steal him right back.

CHAPTER
10

~~~

AMARANDE pushed out of the red hall, heart pounding but head up—Renard's guards waited for her; she was sure of it.

And she didn't put it past this boy, this snake in silk, to order them to stop her. To put hands upon her in her own home. To carry her kicking and screaming to the Royal Council, some forged contract in hand, and dump her at the feet of her future. At Ardenia's future.

She stepped into that passageway as if she owned it—she did.

As if she could do as deadly things with her fists as with the knife in her boot—she could.

As if she had her mind made up about exactly what she was going to do—she had.

The guards stood at attention. They weren't lolling around, deep in cups of actual sagardoa, their own cuts of lamb balanced in plates upon their knees, threatening to stain their silken tunics with savory juice. No. They stood, all four of them facing the great doors, hands on the hilts of their swords. Waiting for a command.

Amarande didn't hesitate when she saw them. She simply turned that proud chin over her shoulder and said loudly, politely, "I shall see you in the morning, Your Highness."

The guards didn't spark at that; they only dipped their heads in honorable nods, spying their master standing—alive—through the glimpse the doors gave as she made her exit as quickly as possible.

With a single word, these men would be on her.

But they didn't know the castle—not like she did. And thus, they didn't happen to notice that the princess did not turn left toward her chambers, but right.

She clasped her fingers together, so that the men wouldn't see them trembling as she walked away, as briskly as possible without breaking into a dead run. Just a princess strolling away for a night of contemplating a generous offer from a boy who would sacrifice her people to satisfy the greed that slunk under every inch of his useless skin.

The trembling didn't still as she turned a corner and away from their eyes, the tower stairway she'd been seeking straight ahead of her. Rather, she almost shook harder as she closed in on the stairwell—the one that took her to the arena side of the yard and then in a quick diagonal down the hill to the stable—her body reacting as much to her anger at Renard as to what she was about to do.

She pressed open the door into the courtyard, the crisp night air filling her lungs, stinging at her eyes, whispering at the fear creeping up her spine. This new fear.

She knew the brand of fear she felt whenever her father left for a battle. Though she knew he was the strongest, the most capable, there was always the fear that he might never come home. That fear rumbled low, like an ache in the temples before a thunderstorm—something common yet painful.

This fear had come with her father's death. It hadn't been there that day, waiting, creeping, auspicious. No, it'd appeared later, once the shock wore off and the consequences settled in. It was this fear that sent her mind to places that had her questioning everything.

What if this isn't the right thing? What if this isn't the right choice? What if this makes it worse?

That fear pulsed through her mind as she ran. The moon was weak and unhelpful, but her confidence grew with each step.

Yes, this is right.

Amarande pushed the questions down—locked them away deep.

She was the daughter of the Warrior King and the Runaway Queen, and she had made her choice.

These people were poised to steal her crown, her independence, as they had stolen her father and Luca.

And that was their mistake.

She was going to prove to them that they couldn't steal from her. Not again. She was strong enough to take what was hers—her love, her throne, her future.

Amarande was going to claim it all, while letting these vipers devour one another in the chaos of her wake.

Renard, his mother, his brother—they could poison one another with their ambitions.

Domingu and Akil could gamble capable men for half-baked attempts at conquest.

Koldo wouldn't fail the kingdom. She'd keep it as strong and protected in the princess's absence as in her presence.

The princess ran straight into the arena, to her father's casket, more silver than gold in the quarter-moon's silky touch. And there, crossed atop it, were exactly what she needed—Egia and Maite. Waiting patiently as if Sendoa had told them of their quest long ago.

The swords felt perfect in her hands, the weight of them matching the fury roiling beneath her skin. Amarande crossed her father's fabled weapons tight against her back, using the leather straps that held them to the casket's form as her scabbard.

If Renard's men did trail her, they would be in for one hell of a fight.

No hint of that new fear remained when the princess stepped out of the arena and back into the open, her feet quickly retracing the steps she'd taken only hours earlier.

Amarande ran straight into the stable, not a single hesitation in her gait. She had spent hours in that building and knew exactly where Luca kept everything. Saddlebags. Provisions. Exactly what she needed.

In minutes, she had packed bags with salt cod, almonds, and dried cherries. Filled two waterskins in the stream behind the stable. Pulled Luca's chest plate off the wall and slung it across her body, tightening the straps as best she could against the garnet lace and silk of her dress. It would have to do. She tucked the diamonds at her throat beneath the lace neckline of her dress—they would be a decent trade if needed but no good to her if seen and stolen.

Loose armor clacking against the bones of her corset, she ran to the stall where Luca kept her horse, Mira, a filly black as the night that stood between her and her best friend.

Her love.

Another of her father's tenets flashed forth in her mind. It had only been days and yet in death he seemed with her sometimes more now than in life, entering her thoughts as if he'd never left them.

Track prey as if your life depends on it, not theirs.

Amarande came to the edge of the stable and looked into the starry night, ready save for the first step. The princess was still, the girl her father had trained her to be waiting for just the right sign.

At her side, Mira was anxious on her reins, the filly shifting in the torchlight.

The wind changed and a fleck oh so small kicked up from the ground, like the first whisper of snow on the edge of winter. Though it was summer, high and stinking and dry. Amarande's training seized upon the seeming snowflake and the princess bent to the dirt.

An oat.

The kernel was flat and floured—just like the kind Luca saved for certain horses.

In a blink, Amarande spied another white speck yards away. Then a cluster of them just outside the first of the juniper trees that marked her and Luca's little meadow. The wind rustled down from the mountains, driving the flecks into the dark nothingness.

Her eyes adjusted again. *Yes. There.* The faintest of horse tracks there in the swirling, fluid mountain dirt. Even in broad daylight, they would've been nearly impossible to notice.

But they were definitely there.

Three horses. Not headed north toward Pyrenee but west. Toward the dunes and drought of the Torrent.

Maybe she wouldn't just find Luca there but also the truth about her father.

And so Princess Amarande of Ardenia mounted her horse, pointed Mira toward the juniper grove, and followed her heart into the night.

CHAPTER
11

THE night seemed to race across the sky as Amarande moved relentlessly forward.

She didn't bother to sleep.

She didn't bother to eat.

She didn't bother to drink.

Instead, she pushed through the mountains, saddlebags heavy but eyes wide. Always searching for another hoofprint and corresponding oat.

One would think there should be only a single path through the mountains to get to where she was going, but no. There wasn't even a *main* road. The path dividing Ardenia from the Torrent was a web of alternate routes, all of them spidering out from one another in every direction like a cracked mirror.

Worse, all of the paths were well traveled this time of year and it hadn't rained in weeks—meaning they were pitted with footprints and carriage wheels. Summer was when people here did their business, stuffing in a year's worth of trade—mostly in diamonds—before shutting down for the winter's snow and ice.

Amarande couldn't let her focus dip. Adrenaline was her friend, and she had plenty of it. Bitterness and indignation, too—one could run on that particular mixture for days on end.

The princess was alert, moving fast and sure. And even better, as the sun crawled past dawn in the sky, Amarande had an inkling that she was catching up.

She'd played over all the scenarios in her mind and she still had nothing definitive. She knew based on her own timeline of finding the note and then suffering through that absurd meal that she was likely at least two hours behind. But, in truth, that number might have been closer to five. She'd locked eyes with Luca at the funeral, but there was a three-hour gap between seeing him then and being able to slip away from the clutches of an angry council.

Amarande's heart dropped at the lost time—she shouldn't have even attempted diplomacy with that boy. It wasn't worth it. Guilt fluttered in her stomach, which was empty save for a single swig of spiced apple juice. Egia and Maite pressed into her back with all their weight, almost as if to say, *For every moment they made him suffer, you will return it in kind.*

That was another of Sendoa's sayings: *If not an eye for an eye, a lash for a lash.*

Amarande didn't let herself think about what would happen to Luca if Renard were able to reach the kidnappers before she did.

The road in front of her yawned open, into the red mouth of the Torrent. Her most recent mountain path evaporated into the dust of a much different land.

Amarande had seen the Torrent before, of course. Plenty of times. But she'd never actually set foot in it. Her father and Koldo had only ever shown her it from a safe distance, at the top of a peak claimed by Ardenia.

For as trained as she was, she suddenly realized how sheltered she'd been.

From afar, the Torrent looked like nothing that could bear its name. There was no water in the dusky landscape below. Nothing that could deluge, flood, cascade.

But here, with Mira's hooves touching the first specks of red sand, Amarande could understand. It wasn't that the former kingdom had been called Torrence, though likely that played a part. No, it was the other definition of the word that gave this place its name.

It opened wide and presented itself as something sudden, violent, unflinching. The red sands that seemed like a painting from afar shifted like liquid in the wind that barreled down from the mountains on every edge of this bowl, before being trapped, howling, with no way to get out.

The Torrent.

The fallen kingdom of the Otxoa. The lawless desert of raiders, bandits, and the people too stubborn to leave. The Warlord's domain, with his fire pits and caravans and stolen power.

Amarande reached into her saddlebags for the first time. Not for sustenance but for something she was thrilled she'd thought to pack—a linen kerchief.

She wrapped it atop her nose and mouth, lacing it behind her head, mussing up the careful braids that were already coming undone with a hard night of riding.

Set, Amarande gave Mira a pointed tap with both her heels.

And pushed on.

CHAPTER
12

❧⟨◉⟩❧

THE sun was a searing slash across the sky when Luca's eyes fluttered open. He blinked to catch his bearings, trying to stay as still as possible. General Koldo's pity lessons were the first thing in his mind: *Lack of preparation can squander the element of surprise.*

His cheek was pressed against someone's back, the sun's rays hot enough that his sweat mingled through fabric with that of one of the pirates. His ear was damp against that person's spine. The pirate swayed gently beneath the weight of Luca's body as they moved forward across earth the color of shattered terra-cotta on a horse that was at least seventeen hands high.

The Torrent.

Luca knew enough of his homeland to know that much of it was burnt and barren. The continent of the Sand and Sky had been named to encompass the closer-to-the-sun locations of the mountainous Ardenia and Pyrenee and the lowland beaches of Basilica and Myrcell, but truly the Torrent captured both. It was the Sand and Sky on the most extreme palette—skies so clear they blinded and burned, a landscape of nothing but sand scorched sienna. Mountains ringed the bowl that made up the Torrent on all sides, coolly standing sentry in the distance. The only variations here were flattop plateaus scattered at intervals across the terrain.

The pirates had been overly cautious in securing Luca—his

hands were bound and latched to the saddle, another rope connected his midsection to the horse, too, and his legs were tied to the rider's stirrups. One rope would've been enough to keep him from sliding off, but they clearly weren't taking any chances. Which was funny, because he hadn't put up much of a fight in the stable—the evidence was undeniable in the bruises that had bloomed across his back, the knot at his temple, the pounding behind his eyes. Not to mention the blood that coated his mouth, drier than it should be thanks to the arid climate.

His periphery was such that he was able to see a rider next to him, but that horse was just enough ahead of the one he was strapped to that he couldn't make out the rider. Figuring he'd learned all he could know while still, Luca finally raised his head.

His rider reacted in an instant.

"The cargo's awake!" It was the girl's voice—he was tied to her back. Both she and the parallel rider, who he could now see was the tall Myrcellian boy, came to a halt. Luca expected the Eritrian's voice to come next from up ahead, leader that he was, and the boy didn't disappoint.

"Welcome. You missed the breakfast we weren't going to feed you."

Luca's stomach rumbled loud enough that he felt as if it shook the sand beneath their horse's feet. There was no way the girl didn't feel it, close as they were. But Luca didn't say anything about that. He needed to get more answers before they decided they didn't like him awake.

"I suppose you will be taking me to your ship?"

He'd aimed the question at the girl, who was turned in their shared saddle so she could lay an eye on him. From the twist of her body he could see her curved sword stashed in the well of her lap. Close, but not anywhere he could easily snatch it away. Yet it was the tall boy who answered, sneer on his face. "For this trip, we're land pirates."

Luca's mouth opened—he couldn't help himself; there was something about this boy that demanded an argument, even with dried blood clinging to his tongue from their first encounter. "Do you even have a ship?"

"We have a ship," he spat back, chin high.

"Do you? Where is it? We're a hundred miles from the nearest harbor."

"It's docked. Now will you stop asking questions?" the tall one said. "Or I'll knock you out again."

"No you won't," the girl said, coolly, fingers wrapping around the hilt of her sword. "You'll be the one to ride with him if his brains are sliding out of his nose."

"You're just afraid I'll ruin his pretty face, Ula," the boy said, teeth bared.

"Hitting him doesn't make you any more attractive."

The boy's jaw tensed and then he was moving ahead of her, up with the Eritrian, whose peeling neck was already a deeper red than the day before and the morning was only half-over.

When the Myrcellian boy was gone, the girl's fist loosened on her sword and her other hand dug into a pocket sewn into the front of her tunic. And then in her palm were dates—plump but dry and cracking.

She slipped them into Luca's bound hands without comment.

"Thank you, Ula." It was probably dangerous, but if she was to be his ally for any reason—whether it be his looks or the fact that they'd both been born to people from this place—he wasn't going to squander it. "My name is Luca."

She barked out a laugh that was just wry enough to remind him of his princess. "Your parents didn't waste any time on Ardenian assimilation, did they?"

Luca didn't know if he should tell her that he'd been given that Ardenian name before they'd fled the Torrent. In the end, he decided vague was best. Even if she was kind, she was still willingly aiding in his kidnapping. And she'd held a sword to his throat.

"I suppose so." He took a bite, the sugar immediately vanquishing the bloody taste in his mouth. He spat the pit to the red earth and swallowed. "So—"

"Save your saliva, Luca. We won't be to water for a few more hours. Just because you're of Torrent doesn't mean the Torrent will be kind to you."

With that, Ula turned completely away and kicked her horse to raise her speed over the endless red sands.

Luca took her advice. He simply put another date into his mouth and then peeked over his shoulder at the vast desert wasteland behind them, the mountains cradling Itspi straight behind them, covered in the same golden light that haloed them every morning.

The wind echoed with emptiness as Luca moved his lips, no sound daring to come out. *I'm here, Ama. I'm here.*

CHAPTER
13

❧◦◉◦❧

BY late morning, Amarande was regretting her choice of clothing.

She should've changed out of her evening dress and belted on something of Luca's besides just his chest plate. Anything of his would've been too large, of course. But it would've provided more in protection than the lace that covered the whole upper half of her body. It was finely made, but even the best lace was by definition full of holes. Even with armor covering her chest and leather guards at the shoulders, her arms and back seared bare to the sun through the beautiful design.

There was a matter of its distraction, too, garnet red that her dress was. An unusual variant in the range from deep umber, to sienna, to buff and copper highlights of her surroundings as she pushed into the Torrent. Up close, it was worse, she knew. Only the highest members of society owned a dress like the one she had on. And only someone expecting trouble would be strange enough to top it with a too-large chest plate and swords crossed over her spine.

It made Amarande glad Renard's kidnappers had forged their own trail, the oats and three fresh sets of footprints leading her along the southern side of a rock formation that jutted up like the skeleton spine of a long-ago fallen dragon—rigid, rocky, and whispering of death.

The north side held more shade in the morning sun, and thus, every few miles when the dragon's spine dipped to its lowest point before the rock face climbed anew, Amarande occasionally glimpsed travelers going this way and that on the other side. They saw her, too.

And therein lay another problem: The Crown would be searching for her.

If not Koldo, gone to the border, then one of her seconds. Serville, Xixi, or the like. Whoever it was, he or she had been trained just as well as the princess herself. There was no getting out of the idea that this was a three-way chase. Her tracks would be much easier to follow. Fresh, and straight from the stable. There wasn't much she could do to obscure them other than pray the winds picked up—but only after she found the next hint of Luca's whereabouts.

Not for the first time Amarande wondered how her mother had managed to vanish completely. Queen Geneva had left in the dead of night, too, or so the story went. Stealing away while King Sendoa was off on the front, leaving her baby in the care of night maids and the hands of the Itspi.

That tendril of anger at Amarande's father flared again in her empty stomach. For not telling her his plan, just leaving her with a puzzle of laws and the council and the ambitions of many. She was angry at herself, too—for not asking enough questions.

About his succession plan. About her mother's disappearance. About everything.

But then again, he was the Warrior King. Invincible. Though she worried for him as any daughter would, Sendoa always returned with a scar and a story. The lack of time was not something she'd ever truly feared.

Now it was what she feared the most.

The princess swallowed that fear and pressed on as the sun made its turn for the afternoon, her stomach growling and throat parched. With each passing moment, the trail became more clear, the hoofprints fresher, the winds having less time to disturb them.

She was closing in.

Mira gamely moved ahead on sure feet, trusting herself to navigate the deep wounds scraped across the landscape, brutal skies and wind leaving parts craggy and sunken. The filly climbed nimbly over rocks when it was the best path and pressed on, the unfiltered sunshine hot on her neck. Amarande had been riding for hours and had yet to come to water, but Mira hadn't taken a misstep, finding a way through anything.

Until the obstacle wasn't the terrain, but the people and horses upon it.

Not long after yet another view of the road more traveled, three riders came sprinting through a gap ahead, forming a tight V and heading straight for Amarande and Mira.

The princess saw them coming before they even truly appeared, her senses always at the ready, her training at the forefront. She knew when they turned that they were coming for her, not merely carving a path back to the mountains. But Mira didn't have the training to know that, and she drifted to the side, as if to let them pass. To go around them, and keep working her way forward at her rider's direction.

But as Mira swerved, the riders swerved, too. Amarande drew high and hard on her reins, and the horse slowed to a stop, albeit reluctantly. As a cloud of copper dust settled over the riders, the princess held tight on her reins, appraising them.

Three horses. Three riders. Luca nowhere in sight.

Either these weren't the bandits she was looking for or they'd ditched Luca before accosting her. Whoever they were, they stood between her and her best friend and they had to go.

Each of them had kerchiefs pulled over their noses, mottled a strange mixture of pink, from the pounding sands, and white, bleached from the hard summer sun. Their clothes were a mishmash of canvas, camouflage against the landscape, their horses all shades of cider brown like newly poured sagardoa.

The princess knew they expected a girl dressed as she was to politely request that they state their purpose in stopping her. Or maybe to announce who she was in exchange for respect that surely would be given. Or maybe to offer them gold for no trouble, or even to flip it all around and use that gold to gain an escort.

But Amarande just wanted the bastards to move.

"You're blocking the path."

The man in the center made it a point to look around. "I see no path. I simply see a girl in a fancy dress out for a ride on a fancy horse in a decidedly un-fancy place."

"You're blocking *my* path," Amarande tried again, ripping down her own kerchief so that there was no mistaking exactly what she said. She didn't yet reach for Egia and Maite, though she knew these men could not mistake the shapes of the pommels peeking out above her shoulders. The blades pressed into her back, and her blood sang to use them. She nearly whispered to them, *Not yet.*

Though Sendoa always told her to make the first mark, he balanced it with: *Hang back and listen for the time to be right.*

When one couldn't strike first, it was best to wait for the perfect opening. Moreover, it was Koldo who was in the forefront of Amarande's mind now. The king had never known what it was to travel as a woman, of course. He hadn't experienced that the way a man appraised a woman—even one with steel at her back—was always something *else.* A sizing up having much more to do with the specifics of the situation: setting, audience, perceived station, vulnerability.

Amarande was the Warrior King's daughter, yes, but she was also a sixteen-year-old girl riding alone. And even someone as strong as Koldo knew how that felt and what it meant. If a man had a certain lack of respect for women and a certain amount of entitlement in his heart, then another danger would add to the fray.

The leader barked out a single laugh. *"Your* path? This is the

Torrent, dearie. Nobody owns anything except the Warlord in this dump."

This was true. From what she understood, shiny things bought much in the way of favor in the Warlord's realm. If not from the Warlord himself, from other souls within it, trying to get ahead.

The man inched his horse forward. "But you, my *lady*, seem to own quite a bit for these parts. Pretty horse. Pretty dress. Saddlebags fat with more than sandy air."

Beneath her, Mira stirred, looking for a way out, but Amarande would not run. The princess tipped her chin up, defiant.

"I shall give you nothing but my gratitude if you let me pass."

"I wasn't asking what you'd *give* me," the leader said, before nodding to one of the men beside him. "How much do you think we could fetch for those yards of lace? Five years free of tax? A dozen moons in the nicest carriage available, no matter the caravan? Passage on a ship straight off this blasted rock of a continent?"

Amarande didn't blink. Every educator she'd ever had—her father, Koldo, old Zuzen—told stories of the Torrent filled with men like these. Bandits with aims forged while living under a single law: Survive or die. Of starvation, dehydration, or at the hands of the Warlord as an example. The storied fire pits were not for show.

The man answered without hesitation, "I'd say double any of that for the dress itself."

Neither man looked away. The third one joined in with his own unblinking appraisal.

A curl of fear spread through Amarande's empty stomach. They would take her clothes and her armor and most likely the diamonds they'd find underneath. They'd leave her naked in the roaring sun. Or they wouldn't leave her at all. Amarande wasn't aware as to whether the Warlord had a sanctioned, active slave trade, but she knew enough of the world to know there was more than one way to sell a girl who'd come of age.

It was time to draw her swords.

Though they'd been made for a much larger person, Egia and Maite felt right in her hands. With them drawn and raised, she knew she looked intimidating, and if anything, that was a way to survive. *Look larger than you are and don't back down*—if it was a valid way to survive a mountain lion, it had to work with run-of-the-mill highway robbers.

The leader laughed again.

"I don't give a damn about those swords. It's three against one— the numbers don't give a damn either."

They came without hesitation, without a signal between them. The leader and his clothing-appraising second each aimed for Egia and Maite with long swords of their own.

The princess met them both in a high block, the men much taller and using their leverage to press down upon her.

"The thing about having two arms," the leader said, grinding his teeth as his mask fluttered aside, "is that one is always weaker than the other."

Rather than trying another blow, both men bore down as hard as they could. Amarande's arms began to quiver in their lace, accustomed to the constant motion of a fight—not the relentless press of two men twice her size.

She couldn't see where the third man had gone, and she couldn't worry about that. If she didn't change tactics right that second, her own steel would soon be hard against her unprotected forehead, their blades behind it.

"That's the thing about arms," the princess said. "They aren't all we've got."

Amarande placed her right foot on the leader's horse and shoved with all the might of her own strong leg. At the same time, she immediately dropped her sword on that side, swinging low and away. The leader was suddenly left leaning forward off his horse with no purchase, his sword heavy and touching nothing but air.

Before he could catch himself, his far leg slipped out of his stirrup and he plummeted face first toward the ground, his hands stuck uselessly around the sword grip. The leader's horse bucked wildly, stunned at the loss of its rider, front legs crashing down upon the man as Amarande turned her attention to bandit number two.

She brought her right sword up and around, slashing. The meat of the man's shoulder flashed in the relentless sun, exposed with the hard blow.

His sword clanged to the ground as he reacted, and Amarande thrust a sword tip immediately to his throat. Her left-hand sword was pressed blade side against the meat of his belly—no armor there.

Amarande felt the knowledge hard in her gut: She could kill this man.

She knew how using either sword. A quick slash of the jugular and his life force would tumble out in less than a minute with no way to stop it. A stab to the liver and this man would languish for days, fading yellow with jaundice before gray with death.

Still, she wasn't sure she could do it. Not yet.

"Have you seen a group of three riders with a hostage?" Amarande asked him, needing him alive to answer.

The man seemed to look past her. "Nope."

WHAM. The stiff leather sole of a boot heel connected with her knuckles. The sword in Amarande's left hand tumbled out of her grip and bounced off the rib of her chest plate as her hand stung with pain, white and hot. The falling sword caught the second's unprotected side, slicing open the fabric and skin there as the man yowled, before it clattered all the way to the ground.

Someone was clawing at her free hand now, trying to pull her off the horse. She knew if he managed that she would most assuredly lose her dress, her diamonds, and maybe more.

Beneath her, Mira reared onto her hind legs, fighting for herself.

That had the desired effect of dislodging Amarande's hand from whoever yanked upon it but also sent the princess scrambling to hang on to her reins, her other hand still clutching a sword. She wrapped her throbbing fingers around the reins just in time, as Mira reached her full height with a cry.

But just as the horse hit near vertical, there was something else Amarande felt—this from behind. She wrenched around to look over her shoulder only quick enough to watch both her saddlebags slide off Mira's backside, belt sliced free, the third robber catching them in his thick hands.

The third man ran to his own horse, already mounted with the hanging form of the injured leader. He slid atop the saddle with all her provisions and kicked off into the afternoon. The second followed, one hand pressed to his bleeding gut, the other awkwardly holding his retrieved sword. The pack of bandits aimed themselves straight south across the open terrain.

Breath straining hard against her bodice, the princess surveyed the site. Blood was splattered on the ground, but none of it was hers. Not much of it was theirs either. The third horse had run off, and if they let it stay missing, Amarande knew the horse wouldn't survive long—it'd likely broken a leg as it stomped on the lumpen shape of its master.

To her relief, her missing sword was at Mira's feet. She climbed off the horse to grab it and collapsed into the dirt, her legs giving out, shaky with the kind of adrenaline she'd never before felt.

Red dust swirled around her as she shook out of the heap she'd become. Crawling, she retrieved the sword—Maite, *love*—grateful to have it once more in her hand. On her knees, she sheathed both swords in their cross at her back and then pushed herself to standing. Her legs held, and she dusted off the length of her dress. She immediately regretted doing so, both palms caked in russet powder.

Amarande punched out a breath and checked Mira's haunches,

searching for any injury from their ordeal. But the horse seemed untouched. No nicks, cuts, or slashes, no welts or sure-to-be-bruises. The princess patted the filly's back and sighed.

"So that was battle," she said to the horse, resetting the straps of her saddle that had loosened in the ordeal. "Not quite as we'd practiced."

Which was true—Amarande had never lost her sword in sparring.

She hadn't been smashed in the hand either.

She also hadn't ever felt vulnerable like that before. Not in practice. Not in voicing her demands in front of all those people at her father's funeral. Not ever.

Worse than that, though, was something else: In practice, with a dull sword, she'd never once hesitated to deal a killing blow.

But here, with her life in danger—with Luca's life in danger—she couldn't manage it.

Amarande had looked that man in his eyes, his life in her hands, and she couldn't do it. Even with all he wished to do to her.

The princess's heart skidded with the truth of what could've happened—what could still happen. She took a deep breath. Whatever the unknown threats out here, the present one was clear: Someone had seen her.

These men had her description, Mira's description, and her saddlebags in hand, which they could likely trace to the Itspi. Plus, that man she didn't kill knew exactly who she was looking for because she'd told him.

Amarande had survived her first battle with her life, yes. But she'd lost much more than water, food, and time.

CHAPTER
14

⁂

The contract proclaiming Princess Amarande's union with Prince Renard sat on the polished table inside the council room in the Itspi's north tower. Outside, the grounds of the castle were blinding white with late-morning light.

But inside, the mood was edged in coming dark.

And the prince thought he knew why.

The parties from Myrcell and Basilica had moved out earlier, the news of the signed contract an invitation to exit. A chance to go home, regroup, and decide if they really wanted to try their men on General Koldo, who Renard understood had left for the southern borders immediately after the funeral.

Renard had wasted no time in informing his competition of his victory for the princess's hand. It was that confidence that held him up, casting him in the brightest light from the open window, as he stood before the council, each member's shoulders sloping, grave.

He'd taken on Princess Amarande last night, and for all they knew, he'd won. And now he was before her council, verifying his prize.

His throne.

Her throne.

And his mother watched it all, sputtering in her stays as she pretended to be pleased.

Councilor Satordi looked up from the final words of the agreement, dark eyes falling heavily on Renard. The prince stood tall under the weight of them, shoulders straight and back, one hand cuffing the opposite wrist, his emerald-tipped sword resting silent at his hip. His younger brother, Prince Taillefer, was planted to his right; his fleet of guards was lined up at his back, Itspi castle guards fanned out in front on either side of the council table.

Dowager Queen Inés sat regally behind—she would not stand for a meeting such as this. The princess was not in attendance, but Renard did not expect her—she'd been absent from every meeting he'd had with the council thus far on the subject. Even after her impassioned plea literally over her father's dead body, he did not expect the council to invite her unpredictable energy into a discussion such as this.

"Your Highness, she signed this? Last night?" Satordi prodded, and though Renard worked not to show it, he was disappointed in the man's arched eyebrow and sardonic tone. Taillefer had perfectly copied her signature from the letter she'd sent following the death of their father. The signature had years between now and then, but the prince doubted Satordi or any of the council would have something more recent to compare it to. Among the network of Sand and Sky royalty, the princess was known for her love of being outside, playing in the yard, not for sitting inside, scribbling on parchment.

Renard bowed slightly for emphasis. "During our lovely dinner."

"Is that so?"

"Yes, Councilor."

Renard tried not to peer at the other councilors—an old woman and a young man, both swaddled in their robes, silent—for a sense of why this line of questioning was occurring.

After dinner, it had felt like the right gamble—to appear a winner at the feet of Ardenia's council before the princess could call his bluff—but now? Stupid. Would Satordi and the others truly believe the Warrior King's daughter would sign a contract without loudly demanded amendments and a notary on-site? They might want to keep her energy out, but *could* they?

Still: He was the most natural suitor. Similar age; her nearest neighbor; as handsome as she was beautiful. And despite what the princess had spat at him last night, he knew from earlier meetings that these councilors did not object to any of the provisions in his contract.

The lead councilor's eyebrow arched impossibly higher. "And you haven't seen her since your *lovely* dinner?"

A whisper of uncertainty crawled up Renard's neck.

What did Satordi know about last night? Renard was unsure of the correct answer here. Did *no* admit that perhaps Amarande wasn't enamored with him? Did *yes* mean he was being improper?

So, instead of uttering either the truth or a lie, he simply looked each councilor in the eye and carefully asked, "Where is the princess?"

It was a simple question, but no one—not Satordi nor any other member of the council—answered it immediately.

As the silence stretched, that cold uncertainty blew the length of Renard's spine.

After far too long, Satordi spoke. "We are unsure. The castle staff has not seen the princess since the maids dressed her for dinner . . . with you."

"What do you mean, you haven't seen her?" Renard grasped hard to his internal script, his stomach plummeting into his well-shined boots. "She left our meal in great spirits."

"Regardless of what actually happened at this dinner," Satordi said, each word as distinct as a footfall, "the princess is missing."

"*Missing?*" The word felt fat on Renard's lips. Behind him, he was sure he heard a crack of wood settling as his mother shifted in her tiger's-head chair to get a better view.

"Yes. Missing."

"There must be some mistake." Panic was rising in Renard's voice, and he fought with every inch inside him to keep it down where it couldn't be seen. "She would not disappear after the night we had."

"No mistake. The night maids never saw her. The morning maids met unused sheets. And her horse is gone from the stable."

As that news settled over the crowd, Renard knew what they were all thinking: another Runaway Queen, this one a queen-to-be. Maybe Amarande was more like her mother than anyone knew. Or maybe they suspected he knew something about her disappearance. He'd suddenly made himself a suspect.

Renard began to sweat. Possible responses swirled around his mind—a weak defense, an excuse, a threat. This was not good.

But then a voice he didn't recognize broke the heavy silence. "The stableboy is missing as well."

It was an Ardenian guard up front. He stood slightly out of line from the other guards—the man in charge with General Koldo out.

At Renard's shoulder, his younger brother spoke. "I saw the princess with this boy yesterday morning. He very clearly likes the look of her."

Renard was unsure as to whether Taillefer had actually seen such an interaction, but the muted reaction among the councilors was enough to confirm that it was a likely scenario.

Satordi scratched his nose. "Princess Amarande and the stableboy have a close relationship. They were babes together."

Dowager Queen Inés shifted in her chair with another crack. "And King Sendoa allowed this?"

The old woman on the council spoke up next. "Our king," she said, as gently as she would if speaking to a child, "did not subscribe to separation of social classes."

Renard's mother huffed but said no more.

"He must have stolen her away—this boy. Jealousy affects commoners much differently than those of us with means," the prince said, his voice gaining steam as he sensed an opening. "The princess must have informed him of her impending marriage to me and his jealousy took over."

"There is no evidence to indicate that." This from the young man on the council. Joseba.

"What do you mean there's no evidence?" Renard knew he sounded distraught. It wasn't a bad thing.

Joseba continued. "As you know, the princess is a very strong-willed young woman, who often does as she pleases. It could be—"

"Both of them are missing, as is her horse. We must search out their path as soon as possible. She could be in danger." Renard took a step toward the council table. "I do not understand this *inaction* of yours. Her whereabouts should have been questioned the moment she didn't return to her chambers from dinner. How can you sit there?"

His voice grew louder as he spoke, but the council remained in silence.

"I will go after her," Renard announced, placing a hand on the hilt of his sword. The way he said it might have sounded just a little bit like he loved her. "I will follow her path. There must be tracks. A single set—leading somewhere."

Satordi seemed unimpressed. "With the parties from Myrcell and Basilica heading out this morning, any tracks her horse left may be gone. It might be best to wait and see if she returns."

"Is this what you said when her mother rode off in the dark of night?" Renard's mention of the Runaway Queen was met with complete silence. All but Joseba were old enough to have been on the council when Queen Geneva earned her nickname. "We cannot gamble on her return. If that stableboy fancied himself with her, he could have stolen her away. Decided if he couldn't have her, no one could. This is a very grave situation."

Renard was breathing hard, his anger and frustration escaping into the room. He was usually so good at remaining placid in public, though in that moment he was anything but. Again, not a bad thing, given the circumstances.

Finally, without a word to his other councilors, Satordi spoke.

"You will bring Captain Serville with your party," the councilor declared, looking down his hooked nose at Renard and gesturing with a sweeping hand to the guard who had mentioned the stableboy.

Renard nodded at the captain. A babysitter. Insurance that he would do as he said he would do.

Believe me, I need the princess more than you people do.

It was done. He would retrieve Amarande himself.

"We leave within the hour," Renard said before anyone could question him and his intentions again. He turned to the leader of his own guard. "Captain Nikola, ready the horses and begin the search for her tracks." The captain led the royal party from Pyrenee out of the council room in a swift exit.

This was what ruling was, Renard was sure—being of action. Making decisions. Getting your way.

As they walked down the passage to the guest chambers to prepare, Renard's mother made all the right noises at his side. But the prince knew she was happy to see him off—if something were to befall him in the Torrent, it would only make her path to permanent rule that much easier.

A son dying on a brave quest? All the more heartbreaking.

And if anything, her final statement before she retired to her chambers made it absolutely clear the opportunity she saw in her son's bravery.

"Take your brother with you."

CHAPTER
15

❧

THE adrenaline from her first battle shook everything loose that Amarande had been ignoring on her way to this point.

Her stomach rumbled.

Her dry throat ached with thirst.

The princess was happy to be alive, clothed, safe. But suddenly she wished she'd bothered to pause long enough that morning for a bit of food or a sip of water. Or, at the very least, to afford those things to Mira.

The princess's eyes wandered to the filly's shiny black flanks.

The saddlebags were perfectly filled.

It didn't do to dwell on their loss. Comforts were the last things to mourn. Especially on a journey such as this. But a thread of sadness ran through her still—she'd learned how to pack a saddlebag properly from Luca. He was excellent at matching every need to a crevice and fitting a plethora of items that gave everyone else trouble. There was an art to it, if you had the patience. She didn't, not naturally, but she admired Luca's talent for packing things away so that everything had a place, nothing squeezed, squashed, stuffed. And so she had learned.

But she'd also told it true when she'd reminded the Royal Council that she could track prey as well as she could hold a sword and throw a knife.

Human or animal, she could find it, and those skills in this environment could lead her to exactly what she and Mira needed at this moment: food and water.

The princess mounted her horse and reset her focus.

Birdcalls, bees, animal prints, vegetation—all proved useful in tracking down what she needed.

The landscape was in a heavy, dry roast under a climbing sun. To the north, the dragon's spine. To the east, the mountains and home. To the west, Luca's trail. And, to the south . . . nothing but russet dunes. That was the direction the bandits had gone.

No birds circling. No animal prints. No vegetation.

Somewhere out there were landmarks—the Hand, standing as high as the tallest juniper tree in Ardenia, its stone fingers reaching for the stars. The Warlord, pulling strings from his caravan. Great fire pits dotting the landscape, littered with the bones of the defiant.

These were the things Amarande was certain to find in the Torrent, along with Luca. As for anything resembling sustenance and hydration? Even if metered by the Warlord, they were necessities. They existed, too.

But where?

Luca had once told her horses could go ten days without food. Without water that span dropped to three days—the same time frame for a human. But all those estimates considered ideal conditions, not the Torrent, with its heat and open spaces and unrelenting sun.

More than a half day, gone.

"I'm coming, Luca," she whispered as she tapped Mira into motion, and pulled her handkerchief up over her nose and throat. "I just hope I won't be near collapse and dragging a dead horse when I find you."

Amarande pointed Mira's sand-dusted nose to the north and west, back along the dragon's spine, which was now splitting the sun's rays in equal measure. *Noon.*

Accounting for the fight and the cleanup after, she'd likely lost all of the time she'd gained over the course of the night and into the morning. Fifteen hours riding, yet still three hours behind. Maybe more.

But she'd get that time back.

As the sheer umber face of the long spine of plateaus neared, Amarande searched the ground for any hint of the three horses of the bandits carrying her love. The winds had whipped the trail clear, fresh red dirt blanketing what was there only an hour earlier. It became obvious to the princess after about a mile of combing along the rock wall as she'd done previously that the trail was gone. There was nothing now, not even an oat.

For the first time, panic clawed at Amarande's throat.

The princess swallowed and shut her eyes for a moment. She was not helpless. It was not hopeless.

Again, her father came to her. *A warrior made is a warrior alive.*

The tenet was an obtuse one, but said plain, the meaning was: Use what you have to your advantage to survive.

The princess's eyes sprang open.

She had herself. She had Mira. She had the terrain.

Cobble them into an advantage, Ama.

She blinked again at the tail of the dragon's spine. *Yes.* That was it.

She would guide Mira up the narrow rock ledges until they either reached the plateau or could go no farther and search the horizon. Whatever she saw there had to be more informative than what was left down below.

Amarande and Mira made the turn to climb, angling for the first ledge leading up the mass of rock, the heavy light casting the path in little relief. Which was when Amarande realized there wasn't enough room for them to safely maneuver. The ledges grew increasingly thin toward the top, a true path crumbling into a careful hop and skip.

There was no way they were making it together.

Amarande peered at their surroundings. She didn't have the perspective she craved, but she had enough of a view to see they were alone.

"Don't worry, I'll only be a moment."

She looped Mira's reins around a craggy thumb of burnished rock and edged her way around the filly, to the first gap between ledges. It was just short of a full split leap's distance, and the princess leaned hard against the rock face as she tested the weight of a single foot against it—a fall would be another disaster.

But her weight held, and she hugged the rock face, skirting around, picking one ridge and then another, boot tips freeing fresh red dust with every side step and balance check.

The fourth ledge was the leanest—the width of an Itspi windowsill, and at the height of three of Luca's best stallions placed one atop another. Her fingernails clawed at porous stone, combing for every available groove. Her grip wasn't the best, bruised knuckles smarting, functional but cranky. But she was spry and had plenty of childhood moments spent in trees—most of them with Luca, of course. Picking lemons to deliver to the kitchens along with a heavy-handed suggestion that they'd go to rot if someone didn't make cake. Rescuing a gray tabby who'd chased a bird too far. Spying on Koldo's meticulous methods of reducing new recruits to tears.

By the sixth ledge, she had the top of the plateau within literal reach. Sweat slid down her temples; her hands were wet, too. She dried her palms one by one on her dress, the coating of russet dust adding much needed grit to the slick. She shoved her kerchief up from her nose almost to her hairline, blotting sweat before it could sting her eyes.

She wiped her palms one more time, hooked her hands at the wrists above, and dug her grip into the windblown rock of the top.

Amarande closed her eyes. Her breath came in puffs. She could do this.

To the top or not at all.

Her father had never said such a thing, not to her, but the sentiment fit with everything he taught her.

The princess opened her eyes. Readied her worn arms above her head. Squatted as deep as her balance dared. And sprang for the top.

The upward momentum gave lift she wouldn't have had from a dead hang. Her fingers gained tenuous purchase on the plateau, just deep enough that she was able to drive her left elbow into the graveled skin of the flattop, lace shredding as the bent joint skidded to a delicate halt.

For one sick moment, her entire body weight, plus the heft of her crossed swords and her boots with their hidden knife, was suspended on three points.

With everything she had left, Amarande's right hand left the safety of her grip and shot forward, her elbow jutting out and catching the plateau's lip.

Teeth grinding, she hauled her upper body toward the bend of the edge, and swung her right leg on top, and then rolled onto the table of rock.

Breathing in ragged kicks and starts, she lay on her back, swords pressed in an unforgiving cross over her spine. The air she sucked in was sweet and clean, even mingled with a harsh cut of new perspiration from under her arms.

She made it.

A smile touched Amarande's lips as she sat up and opened her eyes, eager to peer over the edge, hoping for three horses at a distance and therefore more pointed guidance on the correct direction. The barest sign of water along the same general path would be even more desirable.

So much to gain. But when she stood, something came that she didn't expect.

The sudden sensation that she wasn't alone.

The princess immediately extracted both swords and whirled a quarter turn to her left, Egia and Maite out in a high blocking cross.

Between the intersection of glinting Basilican steel, the princess saw a ghost.

A wolf as black as night.

Her breath caught and her swords quivered.

Dehydration might kill a person in three days, but the princess knew not how long a person could go without water and maintain sanity.

This couldn't be real.

There were no black wolves left in the Torrent or anywhere else in the Sand and Sky. All had been famously murdered and their pelts made into various fluffy gifts to the Warlord. The symbol of the Otxoa, eradicated right along with the family that held it dear.

Yet the wolf's eyes narrowed.

Its canines flashed, the length of her hand from wrist to middle finger.

It took a step forward, onyx paw landing in a whisper of cinnamon dust.

Amarande's mind raced. This was the face of something that didn't exist. "Extinct" didn't mean lying in wait atop a plateau the height of the Itspi's tallest tower.

"You're not real."

The wolf took another step, its carriage lowering, power coiled in its hind legs.

"You're not real," the princess repeated, this time a whisper. An appeal to the stars. Amarande couldn't attack an actual black wolf. She couldn't. She had her swords, yes. But this creature might be the last of its kind.

Like her.

The wolf's grin spread, snout crinkled. Yellow pupils just slits now. It didn't howl, and it wouldn't, not if it was real. Real wolves attacked in silence. In packs, too—if a lone wolf was spotted, more were near.

But here? On top of the worst part of the world? How could there even be one, let alone a pack?

Amarande backed up on a curve. In her periphery, there was a mass of some kind—a crush of rocks. Koldo's voice stuck in her head, the advice the same for any fanged beast: *Cover your flanks.* She needed protection on one side, and without a tree—ideal— anything upright would do. Looking bigger than she was would help. Her left hand scrabbled at her skirt, pulling the fabric out to the side.

The wolf hesitated. She was wider. Bigger. Flank covered.

It didn't matter.

Before she got to the next viable tactic—be as noisy as possible— the wolf sprang forth.

Amarande dove right.

A mistake.

The promise of a bone-shattering fall blew in an upward gust against her cheek as she landed on the edge of the plateau, the width narrower here. Her hair dangled in the breeze, the lip of stone spilling pebbles to the ledges and earth below.

The princess rolled onto her back to distance herself from the plateau's edge and certain death. Her boots and palms struggled to gain purchase as the wolf bounded off the mass of rock she'd used as cover and vaulted back in her direction. She crab-walked back, sword pommels scraping the dirt from an indefensible position, heels shuffling as she tried to get the balance to stand.

"No, don't—"

Again, the wolf came. Its paws connected high on her chest plate, the metal driving into the diamond necklace beneath the lace of her gown's neckline. Her heels released as she fell, and she whipped her shins and boots up, hitting the animal broadside against the concave target of its belly. The creature flipped, head over heels. Amarande spun to her feet and stood, swords out, the scent of the wolf's rank breath full in her nostrils.

The creature regrouped, teeth bared. But before it took the first step in a new attack there came a piercing whistle—so high Amarande thought it might be a keen of pain. But then the wolf sat, as docile as a dog, its eyes still over her shoulder.

The princess turned, now half-recognizing that stand of rocks to be not a boulder and stones, but the makings of a rock-hewn lean-to. A whoosh that was not the wind came and, following it, a sudden, intense stinging at her neck, right beneath the edge of her kerchief.

The princess dropped Egia, her hand flying to her hair and brushing it aside to find a dart, sticking straight out from the cluster of veins that made up her jugular.

"Who—" she started, her voice slipping from her lips before petering out, her thought dying with the sound.

She couldn't speak; she couldn't move; she couldn't even blink—everything was still beyond her breath.

Amarande fell then. The red dirt coating the plateau top swirled before her eyes as her body hit, Luca's chest plate clanging as it made contact with the unforgiving rock.

As the edges of her vision bled into darkness, a face appeared before her, only the proportions and stature giving away that it was a man.

"This one is both our penance and our entrance, Beltza. Yes. The stars have given us a mighty prize indeed." The voice was haggard but pleased. Amarande heard it like an echo, her ears not complying. Not the men from before. A new threat.

And then her vision died out completely.

CHAPTER
16

GENERAL Koldo sat atop her horse, paused for a moment after a night and half a day of relentless push.

She'd arrived at the junction of the southern kingdoms' borders with her troops ahead of the caravans from Basilica and Myrcell with intention. She wanted King Akil and King Domingu to get a good look at her and her regiments before they passed into their sanctuaries of home.

Sendoa's voice whispered in her ear, loud enough to startle, though it was just a memory of him and his sayings.

Sometimes a look is all it takes to halt something unsavory in its tracks.

These kings had bold plans to satisfy their greedy hearts, but they also wanted nothing more than to survive. No way to enjoy new, far-reaching power while bleeding out on the throne.

Thus, if they were to strike, the kings would need to believe with absolute certainty that they'd win.

It was her job to stare them in the eye, her trusted men and women at her back, and give them pause.

King Domingu was old enough to know the price of war. King Akil was young enough to fear the cost of failure.

And so she would wait. Her encampment was already set, the ornate garnet tent perched above the road that split to divide the kingdoms from Ardenia—left to Basilica, right to Myrcell. It gave her the perfect vantage to be seen by those kings as they passed, but even better, it afforded her a fantastic view of both the kings' encampments. Soldiers huddled at the mouth of each border like silt in a delta.

One command from attack. One command from banding together, the southern kingdoms assaulting the north. One command from turning on each other.

But not yet.

General Koldo idled long enough for her horse to graze at the stomped-in grass beneath its hooves. In her gloved hands was a spool of parchment delivered to her by a lone rider who'd come so far, so fast, his horse nearly collapsed.

The note was brief but informative. Sealed with blank wax and unsigned. The news within delicate enough to require all of those precautions plus a cipher. Though this was one Koldo had learned long ago.

The girl has run away. The boy may come home.

Koldo read the rest one time over, her face kept blank only because of decades of practice.

The general reached into her saddlebag and pulled out a small flask. She took a long pull of sagardoa, reveling in the burn on her throat for a quick moment before turning the acidic cider on the parchment's ink.

Just a few good drops and the words withered into black tears on the page. It would be enough until she could put it to flame.

CHAPTER
17

❦

THE water stop was at a furrow of trees that ran like a stubby scar along a mostly dry creek bed. Mosquitos clung to the spotty stream right along with other travelers, all squint-eyed and haggard from the pervasive sand and too-bright sky as they navigated the trickling waters.

The relative shade was nice, but what Luca really appreciated was the idea that there were people here. Surely someone would notice his predicament and realize something wasn't right. Though he wasn't sure what to make of the fact that the pirates hadn't taken any care to hide that they were carrying a hostage.

The tall boy untied Luca from Ula but left his hands bound. After he took a few good swallows and had one extended coughing fit from the silt in the water, the dried blood was washed from Luca's mouth. The water seemed to have a pleasing effect on all of his injuries—the knot on his head pounded a little less; the pain at his midsection seemed to ease the tiniest bit, though he was sure he had at least one cracked rib.

Another swallow and he finally felt he had enough refreshment to spend a moment looking around. His pirates were filling waterskin after waterskin as their horses grazed on thin shoots of grass. Beyond them, other travelers were doing the same. There were no children here, and only one girl besides Ula. The kidnappers' attention had wandered her way at first, but when it became obvious this girl was of Basilica—dark hair, skylight eyes—and that she was with a party of men, the worry (or hope) that she could be the princess in disguise dissolved. Everyone kept clustered to themselves and no one seemed to bat an eye that they were in the company of a bound and bruised boy.

"Do you come here often with hostages?" Luca asked the group as he wormed sand and silt from his teeth.

"Why?" the tall boy spat back, swallowing down a whole cheekful of water from his newly filled waterskin.

"Because you're parading me around with my wrists tied together and no one seems to think that's strange."

"We're in Torrent. Prisoners aren't unusual. There's probably one or two among them," the short boy answered, wetting down his white-blond hair before wrapping his whole head in a length of linen borrowed from Ula to deter the sun. Too little, too late. "No matter who they are, they likely think you're either a criminal or a penance, and either way you're being escorted to the Warlord to meet the fire pits."

"If anything, they're surprised that we're letting you drink," Ula added, something in her tone like a memory. The hint of it was gone as soon as it came and she turned her back, shifting the ropes that had bound him to her from her gray mare to the one ridden by their leader.

Luca took another draw of water before continuing. "And why exactly are you letting me drink?"

"Because it's not time to kill you yet," the tall boy answered with a ferocious grin.

Luca returned the grin in kind. "I'm no good to you dead. If you kill me too soon, my princess won't have any reason to marry your man."

"I said 'yet.'"

"What my friend means to say," the blond boy started, "is that if your princess doesn't do as was requested in that letter, we'll give her a nudge with your head on a pike."

Luca stood from the creek bed. He knew his full height was impressive to most people, though he wasn't in the habit of using it to intimidate anyone except maybe the occasional opinionated horse. He drew himself up, chin up and shoulders back, and leveled his gaze on the leader boy. "And what will you do when my princess comes for me?"

The short boy made a show of looking around at the decidedly uninterested travelers, the pounding sun and barren cargos and steep plateaus beyond.

"It's been eighteen hours since we stole you away. That's plenty of time. Where is she, stableboy?"

Luca didn't let his gaze waver, though the number of hours that had passed rattled through his mind. Longer than he'd thought.

"My princess will come."

The Eritrian boy waved a ringed finger and snatched a rope from Ula, latching it around his horse's undercarriage—Luca was to ride with him after this break. "Sure she will, right after she finishes her tea and cake. Or perhaps her embroidery calls first?"

Ula stopped short of what she was doing and glared over the horse's back at the blond boy. "Spoken like a man who has never been with a woman."

The tall boy snickered, drawing the ire of both Ula and the short boy.

"Can it, Urtzi," the short one snapped.

Ula rolled her eyes. "You know no more about women than he does."

"I've been with plenty of women," the tall boy—Urtzi—shot back.

"Lying in bed with a woman is completely different than *knowing* a woman." Ula waved her hands, done. "You both talk about them like they're inanimate objects."

"I wake every day to your smug face—are you not a woman?" Urtzi tested Luca's binds for slippage around the wrists where the ropes got wet.

"I am, and if this princess is anything like me, she'll castrate you before she kills you."

Urtzi huffed out a non-answer while using every inch of his lanky arms to deposit Luca on the horse's back. Like his rider, this horse wasn't cut out for the sun—a pebbled white gelding whose pink skin shone through his coat.

"*If* she arrives," the leader said, mostly to Ula. As if he could get on her good side. Luca didn't think it possible for him to talk his way out of this. He wondered why she put up with this crew at all. "I'm not questioning the girl's strength—she's the Warrior King's daughter. I'm questioning how much she cares."

"No, no you're not," Luca countered from atop the horse. He was aware that any one of them could knock him off in anger, his arms useless to break his fall, but it was worth it for what he had to say. "The first moment I said that she'd rescue me, you mocked me and insulted her over the basis of her ability, not because you believed she was too busy sipping tea and minding embroidery to come after me."

The boy from Eritri simply laughed. It was loud and exaggerated, and a few fellow travelers took the time to peer over at their group. This included the Basilican girl, who Luca now saw was tied up just the same as he. Maybe the pirates were right—he wasn't the only prisoner around. Still, that any of them had been moved by laughter but not by captivity confirmed for Luca all that he'd heard about what had become of his birthplace.

Ula pressed forward, even as Urtzi gamely tied a slip of fabric loosely around Luca's throat. "Luca has a point. If he's important enough to kidnap, he's important enough to save."

"Maybe I should gag you, too," the short boy deadpanned.

"If you want to keep both hands, Dunixi, you won't," Ula said with a smile, but her tone was enough that no sane man would laugh.

Instead, the leader—Dunixi—changed the subject. "Let's keep moving."

"Where are we headed?"

Luca didn't expect an answer. But all three pirates responded in near unison. "To our ship."

That was not the response Luca had gotten when he'd asked them before. He wondered what had changed. Or maybe nothing had but their tune. "And what will we do when we get there?"

"Sail, of course," Dunixi said, swinging up onto his horse and lashing Luca's middle to his own. This close, his skin wasn't just bright pink—it was burned badly enough that blisters had formed, stretching in looping rings across his skin, all up his neck, crawling beneath the linen he'd applied.

This boy was no sailor.

"I thought you'd been hired to keep me until my princess marries your man?" Luca asked. "If that's true, why would we need to flee? Wouldn't you return me home—in whatever state I'm to be in?"

"Ah." Dunixi wrenched around in the saddle, grinning wide and gap-toothed at Luca. "You're thinking she's not coming then?"

"No, I'm asking because if you're planning to take me on the water, you aren't expecting for your man to get what he wants," Luca said, "which means you actually think my princess *is* coming and you need to keep me from her."

Ula cocked a brow. "Luca has a point."

"Or I think she's not coming and she's not marrying our man either." Dunixi kicked his gelding into gear with more force than necessary. Luca bit back the urge to admonish him for treating the animal in such a way. "Which means you, my friend, are up a creek."

They left the gag dangling loose around Luca's neck as the three horses pushed back into the full sun.

CHAPTER
18

·~⟨❧⟩*~·*

ROCKING.

Amarande blinked her eyes open to a violent swaying that was not Mira's practiced steps. Her vision was nothing but white. The sun's rays seemed to pry through her skin, burning her throat, lungs, heart.

Again, her eyes closed, the unrelenting heat wrapping around her like a shroud shorn from the stars above. And then the world shriveled to a pinpoint behind her eyes, the heat evaporating, the rocking, her sense of place.

Everything became black.

AMARANDE awoke to darkness and dirt. Her back and neck ached; her skin burned; her throat was dry. Blinking into the new night, she sat up—she'd lost all of the afternoon and most of the evening.

Gone, in an instant.

Luca.

The princess's head swam as she righted herself, and it was only then that she realized her hands were bound. Her feet weren't strung together, but there was a manacle around one boot, a long chain tying her to some sort of wire wall erected against a rock face. The wire curved in a half-moon within the bounds of three rock formations that formed somewhat of a gapped circle. A holding pen.

Around her, a half a dozen girls sat, awake but unseeing, visions of what was to come next in the faraway looks in their eyes. All were young, all were bound in the same way, and all but Amarande were dressed in dirt-clogged linens.

Across the way were two men. They appeared to be guards, lacking uniforms but clearly there to mind prisoners, mugs in their hands and gossip on their lips. There were no horses near, and her stomach dropped with the realization she'd likely lost Mira. Sold off along with her by the man living on the plateau with the black wolf.

Those words stitched together were one impossible improbability, and yet here she was.

Amarande swallowed, Koldo's voice in her head. *Know your surroundings as well as your opponents.*

Next to the guards was a cart, piled high with items that weren't theirs, collected and likely to be shuttled away. The hilt of a sword, maybe one of her father's, stuck up from the pile. Maybe the other and Luca's chest plate underneath. *Maybe.* With some relief, Amarande realized they hadn't found her boot knife or her necklace, still safe under the high collar of her dress. If she had any luck in this, it was in that.

Her movement got the guards' attention.

"If the lady isn't up from her beauty rest," one of the guards said, not really to her but to the other man. "That's quite the dress."

Up until this point in her journey, Amarande had thought she wouldn't voluntarily give up her identity at any point. The most important thing was Luca, and her name almost seemed like a hindrance to finding him. But given they'd stripped her of her weapons, her horse, and her best chance to stay on Luca's captors' tails, her name might be all she had to use.

True that she still had her knife and her diamonds, but the

second they were revealed any advantage they gave her would be lost. If they didn't work, they'd disappear. But her name—that was one thing that couldn't be physically removed. Her title, too.

Amarande stood, and the world spun slightly—the sleeping poison's last gasp. With a steadying breath, she tested the length of the shackles at her ankle. Three feet. Maybe. Her throat was still parched, but she gathered what she could of her voice and projected it proudly, like she had the day of her father's funeral. Yesterday.

"I look like a lady because I am one. A princess, in fact—and I demand to speak to your leader at once."

The guard who'd spoken first pushed off the wall, discarding his cup on a toadstool boulder. "That's quite a lot of privilege to toss around with little proof. I was having a laugh at your expense when I named you 'lady'—a nice dress doesn't make you a believable princess."

Amarande gritted her teeth and set another gamble. She had no clue how she'd gotten here and if Mira had been with her. But it was worth a shot before showing her final hand. "My horse's saddle and horseshoes are marked with the royal brand of—"

"So you stole a horse." The man laughed, and so did his friend, cutting her off. "If I check its teeth, will it cry your name? Pledge fidelity? Offer proof?" The man advanced until he was right in front of her, the bootleg sagardoa on his breath heavy and sour. "No? Perhaps there's more than one way to extract the truth. . . ."

The guard's curved finger ran the length of her jaw, the other hand moving toward her chest—covered now only by thin lace and the sturdy boning of a well-made bodice.

The guards had tied her hands together, yes, but they hadn't bound them to her body or wrenched them behind her back.

Which was their mistake.

Now wasn't the time for the knife, not yet, but there was still much she could do bare-handed and bound.

Amarande's arms shot up, crashing into the man's forearms and breaking through his reach. Surprised, the guard fell forward, his hands paused at his sides. In that space of hesitation, Amarande's hands were reset for another strike, and she thrust the heels of both palms out and upward, dislodging the man's nose from its spot on his face with a bloody crunch.

"Aiyyyy!" The guard stumbled back, voice misshapen along with his face. His partner rushed forward to grab him, and Amarande advanced as far as her foot chain would allow, threat clear.

"Your leader," she spat at the uninjured guard as he stumbled under the weight of his shrieking friend. "Or you're next."

The man looked up from his cohort long enough to bare his teeth at her. They were whiter than most and would bloody nicely. "The Warlord doesn't take kindly to mouthy brats."

Amarande's breath hitched for the barest of seconds—she was in the Warlord's camp.

The Warlord who met her father years ago and released him. If he could survive, then so could she.

"And I don't take kindly to anyone who calls me a mouthy little brat. Make sure the Warlord knows my name—Princess Amarande of Ardenia, daughter of King Sendoa, long may he rest."

The guard who hit her started laughing but then thought better of it, howling as that decision sent more blood streaming out his nostrils and down the bare-knuckle jags of his chin. His cohort tried to calm him, righting the man and tugging him away. "We've heard some lies on this caravan, but that one is massive enough to win a fistfight with the Hand. The princess has never left Ardenia. Locked in a tower the day her mother ran away. Even the spiders crawling the Hand know that."

Amarande drew in a thin breath. Was that really what others thought of her? Locked away, a prisoner in her own home?

"Nice try, mouthy little *brat*."

CHAPTER
19

By nightfall, the pirates were pointed along a new track.

Luca didn't know if they had a ship; all he knew was that there was absolutely no harbor in the direction they were currently headed. The Port of Pyrenee would've been the closest, and even that was far. Torrent's single functional port was to the north and west, but it was still a week away at this rate. Maybe.

But then, just as the dark settled in tight, stars guiding their way, Luca saw that they'd changed course not to find their ship but something else—a ranch of some sort. One with a main house and little outbuildings. More than one campfire flickered through the privacy fence encircling the property.

"I thought all of the Torrent was nomadic. This looks like a compound," he whispered to Ula, who'd taken him back from Dunixi a few hours before. No permanent settlements, only caravans, as dictated by the Warlord. *Control by chaos*, as old Zuzen called it in his Itspi lessons—move or die. If one stopped long enough to make a stand, he or she was already dead.

"There is much that is misunderstood about the Torrent, Luca," Ula said. "Those who pay their tax and live alone are let be."

Luca had so much to ask but didn't when Dunixi confounded him further with what he did next. The leader dismounted and handed his reins to Urtzi. "You know the drill. Come for me with your daggers in five if I'm not out."

And then the Eritrian walked toward the compound, alone.

"Why five minutes? Why aren't we just going in there with him, daggers drawn now?"

"You ask too many questions," Urtzi answered, one hand snaking into Dunixi's saddlebags. He pulled out a palmful of dried meat made from an animal Luca could not identify and stuffed it straight in his mouth, as if he believed that eating it before Dunixi came out would prevent the boy from noticing that it was missing at all.

"You don't ask enough," Ula shot back. Rather than grumble at her, Urtzi laughed. It was true—from what Luca had seen, the Myrcellian took orders without ever thinking them through. He just collected them like sips of water—or pieces of dried meat—until there was a break in action, and then he did it all over again. Ula shifted so that she could look Luca in the eye. "He's getting us a spot for the night."

"And we're not in there because . . . you showed me off in my restraints at the river but don't want to do so here?"

"Not everything is about you, Luca," Ula replied with a smirk.

"No, it's all about me," Urtzi crowed over his chewing, delivering the full-mouthed words with some sort of faux self-disparagement that didn't work with his overconfident nature. At all.

Ula ignored him and the boy seemed to shrink a little when she didn't punctuate his answer with her bell-like laugh. "You outsiders see the Torrent as this lawless place, but the truth is it has more rules than the rest of the Sand and Sky put together."

Luca cocked a brow. "And what rules live here?"

"Wouldn't you like to know." Ula turned away from him, trying to play coy. She wasn't very good at it. He'd spent a little more than a day with her, and he'd learned she was one who loved to tell it like it was, and loudly. Making someone work for her thoughts was not something she was terribly gifted at.

So he waited. There was a sign several yards from them, but he couldn't read it with the lack of light. And even if he could, a conversation like this was one way to keep in her good graces.

As she began to turn, Urtzi swallowed the last of his pilfered snack. "I'd like to know. All I know is that I hold the horse here."

Ula sighed. "The key words when I described this place were 'tax' and 'alone.' The proprietor pays his taxes on time and the Warlord turns a blind eye to the fact that he lets people congregate— renting rooms or campsites at this place. It looks like a compound, but it's technically an inn. The key is that one must enter the main structure alone to purchase a night's stay."

Luca's eyes fell to the leader's saddlebags. He hadn't rummaged through them before he dismounted. If Dunixi had gold pieces in his pockets, they were small in number—there'd been no telltale jingling as they rode together. No bulges in his pockets to account for larger bars tendered in troy ounces either.

Urtzi, though, did not have this information. "But we don't have any gold. We never have any gold. That's why we have him." The boy nodded at Luca.

Ula pursed her lips. "This man takes more than physical valuables—if you have useful information, it's as good as gold."

"That's quite the business model."

"He's survived on it for many years. I wouldn't disparage it, Luca."

Just then, Dunixi returned, a key dangling from his hand, the metal catching the starlight with a blink of shine as he walked.

"That one nearly cost me a dip in the compost." It was a funny thing to say, but he delivered it with a tic of nervousness and something in his eyes that made Luca believe that there actually was the possibility of him becoming worm food, though it didn't make much sense.

Dunixi relieved Urtzi of his reins, mounted his horse, and made another announcement as he led the way to the compound's east gate. "I'm off watch tonight, folks—I'm spent. Ula, you're set until midnight. Urtzi, until sunup. Then we push on."

THEY settled in a camp on the northeast edge of the property. The key went to a gate to the fence that surrounded them, and then again to their lodging. Somehow, Dunixi had secured them a spot surrounded by a privacy fence tall enough that the horses couldn't peek over. They lit a fire, feasting on pistachios, dates, and dried meat—taken from Urtzi's saddlebag, interestingly. Ula fed Luca a handful from her stash before Dunixi caught her.

"No more, Ula. He doesn't need to be plump, just alive."

Then the leader draped a wet scrap of linen over his burnt skin and turned over for the night. Urtzi did the same minus the cloth. Within the space of just a few minutes, both boys were snoring. Ula stayed seated upright and awake—on watch.

Luca lay back and attempted to join them in sleep, but his mind was racing. Trying to make sense of these land pirates, where they were headed, and who exactly had come up with the plan to use him to coerce Amarande's hand to begin with. Moreover, there was the fact that for the first time in his life since his mother left this place with him lashed to her back, he was in the Torrent. He'd thought many times of what it would be like here, fed on stories from the childhoods of Maialen, Abene, and Zuzen, not to mention the more recently wrought tales of King Sendoa and General Koldo.

He lay on his back, watching the stars. The pirates had left the fire going. Luca had thought this strange at first, but after the meal, with the sun fully devoured by the horizon, it was clear why. Because though it was summer, warmth here fled fast when the sun set, the heat evaporating from the parched ground, leaving it nothing but scorched embers, cold and dusty.

The winds picked up in the night, too, howling through the open spaces, between the boney plateaus, winding loose soil into flowing rivers of earth. The fence provided some insulation, but not much. Though he'd grown up in the mountains, Luca never knew summer could be so cool.

"Luca, shut your eyes and dream of your princess."

Luca could feel his cheeks grow hot with Ula's quiet suggestion, though in truth he didn't need to shut his eyes to dream of Amarande. He sat up.

The pirate was sharpening that curved sword of hers, the gentle *swish-swish* of steel on the blade a complement to Dunixi's pig-squeal snores. A bound journal and pencil sat half-pulled from her saddlebag, and Luca assumed that she was waiting for him to sleep before writing in it, preferring privacy for whatever she wanted to record. He spied the bald rope of the oat bag, a few fat flakes escaped and clinging loosely to the canvas. *Good.*

"May I ask you something?" Luca whispered after a few moments of watching her work.

She didn't say yes. Didn't say no. Didn't tell him to shut up. So he continued, mindful of his volume with Dunixi and Urtzi snoring in the shadows.

"Did you grow up there—*here*, I mean?" He still couldn't believe he was actually in the Torrent.

Instead of answering, she asked, "Did you?"

"No, I came to Ardenia with my mother as a baby. This is the first I've seen of it."

Ula's attention shifted to her blade. She held it up close to her face, inspecting its new sharpness. Once satisfied, she spoke. "It's beautiful. This part. The coast. All of it."

"I believe you."

Ula accepted that with a chin tip, eyes so much like his own glued on the firelight. When she spoke again, her voice was barely above the exhale of a breath—as if the Warlord himself could hear the shape of her words. "I'm going to get it back."

"The Torrent?"

"Torrence. That's its name, you know. The Kingdom of Torrence. Ruled by the Otxoa family for a thousand years."

Luca nodded. The Otxoa—*the Wolf*. It was actually a whole clan of them, a royal family ruling just as long as Amarande's.

"What happened to them? The Otxoa?" Luca knew what the people in Ardenia had told him—that the Warlord rose to power in such an insidious way that by the time the coup physically happened, everything outside the wolf den had already turned. The disease of dissent against the Otxoa was so thick within every city, town, settlement, that by the time warning bells were rung, the people ringing them were the last loyalists to pick off. The Eradication of the Wolf, the Warlord's people called it. They even destroyed the castle—Otxazulo, rendered to ash and rubble.

He knew all that, and yet he expected Ula to have a different point of view. She did.

"*Your king* left them to rot, that's what happened."

This wasn't the King Sendoa that Luca knew, but he held his tongue and let her continue.

Ula kept her words low and swift, the rumble of pain a tremor beneath it all.

"Your king, exalted protector of the Sand and Sky, found it too difficult to restore order here." When Luca didn't balk or go on to defend King Sendoa, she continued. "Oh, he made a show of it in the beginning, when you and I were babes, running for our lives on our parents' backs, as our towns crumbled and our homes burned. But then he lost his queen and he gave up. Didn't do anything more than run interference. Kept raiders at bay from the kingdoms ringing the lands the Warlord took but never struck at the root of the problem."

Luca frowned. King Sendoa had met with the Warlord. That was how he had gotten the scar on his face.

The wind kicked up beyond the fence and Dunixi rolled over in his sleep. When all had settled again, Ula sheathed her sword.

"You know what I think? I think *your king* didn't think it was worth it, to save the Kingdom of Torrence. So he let a royal family like his disappear into dust. Let the people fall to ash." Ula's eyes flashed to Luca's. The undercurrent of anger in her whisper was matched now with sadness. She didn't answer when Luca asked about her family and what she'd been through, but clearly none of it was good. His life hadn't been roses, but his situation at the Itspi had never let him feel lost, displaced, unloved—all the things that Ula didn't say. "No Ardenian diamonds here. No Pyrenee gold. No Basilican iron or steel, or pearl-rich Myrcellian beaches. Just people cowering beneath the shadow of a tyrant in a place without anything but the forever sun."

Ula nodded to herself, grimace set. Something as deep as the sea shifted in her golden-brown eyes.

"This is my home. And even if *your exalted leader* didn't care to save it, nor did any of the other men ruling this continent, I do. I care. And I'm not alone. The Otxoa are the rightful rulers of this land, but in their stead it belongs to the people who loved them. It belongs to us. And eventually we will regain it."

Luca met her gaze, which didn't flinch. Ula was nothing if not solid and sure. Unblinking, he repeated his earlier affirmation: "I believe you."

CHAPTER
20

❧⟡❧

THE guard's howling would not stop, and five minutes after he'd been beaten by Amarande the men left to find aid. They turned their backs on the princess and the other prisoners, leaving only their binds and fear to hold them.

It was their mistake.

The second the guards disappeared around the rock formations and into the maze of tents and to a roaring fire beyond, Amarande began testing her bindings. As she did, the steel wire structure they were attached to shuddered, bending slightly toward where the guards had been stationed. The princess stomped to the end of her bindings, dug in her boot heels, and pulled. The structure more than shuddered—this time it definitely wavered.

The light was weak, the only source distant fires, but it was enough to reach through the crevices between the rock walls. The illumination proved the structure was crudely mounted—something lightweight the Warlord's caravan could easily dismantle and haul from place to place, using it to stabilize prisoners from one edge of the Torrent to the other.

They must not think highly of their prisoners. Or maybe it was this specific set of prisoners—all girls. All around the same age—middle teens. Pretty. All likely dumped at the Warlord's feet as payment of one kind or another. The wolf man's craggy voice came to her—*penance*. The bandit's sneer—*tax*.

There was likely a single use for so many girls of a similar age to a man as powerful as the Warlord.

That only made Amarande want to flee more.

If she could escape, she could steal a horse and be on her way.

Back to Luca. Always to Luca.

"Help me pull," she whispered, eyeing the other prisoners, all slumped in their chains against the structure.

No one stood to join her. No one answered. Many of the girls had their eyes closed, and the ones who were awake simply eyed her as if she were speaking ancient Torrentian.

Fine.

Amarande braced herself again and pulled. The wall quivered.

"What's the point?" one girl asked, the whites of her dark eyes flashing from the far corner. "You're just going to tire yourself out before we're marched into the fire pit."

The fire pit. Of course. That was how the Warlord kept his power.

Supposedly, these fire pits dotted the Torrent landscape, waiting for their turn to host the Warlord. Only he was allowed to light them—do it yourself and risk your own death within the flames.

The pits were all a day's ride from one another—spread across the Torrent in roughly the same formation of where its cities and towns had once been. And kindling was scarce in the tree-deprived Torrent. Rumor had it that the fires were lit with the most abundant flammable substance around: human flesh. One sacrifice going before all others to literally get the party started. The others coming at intervals all night long to keep the flames licking the sky until dawn.

If they were to be sacrificed, the princess didn't want to think what the Warlord might do to them before they stoked the flames. Not one use as she'd guessed—two. One, and then the other, final one.

Amarande looked the girl right in the eye with everything she had. "I'd rather march to my death exhausted than full of energy I'll never use again. Wouldn't you?"

Rather than wait for an answer, the princess turned and pulled at the end of her chain a third time.

Again, the wall moved. But as strong as she was, her leverage wasn't enough without more support.

"Come now, we know the worst that can happen. Why not try for the best? We won't have long before the guards are back."

At this, a girl with tumbling dark hair and the blue eyes common in Basilica—and similar to her mother's, so she'd been told—stood and modeled her posture off Amarande. The princess kicked up a smile. "Thank you . . ."

"Osana."

Amarande nodded. "Osana, one, two, three—pull." The whispered command worked, and together they were enough to slide the pen wall an inch.

A girl on the far side of the flat U shape stood. "They have a rock over here fortifying this end." She turned to the captive next to her. "Help me move it."

Reluctantly, the other girl stood and strung herself to the end of her chain—just far enough to kick at the rock with her unchained ankle as the first girl shoved against it with bound hands. Everything men could move and erect, women could, too. The rock slid a couple of inches and that whole side of the structure wobbled, looser than before.

Amarande nodded at them. "Excellent. Now, pull."

The two girls on the end braced, as did Amarande and Osana.

The whole structure bowed.

Amarande turned to the last girls on the other end. The one who'd told her not to waste her time and a girl next to her who looked so similar they could be sisters. Neither had moved, not even to inspect the rock fortifying their end.

"We're almost free."

The one who'd protested spoke again, not moving. "It'll fall on all of us. And then where will we be? Flat as heel-stomped beetles and burnt to a crisp. No thank you. I want to haunt these bastards from the afterlife as beautiful and robust as I am now."

Amarande turned her full attention to the girl. "If this comes down we have a chance to be free of our leg chains."

The girl sneered. "Or when they hear a loud crash and find us caught under the weight of this thing, you'll think you're special just as you did before—throwing around titles in hopes of an audience. You and your title will escape and leave the rest of us to suffer the consequences."

The princess leveled her gaze at the girl. She was as blond as Renard—of Pyrenee, or maybe from across the Divide. Wherever it was, it was a place where teamwork had let her down.

"You have my word that I won't leave you." She eyed the girl next to that one. "You either."

This promise was enough for the younger girl, who stood. Her sister's whisper was out before she'd reached her full height. "Sit down, Kiri."

The younger one shook her head and began testing her leg chain's length. She couldn't get to the rock on that end—her sister blocked the path—but she tried.

"We have another, thank you, Kiri," Amarande whispered to the others. They reset while the mouthy girl stewed in the far corner. "Let's try it again on my count."

Now when they pulled, the wires twisted together to form the quilted structure began to snap. *Ping. Ping. Ping.* Better. Definitely better. But they were still only getting tension from the bottom half of the wall.

Amarande had an idea.

"You two," she whispered, pointing to Osana and Kiri. "Can you climb and pull with me? Like this?"

Amarande hooked her fingers between wire slats until she had climbed up as far as her leg chain would stretch. The other girls did the same. The structure bowed against their weight. Nerves flashed across the faces of the girls still on the ground. Even the mouthy one shot to her feet, spurred into action by the desire to get out from where Kiri's section of the wall bent toward her forehead.

"On my count, those of us up the wall will jump down and pull. Meanwhile, the rest of you will come to the ends of your chains and yank. If it begins to come down, cover your heads and rush toward the wall ahead. If we do this correctly, the tension will dislodge our leg chains and we'll be out and gathering our things before anyone can check on the collapse."

Not even the dissenter had anything to say to that. It was a plan, plain and simple.

"One. Two. Three."

The girls did as they were instructed—three falling to the earth and three yanking, the mouthy girl included.

With a great creak and chorus of pops, the steel snapped along the lower third of the wall. The girls' leg chains lost their anchors with them, and, as the wall fell forward with a massive clang, all six girls sprinted straight for the opposite rock wall.

One sword was an easy find in the cart, its pommel a beacon and the makeshift scabbard dangling off. The other sword proved to be more difficult to locate, hidden under a pile of cups and saucers and jugs for trade, but soon Egia and Maite were in Amarande's hands and she began sawing at the girls' wrist binds. The leg chains were another matter, and the girls realized within a matter of seconds that loosening the anklets wasn't going to be easy, with a sword or otherwise. The first girl in the line to get her binds cut—Kiri—simply gathered the chain in one hand and began to run. Her sister followed and then each girl after that.

In less than a minute, all the prisoners were free and scattering into the darkness as men's voices and footsteps charged at the noise they'd made, alarm sounded. Osana lingered, her blue eyes drilled into Amarande's face.

"Lend me your sword and I will cut you free."

The princess hesitated. She could do it herself, but it was an awkward reach, and her swing from that angle would not be efficient. It would take her longer to be free of where the leg chain attached to the wire frame than it had taken the other girls.

"Amarande, was it?" the girl said, and suddenly the princess felt naked with the use of her name. Though she knew it, the girl didn't use her title, and somehow that made it as intimate as if she were using the nickname Luca and Koldo were allowed to use. Stunned into action, the princess nodded. Osana went on. "On my honor, I'll return your sword and I won't cut your hand off or spear your heart first. You just rescued me and I won't hurt you. Trust me—I trusted you."

Osana was right.

Amarande handed over one sword but kept the other in her grip, threat clear, as Osana righted and raised the sword she'd been given.

The Basilican girl didn't say anything, just made her cut with her lips curling up slightly at the corners.

Binds shredded, Osana returned the sword. "The horses are this way."

Amarande fought back the tendril of fear in her belly telling her not to outright trust anyone, even this girl, but the direction Osana ran was away from the thunder of footsteps, and so it seemed like her best option anyway. She had still been unconscious when they'd come into camp and she had no idea where horses might be.

The princess stowed one sword in her makeshift scabbard—Luca's chest plate wasn't worth the time it would take to find it and get it on and tight—hauled up her leg chain, and followed, remaining sword out and on guard. She followed Osana around the perimeter of the camp, sticking to the darkest corners as chaos ensued, a thousand men and women rushing around against the backdrop of a roaring fire that almost appeared to leap from the earth's center itself.

Human tallow made quite the kindling.

As they darted around the camp's edge, the spires of the greatest tent Amarande had ever seen came into view.

The Warlord.

It could belong to no one else.

The tent was a lush blue like the waters that were so absent in the Torrent. The thick canvas held fast against the tug of the night wind and the commotion, men running through openings on all sides. Each time someone left the tent, there was a slim firelit glimpse of the inside. Furs swaddling the floor, a figure in the center.

Before she knew it, Amarande had veered off course by a half-dozen steps, drawn by curiosity.

This was the Warlord who'd met with her father. The one who'd let him go with a scar on his cheek and a censored story to tell. The one whom Sendoa had mostly allowed to rule unbothered.

Amarande stopped running.

She stood, heart pounding and sword lifted, as three women pushed out of the tent together, providing her with the best view yet.

The figure was slim and small and facing away. Clothed in swaths of blue, linens draped across slight shoulders, up to an elegant neck, draped in extra linen. Hair piled into a bun slashed through with a dagger.

The Warlord was a woman.

Granted, this person could be the Warlord's mistress, but something about the cushion of space surrounding her, the dagger, the extra linen, the strength of her posture even while sitting, added to the press in Amarande's gut.

Yes, a woman.

A grain of something shaped like hope dropped in the princess's stomach.

Amarande took another step toward the tent, toward the War-lord, wondering if the timing of the Warlord's rise to power wasn't as important as it seemed. Her mind reached back, back, back, for her mother's face. There were no paintings of her in the castle—not anymore.

Could it be? Or was it hope that shaped what her eyes thought they saw?

All Amarande knew of that face was what others told her. Facts, rattled off. Queen Geneva of Ardenia: dark hair, blue eyes, petite frame, punctuated by her youth at the time of her marriage.

The tent flap swung closed, swallowing the figure and the light, and a palm pressed against Amarande's shoulder. The princess startled, hand to her sword hilt as dark hair, blue eyes, and a teen-age face swam into view. Not a trick of her taxed memory but Osana, pointing to a shadowed mass ahead.

"There," she whispered. The gate to the enclosure was already gaping wide, the other captives having found it first.

Amarande hesitated.

The timing didn't make sense, no. Yet so many other questions could be answered by the Runaway Queen wearing the Warlord's name.

But it couldn't be. And staying on a wild scrap of hope would mean another chance at capture. Another chance at death in the fire pit. Still—

"There! Get them!" Men's voices. They'd been spotted.

Osana yanked on Amarande's arm, pulling her into a run. They stumbled over the landscape, rocks and dips and undula-tions catching their stride, which was already hampered by one leg cuffed in the heavy chain they slung in their opposite grips. Still, they careened into the pen, dodging newly woken horses, edging toward the open gate, escape in their eyes.

Osana dropped Amarande's wrist and went for the first horse available, a chestnut gelding.

"Mira!" the princess screamed over the churning equine mass. It wasn't a given that she'd be here. But Amarande had to try. They'd been seen—she was most definitely going to call for her girl now.

After a pause that seemed as long as a moon phase, a rustling came from the back corner. Amarande bit her lip and ran in that direction.

And, there, rising from a stiff sleep, was the midnight filly.

Amarande mounted Mira bareback, picked her way through the crowd of horses angling toward the exit, swooped up someone's reins from a fence post, and took off into the night.

CHAPTER
21

AMARANDE was in a silent battle to stay awake longer than Osana.

The girls rode side by side through the night, into the dawn, and though they both drooped against their animals, neither dared to stop. The risk of betrayal was too high.

Amarande was certain she herself was leading them, going in the general direction she had been before she'd been captured—to the north and west, though she had no idea where within the great Torrent she'd been taken when she'd been dumped in the Warlord's camp. Osana didn't question Amarande about the particulars of where they were headed. Nor did she seem eager to make a turn elsewhere.

The threat presented by company outweighed the positives, even with the small trust they'd built in their escape. The princess was losing time and wasting energy on the girl. This worry only added to the mountain of frustrations that'd grown in the void created when the adrenaline of freedom had bled away.

The frustration that her tracking skills were useless at the moment—no oats, no hoofprints, no pinpricks on the horizon to lend guidance.

The frustration of possible failure. Of losing Luca—to the wilds or to the promise of the blackmail note still pressed to her skin beneath her bodice.

The frustration that she'd come all this way, fought so hard, and that she'd have nothing to show for it but heartache and an empty-handed return to the Itspi, where she'd have to accept Renard's offer to get Luca back.

Even if it were successful, that in itself felt like defeat.

And who knew if he'd make good on returning Luca in one piece? Who knew if that was ever the intention at all?

All those frustrations wound onto themselves until they were a hard lump at the base of Amarande's throat. The weight of it all pressed tight on her ribs, already constricted under the stupid stays of the bodice, and tears sparked against her eyes.

The princess tried and failed to clear the lump from her throat but then spoke anyway to Osana, her voice strange to her ears. "The sun is up now—go your own way. Surely you have some-where to be."

"There's water up ahead."

Amarande didn't respond other than to scan the horizon again. In the cool blue of the new morning, the red dirt looked the same as it had the day before. Shifting, tugging, blowing. She'd fixed her position against the fuzzy gray of the mountain in the distance—home—and noted the tail end of the rock formation she'd dubbed the dragon's spine well behind them. She didn't see the Warlord's camp. No one trailed them—a small miracle forged by the chaos of their mass escape.

Mostly, this patch of earth was the same as any other, rusted and red and dry as a bone, over and over.

Another mile, and a dark smudge appeared on the horizon. Trees.

The girl was right.

An hour later and they were there, a small creek tinkling up from the ground through an improbable stub of trees.

"The Cardenas Scar," was all Osana said in explanation as they watered the horses and themselves.

No one else was at the watering hole in this early hour, though signs of a camp hung with fire smoke in the air. Amarande used one of her swords to finally remove the chains from where they cuffed their ankles. After that chore was finished, Osana disappeared to relieve herself behind a tree. Amarande pretended to do the same, though she was so dehydrated it was an impossibility— the water she'd just ingested only replenished what was missing. Still, she needed a moment away from the girl's eyes to plan for what was to come.

Mira and a tree blocking her movements, Amarande wrenched her necklace out from its position underneath her lace collar and tugged the clasp apart. It had occurred to her somewhere in the endless inky night that if she were truly going to use the necklace to her advantage, she'd need to do so with it in pieces. She couldn't just haul the thing out and present it, asking someone to choose a diamond the way they would their preferred lemon cake from a platter.

She laid the necklace on the bug-eaten stump of a long-dead tree, unsheathed one of her swords, and knelt close to her workspace. Raising the weapon, she brought the butt of it down hard on the soft gold setting, which served as the framework necessary to keep three pounds of diamonds—a hundred carats—clinging in their arrangement. Over and over she went like that, wiggling diamonds free and stowing them in the hidden pockets within her skirt as she went—she'd need a pouch of some sort eventually; pockets were not a safe place for loose diamonds, even of these carats and weight.

"Amarande?"

At Osana's call, the princess scooped the last diamonds into her pocket, sheathed her sword, and shot to standing, fingers scrabbling to dump and hide the mangled golden setting. She dropped it within a narrow hole in the trunk. A handful of silt earth stuffed over it was all she could do to hide it from view before the girl appeared, holding her horse by the reins.

"I thought you might have run afoul of a Quemado Scorpion. They like the water."

Amarande rushed out a lie. "No, just thought I might have seen a quail egg. The light and my hunger playing tricks."

The girl chewed on that. "If there was ever an egg to be found here, a Harea Asp has already claimed it and its mother."

Amarande stilled. She'd been so distracted by the obvious threats—the people, the terrain, dehydration—that she'd completely discounted the animals lurking here.

Beware or be dead.

It was her father's rule number one, and she hadn't applied it. Even after her brush with the black wolf. Quemado Scorpion. Harea Asp. Osana had pointed out two immediate threats in less than a minute and both were as deadly as the men possibly following them. Or as deadly as they could be to each other.

"They like the rare vegetation as much as we do," Osana added when Amarande didn't respond.

"Yes, I suppose so."

Amarande grabbed Mira's reins and realigned herself with her course—through the water, up the other bank, and cutting back into the sun. When the girl followed, sloshing through the meager water, Amarande mounted and then hesitated before kicking Mira into action.

It was dangerous enough that Osana knew her name and title. If she'd been bought and sold within the halls of her own castle, the same could and would be done here. She'd misjudged when she'd shared with the guards. And having a companion she barely knew was another danger.

She looked the girl in the eye, suggestion in her tone. "Are you sure you don't have somewhere to go?"

Osana pushed her dark hair behind her shoulders. Like Amarande, she wore it loose, letting it blanket her neck from the sun. "We left Basilica in debt, moving our sheep over the mountains." Into the Torrent. "That lasted a year."

Amarande's mouth dropped open, her heart clenching at what must come next. The girl's words didn't have the skew of a lie. "The Warlord's men?"

The girl smiled tightly. "None other. My father sold me off as penance for squatting unapproved." *Penance. Again, that word.* Osana continued, her eyes meeting Amarande's in a heavy way. "But I wasn't enough, so they murdered him anyway."

The princess's heart, already so low, dropped further. Their meager trust had grown in the daylight, to be sure, but it was still fledgling. Discomfort rose in Amarande as she processed this new information. Sharing like this was an invitation. And Amarande had already shared enough. Still, she asked more. "And what of your mother?"

"Somewhere in Basilica—new family, new life."

Amarande nodded and let the girl follow.

CHAPTER
22

~❦~

A few hours later, the sun high and Mira's black coat burning to the touch and baking into the silk of the princess's skirts as she rode bareback, a compound rose above them. A mirage. It must be.

A rambling building of blocked mountain stone, plunked down in a blanket of basin-flat desert terrain. Though she'd yet to see the fabled Hand in person, this house was possibly an even more stark anomaly against the flats of red earth. Almost as amazing, a barrier made of wood—*wood!*—stood tall in a large, circular wall around it.

"Is this place real?" Osana asked, her voice barely above a dry whisper beneath the cowl she'd made from a ripped scrap of her pant leg.

Amarande tugged away her own cowl, fashioned from her skirt hem. The one she'd made from the kerchief hadn't been with her when she had awoken in the Warlord's camp. "I believe so—you knew about the Cardenas Scar but not this?"

Osana pulled down the fabric, licking her lips and shrugging. "My captors took me to the watering hole and called it by name."

In answer to Osana, Amarande simply tapped Mira forward in approach.

Ten horse lengths from the compound's entrance was a sign meant to address anyone looking to enter, written in the chicken-scratch equivalent of the etched text found on steel historical markers throughout the standing kingdoms of the Sand and Sky. Only this message was written in what appeared to be blood— human or otherwise, it was a commodity that had been used to paint over and over as the sun bleached the words away.

ONE AT A TIME AND YOUR LIFE ON THE LINE.

Amarande dismounted and tied Mira to the post. She tipped her chin at Osana. "Stay here."

The girl didn't protest, and Amarande felt confident she couldn't steal away Mira without Amarande hearing and preventing her from getting far. Feeling the weight of the girl's stare against her father's crossed swords at her back, she tested their modicum of trust and walked away.

As the princess's boot heel hit the single-plank step leading to the building's shade portico, a voice came from within. "Remove your weapons before entering."

Amarande hesitated, her father's swords pressing into her back.

"I see those swords, girl. Drop them where you stand."

The princess brought both boots back to solid ground. The voice came again, male and even. "I am alone and unarmed and so shall you be. Or you won't enter at all."

The princess directed her words, clear and just as stern as the man's, at one of the two front windows situated on either side of a massive wooden door, both shaded and dark from the overhang. "How do you expect me to enter weapon-free when your sign clearly states my life is on the line?"

"Enter that way or don't. I expect your wits to be the sharpest thing in the room."

Egia and Maite each came out of her makeshift scabbard with a quick metallic swish. She set them gently on the wood slats of the portico, marveling again at the materials this man possessed in such a place. In all her father's stories of the Torrent, nothing like this had ever been mentioned. It was nearly as big a surprise as the black wolf.

Feeling naked without her weapons, Amarande entered, blinking, her eyes adjusting from the fierce sun to extreme shade. The building's windows were nothing but pinpoints of light within, thanks to the portico overhang. As the door slammed shut behind her, a dozen lit candles within flickered from their positions atop built-in ledges and pedestal tables.

As the flames recovered and grew, she saw she was standing in some sort of grand entry, the rest of the structure peeling off in a series of closed doors. This room, though, was a presentation of wealth, each candle strategically placed next to a fine vase, shade plant, plush chaise. At the very center, at a slight angle from the door, was a broad marble-topped desk, and a man sitting behind it with his elbows trained along the top, hands gently clasped together. This man was the same age her father had been, but soft with comfort.

"Welcome to the Warlord's Inn. You have come alone, yes?"

The Warlord's Inn? That went against everything the princess knew about the ruler's decrees. Movement was key; housing people who could use close proximity and routine to conspire? Definitely not. But in the past day, it had become as clear as the diamonds hiding in her skirts that there was so much about this place—and the Warlord—she didn't know.

Amarande didn't react. She simply replied, "Yes."

"And you have no other weapons upon you?"

The princess's knife sat heavy in her boot. "As demanded, none but my wit."

"We shall see about that," the man said. "These are not my edicts; they are the Warlord's. No one is to be stationary unless they are alone. One in and one out, and a tax upon each head. At the inn you can purchase shelter, food, supplies, and information. Now, I ask you, what do you require?"

The princess didn't hesitate.

"Food, supplies, information."

He laughed, long and hard, everything echoing off the empty hollows of a place filled with nothing but this man and other people's belongings. "That's a heavy load for a girl who looks as if she's just come from a celebration."

The princess's muscles stiffened under her ruined skirts—again with cracks about her gown. If the Warlord was a woman why did she elevate men such as these who didn't have the capacity to comment on anything other than her appearance? Surely the Warlord could find better. Or women—Koldo could stop this man's heart with the right expression.

Amarande's eyes narrowed—both she and this man were visibly unarmed, but they were not equal in training. "Do not let my appearance deceive you."

The man reset, tenting his fingers. The more she watched him, the more he reminded her of an aged Renard—lily white and bland, the lines of his body fading along with his coloring. "The majority of my guests can only pay for one of the four."

Of course. That lump crawled back into her throat. Tears pressed against her eyes. It would cost all her diamonds just to get what she needed to continue this journey past the morning.

The man continued. "Of your requests, which is the most important?"

The princess answered immediately, swallowing that lump away. "The information."

"And what is your payment?"

"Nothing until I know you have what I need."

The man smiled, thin. "You're the chicken or the egg kind, I see." He untented his fingers, his posture hardening. "But let us remember the particulars of the sign beyond my door. The second portion of that sign isn't simply for a rhyme. By standing here, you are gambling your life. If this transaction doesn't go your way, it's off to the compost garden with you."

The princess coughed out a laugh at the utter lack of drama in the name. "The compost garden? Am I to do manual labor or become worm food?"

The man was not impressed with her reaction.

"Not quite either. If you run afoul of me, you will be unceremoniously dumped into the very special white sand at the center of my compound. It's fed by a geyser that runs as hot as the Warlord's fire pits. The second you slip through that earth, you'll be poached right in those beautiful clothes. An hour later, the earth will spit you into my garden and you'll become stock for stew, tallow for candles, marrow for horses. I'll use every single piece of you until there's nothing left."

It was so over the top that Amarande didn't believe it. But she'd already laughed at the man's name for the place, and she needed to get whatever information she could before she broke a vase over his head or retrieved her swords.

"Noted, sir—"

"Innkeeper."

Stars, of course.

"*Innkeeper,* how do I purchase information from you?"

"It's a simple exchange. You tell me what you want. If I confirm I have what you need, you give me information in return before I give you an answer."

Not ideal, but her father had taught her to play. *If you underestimate your opponent, you overestimate yourself.*

"I am looking for four riders on three horses. They should've come this way last night. One boy, my age, of Torrent, is a hostage."

The man's posture relaxed. It was as if he only had two settings: cold and stubborn or sagardoa warm and ready for gossip. He leaned back and, though he didn't have a mug in his hand, she imagined him at one of the cafés lining the market outside of the Itspi, trading information of a less valuable kind. "That is something

I know about. The only question is how you plan to pay for it. I trade in like. In this case, information requires more information. I will accept nothing else."

The diamonds lining her pockets clicked together, at the ready to test his policy. The knife in her boot, too. Amarande chewed her cheek. Somehow, she thought her news would hit this man differently than it had the guards. Finally, she spoke.

"I am the information. Princess Amarande of Ardenia, running away from my castle after someone dear to me was kidnapped to push my hand into a marriage contract." She lifted her chin. "Surely you can find value in that."

The man leaned forward and again tented his fingers. Amarande's knife hand twitched.

"You were correct earlier—your looks do not deceive, Princess. What do you think those who you seek paid for their time here? I already know all about you and your stableboy."

"Good, then which direction did they go?"

The man clicked his tongue—*tsk, tsk, tsk.* "Tell me who they work for."

"Pyrenee."

The man tilted his head. "I said *who.*"

How was that answer incorrect? "Renard."

The man tilted his head farther. Clicked his tongue again. *Tsk, tsk, tsk.*

Amarande's guts turned to water. Had the kidnappers lied to him?

"Where are they? Was my . . . was he hurt—the hostage? What did they tell you?"

The princess's questions died on her lips as a door opened to her left and she realized they weren't alone. The innkeeper made the rules, but he didn't abide by them. A man twice the size of her father staggered out and grunted, "Pretty compost."

Amarande's hand was in her boot in a flash, but the ogre was much faster than he looked, picking her up as she grappled for her knife. His massive hands grabbed her about the waist, an arm curling around her back and across her stomach as she knelt. She was upside down, several feet in the air, knife jiggling against the slit of space between her stocking and the top of her boot shaft. The giant man belly-laughed, and she shook with it. "No weapons, girl. No weap—"

The repetition died on the man's lips as Amarande kicked back and up *hard*, heel of one boot and then the other smashing into his jaw from the underside. The giant's head cracked back, spittle and blood flying along with maybe a tooth or two, and his arms failed.

She fell to the floor face first, getting her arms out in front just quick enough to roll forward, backbone smacking against the plush rug and wooden floorboards with a thud, and to her feet.

The giant stumbled into a vase and marble pedestal with a crash, knocking the candle there to the floorboards. Amarande didn't see if the flame caught, because the ogre was moving toward her again, the man behind the desk screaming orders now. The giant tossed the sharp remainder of the vase at her as she reached again for her knife, and Amarande turned in time for the large shards to hit her back.

The man stumbled forward and dove at the innkeeper's orders: "Catch her before she gets that hand in her boot again. You're no good to me with a knife in your eye!"

The giant was so long his fingers were wrapped around Amarande's ankles in the next instant. She kicked, but his hands were large enough to void her movements, and he pulled her forward as if she were a rag doll, the silk of her skirt slick against the expensive weave of the rug.

"No . . . don't. . . . I-I . . . ," the princess stuttered. She'd been taught to fight much larger people, Koldo always emphasizing that for women technique was everything, but they'd never taught her how to survive an eight-foot nightmare.

Scrambling, Amarande put a hand in her pocket for her diamonds—the innkeeper's greed was the only thing that might get her out of this now.

But then there was more movement, the ring of steel, an extended spray of blood.

Osana.

Osana, standing there with Amarande's swords, one downturned and scraping the floorboards, the other straight through the giant's back.

Impossibly, the big man got to his knees, then to his feet. Osana whistled and tossed the untainted sword to Amarande, who caught it as she stood, and then, using two hands, the girl pulled the other sword straight out of the man's back before he made it to his full height.

Amarande got her sword up in a high guard, ready for the giant to turn and lurch at them. Osana followed, trying to copy, but clearly she'd never held a sword in her life until the moment she decided to thrust one into the ogre's back.

But he did not lurch at them. Instead, he pressed a massive hand to where the blade had come out of his stomach, eyes flicking to the innkeeper, who was frozen behind the desk, his melty-soft features waxen.

"No good. No good," the giant grunted, and then collapsed forward. He fell onto the marble desk, which buckled under the weight, and onto the innkeeper, too slow to move out of the way.

Amarande grabbed Osana's hand then. They ran for the door, pausing only so Amarande could stamp out the knocked-down candle, which had, from its side, tipped melted wax onto the floorboards, its flame now a mere hairbreadth from lighting that runaway wax and setting the wood on fire. Then they sprinted out of the inn, across the portico, and into the sun. The horses waited, shifting on nervous hooves.

"Thank you," the princess coughed out as they mounted their

horses, swords out and ready for the innkeeper's retaliation until they got their horses going into a hard gallop.

"You saved me, I save you," Osana answered, though her face went pale as the giant's blood dripped from the sword to her hand. She'd killed him; Amarande was sure of it.

The girls looked back as they wound around the edge of the wooden wall, waiting for the owner to come rushing out—or to perhaps send out more lackeys, because if he broke his own rules with one man, there were likely more.

But the innkeeper didn't come, and he didn't send anyone after them. He was a man who waited for prey rather than one who gave chase after it—a spider instead of a tiger.

Osana yelled to Amarande over the rushing wind, "You said four riders on three horses, yes?"

"Yes, so?"

"They've gone this way."

"How do you know?" Amarande asked, sheathing her sword. Osana had nowhere to put hers and kept it out, the wind peeling blood off the Basilican steel.

"You aren't the only one who can track."

Headed due west, they raced for two more minutes, until the compound could be fully seen behind them, along with any possible retaliation. Amarande slowed Mira, and Osana slowed, too, pointing to a line that cut through the shifting sands. An indentation large enough to be a path.

And there they were, three pairs of horse tracks, and one person walking. All away from the compound, their path leading back to one of the doors in the wooden wall.

It wasn't a perfect track, not really. More like an educated guess than something that could be corroborated.

Several yards away, the footsteps stopped and simply became three sets of hoofprints.

But then Amarande saw it—a small cluster of white flecks.

Amarande pulled Mira to a hard stop and dismounted to check, plucking a tiny beige grain from the scorched earth. Yes, a few oats, slipping through again.

Luca leaving clues. Which meant he was still alive and coherent. *Thank the stars.*

"What is it?" Osana asked.

"Proof."

"Is it true what you said? That you left your kingdom because your stableboy was kidnapped to push your hand into marriage?"

Amarande nodded, her earlier concerns about what this girl knew assuaged by her very recent actions. "Yes. All of it."

The girl chewed her lip. "I don't know much about being a princess, but . . . can't you just get another? That would be a good job for anyone."

Amarande mounted Mira so that she could look the girl in the eye. "I can replace the stableboy, but I cannot replace what he means to me."

Osana's eyes widened. "But you're a princess. You can't . . . you wouldn't . . ."

"Love a commoner? Of course I can, and I do. Love doesn't know anything about class, nor should it be bound by it."

Osana was quiet for a moment. "If I help you find him, may I earn a place at your home?"

Amarande looked at the girl then, covered in the giant man's blood, hand still gripping the sword. *Egia—truth.* "Osana, you have earned that sword, and you most certainly have earned a place. But this journey is my own, and dangerous enough. You've been good company, but I won't have you risk yourself for me without training. You've done enough already."

"But I want to come with you."

"And I want you to find a place at the Itspi, and the truth is . . . I'm unsure what will happen when I find these men and my love."

The girl's lips parted, but she stopped, giving Amarande space to continue.

The princess appreciated all the girl had done, but something in her gut told her that she must be alone to get Luca. She might die at the hands of the kidnappers, but she couldn't see this girl do the same. Not for her and her quest. Not untrained and exhausted.

"You say you can track? Head east to Ardenia, and to the Itspi. Ask for a man there called Serville. He is the head of my castle guard. Tell him what you know about me, show him the sword, and tell him this is Egia, and that I have Maite. He knows where to find the inscription that proves it. I wish I could send you with more proof than that, but hopefully all those things will combine to him believing you—he's a smart man and he will see you for a clever and loyal girl."

"Please let me come with you." Her voice was small, eyes downcast, as she made her plea yet again. So young yet so very weary. "I . . . I don't want to be alone."

Amarande placed a hand on the girl's shoulder. "On my honor, you have a place in my home, and after you make it there, you won't be alone again. Now, go."

Osana nodded, accepting her first order. "Until I see you again, Princess."

THE princess was closing in. She couldn't see them, not yet, but the hoofprints in the russet earth grew deeper with each passing minute, the wind receiving less time to wipe the earth clean of the riders' path. A loping angle toward the only functional port in the Torrent.

At least that's where she thought they were going.

It made no sense, but she followed. It didn't matter the kidnappers' destination—they wouldn't get there with Luca.

The sun was barreling toward the horizon now. Sunset was still hours away, but with each passing moment the lack of sleep pressed deeply into Amarande's eyelids. Her father had trained her to track prey like her life depended on it, yes, but he hadn't simulated the other parts of a journey like this—she'd always gotten as much sleep as she needed.

In the new light, the sands changed, too, the flowing seas of dust and earth becoming more irregular. Shrubbery brave enough to survive here poked up toward the coming night. She'd been told the Torrent was nothing but sand and sky and plateaus for miles on end, but this vegetation multiplied with each horse length. Amarande squinted ahead and saw the cut of a clear path through the scrub as it grew thicker, and the smudge of trees on the horizon.

The watering hole, the innkeeper, and now a change from the endless red dirt. What else would she find?

The wind kicked up and brushed a fine spray of sand into her eyes. Mira halted, her nose peeled back against the gust, her own eyes tightly closed. Amarande pulled her cowl up tighter and waited for it to pass, tears sticking in her eyes as her body sagged with exhaustion. Her stomach rumbled once again—if her adrenaline failed, at least her hunger would keep her awake. Like sleep, food was something of which she'd never been deprived, even in her training.

A weakness among many. She'd been highly trained, yes, but she was still completely unprepared.

When the air quieted down and it was safe to open her eyes, the princess did so, blinking to reorient herself before moving on. Mira waited patiently for her nudge.

Home, in the gray shadows of mountains to her right.

The Port of Torrent, somewhere up and to the left.

And there, angling toward the thick stain of trees on the horizon, were three little specks.

CHAPTER
23

❦

By the time the sun was beginning to set on another day and twilight fell in a silver cloud over the rushing red dust, the first thread of doubt looped its way around Luca's heart.

Amarande still hadn't come.

A second full day had passed now—Luca could no longer be ignorant to the length of time that had expired between his kidnapping and the present.

He pictured the princess as he last saw her, in the arena, jaw set, appeal unwavering as it lifted above the crowd. That girl wouldn't give in to bribery. She wouldn't trust the words of some unnamed letter writer to ensure the safety of her best friend. Deep down, that thread plucked itself into something resembling a sound, a fiddle string loose and thumping.

Luca glanced over his shoulder. Ula was riding beside him—he'd been pawned off on Urtzi in the late afternoon. Beyond her, the world was growing dark. The distant mountains to the east—Ardenia—had swallowed the last vestiges of the sun there, darkness consuming them. To the west, the last hour of light. Behind them, the wind shifted the dust in swirling clouds that gave the appearance of travelers on the horizon where there were none. Before them, their path was opening toward a thin ribbon of trees, jutting up from the earth like fingers pointed crooked toward the darkening sky. In this landscape, it almost appeared to be a forest, though nothing so robust was supposed to exist in the Torrent.

"She's not there, Luca." This came from Ula, who didn't glance his way, nor did she bother to look behind her to confirm what he wasn't seeing.

"Oh, but she is, Ula."

Ula's golden eyes slipped into their periphery. After a moment of watching silvering night, she looked back to Luca, trying to read his face across the distance. Luca wasn't sure what exactly she was trying to deduce, other than possibly to see if his viewpoint would project itself across his features for her.

"My princess is one of the best-trained hunters in the Sand and Sky. She won't let herself be seen."

At this, Ula shook her head, the linen she had wrapped around the fall of her long dark hair snagging gently against the pommel of the curved sword, which was slung across her back without Luca in the saddle. "Your confidence in her is more than I have in the sun continuing to rise."

"I—" Luca started, only to be cut off by a guffaw from up ahead.

"To the stars, you are the absolute sappiest male in our entire species. Stableboy, why are you still looking for her?" Dunixi wrenched his whole body around, his neck red enough again that clearly it hurt too much to fold the skin with a turn of his head. The linen had done little to protect his skin, which was still a vibrant pink beneath the cloth and in the waning light. "Your princess may be *different*, but she's not coming, because *she doesn't care*."

"I would like to remind all of you," Urtzi said, voice proud and projected from his spot inches from Luca aboard a honeyed-butter palomino named Ferri, "that I thought we'd snatched the wrong boy. And perhaps we did. The stableboy isn't her love."

"If she doesn't care, and I'm not her love, then you must let me go," Luca argued, knowing quite well that his cheeks were pinking at the thought of Amarande's heart finding him so. "I'm not worth it for you to drag around. I'm a liability, even—your man will be very disappointed that you've been hauling around no one of value. Return me and I'll help you find your rightful hostage."

Dunixi laughed again, but it was stiff, his shoulders still so as not to disrupt his neck. "Nice try, stableboy."

The trees they'd been pointed toward were suddenly upon them. No water here, but shade, not that they needed that now—the sun had dipped below the western horizon, the mountains' shadows falling long across the bowl of the Torrent.

Though this copse of trees was a respite from the wind and exposure, there were no other people in sight. Wherever they were going, whether it really was toward an actual ship or somewhere else entirely, was not somewhere many people seemed to want to go.

Near the middle of the strip of trees, Dunixi slowed his ghostly gelding, Boli, and swung a leg around. "Urtzi, rustle up our meal and secure the perimeter while you're at it. Ula, graze the horses and double-check that bonehead's perimeter work. Boy, sit down and watch me cook a meal you won't enjoy."

"Is that because you're an awful cook?"

Dunixi grunted. "No, it's because though we'll give you enough water to keep you around, the truth is you can survive weeks without a morsel to eat."

Luca decided not to remind the boy that Ula had given him dates for breakfast both this day and the last, plus part of her meal the night before. Perhaps the pain from his sunburn was making him forgetful.

The light died faster than Luca felt it ever had in the Itspi, the trees and high western mountains leeching it out in record time as the blond boy piled together sticks for a fire. Luca was surprised that he'd go to the trouble but didn't question it—maybe Dunixi believed they weren't being followed, that nobody cared that they were there, but Luca wouldn't stop the boy from announcing their presence with flame and no protection such as what they'd had the night before.

Ula returned first and tied the horses in careful intervals around the camp, a makeshift fence against the interests of the night. Urtzi returned almost a half hour later, four dead hares hanging by their ears in his huge hands.

"This is exactly why I keep you around, my friend," Dunixi said, snatching the hares away in greedy hands. "Don't get excited, stable-boy. There are four hares only because the hunter eats twice as much as everyone else."

The Myrcellian smiled wide at Luca, but it wasn't necessary; he believed the boy would have no trouble downing both hares. Urtzi had at least a head of height on Luca and was made of only hard things—muscles, bones, and ligaments. There wasn't an ounce of fat on him. Even Koldo would covet the chance to mold a soldier with a body like this one. Though, considering both his attitude and his opinion of women, she'd likely have much to mold.

Dunixi went about skinning and preparing the hares for the fire. And he *was* a capable cook—his knife skills were as good as Maialen's, and that was saying something. The hares were on a spit in record time and dressed with curds and whey pulled from a pouch within the blond boy's saddlebag.

Urtzi made it a point to squeeze in next to Luca. The lean bodies of his two hares swam in sauced cheese curd upon a wooden plate pulled from Dunixi's saddlebag. The Myrcellian ate them with all the gusto of someone who knew he was being treated, and it was clear he hoped Luca was watching, mouth watering. In truth, Luca was starving, but he didn't show it, his body relaxed against the base of a tree, eyes set on the fire.

Ula sat next to him, savoring her food slowly, while Dunixi sat across from them, trying very hard to put on the same sort of show that Urtzi was. Luca watched as he tried to drink from his flask without tossing his head back at any angle that would upset the blistered skin. Luca drew in a thin breath, thinking back to many dinners in the kitchens at the Itspi, and Maialen healing more than just nightly hunger. Medikua Aritza was talented, but she cared little for a stream of worn castle staff. "Dunixi, if you'll let me, I can calm your burn."

Luca was surprised when the boy didn't bat an eye at his name falling from his captive's lips. Luca may have been a "stableboy" to him, but they were on this journey together and he would address both Dunixi and Urtzi with respect, even if they didn't give it back to him in the same way Ula did. Moreover, he was quite sure the names every one of them preferred weren't the ones they were given at birth. Not that it mattered.

"My burn?"

"Your neck. I can help your neck. You don't even have to untie me, just allow me to use my hands."

"I don't—"

"Stop talking for a second and listen to Luca," Ula snapped, tossing a hare bone into the fire. "You've looked like you might pass out all day."

That shut him up. Luca met the Eritrian's eyes across the fire.

"How about I describe what I'm going to do before I do it so you're not surprised and you can decide if it's worth it or not?" Luca offered.

At this, Dunixi didn't say a word, which was actually slightly stunning to Luca. Unsure, he met Ula's eyes for a moment and then pressed on, knowing the answer but asking it anyway. They didn't need to know what he'd done with the oats. "When you knocked me out, I had a bag of rolled oats in my hand. Do you still have it?"

Luca knew they did, but he didn't want to let on. Any oats that escaped beyond what he'd released would find Amarande's notice. He was sure of it. That bald rope was a stroke of luck he didn't want to ruin. Ula nodded and held up her bag.

"If you allow me access to those oats and give me some of the whey from the cheese, I can make a paste that will take the sting out of the burn on your neck. It may help dry the blisters as well."

Dunixi swallowed. "Oats and whey? That's all you need?"

Luca nodded. "Honey and a mortar and pestle would be ideal, but those are the basics, yes."

"And why would you do this?"

"Because you're in pain and you need help." It was true.

Dunixi's eyes narrowed, shadows falling over the near-colorless blue. "Kindness won't keep me from killing you."

"I know."

The Eritrian laughed. "That's it? That's all you're going to say?"

"Yes. Now would you like to stop questioning me and let me help?"

The boy's attention skipped to his seconds. "Urtzi, watch his hands. Ula, you apply it. I don't want him anywhere near my windpipe."

Luca nearly smiled—the girl was a much bigger danger. By the time Dunixi figured that out, he might already be dead.

CHAPTER
24

❦

By the time Amarande hit the trees, her eyes were closing for long periods, no matter how much she told them not to. Her grip was slack on Mira's reins and she knew sleep would come for her soon—she was her father's daughter, to be sure, but even the Warrior King needed rest. Ardenian tigers couldn't stand forever.

She shook it off.

The three specks had disappeared into those trees. She was sure of this, even with her eyes failing her.

Either they would emerge on the other side, or they would break for the night. They were human and they didn't realize they were being chased, and so she hoped for the latter.

This was her chance to see what she was up against and then plot her attack.

Amarande dismounted Mira, patting the filly on the nose before guiding her between spindly trees that grew toward the cobalt blue of a new night. This was the type of brush that provided cover but also hid the worst of what nature could provide. Things with fangs, and claws, and venom. Everything Osana had made her recall, plus the impossible black wolf and more. The sun and the Warlord and mongrels like the trio of thieves weren't the only dangers here.

The princess and her horse walked slowly, carefully, quietly, for an hour before Amarande saw it. A flash of orange light.

She paused, unsure whether it was real or simply hope manifesting in her exhausted eyes.

When it flickered again, she knew it to be true and tangible.

Flame.

A fire.

A distance of maybe a hundred yards.

Amarande tied Mira's reins to a nearby trunk and pressed her hand to the horse's nose. She hoped she didn't have to order the girl to be silent, because this close, she didn't trust even a whisper not to carry. Mira blinked patiently and let her master go without a single neigh of protest.

The princess reached into her boot and brought out her knife, leaving her sword strapped to her back—a long sword wasn't made for stealth, unless that was all one had. She kept her pace measured and careful, navigating underbrush that might give her away if met with the weight of a step. The ground here was soft and swallowed her steps, the earth sparkling with dew as the temperature dropped, the moisture-starved climate appeased for a moment.

The closer Amarande got, the more confident she grew that this was right. Three horses were tied up at intervals around a natural campground, brush pulled away and space for a fire in the middle of a ring of trees. Long ago, a tree near the center had fallen, and someone had cleared everything but a stump, creating a pocket among the tightly packed spindles that allowed for this kind of space. Which meant, Amarande realized, that these kidnappers had been here before.

The exhaustion she'd felt just moments earlier receded, her eyes wide open and heart pounding. She held fast to the knife, ready to act—*Make the first mark*—but hoping for the opportunity to take a more measured approach.

Ten feet out, she sank into a near crawl, crouched into the shadows and close to the ground as the people came into view.

There were four bodies surrounding the embers of a fire.

A boy with white-blond hair that shimmered in the bare light. His back was to her as he lay on his side, some sort of medicinal paste flaking from his neck. He appeared to be asleep.

Toward his feet lay another boy, this one long and lean, with smooth tawny skin and a mop of curls that shaded his eyes from the firelight. He also seemed to be asleep.

Closest to her, a girl, propped up with her back to Amarande, long dark hair spilling out of a linen kerchief and over her shoulders. From the gentle movements of her right forearm, the princess knew she was awake, and writing or drawing. Amarande shifted to the right to see, and, yes, the girl was scratching at a leather-bound book with the stub of a pencil. It wasn't the only thing in her lap, though—a long curved blade lay across her knees.

It was such a casual place for a weapon that Amarande knew at once that this girl could use that blade as well as she could use her own.

Amarande sucked in a deep, quiet breath and shifted her gaze to the last body in the circle—sprawled out on the ground next to the lookout and her deadly weapon.

The moment of truth.

Raven hair, the right build, clothes that seemed familiar.

Heart pounding hard enough that she thought the girl might hear, Amarande took two careful steps to the right and squinted across the short distance to read what she could of his face.

Amarande's heart stuttered.

Luca.

Relief spread across her shoulders and down her back as she saw his chest rise and fall. Luca, alive. In front of her.

He was rolled onto his side, one arm wedged beneath his ear as a makeshift pillow. She couldn't tell from where she crouched if he was awake or asleep, unharmed or injured, but considering how they'd secured him, he had either put up a good fight or given them quite the reason to believe he would. Both his hands were bound, as were his feet, meaning that to use one arm to buffer his face from the ground, the other fell across his face at a slanting angle. The ropes that held his limbs were secured to *another* rope that was tied to the tree behind him. Amarande made note of each restraint, running through the blocking in her mind of what she'd have to do to pull him free—sawing and hacking at the restraints would take only marginally less time than releasing the knots.

Ropes cataloged, she began to document everything else, crouching against the trees, melting in with the shadows, forming a plan. Much of good reconnaissance was in training, but part of it was in luck—and here she'd been lucky, approaching the lookout from behind.

The girl stowed her pencil and journal in the saddlebag at her side, then sheathed the knife at a slant across her back as she got to her feet. Out of instinct, Amarande sank back farther onto her heels, watching as the girl picked her way around Luca and the fire before crouching over the lanky boy asleep on the other side of the flames. Her back was to Amarande as she tried to nudge the boy awake by tapping his calf.

The boy startled, hands out and ready to throw a punch. As if she'd done it before, the girl caught his knuckles in her palm.

"Your turn, you big oaf."

"You like me more than your nicknames let on," the boy answered, a smile sliding across his face. In the dark his teeth were the same brilliant white as the moon.

The girl dropped his fist.

"Keep telling yourself that," she whispered, and stood, turning her back on the boy and heading back to her spot next to Luca with a bemused turn to her lips.

Amarande dared not even breathe with the girl facing her now— she was exposed more than she'd been at any previous moment. The knife's weight seemed to double in her palm, her training flashing her through the motions she would use if the girl saw her.

Lunge and stab, straight under the rib and into the girl's left lung as she raised her hands over her head to draw the sword from her back.

Immediate release and drop of the girl, freeing the knife to throw it straight to the boy's stomach, chest, or neck depending on how quick he was to get to his feet.

Slash of a sword tip against the girl's throat to finish her, then the same to the boy where he fell.

Next, the sleeping blond boy. If he woke, it would be the boot dagger to his chest as he sat up; if he slept, a clean assassin's smile carved across his windpipe.

Amarande's hand trembled around the knife as the boy brushed parched leaves from his foppish curls.

"Why do I always get the middle shift?" he whined softly to the girl's back. "It's so hard to fall asleep twice."

She did Amarande a favor and turned, glancing over her shoulder while eviscerating the boy and his complaints.

"Because you haven't figured out yet that you could disembowel the Eritrian as easily as those hares you caught for dinner, and he's the one who gave you the middle shift."

Despite herself, Amarande grinned just a little as the boy shrugged and glanced at the blond one, snoring across the way. "If he leads, I don't have to make decisions. Easy enough life being a follower."

The girl plopped down, her back to Amarande as she lay all the way to the ground, her head cradled in her hands, elbows jutted out toward Luca's soft breaths.

"One day you might wake up to how sad that statement is," the girl said, shaking her head, "but for now, enjoy the sounds of midnight. See you at dawn."

And that was that.

Amarande's plan began to form. She knew her foe. She knew when they would leave. And that gave her time to rest up and prepare for a proper attack, her father's words again appearing in her head.

Lack of preparation can squander the element of surprise.

It was a gamble, because if she was rested, they would be, too, but she had one chance at this. And she wouldn't miss.

The Warrior King's daughter backed away from her opponents and shrank back into the trees. Back to Mira, to the chance to recover enough to be at her best when saving her love.

She removed the slip of fabric she'd used as a cowl, unknotted it, and tied it to the black filly's bridle and her left wrist, hopeful that the predawn feeding routine Luca kept with his horses would mean Mira would grow restless at precisely the time Amarande needed to attack.

It was the best she could do.

And if it failed, she was on the right track and would adapt.

Boot knife tight in her right hand, the princess lay in the dirt, the pommel of her father's sword digging into her back. Rather than move it, she shut her eyes and finally fell asleep.

CHAPTER
25

❦

AMARANDE'S left hand dragged through the dirt, and her eyes immediately shot open, her body rocketing up until she was sitting, knife out, blinking into consciousness.

It was still dark.

Oh, thank the stars.

There was Mira, up from where she'd lain down the night before, muzzle digging coolly through the underbrush for something worth eating. Right on time.

The princess took a deep breath and squinted over her shoulder—the fire was still burning in the distance, hot enough that if the kidnappers had moved on, they weren't far. To the right, the horizon beyond the thick cluster of spindly trees was slightly lighter, the first blues bleeding into the night's endless black.

Relief flooded through Amarande's body. She blinked again, eyes renewed, though being rested was not something she could claim. Three hours, that was it. But that would have to do, and it would have to last her—the second she had Luca's hand in hers, they were on the run until they were safe or they were captured.

The princess removed the cowl from Mira's bridle, looping the excess around her wrist. The horse huffed, hoping for the breakfast Luca always had prepared for her at this hour. "Soon, girl."

She stowed her boot knife for the moment. The sword stayed on her back as well. She guided the horse through the trees and wound around to the very edge of the slip of forest, walking along the border, feet in the sand that sloped out to the desert she'd ridden through the day before.

Amarande couldn't risk taking Mira into the kidnappers' camp. Though she was a very good horse indeed, she was still too loud and too smelly—the other horses would notice her in an instant. What's more, there were too many variables to getting Luca free from his ropes and onto the horse while potentially fighting three people who likely would only get paid if they held on to Luca—or captured her to go right along with him.

And so the princess tiptoed along the dirt, keeping Mira at a wide berth of the tree line and the crackling debris that would snap under hoof. Then when she was right in line with the orange glow of the fire, she tied Mira to another spindly tree. Not too tight that she couldn't get her free when she came back to her with Luca in hand. The idea that the knot had to be loose in case she never returned to Mira blinked in the recesses of Amarande's mind, and she shut it away just as quickly as it came.

Warriors didn't make concessions like that.

Mira taken care of, Amarande turned her attention back to the fire. Using the orange glow as a beacon, she snuck toward it on soft steps, her movements sharper than they had been only hours earlier, her senses heightened, her focus clear.

The princess's steps slowed, her center of gravity becoming lower as the fire grew closer. Her fingers slipped into her boot yet again, the knife at the ready as she came within striking distance. She was approaching from an angle that put her between where Luca and the girl had been on the sundial, and the blond boy— the Eritrian, who apparently was giving the orders.

Amarande didn't know how long the watch shifts were for the party, but she guessed by the conversation between the girl and the Myrcellian boy that it should now be the Eritrian's turn. And so she scanned the site, hunting for movement, especially from the blond boy, whose form she pinpointed at the tenth spot on the sundial.

No movement.

Good.

She could see the lumpy shadows of the horses and their owners, forged in the fire they'd left burning. They hadn't left camp, and if they were awake, they weren't alert yet.

The opportunity was exactly what she needed.

Her father's words rang in her ears, and it made her smile.

Make the first mark.

Yes, she would.

The princess's heart kicked into high gear, the promise of a fight approaching. The Warrior King's blood was her blood, of that there was no doubt, and it sang and danced in her veins with a life of its own.

Her fingers tightened on the knife.

She came to a tree on the very edge of their camp circle. The horses stirred but didn't alarm, as tired as they were and quiet as she was. That knife tight in her fist, she cataloged each of the people, closer than she'd seen them even last night.

The girl—of Torrent, it appeared.

The tall boy—Myrcellian to be sure.

The blond boy—Eritrian, as burnt as the landscape.

And Luca, breathing but bound, a massive bruise blooming across his temple. That had to be the tall boy's work. And for that he would pay.

All of them still, but more than that—*asleep.*

There'd been a breakdown in communication on their watch. The tall boy's handoff to the Eritrian either hadn't happened or had and the blond boy fell back to sleep.

Either way, it was to her advantage.

They were sitting—*sleeping*—ducks, vulnerable in ways that may very well be their end, should her knife blade go to work.

The hesitation that she'd felt when she encountered the robbers crept forward in her mind—that instant when she'd held two swords to one man and hadn't managed to kill him, getting nothing from him in answer to the question that initially kept him alive, all the while losing her provisions and the security they provided.

She'd most definitely suffered from her choices.

The princess shook free of the thought.

Retrieving Luca was the only goal. Punishment to the kidnappers and anything else would only be secondary.

And so she set her eyes upon Luca with the aim only of getting him out alive. Not starting a fight. Not settling scores.

Just Luca. Only Luca. Forever Luca.

Amarande crept forward, knife out and ready, attention skipping from one sleeping body to the next. She approached in such a way that she could go directly to Luca and meet him where he would see her the second he opened his eyes—approaching him from behind might startle him too much. But with that tactic came an additional hurdle.

The girl.

She was sleeping next to him at arm's length—close enough that she could grab him if she sensed movement. Which meant to get to Luca this way, Amarande had to step over the girl, or go around her and then squeeze between their bodies, crouching down with either her back or her weak side to a girl who slept with a curved sword of Torrent like it was a babe at her breast.

Not ideal.

But it was the most direct path to her goal.

The princess crept toward Luca and the girl, sweeping around their feet. She paused in the space between them, squinting at the shadows that separated them. On further inspection, Luca's binds hadn't just been attached to a rope that had been tied to a tree, but to the girl herself after her watch, an additional rope tying his bound wrists to her left hand.

Again, not ideal.

But she would make it work.

Amarande crept forward, her footsteps as soft as a wren's in the mud, though the brush was dry and she had the weight of what she wanted to do pressed down upon small-but-mighty shoulders, her sword, her long gown, and the hidden diamonds.

She swept her skirt close to her body with her non-knife hand, willing the fabric not to splay out and brush the wrong arm, and then sank all the way into a squat—split stance and ready to run. She angled her shoulders so that her left one faced the girl rather than her back, and then brought her hands within an inch of Luca's sleeping form. So close she caught a whiff of the lavender oil he used on the Itspi's horses.

Stars, he's real.

He was really here. This was happening. Her love was before her and they were minutes from going home. She'd have Luca, and Renard would have nothing except a ruined plan.

The princess took a calming breath.

Always forward, never back.

Simultaneously, she gently placed one hand over Luca's mouth and one on his hands, spreading her fingers so as to keep any startled movement at a minimum.

His eyes flew open, gold and alarmed.

His hands fluttered as she expected they would, and though she kept even pressure, the rope skittered across the dry dirt. She subdued it with the toe of her boot, attention shooting to the girl. She didn't stir.

When Amarande looked again to Luca, he'd gone completely still, except for those eyes, which rounded.

In recognition. Wonder. Joy.

The princess could feel his lips moving under her palm, and she gently pulled her hand away, revealing a smile and words formed yet soundless.

Ama, you came.

Her own grin was stretching before she could stop it—she was so relieved to see his face, his surprise, his happiness, that she answered his joyful silence with a whisper. "Yes."

And that was when the princess realized her goal was also her biggest weakness.

Luca's eyes grew wider, smile faltering at the same time he jerked himself up onto his elbows. "Ama, watch—"

She didn't hear the rest of it.

Luca yanked hard against the rope with his bound wrists, and suddenly there was a body crashing over Amarande's upper back.

The princess shot to her feet as the body rolled over her, sending the girl to the ground with a hard thump. The girl managed to keep hold of her sword, and Amarande immediately stomped on it with both feet, pinning it and her right hand beneath it to the ground.

Knife out, Amarande silently beckoned to Luca, using the few seconds they might have before the girl began screaming to draw him close and begin sawing at his binds. He lunged toward her, wrists presented, but Amarande only got in a single hack at the ropes before the girl found the breath that had been knocked from her lungs.

"Attack! We're under attack! Urtzi, Dunixi! Up!"

The rope binding Luca's wrists began to fray and Amarande hacked and sawed at it again.

"Wait!" Luca said to Amarande. The princess immediately froze, and Luca lunged back deeply, yanking and twisting with his whole body just as the girl's fingers scraped the hilt of her pinned sword. The girl's entire left arm lurched back, threatening to come out of the socket—her wrist still attached by rope to her prisoner.

She cried out at the tension, and suddenly Luca was falling backward, stumbling into the Eritrian, who was pushing himself up, out of too-deep slumber.

Luca rolled over the blond boy, shrugging his hands free and apart, the rope dead at his feet. Then he pitched them in front of his body, ready to catch. "Ama!"

And suddenly the princess was back in their meadow, but working with Luca instead of against him. Her boot knife left her grasp without a whiff of hesitation, wheeling hilt over blade, straight for his outstretched hands. Beneath him, the Eritrian boy scrambled to his feet, blood spurting out of his moon-white nose and down into his mouth, the mass of Luca having dealt quite the blow.

"Urtzi!" he screamed in a gurgle at the Myrcellian boy, who clearly woke much easier by touch than by sound.

Hands free, Amarande began to draw her sword just as the girl decided to change tactics and kick backward, curling her legs over her head and springing up from her shoulders, nailing Amarande's shins with the full might of her tumbling body. Amarande flew back right as, across the fire, the Myrcellian boy jolted up to his feet.

Amarande lost sight of both the tall boy and the girl as she hit the tree behind her hard, shoulder and hand smacking hard enough to shed bark from the trunk. The girl stood, sword out and ready as Amarande rolled off the tree, willing her stinging hand and throbbing shoulder to listen to the commands of her brain and grab the sword at her back. A second passed and the girl took advantage, lunging, curved sword striking straight for Amarande's heart.

The princess's left arm shot back, grabbed the sword, and met the girl in a hanging parry. She cut up with all her might, right hand joining the fight, flinging the girl's sword up and back.

"So it is true—you can fight, tiger cub," the girl said, bringing in a high guard as Amarande's sword swung toward her face.

"I am my father's daughter."

Their swords rang out again, and Amarande called out to Luca over the girl's shoulder. He'd just kicked the Eritrian back to the ground, sending the boy sprawling and more blood spurting. The sky was suddenly a shade brighter, everything coming to light. The Myrcellian charged at him, and Luca held his knife out against the boy, who had no obvious weapon except those meat-paw fists at the bases of his long arms.

"Don't kill him! We need him! Fists only. No daggers." The Eritrian blubbered from the ground, trying again to get to his feet but dizzy enough he swayed every time he nearly got there.

"Dunixi, if you haven't noticed, we're fighting *the princess,* so I don't think we need him any longer!"

"Ula, and here I thought we were friends," Luca said, and it almost sounded like he was laughing.

Amarande thought she saw a whisper of a smile as the girl met her latest blow. "Nothing personal, but you're worth the same to us alive or dead at this point, Luca."

Luca dodged a running swing from the tall boy, the Myrcellian's long arm finding nothing but air as Luca rolled. Through the movement, Luca's blade slashed the boy's shirt from his skin, blood blooming under his rib cage as he shrieked, "If you don't need me, let us go. I'd rather not hurt any of you."

That surprised Amarande a little, considering what they'd done to him, but Luca was nothing if not kind to the most difficult creatures—human, equine, or otherwise.

"If we don't have either of you, we don't get paid," the Eritrian bellowed, finally getting to his feet. "Ula, Urtzi, capture them both and let's collect."

"Capturing would be much easier if it were *three on two,*" the girl spat through clenched teeth as she crossed swords yet again with Amarande. Up close, her eyes flashed, furious despite her sarcasm. If Amarande were her, she'd be furious, too.

"Hold the stableboy, Urtzi," the Eritrian ordered the lanky boy, forearms and hands bloody with more direct slashes from Luca's knife work. Luca danced around, pulling the Myrcellian toward Amarande, as the Eritrian came their way, drawing a flaming stick from the fire and coming toward Amarande and the girl as if brandishing a torch.

Amarande's eyes rolled. *Just like an ineffective leader—kill it with fire.*

Middle guard and cross, and she pushed the girl back toward the advancing boy, so that he'd have to work around the swing of their swords to do any damage. At some point, he'd wiped the blood from his nose into his eyes, and with the change in blocking he misjudged, swinging and nearly catching the tips of the girl's long hair with the flames. The girl wrenched herself away, giving up ground on Amarande's advance, and the princess's sword came down at an angle that grazed her forearm.

As she cried out, the Eritrian tipped off-balance, hitting only air and tumbling forward into some brush, spinning as he fell to keep from landing on his flaming stick. It dropped out of the boy's hand as he hit the ground with a smack, a violent *oooof,* and a hiss.

More than one hiss.

"Dunixi!" the girl yelled, her slashed arm really bleeding now. But the boy was slow to take her warning, the air and all his motivation vacating as he landed hard.

And just beyond his far shoulder was the reason for the hissing—three snakes unsettled and unfurling.

Amarande's eyes widened.

Squat body, zigzag-patterned scales, buzzing hiss—unmistakably Harea Asps.

Owners of the deadliest venom in all of the Sand and Sky.

Able to strike and reset within a tenth of a second.

And very, very easy to anger.

Suddenly the princess was in motion, lunging for the stick and its remaining flame. She scooped it up in her right hand and tossed it at the snake just as it struck at the Eritrian. At the same time, the girl yanked him hard and pulled him toward her. He tumbled into her and in an instant they were both flat on the ground, him pinning her, as the flaming snake hissed back.

The asp's brethren scattered—right toward where Luca and the tall boy still exchanged blows.

"Luca!" Amarande yelled as he ducked from a long swing of the tall boy's fist. She ran toward both Luca and the fire. "Move, move, fire incoming!"

The Myrcellian boy just grunted, his attention squarely on Luca.

But Luca had his wits about him, and just like during those faux battles back home in their little meadow, he knew everything Amarande was thinking before she did it.

When the tall boy's next automatic punch sailed toward Luca's face, instead of ducking, Luca grabbed his opponent's fist in both hands and used it to swing them both out of the way. As they stumbled in the opposite direction of where the girl and the blond boy were trying to untangle themselves, Amarande scraped the fat edge of her sword through the fire, scooping up embers and ashes on the thick Basilican steel. In one broad heave, the flaming kindling sprayed the advancing asps with a crackle and hiss.

The snakes shuddered and retreated, scales smoking.

And, suddenly, Amarande and Luca's window of escape was open.

Luca extricated himself from the Myrcellian and grabbed Amarande's outstretched hand. She yanked him in the direction they needed to go, sword out. As they ran to the edge of the camp, she dropped his hand and lifted a saddlebag from the ground—the girl's, her journal spilling to the dirt with a thump. Luca seemed to startle at the sudden loss of her fingers in his until he realized why she'd done it and dipped down to grab another saddlebag, just a few feet away.

Then Luca fell in behind Amarande as she raced them through the forest, freedom stretching before them, his captivity at their backs.

CHAPTER
26

❦

THIS was taking too long. Far too long.

Prince Renard fell asleep yet again to that thought, curled into himself on his bedroll, a million stars twinkling overhead and the wind howling all around. And he woke to the thought, too, a sick feeling wedged deep in his stomach, strong enough that he felt it even before the thirst that had a stranglehold on his throat. The arid landscape and hard travel were catching up to him.

He blinked awake and pushed onto his elbows. The sun was up, as was everyone else in his party, toiling around a breakfast fire, water for coffee merrily boiling. And suddenly he was furiously, inexplicably, frustrated.

"This is all wrong," Renard grumbled, his voice cracking. He needed water. The prince got to his feet and yanked a mug out of the hand of the nearest guard, took a swallow, and then spat it down the front of his breeches.

"Tremaine! *Madiran?* This early? *Here?*" The bloodred Pyrenee wine would leave an impossible stain on the pearly white fabric. The prince rubbed uselessly at his pants.

"Your Highness, I suffer from headaches; it helps—"

Renard knocked the guard upside the head with the mug. "You deserve more than a headache for thinking this conduct proper." The prince lobbed the mug straight to the red dirt between them, the pottery shattering as wine sprayed their ankles. "Considering the time of day and the seriousness of this quest, I expect water, coffee, or blood to wet your tongue and nothing else."

"Easy there, Your Highness," Taillefer chided, standing from his place by the fire and offering Renard his own drink. "Coffee?"

"No," Renard spat. "Water."

Bemused eyes never leaving Renard's face, the younger prince knelt down and snatched a waterskin from beside already-packed bags. He tossed it to Renard, who took a healthy swig before wasting a conservative amount on the stain streaking his lap. This action did nothing but spread it, now pink and reaching at the edges. Renard drained the rest of the water and tossed the skin back to Taillefer, whose face was smugly recording the worsening splotch.

"Pack it up!" Renard barked, throat moistened and voice recovered. "There's no time for breakfast—we need to keep going. The princess awaits. Kill the fire; ready the horses. Let's move!"

His men screeched to a halt in their various movements— drinking coffee, slicing sausage, even midstream with a chin thrown over a shoulder to receive orders.

And that's when Taillefer began to laugh. "That's rich from the last man to wake."

Renard's eyes narrowed and his voice dropped into a fierce whisper. He grabbed his brother's wrist, coffee splattering onto the rusted dirt between them. "I will not have you openly question me on this trip. I am your leader. Treat me like it."

Taillefer's quirked lips hardened into a line, and a single brow arched as he wrenched his arm away, purposefully spilling the rest of the coffee down Renard's pant leg and onto his newly scratched boots. "Then act like it."

The crown prince rolled his eyes and swatted at his clothing as the coffee soaked in with the wine. Stained in a way that made it appear he'd wet his pants with something worse than urine. So regal.

"Renard, start the morning over, man," Taillefer said, moving in close—not to intimidate but to implore. "We're going to find her much faster if you don't piss off your crew. Plus, that Serville man will report your behavior to the castle whether we find her or not—you don't want him to describe you as a brat who's lazy enough to sleep in and undisciplined enough to rant without cause."

"I have cause," Renard snapped. "*You* should've woken me, Tai. We should be on our way. We're losing time. She's been gone two days now. And lest you forget, Mother is using every moment we're absent to steal our rightful throne. We can't wait."

"No, but we need to come up with a better plan, because no matter if we're moving or sleeping, it's becoming increasingly difficult to find a princess-shaped needle in this haystack." Taillefer made it a point then to look around them. They'd slept at the base of a perfectly vertical flattop, jutting up from the red earth, reaching straight for the moon. Around them, the only movement was the ever-drifting sands in the current of wind. Taillefer met Renard's eyes—blue on blue, the cheeks beneath them shaded a deep pink above the line of the cowl he'd worn during yesterday's travels. "We need a new plan."

Around them, the men were in motion—his four men plus the babysitter, Serville, picking up the camp. Renard tried to ignore the fact that all bags but his appeared to be packed and ready, the horses saddled and fed. The pot over the fire was for a second round of coffee—most men were already finished with their breakfast. He bristled at the thought that they'd let him sleep—that he'd let himself sleep.

He wouldn't beat his mother at her own game while dead to the world.

Renard closed his eyes. Yes, a plan. It had been Taillefer's idea to head into the Torrent in the first place. It was the most logical place, of course. The stableboy had been born there, and though it was entirely open spaces, it was the most famous place in the Sand and Sky for anyone to hide.

As his brother had suggested, the haystack here was wide and grinding and as impossible as the sea.

Renard took another swig of water, this time from his own waterskin. Let that anger and frustration wane. Those were symptoms of his ambition. He couldn't let the symptoms outweigh the real heart of the matter.

He needed the girl.

He needed to be the hero, bringing her back.

He needed to make her see he was right for her. Make her see that he was her future. That they, together, were the future of not only Pyrenee and Ardenia but also the Sand and Sky.

Renard felt the mask he'd worked so hard to create slide over. The boy who'd woken disappointed enough at himself to take it out on others was now buried deep, with any other inklings of a terrified seventeen-year-old boy.

They couldn't just press on in whatever direction their gut led them. He'd spent the last years of his life learning to outsmart his mother before she could steal away his throne. He could be smarter than what he was chasing.

The prince opened his eyes. His brother stood there, draining his coffee. Taillefer's confidence, wit, and proclivity for plants over people were among his most annoying traits, but they were also his most useful ones. And, as a right-hand man, he was usually surprisingly supportive. Again, Taillefer raised a brow. "So?"

Always prodding, the little brother. Renard preferred Tai poke at the travesties in his natural arts den rather than at the feelings deep within himself, but out here the options to distract his little brother's probing attitude were limited.

Renard placed his own hands on his hips. Glanced around. At his back, the plateau and its disappearing shadow, the sun growing higher with each breath. Ahead, an endless expanse of red, dead-ending at the mountains that he called home. The ones his mother was returning to in haste. At that very moment she was likely in her coach, writing letters to the southern kingdoms, wooing both King Akil and King Domingu to greener, *more landed,* pastures. She wouldn't wait for them in Ardenia. Renard knew that as deeply as he knew his time was running out.

His chance was running out.

As he squinted, Renard's attention snagged on movement on the skyline. Neither wind, nor a single black horse with the stable-boy and the princess, but a long, snaking thing of patchwork and a certain kind of power.

And suddenly the prince knew what to do.

THE promise of payment would get someone far in a place like this. No one had to tell Renard this. He felt it like the rising sun's pledge of heat in the new day.

And he was going to use that to his advantage.

His party packed up and headed out in record time, following his lead with renewed energy, pointed straight toward the caravan they spied in the distance. It was long, snaking, and on the move itself, but slowly and in a crossing direction to their own. The band from Pyrenee caught up within the hour, and the caravan slowed at their approach, recognizing at a distance the purple-and-gold garb of the majority of the group and the garnet-and-gold uniform of the only outlier.

The snaking mass of horses, oxen, and coaches ground to a halt, riders from various connections in the mile-long line abandoning their posts to meet the approaching group.

The riders assembled in a pyramid, with a long-haired, broad-shouldered man at its point, staring down Renard and his men.

"Announce your intentions," the lead rider said, his mouth covered with a fluttering shroud of linen but his words clear and crisp. This was a man who was accustomed to having people listen to him.

But so was Renard.

"I intend to pay your finest men a generous sum of gold each to hunt down something I have lost."

"A lump sum isn't valuable without parameters attached to it," the leader said. "How long will this task take?"

"It depends on how good the men are. A day, maybe two."

The leader considered that. Renard's heart snagged mid-beat on the worry that these men might have no use for gold. But in truth, gold could always be of use—melted and molded in a way diamonds could not. Or at least it was what his kingdom had survived on for a thousand years.

The leader spoke again. "And what is it that you've lost?"

"My fiancée." It was true enough. Behind him, Serville coughed into his garnet cloak. "Princess Amarande of Ardenia. Traveling with a young man of the Torrent on a single black filly. Or, if she's escaped from his clutches, alone. There will be a further reward for anyone who has credible information on her."

A man set apart from the leaders immediately nudged his horse forward. "Me and my boys saw her two days ago."

Renard's gaze drifted to the two men behind the speaker, and they both nodded. One looked perfectly fine, the other nursing wounds to his shoulder and flank. Looking at the speaking man closer now, the prince saw that his entire left side hung at an unfortunate angle, a hasty sling on his arm doing nothing to haul it back up. Purple bruises marred his face, sand rash obvious, too.

Renard's heart beat faster, sure and strong. The man's quick response, along with his appearance—as if he'd just met the ghost of the Warrior King—was a good sign. Still, Renard knew to be cautious. If living with his mother had taught him anything, it was that.

The prince pulled a small drawstring pouch from his belt. He fished out a solid gold piece and brought it into the strong morning light. The metal shimmered as he knew it would, and the men's eyes grew hungry with each shining turn as he held it out for them to see. "A troy ounce of pure Pyrenee gold is in this pouch. If you can prove to me the girl you saw was her, it will be yours."

The battered man narrowed his eyes, choosing his words carefully.

"Black horse. Garnet dress of lace and silk. Chest plate two sizes too large. Hair, reddish brown and done up for something special. Blue-green eyes eager to saw a man in half. Two swords crossed at her back"—his eyes flicked to his useless side—"and she knows how to use them."

Behind him, Renard heard Taillefer snicker. It was funny because it was so dead-on. This girl couldn't be anyone but Amarande.

Without hesitation, Renard tossed the pouch at the man. He caught it with his good hand.

"That's her," the prince concluded. "Am I to deduce from your story that she was alone? Perhaps fearful enough to attack any man to cross her path after what she endured at the hands of her vile captor?"

Again, Serville coughed.

The injured man tucked the pouch of gold into his old belt but didn't seem moved by Renard's apparent elation. "She was alone but headed away from both Pyrenee and Ardenia."

Renard rushed in to turn the tide of conversation from this one of skepticism. "After such an ordeal, it is no surprise that she would have been confused. Do you know which way she went?"

The man nodded. "She was confused enough to think she was looking for four riders on three horses. I see seven of you."

Another person urged her horse forward—this one a girl, no older than Renard. Maybe of Basilica—blue eyes, dark hair, clothes in tatters, nice sword strapped to her back in a hasty scabbard.

"I saw four riders on three horses watering themselves and their horses at the Cardenas Scar two days ago. A Torrentian boy was bound and loudly insisting his princess would come for him. It sounds like your princess could have been looking for that group."

Renard drew another pouch of gold from his belt and tossed it at the girl before she could say more so publicly. She'd ripped the rug out from under his repeated assumption of the stableboy's misdeeds but she'd also hinted at what they really needed: actual direction. It was time to leave.

"You two come." He gestured warmly, regally, to the rest of the caravan. "Four men of strength and talent, join us and your own gold awaits. We must not squander these leads."

CHAPTER
27

❧⸎❧

AMARANDE and Luca ran until the sun was strong. Thirst gripped them with the dryness and the heat that had found them in their rush away from the kidnappers—due west, with the forest close enough that they could duck in for cover if needed.

Soon enough, the light tinkling of a thin stream was too much to resist. The water trickled out from under a thick stand of low brush and continued a short way. It was impossible to tell where it had started from, but the water was moving along, not stagnant, and therefore as safe for consumption as they were likely going to get.

Amarande pulled Mira to a trot, and she and Luca both took a long look behind them. No one. Not yet.

Wordlessly, they slid off the filly's slick back and tied Mira to a strong bloom of bush downstream for her own fulfillment. Then they sat and drank and then drank some more, filling over and over the two waterskins they'd found in their stolen saddlebags. They'd found other things, too—food, clothing, a dagger, and, to the princess's interest, a small drawstring pouch perfect for her diamonds.

And when their bellies were full with cool water and the sweat was beginning to dry to their skin rather than continue flowing, Amarande grabbed Luca's hand and pulled him under a rock shelf that shielded them partly from the sun.

They'd run so far and so fast, they'd yet to say much at all.

"Let me have a look at you," the princess said, her tongue curling in an almost embarrassed way as she met his eyes. She usually could be so unguarded with him, but at that moment, with the weight of what she'd done to get him back hanging between them, she found herself suddenly sheepish under his gaze.

He'd ridden at her back for the last two hours, his chest pressed to her spine as Mira navigated through the shifting sand and brush. But feeling his heart slow from frantic to relieved as it thumped against her backbone was completely different from seeing for herself that he hadn't been harmed.

Luca's cheeks were flushed with heat. Sweat shimmered in the usual places—his brow, the dip below his lower eyelashes, the ridges of his cheekbones. There was evidence of what he'd been through—a large knot at his temple, obviously red and angry even beneath the curling ends of his hair. His wrists were bruised and raw where his hands had been bound.

There wasn't more that she could see, though he held himself carefully, as if his back ached, or maybe it was his ribs. Amarande's attention again settled on his temple.

"Does your head hurt?"

"Not anymore." He shook his head for emphasis, but then he thought better of it, a wince sharpening his handsome features. Even if he hadn't given himself away with that reaction or the obvious bump, she wouldn't have believed him.

Luca was honest and earnest, yes, but he never wanted her to worry either. She'd find out about the other injuries only if she asked, though the way he fought the Myrcellian and the Eritrian gave her confidence that nothing was broken, only bruised.

The threat of a fight still coursed through Amarande's hands, her fingers still tense, blunt. She used every inch of her concentration to cast them gently toward his face, pressing her palms softly into his cheeks, fingers trailing into his hair. That feeling in her heart was back, as if it were made of wax, melting into nothing within her chest.

Her Luca.

Amarande kissed him then—forehead first, then the bridge of his nose, the tops of his cheeks.

She'd never kissed him before.

And yet her lips found dust and sweat and fear and *him.*

The princess immediately wanted more, and took. The kisses were slow and spread out, like raindrops in the Torrent desert. Luca sat still, oh so still, as though if he so much as breathed, it would stop.

As long as he consented, she wouldn't.

In time, Amarande's mouth landed on his and it was a relief when he finally moved—to kiss her in return.

The princess was as gentle as she could force herself to be, though she wanted to squeeze him between her body and the rock, until her skin matched his and there would be no way they could ever be torn apart again.

Amarande held back from flattening herself into him, being as tender as her feelings would allow, and after a time pulled herself away so they could both breathe. When the princess opened her heavy eyes, Luca was smiling, dimples flashing.

"I told them you'd save me."

And then Amarande kissed him again. Harder this time—she couldn't help it. He laughed low against her lips and put his hands in her hair, smoothing it off her face.

When they parted, she watched his eyes like she always did in their meadow.

"Did they believe you?"

"They laughed."

"They aren't laughing now."

Luca conceded that but didn't shake his head this time. "They aren't, but we should go—they'll be coming."

He was right. Those bandits had kidnapped him with the promise of payment, and though they'd completed his acquisition, that was likely not all they had to do to be paid. Still, Amarande was slow to move, navigating the idea that she'd lost him and then managed to recover him. That her training was a success—she'd set out to save him and she had.

And more: He had known she would.

Luca stood first and untethered Mira, who was more than happy to finally have his attention, greeting him with an enthused snort. Amarande dawdled, eyes pinned to the muscled curve of his back. The kisses hadn't been a relief so much as they'd increased the want within her.

But he was hers now, and there would be no more kisses if they were captured again. And so she stood and readjusted the sword at her back, the knife in her boot, the pouch of diamonds hidden in the folds of her dress. Luca took the dagger they'd found in the saddlebag and dropped it in one boot.

"Where were they taking you?"

"They're pirates—they claimed to have a ship. They didn't say where, though we were headed in the general direction of the Port of Torrent. If that's true, we were crossing the length of this place to get to it. From there, I'm not sure where they intended to go. Their plan didn't make much sense."

Amarande chewed on the possibility that those three could've survived the trek across the Torrent to steal away Luca in a way that fit the timeline of the past week. Or maybe they'd actually left the ship at the Port of Pyrenee in the Divide, or even at Ardenia's harbor, and weren't actually headed to the ship with him, after all. Or they might not actually have a ship to begin with and everything they told him was a lie. She was puzzling out those threads when the sound of Luca's laughter hit the princess's ears, a strange surprise.

"You're wearing a ball gown." He said it like he'd just now

noticed it. And maybe it hadn't registered until they were at a distance in the full light.

"Easy to track and ridiculous to boot, I know." Amarande grinned, knowing full well that, minus the sword at her back, she looked every inch the Runaway Queen her mother was supposed to be. But she didn't mention that and she knew Luca wouldn't either. "There wasn't time to change."

Luca's lips quirked up. "When did you leave?"

"About ten minutes was all I could survive of dinner with Renard. Left the dining hall and went straight for the stable."

Luca didn't press. He didn't ask why she was having dinner with Renard, though he knew the rhythm of the Itspi well enough to understand the Royal Council would have demanded penance for her display at the funeral. More, Amarande knew *he* knew why she'd abandoned dinner to come to him. It was exactly why she'd rescued him. And how he'd known she would.

He brought Mira forward and grabbed the princess's hand. Folded her fingers into his.

Together they walked like that, drawing themselves to the other side of the little trickling stream, where there was room to walk without a cliff bumping against a shoulder. Leaving the little nest of land that had sheltered them for just long enough. At the mouth of the main stretch, where the scrub faded into wide rivers of sand running alongside the spindly branched forest to the north, Luca stopped. Unless they wanted to lose time in the trees, there truly was nowhere to hide, only a direction to pick. At that moment they were heading west.

Toward the supposed pirate ship and away from Ardenia.

Luca's attention lingered over his shoulder—east and home. "Are we circumventing the forest? Is that what you're thinking? Looping around and back?" He asked it like he hadn't realized their direction until just now, too. Maybe it was like her ball gown—so obvious he'd missed it in his elation. "I'm assuming

King Sendoa taught you a strategy for this situation—how do we circle back toward Ardenia without running straight into Dunixi, Urtzi, and Ula?"

That stopped Amarande cold, a sudden and fierce anger rising in her gut, quick as a surprise. The fight was back, flooding every muscle with tense, swift rage. She dropped his hand so she wouldn't crush his fingers.

"First thing: We don't talk about the enemy like we're trying to avoid them at the market."

Luca raised a brow. He wasn't ever invited to the war rooms. He didn't know the first thing about commanding an army. Or surviving one.

"*Their names,*" she said, arms flinging out. "If Father taught me anything, it's that it's much easier to call someone your enemy if you don't refer to them by name."

Luca's brows fell and then knitted together. "But they're people. And they have names. I can't forget that. They were more gracious to me than they needed to be."

Oh, Luca, so kind of heart. "Their humanity is a weapon they're using against you. You see them as human, you begin to identify with them. Common ground will blind you enough that you won't see the knife until it's already lodged in your belly."

Luca was quiet a moment. "Is that really how King Sendoa thought?"

Amarande sighed. "It's what he taught me, so if he didn't believe it he at least wanted me to."

It was depressing. But it was the way of the world. And it was hard to disprove based on what Amarande believed had happened to her father. Only it wasn't a knife in the belly, it was poison in his blood; she was sure of it.

The princess pressed her eyes closed for a short moment. "The anger in my voice is for them, not you." Her eyes shot open and she offered him her hand. Amarande wasn't really sure why she'd helped the kidnappers when the Harea Asps attacked, though she told herself it was because the snakes were a danger to her and Luca as well. "Anyway, it doesn't matter. We're not circling back; we're driving forward." She squeezed his fingers, a new idea barging into her mind. "Let's run until we find the *pirates'* ship—we can sail it to Indu, or north of the Divide."

New confusion pressed his features. "Ama, you know the ship is not at the Port of Torrent if it's anywhere. . . ."

Amarande's eyes dropped to the sandy earth. "I know. It's just—"

The princess pulled up short and Luca was silent, waiting for the rest. Knowing he'd get it. Amarande tested the thought on her tongue, trying to explain the churning discomfort in her newly full stomach.

"Pyrenee plans to steal my kingdom like they stole you. And if not them, Basilica and Myrcell will try. When we return they'll have confirmation about what I'll do for you and use it." She looked up and brought a hand to his hair, combing it to the side, careful not to graze the knot at his temple. "I believe *you* are much safer without me there."

"Safer from *what?* If you're not there, what's to keep them from stealing it?"

"I—" The princess's reply died on her lips. The wind kicked up around them, as if it had something to say for her. After a few moments, she brushed away the blown sand clinging to her face and tried again. "Please. I want to be with you—every day, all day. And I can't be there. Not if I'm married off—not the way the law is written now. I'm just a pawn, no more than you were mere hours ago. It's just . . ." She glanced down at their hands. "I have you back and I . . . I don't want to lose you again."

Luca didn't blink. "You won't lose me. No matter where we are, you're never losing me again." Amarande's heart swelled, and she suddenly felt like she couldn't look at him without bursting into flames. "But you will lose your kingdom unless you go back and fight. I will help you. Always, Princess. I promise."

Amarande's swollen heart dropped into the pit of her stomach. Her eyes shot to the horizon stretching out in front of her, over Luca's shoulder. The western stretch of the Torrent, reaching all the way to the sea. Then to Indu or across the Divide to Eritri and beyond. Then to a life where no one cared who they were or what they did, and anonymity could cover them like so many blankets.

But Luca was right.

Running wasn't an option. It was a dream.

Amarande let that sit in her gut. Waiting for her father's voice to come in her ear. But this time it didn't. And she didn't know what that meant.

After a long silence, Luca pressed on with a different subject. "How do you know it was Pyrenee? Taillefer saw us in the meadow, yes, but any one of those royals is certainly resourceful enough to find out about . . . us." Yes, they were a secret open to the stars if not to each other. Amarande loved the people who made the Itspi hum, but she knew some among them might be swayed by the right gold piece to share a detail so many knew. "Was it in the letter?" He tipped her chin up with a rough thumb.

She nodded, though she was surprised he knew about it.

"Ama, what did it say?"

That shyness swelled back into Amarande's chest. Though she'd just kissed him. Though he'd kissed her back. Though he held her hand now.

The kidnappers' letter was still tucked into her bodice, pressing right up against the skin protecting her heart. Rather than answering him, she asked, "Did they tell you whom they worked for?"

"All they would say was that I was blackmail to get you to pick their 'man.'" The princess's grip on his hand changed as Luca pressed his other hand against hers—now he was holding her rather than letting her lead. "Honestly, my money was on Basilica, because King Domingu isn't exactly known for playing fair."

She laughed a little. "Kill your brother to obtain absolute power and no one will bat an eye when you propose to murder your wife to marry your own great-granddaughter."

Luca's dimples winked. "Or Myrcell—didn't the boy king float your name as a potential bride two years ago? And King Sendoa told him to wait five years before even speaking with you or risk losing an ear?"

Amarande blushed. Yes. It was true. At fourteen, she'd felt intensely embarrassed by the whole episode—that this man of eighteen would even think of her in that way. She knew now it was so much more than a request of the heart. "Father thought Akil to be just a pretty face. Nothing in his head."

"And then there's Pyrenee." Here, he chuckled to himself and swung their entwined hands. "Honestly, I'm surprised you believe it was them. I have no idea why Renard would try so hard after you stole his own sword and pressed it to his throat in front of thousands of people, including the most important ones on the continent, but I suppose maybe he likes a challenge."

"I believe he abhors challenge, actually. He hates that his mother is making him work for his crown."

"Fair enough." Luca paused for a moment. "Though then there's Taillefer. I'm not convinced he was joking about you assassinating his brother for him."

"True. But that might just be how Taillefer shows affection." Whenever duty had put them in the same place, the princess had always thought the younger prince to be idiosyncratic. Whereas Renard went through the prescribed motions with manufactured charm and stoicism, Taillefer always did his part with a smile on his face like he was laughing at a joke no one else could hear.

Luca kicked out a laugh. "Affection? With hemlock around his neck?"

Amarande's mouth dropped open. "The flowers? Those were hemlock?"

"Yes. There's a grove by the stream behind the stable. I'm always trying to kill it off so the horses don't get into it."

The princess's stomach plummeted. Poison strong enough to kill her tiger father was just steps away from the stable he'd last visited before he died. More she didn't know.

"Maybe he would go the Domingu route, as he put it . . . but they seem close otherwise."

Luca placed a hand on her shoulder, warm and gentle. "I'm sure Domingu and Han were close right up until the moment a knife came between them and Han's lifeblood dripped onto Domingu's boots."

Though more than a half century old, the story was well known in the Sand and Sky and often retold simply for the sensationalism of it: a dagger in the back of the crown prince as the two sons of Basilica paid their final respects at their father's deathbed.

Amarande was sure Domingu encouraged its popularity as a means of maintaining his reputation. The princess squeezed Luca's fingers. "You have a point. And Domingu had one literally."

Luca shook his head, dimples winking. "Every last person of nobility other than you is dirty enough to make you think these pirates were working for someone else."

This was true. Every one of them was as deadly as those Harea Asps. Still, Renard's face at dinner—his exact response when she'd mentioned Luca's name—flashed in Amarande's mind. He hadn't reacted. Not even a little bit. But he was a boy who lived in a castle full of vipers. It was ridiculous not to think he was one, too.

The tide was changing, and Amarande pivoted slightly toward the eastern horizon and home. Luca pulled her all the way there. And then they took their first steps in the direction of Ardenia, walking hand in hand toward the problem rather than away from it.

After a time, Luca goaded her to mount the horse. She did, and he followed. He wrapped his arms tight around her, his broad form shielding her from the sun. They were going back the way of the pirates, but hopefully the three had been confused enough that they wouldn't run into them. Maybe.

When Mira broke into a trot, Luca revived his unanswered question. "Ama, what did the letter say?"

Somehow, with his arms around her and his chin tucked against the crook between her neck and her shoulder, Amarande felt only as if she would melt, not completely combust. She gave Mira a kick to increase her speed and the tenor of the wind rushing around them. She'd definitely feel the need to burst into a million stars if she truly heard what he had to say to this.

"*Marry Renard or you will never see your love again.*"

It might have been her imagination, but though she didn't hear a gasp or swear or other exclamation, Luca's arms seemed to grow tighter about her waist as they thundered across the sand and brush.

CHAPTER
28

❧

"THEY took everything," Dunixi bellowed, kicking at the dirt. It didn't get him anything except for a coughing fit as dust wafted up in a fine, choking cloud. The pirates were spread around the remains of their camp, cataloging it all—what was missing, what was damaged, what was miraculously unharmed.

"Not everything. My saddlebag is still here," Urtzi announced, holding his bag aloft from his side of the snuffed-out fire.

"*My* everything and *her* everything, you moron," the leader spat, gesturing to Ula, who was crouched over where her belongings had been. All of it was missing, save for her beloved sword, plus her journal and pencil, which had slipped away in the struggle. Gone—her food, water, extra clothes. Dunixi had been relieved of his items as well. Smoke was nearly coming out of his ears. "Which amounts to *more* everything than *your* everything."

Urtzi just stared at the Eritrian. "None of those words make sense put together, Dunixi."

"Whatever. They took our stuff. And we weren't even completely horrible to the stableboy."

"*Luca,*" Ula snapped, emphasizing the boy's name. Dunixi didn't amend his statement. Just kicked the dirt with his other foot. When his temper tantrum was mostly complete, Ula spoke again. "They also saved us from certain death."

"It wasn't certain those asps would've bitten us," Dunixi

responded. "Though it is too bad about Ferri." He gestured to where Urtzi's palomino had once been. The horse had been so spooked during the fight that she ran off as the princess and stable-boy escaped.

After a moment of silence, Ula continued. "Losing Ferri isn't for the best, but I, for one, would not trade how things turned out for a chance to go back and repeat it and die of snakebite."

"Me either," Urtzi agreed, sauntering over to Ula and offering up his waterskin.

"Cowards."

To Ula's ears, Dunixi sounded like he meant it, and that was extremely annoying. She caught glances with Urtzi, who finally seemed to be chewing on the truth that he could fry up Dunixi's intestines for breakfast, supper, or dinner.

Ula swallowed a gulp of water, set her eyes upon her leader, and took a deep, calming breath before trying to steer the conversation somewhere useful. In truth, it was high morning and they'd lost their bounty, and each second they argued or dwelled was a second lost in retrieving it. "Dunixi, what's our plan now? Go after them?"

In the moment, they'd raced after Luca and his princess on foot, of course. The shock had slowed them down, and they were too far behind to catch Luca and Amarande by the time they mounted their horse and took off, but they'd been fast enough to see which direction they had gone—west.

The answer wasn't an easy one. Dunixi plopped down in the dirt, forearms propped on his knees. He wasn't ever one to admit he didn't know anything, but when he was silent like this it was as good as an admission. After a minute, he finally spoke.

"If the princess was after him, our employer failed in his aim." Ula rolled her eyes—she'd said as much. "But we should still be paid for completing the kidnapping. That was our job. Kidnap him and hold him until the princess made her choice. We did and she did."

Ula cocked a brow. "Yes, but we were also supposed to deliver him."

This was true. They never were supposed to take him to their ship. That had been an agreed-upon lie. Kidnap him and then keep things moving until nightfall on the third full day—today—when they were to meet an intermediary at the Hand for further instruction.

And payment.

"So now what?" Urtzi asked. "Do we go to the Hand and demand our money without Luca anywhere in sight?"

The Hand was to the east and south. They'd bypassed it in their trip out with Luca. Mostly because caravans liked to converge there and one of the caravans in the Torrent held the Warlord, who had a habit of laying claim to anything of value. And their cargo, as it turned out, was just as valuable as most of them had suspected.

Dunixi had to chew on this one, too. Ula rolled her eyes. "If the princess came to rescue Luca, what does that mean to the politics of the kingdoms? She obviously didn't want to do what the note required. Which means our man didn't achieve his aim. Which also means he may not be sending anyone to meet us—he has bigger fish to fry."

The Eritrian shook his head and then thought better of it, the skin of his neck still raw, Luca's paste flaking, spent. "No. He'll meet us. He likely only knows the princess disappeared, not that she went to rescue the stableboy—"

"*Luca.*"

Dunixi ignored Ula's correction and glare. "If he believes we succeeded in executing the kidnapping and delivering the blackmail note, he will want his pawn to see if he can lure her out. There's more than one way to get what you want if you're creative enough."

"But we don't have his pawn."

Dunixi grimaced. "Ula, *there's more than one way to get what you want if you're creative enough.*" When neither Ula nor Urtzi responded to his twisting the logic back to fall on them, he grimaced more. "We meet the intermediary and inform him we won't give up the stableboy without payment first. They pay us, we tell him the princess stole him away, and then Urtzi bashes his brains if he tries anything other than running to his master."

CHAPTER
29

❦

AMARANDE and Luca doubled back to stick to the curve of the forest, rather than angling into the open, the way they'd come separately the day before. It was a gamble, considering the pirates, but going back was one big gamble anyway, so they stayed the route, treating the forest just as they had in that mad scramble this morning—a guide and a refuge, if needed, but definitely not a path.

Within two hours they were back to where they started. Mira almost instinctively slowed her gait.

"Do you see them?" Amarande asked Luca as they both craned their necks into the trees. The sun was at a blinding tilt, and the shadows seemed impossible. "I'm not tracking movement."

Luca shook his head. He wasn't as trained as his princess, but his eyesight was strong.

Amarande drew in a thin breath. "What do you think they'd do? From what you saw?"

"Dunixi . . . ," Luca started, and then changed tactics as the princess tensed, "*the leader,* he was very concerned with getting paid. So he's either after us with a vengeance to collect or going straight to the source to see if he can be compensated anyway."

Amarande's mouth twisted. Considering they had yet to run across the pirates, if they were after them with a vengeance, they'd pointed that vengeance in the wrong direction.

"Do you think Renard is still at the castle?" Luca asked carefully.

It would be good to think about what was waiting for them at home besides the threat of war.

"He may very well be there. His mother, too," Amarande said, confirming what he had already surely surmised. But there was more he likely hadn't. "I suppose I didn't explain why I even allowed myself to have dinner with Renard. After the funeral and my *stated piece*, the council wanted a stiff word with me."

"I can imagine they didn't find your speech nearly as amusing as I did."

"No. They didn't."

"The sword really was a nice touch, Ama."

"Thank you." She could kiss him again right there. "They told me I must meet with Renard to make amends. I ran to the stable and found you missing and the note, and felt like I had no choice. I thought it was the best way to bring you home. What I found out when I arrived to dinner was that according to Renard, his mother is plotting to steal his throne."

Amarande could feel Luca's mind turning in confusion.

"It's a very convoluted plan involving marriage, and babies within the next year, which is ridiculous, but when you've become accustomed to power . . ."

"And this plot was dreamed up by Renard *about* his mother?"

"Yes. But the important part is the way he believes he needs to circumvent said plot. He must be eighteen to rule as king. However, there's a stipulation in Pyrenee's rules of succession that if he marries before the age of eighteen, he's automatically crowned. Therefore, his argument to me was that we both need a wedding in short order to ascend our rightful thrones, so why not marry each other?"

The princess knew Luca wasn't vain enough to venture something like, *And you turned him down because of me?* He was also smart enough to know that even if there were an inkling of that thought running around in the depths of his humble soul, reasoning like that wouldn't be the whole argument.

Luca was quiet, and so Amarande pressed on.

"I said no, of course. But his desperation was palpable. I can picture him in the Itspi right now, puzzling out how to make the most of my disappearance. Surely if the blackmail was indeed his, he will find out soon enough that it failed."

"Failed . . . or . . ."

The princess did not much like that pause. "Or?"

Luca's heart quickened against her spine. "Ama, did you tell anyone I was missing before dinner?"

The princess's stomach dropped. "No—but you usually eat in the kitchens. Wouldn't they have noticed when you didn't show up?"

"Yes, but that's not enough. I disappeared. And . . . you disappeared." He touched her elbow, his fingertips suddenly bone cold. "Ama, they likely think I kidnapped you."

Oh, stars.

Amarande's breath stilled.

"I'm . . . I'm the only one who knows the note exists and that you were kidnapped for blackmail." Her mind was racing. She tugged on Mira's reins to slow her and the wind rushing past them. "There's only a single horse gone from the stable. And . . . everyone knows how we are with each other."

Somehow that was easier to say than *how we feel about each other* and Amarande already worried she might vomit.

But then, with one careful turn and a quick heave, Luca *did* vomit.

"Are you all right?"

The princess wasn't the sort to be squeamish. She immediately wrenched around to have a good look at him. Beads of sweat sat atop his golden skin. Amarande brought Mira to a halt and pressed a hand to his forehead—hot enough to fry up a quail egg. Fever.

"Let's dismount."

"No, no, I'm just nauseous is all. We can continue."

Amarande ignored this and pulled him down—he barely resisted. She sat him against one of the trees on the edge of the forest, gave him the waterskin, and picked around the stolen saddlebags for something to eat. She found a pouch of almonds and fed them to him one by one while asking a battery of questions about where things hurt and how long he'd felt this way.

When he couldn't give her a good answer, she tried a different tactic. "May I have a look at your injuries?" Internal bleeding was her guess, and that wasn't good—she'd need to get him to Medikua Aritza at the Itspi as soon as humanly possible.

Luca nodded and Amarande carefully rolled up his sleeves, pulled down his collar, and then, with his permission, pulled up his tunic. Despite the seriousness of the situation, she felt her cheeks growing hot at the beauty of him. Hard from work, the ink over his heart darkly perfect against his golden skin. Yes, beautiful by anyone's definition, though mottled with bruises over his back and shoulder to go with the one at his temple. None appeared to be swollen hard—the indication Amarande knew of internal bleeding.

"I'm fine. Please, let's keep moving."

"Does anything I haven't checked hurt? Even just a little bit?"

"No."

"No tingling? Burning? Numbness? Swelling? Anything new?"

Luca licked his lips and tried to stand. Amarande grabbed his hand—clammy and cold—as added support. "The almonds helped. Probably just dehydrated and hungry." He mounted the horse as if to prove just how fine he was.

The princess stared up at him from where she knelt, squinting hard into the sun haloing his head. "Luca, answer my question. Nothing at all?"

Finally, he took a deep breath. "Well, my ankle sort of burns."

"Which one?"

He gestured to the one right in front of her, his tone somewhat embarrassed. "Probably just scraped up in the fight."

Amarande didn't respond other than to say, "May I?" She gestured at his pant leg.

Luca nodded.

With careful fingers, Amarande lifted the fabric, frayed from his life in the stable. And there, right above the lip of his boot, was a scrape, as he'd suggested. Except it wasn't just red—the edges were as black as his tattoo and swollen fat. Amarande blinked and leaned in closer. And there, it became more than clear the scrape wasn't just one little cut but two. Just skimming the surface, but in a pattern that made her heart stop.

A snake's work.

In the tussle, the fangs of a Harea Asp had dragged across Luca's skin. The princess's knees buckled and she leaned into Mira to steady herself.

No. I can't lose him now.

A true bite would've killed him within an hour. But if she didn't find anti-venom in the next few hours, this might kill him anyway.

CHAPTER
30

❦

RENARD wasn't sure what he'd find when he finally laid eyes on Princess Amarande again, but he knew he'd at least appear ready for it.

His party had swelled to fifteen and was looking mighty impressive as they combed the sun-scraped Torrent for the princess. To the seven original riders the prince had added four hired hands—burly enough to earn their gold—plus the three men who had spotted the princess on the run (the single injured man wouldn't come alone but didn't seem bothered by lack of payment for his friends), and the girl who'd spotted the stableboy at the watering hole.

They'd come across several riders in their trip to the Cardenas Scar and stopped for every one of them. Asking questions, inspecting bags, trying to gain more leads. They hadn't, though, and now that noon had come and gone, the first son of Pyrenee was getting frustrated. Their sluggish pace, the lack of answers, the constant scrutiny of Captain Serville, who rode alongside him, his sword clattering at the hip closest to the prince, a reminder in forged steel that he worked solely for Ardenia—it all grated on Renard.

As the next riders came into view and their progression slowed, yet again, Renard felt the urge to lay his head down on his horse's neck and softly tap his forehead against it. But then he heard the girl's voice.

"That's them," she announced as they came up on three riders on two horses.

"Are you sure?" Renard asked, because of course it was all wrong—wrong number of people, wrong number of horses, and no one fitting the description of the stableboy. Taillefer had seen the stableboy up close with Amarande the day of the funeral and had been tasked with identifying him—Renard wasn't about to leave a job as important as that to Serville. Still, Renard had hoped the men who'd seen the princess would spark on something first, but he supposed this was better than yet another dead end. If it was right.

"Yes," the girl—Osana—said, emphatic. "I'd remember that mishmash anywhere. Sunburnt Eritrian, giant of Myrcell, girl of Torrent with a curved blade. That's them, minus a horse and the captive boy."

An important caveat, but she was so convincing that her surety was enough for the prince. Renard tipped his chin at his captain. "Surround them."

The guards of Pyrenee and the hired hands followed orders, while the pair of princes sat still and inspected. Serville settled in next to Renard, awaiting news of his princess.

As the guards took their places and raised their swords, the party reacted with the fear Renard was seeking. The girl drew her curved blade, the Myrcellian a pair of daggers, and the Eritrian put up his hands.

"How can we help you, folks?" the blond boy asked, an insincere grin sliding across his wide face. The girl and boy behind him didn't smile from their shared saddle. Renard launched into the description of Amarande that he liked, mostly because it sounded complimentary and maybe even romantic to strangers' ears.

"We are looking for a girl on a black horse. Hair like an open flame, porcelain skin and rose-touched cheeks, eyes a blue-green only found in the waters of the Divide—"

Taillefer held up a hand and cut in on his brother, having heard his description one too many times. "She's wearing a red ball gown."

Renard frowned and continued. "She may have changed, but yes, she is likely clad in garnet lace and silk."

The blond boy tilted his head. "Funny, because we're looking for her, too."

Renard bared his teeth. "What business do you have with her?"

The blond boy hesitated. The nearest guard saw it and pressed the tip of his sword into the soft spot beneath the boy's ribs. The Eritrian blinked hard and continued, overconfident voice faltering. "We were hired to kidnap her stableboy, to convince her to marry Prince Renard."

The prince blinked.

"I'm Prince Renard," he said, aware that Serville's eyes were immediately boring into the side of his face. "Who hired you?"

The kidnappers looked between each other.

With another nudge of encouragement from Nikola's steel, the leader boy spat it out. "Prince Taillefer."

"I'm Prince Taillefer." Now the younger brother exchanged glances with both Serville and Renard. "And I did no such thing."

The Eritrian dug into his pocket and pulled out a roll of parchment. He unfurled it and held it out, though he didn't let anyone from the Pyrenee party touch it. "Is this not your signature?"

Both princes of Pyrenee leaned forward to inspect what very much appeared to be a contract. Renard glanced at his little brother. They said nothing.

The blond boy looked at them like he was trying to read the princes' faces, both locked up tight. "This contract was given to us by a courier five days ago. We immediately went into action, with the promise of payment tonight at the Hand."

Renard managed to skim the contract across the distance. "Payment for exchange of the stableboy." The prince made it a point to look all around the kidnappers. "You no longer have him in your possession, unless you're hiding him in the girl's hair. Did he escape? Die? Or was he never in your possession at all?" Renard nodded at Serville and avoided Osana's open-mouthed stare. "Did he leave with the princess before you got there? Kidnapping *her*, perhaps?"

At this, the female kidnapper snorted in a way that almost sounded like a laugh.

"What's so funny?"

The girl answered without hesitation, "That boy never needed to kidnap that princess. She's in love with him. And he with her. We don't have him because *she* came and rescued him."

Now it was Serville's turn to laugh. "That sounds about right."

Renard rolled his eyes. The blond boy pressed on, staring down Taillefer as much as Renard. "We kidnapped him successfully, and we ought to be paid."

At this, the Ardenian guard tugged on his horse's reins and made to turn toward the mountains at their backs. Renard caught his arm. "You're staying with us, Captain Serville."

The man simply laughed, dislodged his arm from the prince's grip, and adjusted his reins. "I'm not catching sunstroke while you frauds figure out payment. You princes tried to sway Princess Amarande's hand and put her in danger in the process, and it's my duty to inform the Royal Council. It benefits Pyrenee to let me go—the councilors will likely be more fair to you if they know the story before the princess rides into the Itspi and tells them herself."

The Ardenian captain urged his horse forward. The men who'd had their swords pointed at the three travelers swept them toward Serville. Two moved ahead of him, blocking his path. The captain's smile dropped and he addressed Prince Renard, who was still next to him. "Don't do this the hard way."

Renard looked to the kidnappers. "Does the princess know about your contract?"

All three shook their heads.

"Does the stableboy?"

All three shook their heads.

He leaned into his brother's ear, a whisper on his lips. "You and I will speak later, Tai."

Then, without hesitation, Renard drew his own sword, the bejeweled hilt twinkling in the unforgiving sun, and stabbed Serville right through his side. Under the rib cage, astride the man's chest plate, pinning the edge of the captain's cloak as he ran him through.

Serville gasped, blood immediately soaking his elegant garnet-and-gold uniform. Renard had to yank with both hands to remove the sword. When he did, Serville fell from his horse.

Bile surged at the prince's throat. Still, he forced himself to watch the lifeblood drain from the Ardenian onto the cinnamon sand.

His first kill.

When it was done, Renard looked to his men, who all sat atop their horses with mouths open in surprise. This was the type of uncertainty that rooted both fear and respect. It had to be done. Still, Renard swallowed again to ensure he wouldn't vomit his breakfast into his horse's snowy-white mane. "Strip him of his things, bury him, and give his horse to one of these three. They're going to help us find the princess."

"And then we'll get paid?" the blond boy prodded. He was either overconfident or completely stupid; the prince wasn't sure which. Renard was sure, though, of his growing annoyance. This boy's temperament might not be worth his knowledge. The prince set his sights on the boy and made his voice as icy as possible.

"If we find her, you'll get to keep your life. How's that for payment?"

The blond boy said nothing and the guards went to work.

CHAPTER
31

❧

AMARANDE pushed Mira to the limits of what she could run.

The sun was in the early hours of its long summer descent and the princess had set a course for a place she knew people would likely be in the vast space of the Torrent: the watering hole.

Before they'd begun to sprint again, the princess administered the only snakebite treatment she knew to work: removing Luca's boot in case of swelling and covering the wound in a loose bit of cloth—another long scrap torn from her dress.

And that was it. That was all she could do.

Sucking the venom out was a myth. Cutting away at the infected skin, too—that didn't halt necrosis any more than a pleasant bath. Over Mira's hoofbeats and the rush of the wind, she could hear Medikua Aritza's gravelly voice now, the old woman's sharp eyes fixed on the princess's face to make sure she was listening and not daydreaming about crossing swords in the yard.

Time spent is tissue lost—get anti-venom as quickly as possible.

Keep the person still—movement spreads venom.

The wound should be kept below the heart.

The first two instructions were an issue. Time was not on their side and keeping Luca still was an impossibility while thundering on horseback across the Torrent's rivers of sandy earth.

Luca hung on to Amarande's waist with renewed strength. And he made it a point to talk more than he did before, just so that she

wouldn't worry he'd fallen asleep or passed out or simply died on
the back of her horse.

The stub of the watering hole loomed by midafternoon, and
Amarande breathed a sigh of relief. They'd somehow managed to
avoid the kidnappers, the inn and its keeper, and anyone else who
would slow them down. Mira was running hot, her steps impre-
cise; she needed the break. Even in the state he was in, Luca was
watching her vitals, paying close attention to the horse's breathing
and gait, making sure she wasn't harmed from the hard ride.
Whenever they had to slow to navigate a rocky path or tight,
prickly brush, Amarande caught him detaching one hand from his
hold on her and running it across the horse's side, checking the rise
and fall of her lungs.

Amarande dismounted and walked Mira toward the first of the
trees shading the Cardenas Scar. Luca began to swing a leg off, too,
but Amarande's rebuke was immediate.

"No, no, no—walking will get your blood pumping, and that's
the last thing we need."

Luca didn't argue. "What's the plan?"

"Find the anti-venom, pay for it, administer it, and then deliver
you to Medikua Aritza before I alert the council to my return."

"And if we don't find someone with access to anti-venom?"

"We skip to the final two steps of the plan and hope I don't have
to amputate before we achieve them."

Luca chewed on that. "What are you paying with? I didn't see
gold in the saddlebags."

Apparently the fact that she was in a ball gown wasn't the only
thing he'd missed in those early minutes when they'd paused after their escape—perhaps that inattention was the poison already
at work. The princess grinned softly and plucked the pouch from
her dress. She tugged it open and tipped it his way; the diamonds'
facets shimmered in the light, dancing across Luca's face. "Leaving

right after dinner didn't simply mean riding away in a dress. Until *very* recently, this was a necklace from the Itspi's collection."

Luca's eyes settled on the sparkling gems. "Oh, Ama . . ."

"Don't finish that sentence, Luca," was all she said. Tagging on something like *you're worth it* would only make it worse. That thing that had sat between them their whole lives reared its head again. He was worth these jewels and more in any situation; but as she was the princess of the sometimes-called Kingdom of Diamonds, the gems weren't especially precious to her. All she would have to do was say the word on their return to the Itspi, and five other necklaces of greater value would be brought for her inspection.

And so she didn't add to her sentence either. She wouldn't cheapen what he was worth to her. He was worth literally everything she'd been through thus far, plus what was to come, and more—diamonds, battle, the political ramifications. Everything.

The princess stowed the jewels and guided their party carefully toward the trickling stream. She was after human interaction, but she stayed cautious, gauging the lay of the land before they made their presence fully known.

The banks were calm, everyone minding their own business— nothing unsavory or violent in progress. Amarande tied Mira to the stump of a tree at the water's edge and helped Luca off the horse. Careful not to move too much, he sat immediately and began filling the waterskins. Amarande fished out some dried meat from one of the bags, handed some to Luca, and surveyed her choices as she chewed a piece herself.

There were four clusters of travelers—none she'd seen before. A pair of young men made old before their years by the brutal sun. Two women cradling babes in slings across their chests, traveling with a single man and a boy of six or seven. And three men who at first glance sent a chill up Amarande's spine, because they looked far too much like the men who'd robbed her. They weren't—their clothes and hair were all wrong, and none of them bore the injuries she'd dealt, but just the sight of three men like that traveling in a pack was enough to give her pause.

She decided upon the family. Amarande wasn't comfortable around women with children, mostly because they made her think of the mother she never knew. She wasn't much older than these babes were now when Queen Geneva decided her freedom was more important than her daughter. The tendril of a thought nagged at Amarande then—that when this was all over she should visit the Warlord and put a truth to what her mind wanted her to see a night ago.

Amarande had to cross the stream to get to them. Leaving her sword with Luca, she hiked up what was left of her shredded skirt, took off her boots and stockings, and carried them across. Her knife was hidden in one of the boots, ready should she need it as she waded across the water to negotiate. The women were crouched at the bank, swirling clothes in the waters, cleaning with only the anemic creek's agitation.

Both women stopped what they were doing and straightened as she approached. One of the babies in a sling watched, too, the other child asleep. The man and boy didn't join them, busy filling waterskins.

"*Arritxu*," she began, addressing the women in ancient Torrentian as ladies—it was something Abene and Maialen had always told her was preferred here—"please, if you'd help me. My companion is in need of anti-venom for a bite from a Harea Asp. I have items for trade and can pay very well."

The women said nothing at first. The one on the left—young with hazel eyes and freckled brown skin—swung her gaze over to the other woman before finally speaking. "That was no Harea Asp or your friend would be dead, not drinking water from the banks."

Amarande's smile dropped. "I assure you he came in contact

with a Harea Asp. You are correct that the snake didn't get a full bite—its fangs grazed his skin. Not a full shot of venom, but he's feeling its effects."

The other woman spoke—she was slightly older, with a few strands of silver sparkling in her dark hair. "I know of a healer who is very gifted. What will you give us to lead you to her?"

Here, Amarande needed to be careful. They didn't have the antidote, so they would get no diamonds. The princess licked her lips, waiting for the right words to come.

"We have oats." Luca was sloshing through the water now, holding out what was left of the small sack that had been the spark she needed to track him. He smiled at them, kind as always, then pulled out a few oats to prove the contents. "For your horses—or for your babies."

Genius, Amarande thought. Diamonds were valuable here only for what they could purchase—multipurpose or hard-to-get items were at the top of that list. Oats satisfied both of those criteria, and Luca was cutting out the middleman.

The women eyed the oats and then each other. Finally, the second woman spoke again.

"For the whole bag, we can lead you to the Isilean Caravan, the home of the healer—gifted, very gifted—and her apprentice."

The princess hesitated. Amarande didn't want to waste time trying to find a nomadic city. That might take them in the wrong direction. And if they didn't find the anti-venom there, it could be too late to get to Medikua Aritza at the Itspi.

And then of course there was her last run-in with a caravan. Which had not been pleasant.

But Luca was worth anything and everything.

Any decision she made from here on out would feel wrong, mostly because his life and her heart were riding on it.

The princess swallowed, unsure how to track a meandering city. Locating a caravan, let alone the correct caravan, wasn't something

Koldo or Sendoa had ever covered in her lessons. "How far is this caravan?"

"A couple of hours in the correct direction," the younger woman said. "It is coming our way. We're to meet it at the Hand, where it will settle for the night."

Her best estimate was that there were still about fifteen hours of hard riding between them and the castle.

This was their best bet.

"Can you lead us there the shortest way possible? Please?" Amarande asked quietly, trying very hard to keep the hot desperation out of her voice, afraid it might scare them. Scare Luca. She wrapped a hand around his arm. "For him?"

The women looked to Luca, holding the oats out in front of his body while balancing on one leg. The golden color of his face had gone sallow, a clammy sweat cold over his brow.

The older one nodded. "We will lead you."

CHAPTER
32

❧⁓❧

THE couple of hours to the caravan turned out to be a much shorter distance than Amarande expected because of one thing—the women and babes rode, while the man and boy walked alongside. They couldn't run, only trot slowly.

Frustration built within the princess as Luca's fever raged further. After twenty minutes, she was nearly at her wits' end. "Can one of you please ride ahead with us? I'd like to get my friend to your healer as quickly as possible," she pressed the ladies, who turned out to be sisters.

Amarande hadn't asked their names, but Luca had. Of course he had. She didn't trust them enough to use them. Until the antivenom was in hand, they hadn't earned her trust. "We're almost there," was all one of the women said. No description of where the caravan was supposed to be. No general idea of timing. No nothing.

Luca placed a hand on the princess's shoulder. She tilted her head and he leaned into her ear. "I'm fine, Ama. Let's not test their goodwill."

She didn't believe him. His palm was clammy against her shoulder—its cool dampness seeping through the overheated lace where her neckline and sleeves met. His grip on her waist had loosened, too, and if there was a single reason she was okay with the pace, it was because she was afraid he'd fall off. He'd also vomited up some—if not all—of the water and dried meat he'd had at their stop. This did not quell her serious concerns about dehydration. Every alarm bell she had was a-clang.

Ten minutes more and a disturbance in the sand fuzzed across the distance. The princess squinted and leaned against Mira's neck for a closer look.

The caravan.

It stretched the full length of the horizon before them, snaking across the burnt earth in a southwesterly pattern. It was an entire city laid out in a line. Shops, taverns, service providers, vendors of all stripes, with you wherever you went. Like this, it was a much different creature than what she'd experienced the night before.

The princess pressed a securing hand against Luca's weak grip at her waist and then dug her heels into Mira's side. The horse shot out, a cannonball fired from the bow of a ship. Luca's grip suddenly tightened and his body lurched forward into hers, his face pressed into her hair. He didn't ask what she was doing—but their guides reacted.

"Hey! Wait!" That was from the man, who began running with his wife's horse.

The younger of the sisters sped up to them, one arm lashing her baby's sling tight against her chest. The child was miraculously asleep but wouldn't be for long. Not with how his mother had to yell to be heard over the thumping of hooves and the blast of wind. "You can't approach alone. This caravan doesn't take well to strangers charging in and demanding things."

"Then charge in with us," Amarande shouted.

"Please," added Luca for his princess.

The woman didn't answer but maintained her speed.

Old Zuzen had taught the castle children that Torrent caravans came in two types—the kind that slowed at the approach of riders and the kind that kept going. Supposedly, the caravan that held the Warlord, the one she'd seen for those few short hours, was one that never slowed. This one was in that same camp, and Amarande's blood prickled with something like fear as their escort and her babe pulled in parallel to the caravan. The woman was greeted by every person they passed, and the sideways looks tossed at Amarande and Luca turned into nothing more thanks to her presence.

The princess bit back a lick of regret that she'd been so impatient.

But . . . then the woman halted her chestnut steed, and Amarande had to yank hard on the reins to avoid flying past her. With the sudden lack of motion, her baby jolted awake and let out a cry.

"What—why are we stopping?" the princess asked, working very hard not to sound as frustrated as she felt.

The woman took her time in answering, first caressing her baby's downy head. "The healer is at the back. The caravan will bring her to us."

More waiting. The woman swayed in her saddle, and the child hushed—movement was clearly something he craved. No surprise considering his mother's life.

Meanwhile, Amarande was ready to scream; watching the caravan crawl past was excruciating. By the time the woman said, "Ah, there she is," the rest of her family had joined them, sour faced and breathing hard. The princess's guilt grew alongside her frustration and worry.

The healer's carriage was sunrise pink with a large illustration of a tincture bottle rendered in a bright cobalt on the side. The woman began to trot alongside. She pulled aside the fabric lining the windows. "Naiara, we have a snakebite victim for you. They can pay."

At the last three words, the coach came to a stop and pulled off. Amarande breathed a sigh of relief and made to dismount her horse, but the woman held up a hand.

"A moment." She entered the carriage and pulled the door shut.

"I don't like the look of that," Amarande muttered to Luca.

"Edurne hasn't let us down yet," he said, referring to the woman escorting them.

After the longest minute of her life, Amarande exhaled as the door opened. The woman popped her head out. "Enter, both of you."

Amarande immediately dismounted, unlaced the saddlebags, and then held a hand up for Luca, helping him get off without putting too much weight on the leg. It'd begun to swell a few hours ago, and Amarande hadn't been brave enough to check the snake wound at the watering hole, too afraid of what damage she might see.

The woman held the door open, her baby now wide awake, silent, and watching. Luca made it a point to smile at the child before he entered. Amarande followed him in, her eyes adjusting slower than she liked. The interior of the carriage had been ripped out—no seats, only open floor. Sitting on pillows were two women. One was old enough to be a lost sister of Abene or Maialen, Luca's Itspi-found family after his mother's death. The other was younger than either Amarande or Luca.

"Sit, sit. I am Naiara, and this is my apprentice, Señe," said the old woman, smiling broadly. She still had all her teeth, and Amarande hoped this meant she was actually good at her job. She sighed as Luca sat down, and placed a hand on his face. "Oh, how lovely you are, *kidege*."

Little bird. There was nothing little or birdlike about Luca, and something about the way this woman immediately gave him an ancient Torrentian nickname and pointed out his handsomeness made Amarande uncomfortable.

If Luca felt it, too, he did his best not to show it. His dimples flickered and Naiara seemed to enjoy that, catching eyes with Señe.

Amarande barged right past the pleasantries. She had no interest in giving these people her actual name, nor Luca's. This was a transaction, and then they'd be on their way. But she did try to at least sound respectful. "Medikua Naiara—"

"I am not a medikua. That is a book-earned title of little value to those who know a lifetime of experience. No title can encompass what I know."

Amarande swallowed down her immediate frustration and tried again. "Naiara, my friend was grazed on his lower leg by a Harea Asp about twelve hours ago. It wasn't a full bite, but some venom got under his skin. We need an antidote, please."

As the words left the princess's mouth, the carriage lurched to life, and Amarande immediately clawed at the fabric, searching for Mira. They couldn't leave her. But she saw the man traveling with the two women had grabbed her reins and was walking alongside with her.

The older woman laughed. "It's a caravan; we must keep moving along with the rest." Then she reached for Luca's hand. "Show me the bite, *kidege*."

Luca obliged, rolling up his pant leg. The wound had gone from angry red with black edging to a full-on, no-variation, dead black—necrosis setting in. It was bulbous, too, the swelling taking an angry turn. The old woman leaned in and ran her fingers along the length of the injury. It ran horizontally along the front of his leg, where his shin connected with his anklebone, in the same swift motion of an assassin's swipe across a victim's throat.

"You're mighty lucky it's not deeper. And that it managed to avoid the tendon."

That almost sounded like good news.

"Do you have any sensation around the wound? If I put pressure here, what do you feel?" The healer pressed straight on the gash, burning and rancid as it was. Amarande expected Luca to react as if he'd been stabbed, and grabbed his hand to brace him. But Luca just shrugged. "It's numb. I simply feel the pressure."

"How about here?" Naiara moved her finger to the outside edge of the black. It was swollen there, misshapen and jutting outward off his leg in a wormy line.

"Still nothing?"

Luca nodded.

"And here?" She pressed farther up his leg, where his skin was the proper golden brown.

"I feel that."

The old woman nodded, taking it in. "And below the cut? Can you feel your foot?"

Again, Luca nodded, and the woman continued on with more questions. "Other symptoms? Vomiting? Sweats? Loss of coordination?"

With each question, frustration and impatience grew within Amarande. She swallowed and tried to address the woman as kindly as possible. "Can you cure him, Naiara?"

"'Cure' is the wrong word."

The princess bit back an automatic retort—this woman rubbed her every wrong way imaginable. Though she looked the part, she was not a variation on Maialen and Abene. The princess wished greatly for a similar, easy connection. It was crucial that this visit be successful.

"Anti-venom will work to neutralize what's in his system, yes. Sterilization may help his wound work toward the recovery process. But, *kidege*"—and here she placed a hand on Luca's face—"you may have that numbness for the rest of your time on this earth. There is nothing I can do to recover feeling there except beg the stars."

Luca nodded.

Amarande said, "Let's get to administering, then."

Naiara kept her hand on Luca's face and turned to Amarande. "Payment?"

Finally, down to business.

Relieved, the princess dutifully fished a diamond from her pouch, careful not to reveal the whole contents. The necklace was at least a hundred carats, all large stones, and had been chosen by Abene for Amarande's dinner with Renard specifically because those diamonds were set in gold from Pyrenee. The princess rather liked that it was now in pieces.

"I shall give you this diamond, about twenty carats in weight and of perfect Ardenian clarity."

Seńe gasped, her dark eyes going round. But Naiara simply threw her head back and laughed. "A diamond?"

Amarande exchanged a quick glance with Luca, who was just as baffled as she.

"Two, then." The princess set her shoulders back, trying to be the very image of a negotiation that had met its end, but she knew that this was the type of woman who would be able to see in her eyes that she'd give everything she had for Luca.

Naiara's laugh continued until she was wiping tears from her face. "Little queen, I have no need for your diamonds."

Amarande's jaw dropped—startled at both the nickname and the rejection. No beloved ancient Torrentian for her, only judgment, dismissal, and coincidence . . . she hoped.

The princess drew in a shaky breath and continued, wishing she'd approached this differently. Tongue dry, she finally said, more feebly than she'd like, "They're the highest quality."

Naiara arched a brow. "Can I eat them? Can I milk them for tincture? No."

"Do you have gold, perhaps?" Seńe asked, and then smiled, pointing to her teeth. "We occasionally melt it to fill rotten teeth."

"No." The gold setting was in a tree stump at the water stop. Completely useless.

Luca placed a calming hand on Amarande's wrist and spoke to the healer directly. "What do you require, Naiara?"

The woman's eyes fell to Luca. Again, she looked on him with a kindness she didn't afford Amarande. "Your horse."

"Our horse?"

"She's strong and well kept. To make your anti-venom, we immunize horses with the venom and extract the serum. Once a horse has been immunized, we cannot use that horse again. I will have to make more of this serum for my people; that means immunizing another horse."

Horror flashed across Luca's eyes. He'd been with Mira since she'd been foaled. "She won't be injured in the process?"

"No. She will be well cared for."

Shock rode the princess's face. Turning down a diamond that could buy ten horses in favor of immediate satisfaction? It was shortsighted indeed. There was much about survival in the Torrent that her father, Koldo, and all her instructors combined failed to teach her.

Luca watched Amarande, as did the healer and her apprentice. "Well, little queen?"

They were a sunup-to-sundown ride away from the Itspi now. She didn't know how long that would take to walk, but she guessed four days, if not five. But maybe someone else would be swayed by her diamonds and help them. She'd be smarter about how she presented them and herself.

"Yes," Amarande said, a quiver in her voice. "For the anti-venom, you may have her."

That horror didn't stray from Luca's eyes, though now guilt shaded them, too. "Ama, not Mira. No."

Amarande bent to his ear. "I can't lose you. She will be fine, and this way so will you."

Naiara got to work. Seňe began sterilizing Luca's wound, while the healer rifled through drawers built into the walls of the carriage, finding the right anti-venom. Amarande finally found room to breathe deeply, clutching Luca's hand the whole time. He stayed calm, though a fresh sweat cropped up on his brow as Señe toiled, the disinfectants doing their work. Finally, Naiara produced a vial.

"Drink this down. The whole thing. It does not taste good, but to keep that leg, I think you can stomach it, sweet boy." Luca took it and, without hesitation, swallowed it down. "Good. Now, *kidege*, lay your head down and sleep. You will wake in an hour. Good as new."

The coach was such that Luca couldn't stretch out, not really. He put his head on a pillow, knees pulled in close and feet grazing the opposite end of the carriage. Amarande grabbed his hand and held tight, watching his eyelids sweep closed. In less than a minute, his breathing changed and he was asleep, his cheek lolling against Amarande's knee.

Not caring what the healers thought, the princess pulled his head into the cradle of her lap, fluffing the fabric of her skirt and underpinnings so that he might lie more comfortably. Then she watched him as the women cleaned up their tinctures and dressings. As they finished, Naiara knelt next to Luca.

"Little queen, he must be stationary for a day."

The princess's eyes flew up. "A day? But we need to get home."

The healer was unmoved. "Twelve hours, but then no walking. Riding only."

"You just took our horse. How are we supposed to ride?"

Again, Naiara ignored her question. "His body must have time to accept the medication. And if there are complications—"

The princess's heart stopped. "Complications? What complications?"

"A bite like this is difficult to judge for dosing. Given too much, and his blood might clot more than it should. Or his body may reject the serum altogether and send him into shock."

Amarande swallowed, trying very hard to recover her voice. It was tight when the words finally came. "I wish you would've told us this before you administered it to him."

The woman's eyes met hers. They weren't cold, simply stern. "Would you have not done it?"

"Well, I . . . no, I would've done it."

Naiara nodded, eyes downcast on Luca's face.

"Little queen," the woman said, a drop of kindness finally in her voice for the princess, "I've done all I can to ensure he will survive this. Now you must heed my warning and let him rest as long and as well as you are able."

CHAPTER
33

THE caravan trudged on for hours more until it slowed, the swell of orders and answers pushing past the carriage curtains.

They'd reached their destination for the night—the Hand.

Some said the ashen rock formation appeared after the Warlord took over the Torrent. A metaphor for his—*her?*—power grab over the ousted Otxoa ruling family. But Amarande didn't believe it any more than she believed any other wild tales about this place. She'd learned much in the past day and a half about the Torrent, but nothing to convince her that instant geological phenomena were possible.

And though the Hand was impressive and just as described—seven horses high with four distinctive fingers and a thumb, tapered at the tops and sloping to a wide palm and heel—the princess barely glanced at it.

She only had eyes for Luca, in her lap, dead asleep. Naiara had said he'd be out for an hour, but by the time the Hand came into view and the caravan slowed to a halt, he'd been asleep for at least two, maybe closer to three.

Not a good sign.

Naiara and Señe allowed them to stay in their carriage as the caravan made camp. A tent city went up in a matter of minutes, cook fires started, the smell of roasted meat mingling with the scent of smoke and parched embers. The lilt of a thousand voices came in a buzz of an insect's wings. And it was only then, with the sun hanging low in a sky just as orange as the earth surrounding them, that Luca's eyes fluttered. They focused and Amarande watched, her own face hanging over his head in her lap.

"Ama, you're here," Luca whispered, his voice waking, too.

"Always, Luca." He smiled at her echo of his often-used phrase, and her heart skipped with the hope that maybe he really was saying he loved her every time the words left his lips. She bent to kiss him, awkward and upside down and working around his smile. Execution didn't matter. After a sloppy few seconds she whispered against his cheek, "I wouldn't be anywhere else."

The princess called for the healer then, and Luca's leg was inspected. It was still swollen and flat black, either with no sensation at all or registering a feverish pain—but the necrosis had halted.

"Much better, *kidege*," Naiara said as she gently removed her hands from the injured leg. "Eat and drink well, and rest for the night. We must watch for infection or any delayed reaction to the anti-venom."

Amarande didn't want to stay with the caravan for the night, but she also didn't want to endanger Luca by running too soon. He had yet to test the leg, and she hadn't yet found a solution for the loss of Mira.

Naiara secured them food and a tent. She told them they were welcome to eat with the caravan, but Amarande knew that doing so would mean questions. Who they were, where they were from, what had happened.

In the bag Amarande had stolen from Luca's female captor, she found an extra pair of trousers and a tunic. They'd been worn—sweat stains ringed the waist and under the arms—but they would do.

Luca sat with his back to the princess as she changed into the pirate's clothes behind a few yards of linen, but apparently that didn't keep a blush from creeping up his ears, because after a few moments Naiara cackled, "Oh, *kidege*, you've got your color back."

Amarande blushed, too.

As night bloomed from the horizon, they were led to their tent, set aside on the eastern edge of the caravan—outsiders were literally left to the outside in places like this. Spots such as this were undesirable—open to the wind, open to attack from vandals as well as the animals that roamed here—but it was better than the princess expected. And it allowed them to eat alone.

Amarande made a fire, and when it was good and hot, they roasted the food Naiara had secured them—a skinned fox and wrinkled plums—their stomachs growling side by side as the flames did their job.

Luca's appetite was healthy enough that Amarande could barely pay attention to her own food, watching every morsel that passed his lips to make sure he could swallow it down.

As the sun disappeared for good, Luca disappeared into the tent. When he reappeared, it was with sleeping blankets tucked to his chest.

"What are you doing? Stop that," Amarande whispered from where she was adding to the fire so that it might last the night. She'd seen one black wolf and she wasn't about to let another attack at night—if any other impossible animal roamed these open spaces, it had lived long enough to steer clear of flame.

"I don't think we should share the tent. I'll stay out here."

The princess immediately turned red enough that she was thankful for the night sky. Amarande hadn't kissed him since that waking moment, and suddenly she was feeling both shy and completely emboldened. She stomped over to the tent and pulled out her own blankets. "I'm the one who should stay in the open. You get back in there and protect your wound from the elements."

Luca didn't answer, just plopped down by the fire.

She plopped down next to him.

"Princess, please."

Amarande shook her head. "If you won't use it, I won't either."

"If I didn't know you were born in the Itspi, I'd guess you were born stuck in the mud, Ama."

"Stubbornness is an admirable trait."

Luca's dimples caught the firelight. "I didn't say it wasn't."

Amarande scooted closer to him. Close enough to mimic what the spatial arrangements in their tent would've been. She made it a point to lie in the same direction as Luca, their shoulders nearly touching, as they both looked up at the stars. "Good, because now that I'm set, I'm not moving. I got you back and then I worried all day I'd lose you for good, and now I'm going to take every precaution possible to make sure I wake with you by my side."

Luca rolled over and faced her. He propped himself up on his elbow and looked down at her. Amarande rolled onto her side and propped herself up, too. Somehow it seemed less intimate to face each other in this way than when they were lying on their backs, exposed to the stars and heavens. Still, her cheeks burned as if she'd rolled straight into the fire.

"I will always be at your side . . . unless I'm dragged away kicking and screaming by a band of kidnappers."

She couldn't help but laugh. He laughed a little, too, and then, when it was quiet, reached across the short distance and let his hand graze her face.

Amarande stared back, watching the fire warm his features. She suddenly wished the moon were brighter—she wanted to see this moment as clearly as possible. Instead, it was like the dreams she had—all light and shadows and his eyes watching her like she was the only girl in the world.

"May I kiss you, Ama?"

The princess flashed a surprised smile. "Of course. I kissed you."

Luca was quiet for a moment. "I'm in a position that I must ask."

Amarande hadn't asked him when she'd kissed him after the rescue. She'd just done it. Suddenly it was slightly horrifying to her that she hadn't thought to ask him at all. Power dynamic, emotions, a mutual understanding . . . she wasn't sure what drove her to do it or if any of those things made it worse or generally okay.

Luca's hand swept down her chin. "Ama, I wanted you to kiss me. But I never could've done it first."

"My answer to you will always be yes." She swallowed the lump forming in her throat—*oh, Luca*. "I'm so sorry I didn't think to ask before."

In response, he simply leaned in and made the next kiss his own. Soft. Cautious. Amarande's fingers splayed across his jaw, encouraging him. Her heart seemed to slow in her chest, as if time itself were suspended in amber.

By the time he pulled away, she struggled to open her eyes. She dropped her head to her bedroll with a smile on her face, eyes still closed.

"Ama," Luca whispered, and she could hear him shift around. "What are we going to do when we get back?"

"Well, deliver you to Medikua Aritza," she repeated, wondering if the snake's poison or the anti-venom itself had robbed him of some of his more recent memories, "and—"

"No," he said, voice so low it barely made it above the crack and snap of the fire. "I mean . . . about us?"

The princess's eyes flew open. "I'm not marrying Renard. And if he's convinced the council that I am, they're just going to be disappointed."

Luca drew in a breath, his response measured as always. And quiet. "Even if you tear up his marriage contract and the rest, too, they're not going to let us be . . . together."

"I don't care what they want. This is what we want. My heart has nothing to do with my ability to rule. They don't have to like it;

they just have to accept that this"—she gestured between them—
"is how things are right at this moment in time."

"And the law?"

If she could get the council to see that Ardenia didn't need to
play by the Sand and Sky's rules, they'd be so much better off. But
if Ardenia balked at the laws determined by the union of kingdoms, so could everyone else. Fissures like that would break the
continent apart.

The princess swallowed and set her voice—quiet like his and as
firm as she could make it. "I'll get it to change. I will. I'm not marrying to earn my own power. Not at sixteen, not ever."

Though Amarande loved Luca, and she was sure of it now, she
wasn't ready to marry him. But she wanted the chance to do so at
some point if that was what she chose. More, she wanted to give
him the chance to choose *her*, if he desired it.

What was it about this world that meant neither a princess
nor a commoner could have control over their own lives, hearts,
choices? Was there anyone who could fully make their own decisions without being beholden to anyone else? Even kings navigated
the laws—some were simply more brutal about how to do it than
others.

Luca rolled onto his back and stared up at the stars. They
seemed so much closer here, even though he and Amarande were
thousands of feet below their usual point of view at the Itspi. Amarande rolled over, too, her father suddenly on her mind. Her
father—who seemed to trust her to be who he hoped she would
be. And yet he'd left open the gap that kept her from getting there.

There had to be a reason.

After a time, Luca's hand found Amarande's. He wrapped his
fingers around hers and squeezed. "Ama, if you do marry, I'm still
going to be by your side. I can watch you from afar and serve you
and be in your life as much or as little as you want."

Amarande had never had trouble explaining herself to him before, but now was a different story.

"Luca, I don't want you to *serve* me," she said, sweeping his knuckles to her lips and kissing them gently. "Your *place* has never been who you are to me. I want you in my life, by my side, voluntarily. Not because I've asked you to be part of my household. Not because I've coerced my husband to let you stay. Because it's you and me, together, in this world."

Luca shifted again, his eyes finding hers across the starlit dark. "Always, Princess."

CHAPTER
34

THEY woke to the sun, hands intertwined. Amarande first, her eyes blinking open to the salmon sky. She sat up, not releasing Luca's fingers—after the past few days, she wasn't sure she'd ever let him out of her sight again. He was a foot away from her, his own eyelashes fluttering open.

Beneath them, the earth was cold, and a fine coating of russet dust covered their skin, hair, and clothes. The heat was coming, and with it, more dust and long travel. They'd slept hard and well and safe, and the princess felt better than she had in days. But it wasn't her own health that concerned her the most.

"How's the leg?" she asked as Luca pushed himself to sitting, her voice a whisper, throat parched.

Luca nodded to himself. "Feels stiff but so good that I'm afraid to look and change my answer."

Still, he began to roll up his pant leg, which had drifted down in the night. Amarande leaned over and brushed her hair back and away, the majority of it pulled clear of her crown braid now, the wind swirling a thick sheet of it in such a way that it obstructed her view.

Even the morning light wasn't kind to what they saw. The gash along Luca's shin had shifted from dead black to revenant gray. The swelling from the day before had subsided, yet the whole leg still looked deformed. Like someone had burned a handful of plaster and plopped it on his skin.

"Has feeling returned?" Amarande asked, her fingers hovering above the gash, remembering Naiara's probing hands.

"Less than I'd like," Luca answered, unsure. "Help me stand, Ama?"

Amarande immediately stood and offered both hands. Luca took them and gingerly got to his stocking feet, putting all his weight on his good leg until he was vertical, testing his bad one only then. His fingers dropped from hers and there he was, standing on both legs. He took a step. Then another. Amarande's arms were out, ready to catch him with each successive movement.

He had an obvious limp, but still his dimples flashed, as optimistic as ever. "Like new."

The princess's fingers tightened around his, tears sparking in her eyes, something soft and swift rising in her gut and pushing a lump into her throat. She ripped one hand away to bat at her eyes. Luca wrapped his arms around her and drew her into his chest. She was just tall enough that her ear met the strong beating of his heart as his palm rubbed her back.

Amarande drew in a breath and peered up at Luca, the desire to kiss him overpowering the embarrassment of her tears and the raw emotion found in them: Though they still had a hundred miles to go before they were home, Luca was safe and healthy, and right here with her.

His chin tipped toward her, lips parting, golden eyes hungry in the morning light. She couldn't look away, obeying the want deep in her gut as she drew onto her tiptoes and—

"Before you get too far into that, I have a few questions for the two of you."

Luca and Amarande jerked apart and then back together, startling at the voice. A man revealed himself from behind the tent they hadn't used. He stepped in front of the opening—right in front of where their supplies, her sword, and the Eritrian's dagger with his boots were stashed for the night.

The man was tall and lean, like a tree stubborn enough to reach for the stars on too few nutrients. The rest of him was nondescript: brown hair, skin that started pale but had been tanned by this life, scruff about his cheeks but no true beard. The voice wasn't the same as the man's who'd drugged her two days ago, and the princess wasn't sure if she was relieved or disappointed. She wanted revenge on that one.

"Who are you?" Amarande asked carefully, startled but trying to be polite—they were here as guests of the caravan, after all.

In response, the man crossed his arms, looked to Luca, and said, "Do you always let your woman answer for you?"

"Her question is mine."

The man smiled, but it wasn't a happy thing. "I was to meet a group at the Hand last night for the transfer of a prisoner. The group didn't show. That prisoner is my employer's property, and it's my duty to locate him and bring him in. The only people to join the caravan yesterday were the two of you, and you, boy, match the description of the prisoner."

"There are no prisoners here. We sought medical attention and now will be on our way," the princess said, and reached for the fire as if she was going to fully extinguish it. Dismissing the man.

Her father's voice was in the back of her mind, urging her to squeeze more information from this man—"employer" was an interesting word indeed—but Koldo's advice rang loudest: *Escaping alive is the first priority.* She'd not lose Luca here after everything else.

"Where to?" the man asked.

"That's none of your business," the princess spat, anger now fully on display. She was aware she was making things worse the more she talked to him, since he seemed to think it so unusual that a woman would have an opinion, much less speak for a man, but in Amarande's estimation, that was his own fault. "I don't appreciate your questions or that you believe my friend to be here against his will."

"The group in question was made up of two men and a woman, who I'm told is a savant with a sword." Luca's eyes slid to Amarande's face. She could feel them on her cheek, but she made it a point not to look at him. Not to give it all away. She stared down the man as he completed his theory, growing sicker with each second.

Here—the kidnappers were supposed to deliver Luca here, to this man.

"It's not such a leap to believe that even a woman such as that would let her emotions get the best of her. Perhaps she killed her partners and missed her drop because she fell for the prisoner, who I'm told is handsome enough to catch a princess's attentions."

The man finished with a smile. At her. Amarande did not appreciate what his assumption telegraphed for the motivations of women—her or the girl of the Torrent he was accusing without knowing.

"That's quite the theory, and incorrect when it comes to the two of us," Luca said. "Now, if you'll be going—"

The man drew his knife and shot it at Luca in that moment.

Luca's words died as his instincts drove his body into motion. Though his balance was unstable and his bitten leg clumsy, he ducked out of the knife's way while snagging the hilt, just as he'd done that day in the meadow.

The man was already charging Luca, chasing his knife blade, and going for a tackle.

Luca spun out of the way, and at the same time Amarande launched her own knife—in her boot always—straight for the man's lanky body. But his frame and his movement meant she missed.

The knife grazed his back and clattered into the red earth. Luca was ready and closer, launching the man's own knife back at him in the same instant Amarande's missed. The knife pierced the man straight along the spinal column. Instantly his body went raggedy, his control lost as he fell face first to the cold earth.

Amarande hurdled the dying fire as Luca gathered her knife. She grabbed all their belongings from the tent, stuffing them in her arms and immediately heading due east. No looking back. Not to see if the man was alive or dead. Not to ask him whom he worked for. Nothing.

No good-byes to Naiara or Señe. Or Mira. Luca tried out a jog, catching up and trading the princess's knife for his boots and one of the saddlebags.

"Did I . . . did we . . . did he?" Luca was gasping and looking back, trying to shrug on his boots without tying them. "Did that man just die trying to take *me* captive?"

Amarande wouldn't look back. She couldn't see that body on the ground and guess from this distance whether he was in the middle of bleeding out or if he was about to rise and sound the alarm.

"Someone will find him and know why he joined the caravan. And then, if they didn't know who we were before, they'll know now," the princess said, eyes on the fuzzy line of mountains in the distance. They seemed too far for all they had to outrun—the kidnapper pirates, whomever this man worked for, the murder that may or may not have just occurred, and the elements of the Torrent. Maybe more. There was always more. Amarande caught Luca's eye. "The sooner we get home, the better."

CHAPTER
35

GAUGING by the sun and the landmarks, Amarande estimated they went about ten miles in the first three hours after their escape. Luca kept pace without complaint, but though she could go faster, the princess held back. They had a hundred miles to go, and if she pushed him too hard and infection set in, there would be no one within a day's walk to help. And though she was strong, she couldn't carry him.

Up ahead loomed the beginning of the long, thin rock shelf she'd likened to the dragon's spine during the sprint into the Torrent with Mira. If they could get there, they could find shade if he needed a rest. People too. Maybe some who'd be swayed by her diamonds to sell them a horse.

Or not.

The princess understood now how little she knew about the world outside the safety of the Itspi, but she never imagined a place where diamonds were refused. Especially considering that was one of the reasons suitors wanted *her*.

Diamonds, an army, another throne—her value in a nutshell.

Though perhaps not in that order. That was certainly not Renard's order of priority.

Renard.

Amarande hated so very much *who* and *what* was waiting for her at home. She snagged Luca's fingers and cleared her throat.

"How's the leg?"

"It's fine, Ama. Just like it was twenty minutes ago and the twenty minutes before that," Luca answered. He wasn't irritated, just matter-of-fact. "I promise to tell you if I'm not okay."

She didn't believe that for a second—he'd spent his whole life determined not to be a bother—but she didn't needle.

"It's not *you* I don't trust; it's the possibility of infection." Her mind paged back to one of her father's sayings—one Luca too knew by heart. Everyone in the Itspi did. "*Beware or be dead* doesn't just refer to battle. It applies to everything. It's not just *if* or *when* we get home together; it's what state you are in that matters to me."

"My state is good. Let's get home."

Amarande didn't completely believe that either. But she liked to hear his voice. Though they may have just left a man to die, though they still had a hundred miles to go, when they spoke it was like the old pattern they shared in the meadow when no one was looking and they had hours of training and a fresh slice of lemon cake between them.

"I'm stuck on the timing," the princess announced, adjusting the fall of the saddlebag over her shoulder so that it wouldn't snag her hair. "When were the pirates and that man"—she nodded over her shoulder toward their abandoned campsite miles back—"hired? Father hasn't been gone a week, and the planning of a trade-off points to something even bigger than forcing my hand. Doesn't it?"

"Yes, but either way I'm just a pawn. Though passing me around does seem a little suspect." Luca pursed his lips in thought, his dimples winking as his eyes met the middle distance. She didn't think Sendoa or anyone else would've used the diamond's facets as an analogy with Luca growing up, but just the same, his mind ticked through all the possibilities as they hit the light.

His pace quickened a little as he thought, the rhythm of his limp blurring into something less exaggerated. "Unless . . . the plan changed. Not because you came to get me but before that." Luca stopped dead in his tracks and grabbed Amarande's other hand. "Maybe the pirates weren't originally meant to take me. Maybe they were meant to take *you*."

Oh. Stars. Yes.

The cold possibility of that line of thought sent a shiver across Amarande's overheated skin. The princess thought back to those days, with the vipers arriving in beribboned groups. Pyrenee first, Basilica next, and finally, later in the same day, Myrcell.

"Eliminate the king, kidnap the heir, leave Ardenia and all her spoils open for the taking."

Luca nodded, dark hair brushing his eyes. "Or even cleaner with the laws currently in place: Eliminate the king, kidnap the heir and force her into a wedding, and call Ardenia yours."

Amarande's throat was suddenly very dry. Anger rumbled under her clammy skin. *Father, why didn't you change the law?*

It took her a few moments to revive her voice. Her grip on both his hands was fading her knuckles white in the harsh midday light.

"Either is blatant if true and lends to my argument that we must know the truth about Father's murder before accepting a marriage contract. Both scenarios give me even more pause about our council's reasons to rush me down the aisle and fight me on an investigation of Father's death."

Thank the stars for Koldo's ability to make it happen . . . before impending war took precedence.

"Blatant, yes, but effective."

"Effective, but not *efficient*. There are too many variables— stars, *I'm* too much of a variable. And anything could go wrong." She nodded to the thin space between them. "We're standing here as proof that variables destroy even the best-laid plans. If you have access to hemlock, why not just wipe your foes from the playing field rather than suffer through their constant aberration?"

Luca smiled, though it was resigned. "Because variables make it a game."

These brutal creatures, sitting high atop their furs in gems and silks, plotting how to take more because nothing was ever enough—yes, they would make it a sport. Just like they made one of her courtship via council. A game of compliments, promises, and laughter into always-full cups.

Mountain Lion. Bear. Shark. Not a one of them decent.

The princess sighed. "Have I mentioned I hate every person of royal blood on this blasted continent?"

Luca's dimples winked in the white light. "Perhaps more than once."

The silence between them returned as they pushed forward more, heads angled down to keep the high sun out of their eyes as much as possible. It was a comfortable silence, though, Luca always knowing when to give Amarande space.

They pushed ahead another three hours before finally reaching the tail tip of the dragon's spine. They crept to the shadows and sat down long enough to take deep pulls of water chased by hunks of bread and curd cheese. The rest only lasted five minutes, but it nursed their muscles, stiff from riding in the days before and growing sore from hours on their feet.

They stood, the princess inquired about Luca's leg yet again—still fine, of course—and, as Amarande fussed over her saddlebag, which was caught on the hilt of the sword at her back, Luca whistled. The princess's head whipped around, her blood already rising at the hint of a threat—but instead of the kidnappers or robbers, something completely unexpected approached.

A palomino the color of honey butter.

She appeared like a gift from the stars—her mane was a near-white platinum and her eyes a sweet brown. She was with saddle, but there were no other identifying aspects—no symbols, initials, not even saddlebags belonging to a discarded rider.

Still, Luca grinned as if he'd stabled the horse himself.

"Ferri, is that you?" He held his hand out, fingers offered for a sniff.

"Ferri?" Amarande asked, eyes round.

"It's Urtzi's horse. The boy from Myrcell."

The horse ambled forth and took Luca up on his offer for a sniff, drawing in a whiff of his fingers, and, pleased with what she smelled, allowing Luca to rub the blaze streaking across her nose. "She must have dashed away during the fight. Are you hungry, girl?"

Luca dug into the saddlebag at his shoulder and offered the horse the heel off his loaf of bread. The horse chomped merrily. Sharing a bit of water came next. Ferri happily snuffed at the liquid in Luca's palms.

"Will she let us ride her?" Amarande asked, eyeing the horse. It'd been dark both times she saw the camp. She didn't remember this particular horse, but then again, she'd been watching the people.

"I think she might," Luca said, petting her mane in wide strokes. "I'll hop up first." His dimples flashed. "I won't ride off without you."

Amarande grinned. "You better not."

Luca wedged his good leg into the stirrup and then, with Amarande's help, put all his weight into it as he pulled himself up to mount the mare. The swelling had returned a little with their walking, but his leg appeared leagues better than this time the day before; that much was sure.

He settled and so did the horse.

As the princess approached, the horse whipped her head around, side-eyeing her. She reached out a tentative hand, combing the palomino's mane. "I know you want him for yourself, girl, but we come as a pair. One of us or none of us."

The palomino snorted.

Luca removed his boots from the stirrups, giving Amarande room. She swung up without a hitch. The horse didn't grumble or kick. Luca looped his arms around the princess's waist, and they were off yet again.

CHAPTER
36

An hour later, they were making good time along the dragon's spine. The shadows now were in their favor, and they shared them with other travelers without consequence. Amarande was again thankful for the extra clothes in the girl's saddlebag—without the ball gown, wandering eyes didn't linger so long on her form.

It was a relief, all of it.

Still, Amarande didn't trust the peace or their luck in happening across the pirates' horse. She kept searching over her shoulder. Jumping at every irregular shadow. She was tense and anxious, hungry for it to be over. The next leg of the story would be within the vipers' nest of the Itspi's towers.

"No one's following us, Ama," Luca said, after yet another sweep of her head. "If anything, there's someone ahead of us— Koldo, Serville, *someone*, sent looking for you."

Amarande frowned. She'd filled him in on the posturing at the southern border and how the general had left almost immediately after the funeral. But Koldo was also regent, and that had its own set of expectations, especially after the princess disappeared. The general would likely have had to return to the castle, perhaps personally mount the investigation into the princess's disappearance. But would she have? In Amarande's experience, Koldo saw the bigger picture better than anyone in history save for her father.

"What's more important, locating your runaway princess or managing impending war?"

Luca answered immediately, "You're the most important, always, Ama."

A blush crept across her cheeks and she turned enough to drop a kiss on his shoulder. "To you. But to them . . . peace has to be more important than a princess who can't even rule unless she's wed—"

Ferri slowed as the terrain changed. Because here, north of the dragon's spine, lay a wide pit, scorched black. Embers cold but blowing, the whole bowl was a whirl and puff of ashes, kicked up and reset and kicked up again, over and over, like the sands in an hourglass.

A Torrent fire pit.

Ferri halted altogether.

"Is that . . . ?" Luca started. Amarande nodded so quickly it wasn't worth it for him to finish the question.

How many times had Amarande feared her father would be tossed into one of these, with only his charred remains returning to the Itspi? She hadn't actually seen the one that threatened her that first night, only its flames in the too-near distance. But here, in broad daylight, the carnage was a more impressive reminder of power than a head on a pike.

The base of this pit was at least twenty horses across in any direction. This was the aftermath of what Amarande had seen. The princess had yet to share her capture with Luca, but he, as always, met her where she was, the Warlord also on his mind.

"If King Sendoa relished being the protector of the realm . . . why . . ." Luca trailed off, words implying criticism of his lifelong benefactor dying on his tongue.

Loving her father as she did, Amarande had no qualms about completing the thought. "Why didn't he defeat the Warlord and reinstate the Otxoa?"

"Yes. That."

"I have a theory, but it really is just a theory."

She felt Luca nod into her back, suggesting she continue.

"I think the Warlord is a woman. And not just any woman—my mother."

Luca coughed with surprise and then silently ran it all through his mind. Amarande knew he was paging through the same sort of moonless dark that held her memories about this.

Of what Sendoa had said when rehashing the tale of the scar across his face.

Of what Maialen and Abene had shared with him about their own escape from the Torrent and the Warlord's rule.

Of what those same women told him of his mother and her death the very same night the queen ran away.

Finally, he spoke in his measured, calm way. "Ama, it's a good theory, it is, but the timing—"

The thunder of many horse hooves thumped through the air, cutting Luca off mid-sentence. The clamor shook the ground around them, going from a tremble to a quake in the space of a breath.

Amarande and Luca whirled toward the sound.

A dozen or more riders barreled toward them in a cloud of bronze dust, making it appear as if their horses were riding a wave of earth. No sigil to this group, just a gait that made it very clear they weren't friends.

The princess's eyes narrowed. Someone in the caravan had indeed found the body and figured out who they were. The result wasn't good.

"Hold on," Amarande said as much to herself as to Luca, as she clipped Ferri sharply with her heels. The horse reared, her front two legs picking up off the ground, and let out a cry. And then they were rocketing down the steep edge of the fire pit, toward the flat moor of bones and ash at the bottom.

Amarande hoped the sudden change in direction would buy them enough time to climb back to the other side and gain the type of lead that such a large group couldn't overcome.

They tore down the bank of the pit, the ashen earth coming along with it, crumbling under the collective weight of them. Which killed their speed. The horse stumbled, the soil disappearing the second her hooves made contact, her footing shot. She tripped over herself, front legs sliding out from under her and her momentum pulling her back end along anyway.

And suddenly the earth was rushing up toward them.

"Pull!" Luca yelled, grabbing the reins along with Amarande and yanking back with all his might.

Amarande yanked, too, both of them leaning so far back they nearly fell off the other way. The horse's equilibrium changed, and she tapped the ground and bounced back up, rather than rolling onto her side and over her back—something that would have surely crushed her riders.

They came to a stop in a low heap, Ferri favoring the side that hit, her whole right flank caked in soot. Amarande kicked at her with a leg smarting from being dashed against the ground, the full weight of the horse and riders behind it for just an instant. Feeble as the command was with Amarande's legs not completely in working order, the horse still got the message and tried to get going but stumbled and stamped.

"Come on, girl, come on," Luca urged between coughs. The ash rose in plumes around them, making it as difficult to breathe as to see.

But the thunder of the riders eclipsing the rim of the fire pit was unmistakable. It was steady, but slower than what they'd tried with Ferri—their pursuers had learned from the princess's mistakes.

"Come on, girl, just keep going," the princess whispered, echoing Luca, eyes watering and words weak as a cough chased them out of her mouth. She pulled up her cowl, but it wasn't much better. Luca had one, too, now, but it didn't do him many favors. His coughs were deep enough and close enough to reverberate against her back.

The horse wouldn't move.

And before the dust settled, they were surrounded. The shadows were there, between the ashen plumes, horses snorting heavily. As the fine russet cloud settled, there, in the middle of it all, was a familiar, smiling face. There, on a horse as white as snow, was Prince Renard. That grin widened, though it didn't reach his eyes.

"Princess Amarande, my love, I've found you at last."

CHAPTER
37

 _____

AMARANDE sat tall in her saddle—shoulders back and head held high—and looked the elder prince of Pyrenee right in the eye.

His love? His love? His key to the kingdom, more like it. And she would have none of it.

"I am no such thing."

Renard didn't blink. "*My love*, you are my fiancée, and you've been missing, stolen away by this *brute*, and thank the stars I've found you."

Amarande laughed. "I am only your fiancée if you forged my signature. I went to collect *my* love, who *you* stole away, and now you haven't found me—you've cornered me. Every word you say is a lie."

She hoped Renard would concede—that it was him indeed who paid the pirates to steal Luca—so that at least she'd have that answer. Instead, he said, "It's all a matter of perception, Princess."

"What do you want?" she spat.

"To take you home."

"I'm headed there right now, and I know the way. Now if you'll—"

"To Pyrenee."

"Not in your company. Never."

Renard smiled, blue eyes as cold as a Pyrenee winter. "You don't have a choice, *my love*. The contract was approved by your council."

Amarande's heart sank—this prince wasn't bluffing, and she'd guessed correctly. They'd accepted a forgery without waiting for her to verbally confirm it despite all her efforts to force them to understand her point of view. It was just as she'd both imagined and feared: Her future had been bought and sold, her father's top advisors sealing the deal.

What's more, Luca's conclusion regarding regicide working in hand with the succession laws—*take out the king, kidnap the heir and force her into a wedding, and call Ardenia yours*—seemed a whisper from being plausible.

There was the rustle and huffing of horses. Amarande surveyed those who surrounded her—four men of Renard's private guard, Taillefer, and several hired thugs from the Torrent. Plus, if she was not mistaken, Luca's kidnappers—as good an answer as any to her question of Pyrenee's involvement—and the robbers who'd ambushed her. She saw a girl who looked very much like Osana, but she couldn't be sure, as the girl had a cowl about her face. It didn't matter anyway—there had to be more than a dozen bodies between her and the open road.

The princess held her head higher.

"The choice is always mine."

"Not if I don't let you go."

"I did not consent. I *will not* consent. You've lied to my council and to steal me away would be an act of war. Touch a hair on my head and the fury of the entire Ardenian army will be upon your neck." She gritted her teeth. "And that's only if you survive my blade first. Which you won't."

Again, Renard laughed. It echoed around them, cold and dead. "You won't kill me. You won't kill anyone. Those three right there stole your saddlebags, and you didn't kill them. Those three over this way stole your stableboy, and you didn't kill them. You didn't kill them, and you won't make your first kill with me. Or my brother. Or any of these other people."

With each delineation of the princess's failures, the prince's voice intensified, his confidence in his words fortifying his body language. By the time he came upon his summation, he was staring down on her in such a way that Amarande actually did feel small.

The firstborn of Pyrenee continued, confidence bloated past his storybook features. "No one goes from showing opponents weak mercy to surviving an attack by seventeen men and women who will not only touch a hair upon your beautiful head but relieve it from the rest of your body."

Luca's hands tightened at her waist.

When the princess said nothing, Renard smiled. "Come quietly, marry me, and live."

In response, the princess gathered every last bit of saliva the Torrent had yet to suck dry and spat straight at the hooves of Prince Renard's stallion.

"I would rather die."

The princess drew her sword. Luca drew the Eritrian's dagger from the boot of his good foot. They sat upon their orphaned horse, armed and ready.

"As you wish. There is more than one way to take a kingdom." And then the prince smiled, and it finally reached his blue eyes. "And if you die, I shall make sure your stableboy lives long enough to suffer prolonged, excruciating punishment for your death."

"No. . . ." She said it almost to herself, the word dying swiftly on her tongue.

The prince's eyes shifted over Amarande's shoulder. "Oh yes. You see, Princess, I won't take you kicking and screaming and scheming my murder on my wedding night. Oh no. I'll just go ahead and kill you. And then I'll trot your stableboy back to the Itspi and detail to your council how he stole you away and then murdered you when I tried to rescue you." Renard clucked his tongue. "If he couldn't have you, no one could."

Amarande's gut lurched. She could see it all now. He would do it. He would. Worse, the groundwork was already laid.

She pressed a hand on top of Luca's. She wouldn't let that happen. She couldn't let that happen.

But she had no friends here.

These people would not hesitate to kill her. They'd been paid well and would continue a lie that would end with Luca's head on a pike and Renard drawing control of her kingdom.

"Can you envision it, Princess?" Prince Taillefer asked. He smiled, fox-like, from his brother's side. "You can—I can see the future scrolling across those exquisite eyes of yours." The cheer from his expression dropped, leaving a sneer. "It will happen. All of it."

Amarande swallowed. Not a dozen bodies—seventeen, as Renard had said. Men hardened by the Warlord's rule. Men who swore an oath to the prince. Men, and women, hired by said prince to push her into marriage as a pawn.

The princess's hand tightened on her sword. Renard lacked many qualities, but an eye for strategy was not one of them. He knew the princess had spent her life in the yard, fighting where it wasn't life and death—bruises were the worst of it. He'd called it right. She'd been trained to fight, but she'd never killed a man. Even when she'd come close—the giant at the Warlord's Inn, the man at the campsite—others did it. To get out of this situation, she'd have to kill at least half of these, if not all.

She wouldn't kill any one of them. And he knew it.

"Ama?" Luca whispered at her back. He was ready to stand with her no matter her decision, she knew. But she wouldn't see him hurt in any way.

Her next words determined so much.

The princess drew in a shaky breath. Time paused, waiting.

"I will go with you."

"And you will marry me?" Renard pressed.

Amarande closed her eyes, sword lowered, and she squeezed Luca's hand. Of all the hurt possible here, this was likely the least painful. Because he knew she loved him, and that was something.

"Yes." Her answer was loud enough that every one of them could hear it. There was no mistaking what she'd said.

The prince drew in a sharp breath of relief.

"Nikola," he said to an ox-shouldered guard in Pyrenee purple, "relieve my fiancée of her sword and her stableboy of his dagger. The rest of you, into position. Let's not waste any time in escorting them straight to Pyrenee."

There was a smile in his voice and triumph in the way he held his shoulders. When the princess opened her eyes, she saw that beside him, Taillefer was obviously grinning. She thought of him in the meadow, scheming for his brother's crown, and she wondered if she'd just helped him complete a milestone in his long con.

If she had, so be it.

She could only do what was best for her, and what was best for her in that moment was what was best for Luca. They could be together in death, but there was no way she would leave him to suffer so beforehand. Not to mention what might happen to her kingdom. The rest of the pieces would fall as they may.

"It will be all right," she whispered to Luca. She could feel him nod at her back.

The guards filled in around them, placing them at the center of a large moving diamond. Renard made it a point to slip in right next to the princess and her love. The prince eyed their closeness—Amarande could feel him take in the way Luca's hands rested about her waist and how she kept a hand over his as they were stripped of their blades.

"You know, I've changed my mind. Perhaps the princess should ride with me."

Amarande immediately scowled. "May I remind you what happened last time I came within an inch of your sword, my prince?"

Renard's mouth ticked up. "That does not sound like going quietly, my love." He caught eyes with his brother. "But perhaps you're right and we should give each other space until our wedding night." Amarande rolled her eyes. "Taillefer, would you take the stableboy hostage on your horse?"

"Gladly."

Amarande didn't want to be separated from Luca, but if they couldn't ride together, this was likely the best scenario to keep her fury from fueling something rash involving that stupid bejeweled sword. Taillefer pulled his horse in next to the princess and ordered Luca onto his mount, a white stallion very much like his brother's.

When Luca was firmly bound and in place on Taillefer's saddle, the younger prince moved to Renard's other side. The rest of the group shuffled in around them. As places were finalized, Amarande locked eyes with Taillefer, who winked. *Brutal boy.* Then she looked Renard dead in the eye.

"My prince, as long as my Luca lives, I promise not to kill you."

"All right, my love," Renard said. But then he laughed at her seriousness.

And that was his mistake.

CHAPTER
38

❧

Bʏ the time the sun sank into the horizon over their shoulders, they'd come to the base of the mountains that separated Pyrenee from the Torrent. They looked almost exactly like Amarande's mountains, the ones that cradled the Itspi. If she squeezed her eyes tight enough, she almost believed she was headed home and not being death marched into her very worst nightmare.

But her father had taught her never to dismiss reality.

And so the princess's eyes stayed open as they closed in, and as the base of the mountain range sharpened, so did the reality of the situation. They weren't alone. The knife's edge of war, discussed in theory in the Itspi's council room, was now a tangible thing, made up by camps of Pyrenee soldiers stretched across the range—purple bruises clouding the pass. Koldo faced double the threat to the south. Amarande had no qualms that somewhere very close were her own soldiers, guided by one of Koldo's seconds. Close enough to make a statement, far enough to be ignorant to her presence.

A smile slid across Prince Renard's face as the first Pyrenee camp came into focus. "Look at those fine soldiers. They will make us proud, my love."

"Call me by my name, or this is all you shall hear of my voice until you do," Amarande spat, not looking at him. She kept her eyes forward, taking in the line of soldiers with a warrior's eye.

This camp held fifty men at least; the next fires on the line were a mile away. The border of the Pyrenee stretched a hundred miles through the mountains flush with Ardenia. That meant thousands of men guarding the border, awaiting orders. There would be more behind them; these camps were simply the line in the sand. If she were to run, she'd have every one of them on her back, chasing her in something that would appear very much like the sort of invasion meant to start a war.

"You choose your fights over the most trivial of things, *my love*."

Amarande bit her tongue so she wouldn't shoot back that all of her fights with him had been over things of great importance to her, things that he, in his privilege and greed, would never understand. To snap at him now would be to undermine herself. She was grateful when Taillefer's fox laugh broke in.

"That's perfect, Renard!" Taillefer exclaimed from his spot on the other side. Luca watched with a blank face, his shoulders hunched forward in their binding against the younger prince's back. "Simply call her 'my love' whenever you tire of the princess's insults, and you'll immediately make them stop. A tip for a happy marriage from your clever little brother."

Amarande caught eyes with Luca. She knew he'd understand her expression—*I want to murder them all.*

But she couldn't. Which was partially why they were in this mess.

Renard's aubergine-clad guards led the group toward the first of the camps so that there'd be no mistaking that they were friendly. Still, the leader—a general, based on the stars along his collar— met them at the camp's edge, following the proper protocol.

"Prince Renard, Your Highness, I was unaware you were visiting the front line."

"It was quite unplanned, General—"

"Tousette, sir."

"Very good. General Tousette, myself and my men have been

on an excursion into the Torrent, rescuing Princess Amarande from the misguided attentions of a commoner in her employ."

Amarande's mouth opened to refute this, but Renard's hand was heavy upon her shoulder, quick as a lightning strike. "The princess has had quite a shock and is extremely exhausted. We must forge back to the Bellringe in the morning, for we are to be married tomorrow night." All the saliva left the princess's mouth. *Tomorrow?* That couldn't be. "We would greatly appreciate it if we could fold into your camp for the night, and rest our weary bones."

"It would be an honor, Your Highness. Beds and supper shall be yours within the hour."

"Good man, Tousette."

And then the general was off, barking orders. His men whipped into action around him, restructuring their tent city to fit a prince.

Renard seemed to delight in so many men scurrying around at his direction. The soldiers moved like ghosts in the twilight, a blur of aubergine and white that faded to gray in the smudge of remaining sun. Amarande squeezed her reins, trying very hard not to punch him in the face.

The princess's stomach growled, empty as the howling wind. If she was this hungry, Luca was likely the same, and he needed the rest—that snakebite would take more than the recovery they'd given it. He needed off that horse and a bellyful of good food and hydration.

"I demand full meals for both Luca and myself," the princess said without preamble. "And water. As much as we like."

"Of course, my love, you are not my prisoner. You are here on your own accord."

Ha. "In that case, I request dinner in my tent."

"A lovers' meal. Just as delightful as our first, I hope."

This boy was insufferable. "*My* tent is not *your* tent. Nor are you to be within fifty feet of my tent if you want to keep your blood on the inside."

Taillefer snickered and Renard shot him a look before lifting his chin at Amarande. "Very well. But I won't allow you to sleep within fifty feet of your stableboy either. And you cannot sleep unguarded."

Amarande smirked. "Right, because I'm here on my own accord." Caught, Renard sighed. The princess continued. "I see two women in your party, and I know one is quite handy with a sword. I sleep with them or I don't sleep at all."

Renard's eyes slid to the female pirate and then to the other girl—definitely Osana. Her cowl was still up, but the princess was now sure that Egia was strapped to the girl's back. A thread of disappointment wound through Amarande at this, but she knew it was likely the girl wanted a job more than a place. Or maybe everything she'd told the princess was a lie. It didn't matter, but it did sting just a little.

Amarande wasn't convinced Renard thought of women as his equals, only as something he needed to succeed—for his crown, for his heir—but if he respected anything about Amarande, it was her ability to fight, and these two women were cut from the same cloth in that regard. In fact, the princess thought, they would likely protect her better than any men in the party simply because they wouldn't underestimate her ability while overestimating their own.

"Ula, Osana, set up for the night with the princess. Nikola and Tremaine, you take point outside the women's tent. Taillefer, choose two men to watch the stableboy with you. Everyone else, you're with me."

That smirk nearly deepened into an amused smile—seven people to guard both herself and Luca, seven more plus an entire army camp to keep Renard safe from what he thought they might do to him.

Still, as they separated, the entire camp shifted, men moving things around to surround them in the center. As requested, she wouldn't be within fifty feet of Renard, but she would have a fifty-man layer pressing in on her, as thick as the walls of the Itspi.

Amarande's smile dropped.

If this were how her life was to be—fenced in on all sides by military power—she'd be suffocated by her own dreams, agency, ideas. It could hardly be called a life to live. As if Renard knew what she was thinking, he drove his knife in further, smiling brightly as his brother hauled Luca away.

"Sleep well, my princess. By tomorrow night, the two of us, and our kingdoms, shall be wed."

CHAPTER
39

❧

AMARANDE hated that she couldn't easily see Luca from her tent. True to his word, Renard had placed him completely on the other side of the encampment. He'd set up his own tent beside his brother's, his cushion of seven men filling in the easement between. Through the dark and the glare of dozens of fires, Luca was somewhere in the shadows.

The princess felt his safety was an uncertain thing if she couldn't see him, and so, though it was an impossibility, she kept reading the darkness as she ate a meal of salted cod reconstituted in an olive sauce—the soldiers had pulled out all the stops for royalty in their midst. It was hearty and savory, and she let the juices drip down her chin as she scanned the camp, her heart reaching through the distance to Luca.

The girls she'd chosen as her guards ate in silence, bracketing her. Though she admired both for the way they fought, they were clearly out for gold more than anything else. Osana—that was a disappointment, though the princess didn't dignify the girl's choice by begging her to confirm her betrayal. As for the pirate, Amarande wasn't sure why she was here. Perhaps this was what she must do to receive payment, having bungled the job of delivering Luca to the man they'd met at the Hand.

For a moment, Amarande considered paying the women off in diamonds to whisk her and Luca away from the camp, but given all at play here, that seemed to be a gamble that didn't guarantee much of a return.

Royals and the Warlord were brutal, yes, and their lack of benevolence sowed women and men like these.

Amarande was only half-confident she could close her eyes in the same space as these girls and not wake to her throat being slashed, but she trusted them more than any of the men in the party, and she had to sleep if she was going to figure out a way to survive what was to come tomorrow night. And every day after.

Dinner was finished without a cry of pain from Luca's general direction, and Amarande allowed herself to be satisfied with that. It was the best she could hope for. A soldier came around and gathered their dishes, and then her guards drew the flaps of the tent closed.

"Princess, we must bind you for sleep," Osana said. "The prince commands it."

The girl held out a length of rope, her gaze not wavering. If she was embarrassed about switching sides, she didn't show it. Amarande presented her hands without comment. At least within the castle, she wouldn't be bound. A guard or two at her door, but not a rope every night—she hoped. Osana tied her arms. "Legs, too, Princess."

Of course.

The princess presented her ankles, again without a word. She waited for Osana to steal the knife from her boot—she certainly knew about it after witnessing the beginnings of Amarande's fight with the giant—but the girl didn't take it. Maybe she liked the princess more than she could say in front of the pirate. Or not.

From across the tent, the other girl watched, loosening the handkerchief from her head. The pirate's long hair spilled forward like a lion's mane, and she pulled it back, braiding it, with the kerchief to tie the ends. In her lap was the saddlebag Amarande had stolen from her. She'd already cataloged everything that remained inside but hadn't commented on the clothing of hers the princess currently wore, or on the fancy dress the princess had stuffed inside.

Braid finished, the pirate still watched. Amarande felt uneasy under her glare, as fierce as she imagined a Warlord-lit fire pit to be. The only woman who had a stare more intense was Koldo, and that was only because she had twenty years of practice on this girl.

Amarande lay back onto the furs the soldiers had given them. She shut her eyes, bound wrists propped behind her head. It was still another minute before the pirate spoke.

"You're not going to marry *him*, are you?"

Amarande's eyes popped open and shifted to the pirate's brilliant gold ones. The princess said nothing. The pirate pressed on.

"You love Luca . . . don't you?" Again, Amarande was silent. The pirate's words became more forceful with each syllable. She was angry. "You *came* for Luca. You *fought* for Luca. You nearly *slit my throat* for Luca." Osana was watching Amarande's face now, too, their last conversation together running its course over her features. "Do you know how many times he told us you'd come for him? How much faith he had—*has*—in you? I could nearly pluck his love for you out of the air and slice it up for dinner, it was so solid. He loves you and you love him—true love, simple as that."

The pirate was breathing hard as she finished.

"I can confirm this," Osana said when Amarande didn't answer the pirate. "That's why I remembered the boy at the watering hole—I'd never heard someone speak like that ever in my life."

She'd seen him? Why hadn't she said so when they were together? When she knew what the princess sought?

Somehow this hit Amarande harder than the pirate's words.

A new weight tore at the princess's throat, sad and heavy. She swallowed it down but sat up, feeling as if it might choke her. She caught her breath and stared at both girls. Girls who didn't understand the position she was in. Girls who believed they knew her or Luca or both. They didn't.

"I was born without true love as a possibility. I thought I could change that, and I was wrong."

"Nonsense," the pirate girl spat. "True love is already yours. True love is the most powerful force on this earth—we just forget it because those with power here deal in fear rather than love."

She wasn't wrong—the Warlord, and every other ruler within the Sand and Sky, used fear in one way or another to solidify their power. Even Amarande's father had done that in his own way, by building his army and using force to protect everyone else— currying fear and twisting it into his own currency.

The pirate pressed on, Osana nodding. "If you marry Renard, your true love won't just—*poof*—disappear in a curl of smoke. It will still be there in your heart. You will feel it until the end of your days, and so will he."

That sad, heavy thing solidified and the princess stilled. "Thank you for reminding me how much I am about to suffer. I very much appreciate it."

Undeterred, the pirate girl was forward enough to seize the princess's hand. Her voice was barely a whisper. She leaned over and forced the princess to meet her eyes. "Don't marry Renard."

That fierceness within this pirate wasn't fury. Amarande was struck with the fact that she knew this girl's name and should use it. *Ula.*

"What do you care what I do, Ula?"

"Because when you saved us from the asps, I saw something greater in you. You are a leader who will rule not from a place of fear, but a place of love for anyone in your kingdom. Even someone at odds with you. In that moment, I suddenly had as much faith in you as Luca did. I believed you would not only save him, but you would save me, and my companions." Ula took a shaky breath. "I don't want to see you give in, Princess."

Amarande lay back down. "I'm sorry to disappoint you."

"You haven't. Not yet. And I believe you won't. Your love won't let you."

The princess closed her eyes.

My love is exactly why I'm giving in.

Chapter 40

GENERAL Koldo woke with a start, blinking into the gray wisp of a candle gone cold.

Within the space of that blink, the setting came in.

Her camp desk. Her camp chair. Her camp tent. A home away from home for much of her life, common in its shadows.

She'd fallen asleep with her face to a map of the Sand and Sky. Thoughts of fissures, alliances, and greed still smoldering in the dark of her mind along with the wick before her.

Sleep hadn't been long, but it had been enough that again she dreamed of him.

Sunset hair. Green eyes. Body of a bear though he was an Ardenian tiger, through and through.

Koldo drew in a breath and awakened to something else—the sense that danger hung in the air as sure as the coming day.

The general pulled herself to standing, legs stiff but determined, as she slipped to the entrance of her camp tent. Pulling back the fabric, she peered into the night. The dark was the deep, inky blue of dawn approaching.

The Ardenian camp was quiet, but Koldo had lived long enough—survived enough—to be sure.

Something was amiss.

Whatever it was had woken her when she hadn't meant to fall

asleep to begin with. Her instincts were always razor sharp and never stopped flickering. For that she was thankful.

Vision sharpening, her mind cleared of his face—compartmentalization was one key to her survival. Immediate focus. *Beware or be dead.*

In one smooth, soundless motion, the general released her sword from its scabbard. It didn't have a reputation like Sendoa's twin weapons, but it had served her well enough for some twenty years. It wasn't sung about like Egia and Maite, but it too had a name—Seme—though no one knew it but Koldo. The smooth Basilican steel was an extension of who she was as much as it was a symbol of all she'd lost.

Who she'd lost.

Koldo stepped out of the tent, the sandy dirt silently falling away under her weight. In two blinks, her vision had adjusted to the light of a moon swathed in clouds, light too weak to ever reach so far as the Torrent. That thread of danger pulled against her skin, as gentle as a spiderweb.

She raised her sword in line with her nose—traditional ox guard stance, her favorite. Every sense was on alert now.

That eyesight of hers caught the corners of every movement and cataloged each.

The scent of embers in the wind was noted, as was the direction from whence it came.

On her tongue, taste working via scent, the cool freshness of the water bubbling through the stream near the camp and the coffee grounds prepared for sunrise.

Every breath counted—hers, her soldiers', and probably the distant snore of the men from the opposing camps, along with the call and scratch of mountain life.

The air was dry and frigid to the touch, summer forgetting itself until daylight.

Intuition tugged her right, toward where Myrcell's camp lay past the trees, on the other side of the shared brook. Not that Koldo thought these soldiers better than Basilica's. Neither set was as prepared or as talented as hers. Neither stood the chance they thought they had. That Domingu and Akil thought they had. She'd told it true when she confirmed to the Royal Council and Amarande that Ardenia would be stretched thin by a multi-front war. But she still had every belief that her tigers would win a fight of any kind, no matter how prolonged or multipronged.

Bear, shark, mountain lion, or the sigil-free bandits of the Warlord, none stood a chance.

With Sendoa gone, she now commanded the greatest army in the Sand and Sky and indeed the world. And though Koldo's ego was nearly nonexistent, she had no qualms in admitting she was a big reason for the army's reputation. It was her life's work, and for it she'd sacrificed much.

Thick in the cover of summer-heavy trees, the general cut left. Her vision cycled through the range of her periphery over and over and she scanned the trees for movement. Five horse lengths beyond the outermost tents of her camp, her vigilance and instincts were rewarded with the distinct shape of three men.

They'd blended with the trees and would likely have escaped notice of anyone but Koldo, sticking as they did to the inky swell of mature pines and southern junipers. The soldiers were clustered together, quietly conferring. Reconnaissance. A report back. Which, depending on the information, may mean action.

Not. Yet.

Koldo turned her sword blade out, making the thinnest line possible in their vantage—she wouldn't have the light catch it and give her away. But she wouldn't lower it and be unguarded. She moved as swiftly as she dared—quiet steps, fluid movements, eyes glued to her target.

These men thought they were shadows, but she actually *was*.

A new angle gave her cause for further alarm. One man held out a vial. Small. Dark. He held the cork stopped down with a gloved thumb as if he was fearful of what might escape. The two others—both men, because the other kingdoms still had yet to learn they would be stronger with women in uniform—leaned in, voices low. Though they were on the Myrcell side of the camp, these three wore rich brown tunics. Basilica.

". . . a surefire way to get us killed. And if not, the horses who know not to stay away, or the fish we should be eating—"

"But if it works, we won't be here long at all." This from the man holding the vial. He was barely old enough to be a man, not even the hint of whiskers catching the light. "Ardenia will be defenseless and we'll be on the move."

"Yes, right after we wipe out this water source and every living creature around it."

"That's too destructive."

"What do you think war is, Toma?" the soldier holding the vial snapped at the conservative one.

"A single dose in a kettle would be—"

"Death. It would mean death. Ardenia does not sleep. We'd be caught."

As they continued to argue, something else tugged at Koldo's mind. Not intuition but familiarity.

Sunset hair. Green eyes. A final gasp.

Two steps and Koldo was an arm's length away, sword cutting down at the soldier closest, farthest to the left. The Basilican steel didn't stutter as it drove through the meat of his neck, slicing through skin, muscle, windpipe, and spine, and back out the other side.

With a spray and thud, his head landed at the feet of the one in the middle—who held the vial and the most destructive ideals. The soldier looked into Koldo's eyes a moment before Seme's tip plunged through the soft meat of his belly. A whisper of canvas from his brown tunic grazed her sword hilt for a moment before she placed a boot to the boy's chest for leverage to remove it.

Sword and boot heel released, the soldier's legs gave way and he fell forward. As the man went down, she snatched the blasted vial from his stunned hands. His body hit awkwardly, spinning his partner's detached head into a feeble roll toward Koldo. She stopped it with a boot toe and then relieved the fallen soldier of his head as well.

The third soldier stood there, mouth hanging open but no sound coming out. His eyes were saucer wide, the whites catching weak light from the Ardenian camp behind her. His whole being quivered, attention pinned on the two heads before him.

"Scream and you lose your life."

The soldier's lips snapped shut. His eyes met hers.

The general held out the vial. "Where did you get this? Who gave it to you?"

The soldier's jaw worked. It was the man who'd shown mercy. She'd already forgotten the name the other soldier had used for him. Enemies didn't have names.

"I—orders from our officer." The soldier's eyes didn't waver. The truth, then.

Poison was one way to start a war. That much had been done. But to win one? That was a coward's game.

Without a word, Koldo slipped the vial into her pocket.

The soldier seemed to relax, having expected a death blow the moment he answered.

A mistake.

Koldo grabbed each fallen soldier's head with a gloved hand and tossed them both at the man, who bobbled the first and caught the second, his reflexes overcoming his surprise.

"Deliver a head to each camp as a warning. A preemptive strike is a declaration of war. And neither Basilica nor Myrcell can survive the Ardenian army."

The soldier began to back away but then halted. "Which? They are—were—both of Basilica."

Koldo blinked at the man. "I do not care who you choose to toss where, only that my point is made. No war, not yet. If either camp comes into Ardenian territory again, we will not leave a single soldier standing."

Orders understood, the soldier turned, running first toward Myrcell, rather than toward his camp and the Ardenian grouping he'd have to cross to get to it.

When he was gone, Koldo turned, the weight of the vial in her pocket.

The Ardenian camp was no closer to waking when she returned. Yet her second, Captain Xixi, was stationed outside the general's tent, a mug of something steaming in her hands.

"Is everything all right, General Koldo?" the woman asked in a whisper.

"It is now, Captain." Koldo stowed her sword. She'd clean the blood from the blade later. "I must return to Ardenia. Do not strike until you hear from me. Do not engage. Keep to the camp, except to gather water—a mile upstream into Ardenia. Do not drink here."

The woman had been at Koldo's side for nearly twenty years. She silently cataloged every single thing her commander said with a nod.

"Captain, you have command."

The woman took that command with another duck of her head. "I'll have the grooms ready your horse, General."

Xixi left, straight to the horses, and Koldo entered her tent and swept the map of the Sand and Sky into a roll. When she blinked, her dream remained on the backs of her eyelids.

Those soldiers' lives had bought her time. She only hoped it would be enough.

CHAPTER
41

❧

As the first rays of dawn hit the military camp nestled between the Torrent and the Pyrenee border, Ula was wide awake and agitated.

She hated this assignment.

She hated that they hadn't been paid yet and therefore couldn't leave.

She hated that she liked Luca and even more that she liked the princess.

She hated that they couldn't be together *and* that she had an opinion about such matters.

Because it all added up to a queasy sensation in her stomach that made her feel as if she was on completely the wrong side of things.

The princess was still asleep in their tent, having tossed and turned for hours on end before sleep finally took her. Osana was asleep as well, cradling her sword like a lover—Osana and she were alike in that way. Ula got to her feet, strapped her sword to her back, and exited the tent.

Purple-cloaked men were up and moving, stoking a fire. She felt their eyes snap to her form as she slid out of the tent. Pyrenee did not conscript its women like Ardenia; thus, its military was completely male. Which meant this camp was made up of fifty men a hundred miles from home and the women they held dear.

"Hey there, honeypot, what will you give me for the first cup of coffee?" asked a boy no older than Dunixi as he tended to a kettle hung above revived flames.

Ula bared her teeth. "Call me 'honeypot' again and I'll give you one less hand to hold your coffee cup."

The man next to him laughed and elbowed his friend as he scowled. "Oh, I think she likes you! Anger is how they show love in the Torrent."

Ula ignored them, spying Urtzi across camp, relieving himself against a tree. She waited for him to finish before stepping in behind him.

"We need to talk."

He simply grunted in response—never a morning person, Urtzi.

"Grab Dunixi and meet me by my horse."

Five minutes later, the pirates were together, standing in the cool shadow of Ula's gray mare, Laya.

"Why are we still here? We should leave. Now."

"I'm not leaving until we see our gold," Dunixi answered without hesitation. His eyes were serious, but his hands gave him away—one rubbing at his rings, the other gingerly touching the back of his neck. His sunburn was scabbed and healing thanks to the oat paste. He shouldn't mess with it, but this boy didn't know when to leave well alone.

Ula shook her head. "The prince was clear. 'If we find her, you'll get to keep your life'—that was our payment."

"I heard that, too, Dunixi," Urtzi agreed.

"I don't care what he said," the Eritrian spat before lowering his voice. "He owes us."

"He owes us nothing." Ula's words were rushed and frustrated. "We need to get away with our heads on our shoulders. If we leave now, they won't waste time running after us—Renard clearly wants to get that ring on the princess's finger as fast as possible."

Dunixi let out a bitter laugh. "Rich people, always hurrying off to multiply their wealth through a few words and a marriage bed."

The pirates weren't sure why the prince was in such a hurry, but they'd agreed that he was even before he'd said so while entering the camp. They'd actually been surprised that the party had stopped for the night at all. Renard had been a man possessed from the moment they'd joined him, and even before, when they'd been hired—by proxy, but still.

Ula tried again. "Actually, I'd rather help the princess. He's using her. And he's going to hurt Luca—he's too much of a threat and you know it."

Urtzi's eyes narrowed. "Since when do you care about the stableboy and the princess?"

"Since they saved every one of us from the asps."

Stung, Urtzi snapped his lips shut. Ula's attention swung to their so-called leader—she was having a very hard time remembering why they'd followed him in the first place. "And let's not forget about your neck." Dunixi's hand stilled against his burn, the gems of his stupid rings glittering even in the low light. "We can't just let them give in to that blue-eyed rat's demands."

"Hey," Dunixi joked. "I thought that was your nickname for me."

"There are enough of you to necessitate nickname duplication."

The Eritrian straightened, both hands coming to his hips. He tipped his chin over his shoulder and surveyed the camp, which was more alive now. Both princes were up—Renard tossing orders about, Taillefer drinking coffee while inspecting some sort of weed at camp side. Luca was currently being led out of the tent he shared with the younger prince by the general, Tousette. The princess was nowhere to be seen.

When Dunixi turned his attention back to his partners, all the amusement had fled from his voice.

"You imply that *I'm* greedy, but the simple matter is *we* need the gold," he whispered. "We docked the ship days ago, and without gold we can't release it. We're not out of here until we're paid."

"We're not pirates without a ship," Urtzi mused.

"We could sell one of your rings," Ula suggested. It was ridiculous how this boy wore his only wealth out in the open. A woman could never do that.

"We could sell your sword," he fired back.

That was Ula's hard line. She'd leave before she allowed that to happen—history and ship be damned.

After a long beat, the Eritrian spoke again, eyes on the sun rising over Urtzi's shoulder. "We steal the stableboy away again and hold him until Renard or Taillefer or someone pays us."

Ula scraped her fingertips across her temples. "Renard already has the princess. Collecting her for his own was the whole aim in stealing Luca in the first place. There's no point to taking him now."

The Eritrian smiled that know-it-all grin. "Okay, then, we'll steal *her* away instead."

Ula nearly shot back that Dunixi had a death wish if he hoped to take the princess against her will, but . . . stealing her away was exactly what the princess *would want*.

And so Ula didn't point out the difficulty level in what Dunixi suggested. She simply made him feel as if, as the leader, he had come up with the perfect solution. She could go along with it as long as it kept the princess from marrying that ogre and leaving Luca to whatever fate the Bellringe held.

"That's a much better idea." Then she added, "But the princess is much more likely to go easily if we have Luca, too."

Urtzi smiled. "So we steal both. Easy."

Gold seemed to flash before Dunixi's eyes. "Yes. And if Renard won't pay, we tap Ardenia for payment."

Ula wasn't about to do that, but if it made Dunixi see it her way, then fine.

"What's the plan?" Urtzi asked, dark eyes flashing. This boy was a lot of things, but mostly he was always ready for a fight.

"To wait," Dunixi announced, and the Myrcellian's face fell. "We'll never get out of here cleanly with the two of them. But at the castle? Before the wedding night? Yes."

"But there we'll be in the heart of Pyrenee," Urtzi surmised, brows cross. "Here, we're in the open."

"Have you learned nothing from our successful kidnapping of the stableboy to begin with?" Dunixi whispered, thin lips quick. "Castle grounds are all shadows and people lulled by the comforts of home. Their backyard is the best place to steal away what you desire, because no one is on guard."

CHAPTER
42

THEY sent no party ahead. No rider to prepare the Bellringe for the arrival of Prince Renard and his crew. Amarande understood this completely—the prince aimed to catch his mother off guard. The last thing he wanted was to give Dowager Queen Inés enough warning to set into motion her supposed plan to steal his kingdom.

It was smart, tactical, and it lent credence to why Renard had gone so far in seeking Amarande's hand.

Renard seemed certain his mother hadn't stayed at the Itspi to wait for him after he'd gone into the Torrent after Amarande. The princess wondered if Dowager Queen Inés had expected her son to fail. Or maybe to find himself and his brother tossed into one of the Warlord's fire pits, allowing her to reach her aim without blood on her hands. She'd have a tragic story of her brave sons and live the rest of her life ruling in their stead, a martyr by proxy.

And so the group rumbled toward the Bellringe as one on the thin mountain trails, winding up and up, to the glimmering snow-white castle at the summit of a mountain named King's Crest. Amarande was squeezed between Renard and Taillefer, the brothers exchanging places as the road funneled down to its narrowest points. Taillefer and Luca went ahead of the princess, while Renard rode at her back. Amarande knew this was because they thought she might attack Renard from behind.

The knife pressed against her ankle indicated that they were not wrong.

She watched Luca's back as they trudged up the mountain. He'd glance over his shoulder as often as he could, stealing moments before Renard would yell, "Eyes off the princess, stableboy!" and he'd be forced to turn around until he was brave enough to try it again.

Each time it made Amarande smile. This boy who would be king, so afraid of a mere look from a commoner. Power was relative, and Luca had a kind Renard never would.

One final switchback and the seat of the Pyrenee rose before them, its doors yawning open, aubergine-clad guards in motion on the ground and from the walls above. The Bellringe was carved from quartz-pocked rock, which meant its spiraling towers and dramatic turrets glimmered like diamonds in the high summer sun.

They'd been moving since just after sunup, eight straight hours into the heart of Pyrenee. Now it was past noon and Amarande laid eyes on the castle for the first time in four years. She'd last visited after King Louis-David's death, making the same sort of procession that had just taken place in Ardenia less than a week ago. Then the Bellringe had seemed a dreamlike place—glittering and bright, as if the stars themselves were born in the walls before flying into the skies above. To a twelve-year-old girl, alone while the princes mourned, the secrets and corners of this place seemed celestial, wrapped in clouds and starlight, even under the pall of funeral rituals.

Now, rather than stars, the palace seemed to be carved of ice— cold, suffocating, an end.

As the road widened into a yard running an apron up to the castle, Renard took the lead. He trotted ahead, chin up, a look of triumph stretched upon his face. He'd made it a point to scrub himself clean and change his clothes before they left camp that morning, hoping to look every bit the definition of the new king he would be by day's end.

He was right—his mother and her ambitions were waiting for him, looking down from the ramparts, over the parapet, surrounded by her advisors. Dowager Queen Inés and her honeybees swung into motion as soon as it was sure that the group approaching was indeed her two sons and the princess they'd promised to find.

Renard slowed enough so that Princess Amarande could come up alongside him for a grand entrance. The prince leaned over to the princess, smiling as if they really were lovers sharing a secret. He kept his face forward, speaking to her sideways, so that she was left looking at his profile.

"Now remember, Princess, I saved you from the stableboy and you cannot wait to marry me. Any murmur of dissent from you and your stableboy's life grows more difficult."

She wanted to rip his ear off and swallow it whole.

"The difficulty won't be his; it will be yours. Harm him and I will kill you. I don't care about the show you want to make for your mother, he will not feel an ounce of pain without you feeling it ten times over in kind."

Renard met her with a look fleeting and cold.

"Smile, Princess," was all he said.

Amarande did as she was told, only until the prince faced away. Then she allowed her features to settle back into blankness. It wasn't necessary to put on a ruse for these people. Not a single person cared if she was happy. All they cared about was what transpired. Inés's ambitions would not lessen with a smile from her son's bride.

The party rode into the castle's central courtyard, the guards and castle workers flooding the space to greet the party. As expected, the Dowager Queen and her group made their way down from the battlements and into the yard in a flood that parted the sea of onlookers like water. Surrounding her were clear members of her council. Their rich purple robes and stoic expressions were a dead giveaway that they spent their days in drafty rooms advising on matters of life and death.

Renard made it a point to speak before his mother got the chance to find the right words, preempting her with his perfect smile and a projected voice. "Loyal subjects of the Bellringe, I have returned with Princess Amarande of Ardenia. Rejoice, for we will have a wedding tonight!"

The castle workers and onlookers exploded into a flurry of applause and motion, while the Dowager Queen and the Royal Council stood stock-still in the center of it all, practiced smiles stiff on their faces. But Inés's eyes rounded just enough for Amarande to know she was stunned. Maybe Renard had told the truth when he'd laid out his mother's plans and he'd finally surprised her with a move that she couldn't easily overcome.

A thread of unease shot through Amarande's stomach as the Dowager Queen approached her son's horse—suddenly she realized that until the vows tonight, *she* was the biggest threat to this woman's ambitions. The moment they were married, Inés would have no way of gaining the throne of Pyrenee, no matter whom she coerced into wedlock. She'd simply be relegated to being the Queen Mother. Something to be trotted out for a smile and wave at all official occasions.

Renard dismounted and took his mother's hand. The Dowager Queen leaned in, and when their embrace ended, her eyes danced around the party before settling on her son's face.

"Tonight? I know you're thrilled to have your beloved back safe and sound, but such a wedding simply isn't possible. These affairs take months of planning to be grand enough for such a magnificent occasion." The woman gave a musical laugh, turning as if to say, *Oh, how silly*, to the councilmen surrounding her.

Renard didn't blink.

"Mother, I don't want grand. I want a wedding. The star-born priest, vows, and the keys to my kingdom."

Inés caught eyes with Amarande, searching for help in this madness, but the princess gave her nothing. Like Amarande was to be, Inés had been a bride at sixteen, and though the Dowager Queen's face was still youthful, the worry that slipped across her features now aged her a decade.

The Dowager Queen continued. "That isn't how this works, Renard. There is no envoy from Ardenia. My own wedding took nearly a year to plan, and the dress alone took six months—"

"The wedding is tonight, Mother. Be in attendance or wait a year for the perfect dress, but it will happen." Renard turned to a white-haired member of the council, whose own jaw was hanging as low as the Dowager Queen's. "Laurent, prepare the service."

Inés said no more, only turning with her advisors and disappearing, preparing for her next move.

CHAPTER
43

❦

ONCE his mother's footsteps echoed up the stairs, onto the ramparts, and into the belly of the castle interior, Renard wasted no time in organizing his countereffort.

"Princess, come along. We shall get you bathed and fitted—if it was truly made with such care, my mother's vintage wedding gown will surely do with a few adjustments. Though I daresay you're quite a bit shorter and less voluptuous than Mother was on her wedding day." His eyes settled on her chest in a way that made her want to gouge them out with only her thumbnails and fury. He shrugged. "Only she will mourn the seamstress scraps. Follow me."

Renard turned for a set of stairs mirroring the ones Dowager Queen Inés had just taken. Parallel lives leading up to the wedding and coronation in every way.

In answer, the princess drew Luca's bound hands into hers before moving an inch.

Renard swatted in their general direction, annoyance flickering across his features. "No, no, you and myself only, Princess. This is where you leave your stableboy."

Amarande dug in her boot heels. "No."

The people around them shifted as the atmosphere in the courtyard changed, charged. The open air seemed to press down upon them rather than reaching for the heavens. Renard's eyes shot to his brother as if to get some sort of clue as to how to sway a woman. Taillefer simply shrugged and, always lightning quick to find humor, smiled. "Plants do my bidding, Renard, not women. I don't know how to make her listen."

The would-be king sighed and returned the short distance he'd advanced.

"I agreed that I wouldn't kill him, not that he'd be your pet, Princess. I can't have you preparing for our wedding with your plaything helping to dress you."

Amarande flushed, and that only served to increase her fury—because it validated Renard's decision.

The prince smirked. "The boy—"

"Luca," she sniped, teeth bared. She knew Renard was simply treating him like a servant or maybe like an enemy—Amarande herself had admonished Luca for using familiars with the pirates. But if this was to be their life, everyone in the castle would call her love by his name and nothing else. "Use his name."

"*Luca* will be under the guard of my brother," Renard continued. "I trust no one more. Did he not do a fine job attending to Luca on our trek to Pyrenee from the Torrent?"

Amarande turned to Taillefer. "I shall go with you now and review his accommodations to ensure they're acceptable."

Her grip tightened around Luca's hands as she tugged him in Taillefer's direction. But the younger prince did not budge. His face was as joyful as a hyena's, though his words were firm. "That is quite unnecessary, Princess. I am aware of your threat against my brother."

It was right there on the tip of her tongue—that was what she was afraid of. Renard was an idiot to trust Taillefer.

Renard leaned in, blocking his low words from as many ears—and eyes—as possible. The guards and hired hands hadn't left; they stood at attention, waiting to be dismissed. With them, the horses shifted and flipped their tails. "And I am aware of the threat against you, Princess."

No, she wouldn't play this game.

"This whole marriage is a threat to my power and Ardenia. I—"

"No, to *you*, Princess. To your heartbeat and further." His ice-blue eyes swept the length of her—dusty and ash covered in Ula's clothing—before his warning continued on, rushed and low, confirming what Amarande had already realized. "My mother doesn't want you married to me. My home is a beautiful one, but it will be the death of you if you are not careful. The next few hours are crucial and dangerous. Everyone who is not me is a threat—even my guards can be turned. Marry me and we'll both be safe the second those crowns are upon our heads."

Renard still hadn't learned his lesson, apparently, because he attempted then to sway Amarande with a hand to her wrist. She flung it away the second he made contact.

The prince kept going, pointing now to Luca. "Remember, Princess, if you die, he dies."

Amarande straightened. Luca was watching her, the fierceness in his eyes overpowering every bruise, cut, scrape, and speck of red dirt. That fury was love. Holding his hands now, bound as they were, she saw the boy she'd grown with in the Itspi, the boy who made her blood hot in the meadow, who held her heart with the gentlest of care.

It didn't matter who watched—Renard, Taillefer, the guards, the hired hands, the eyes of the castle ready to report back to the Dowager Queen. Amarande angled into Luca, lifted her hands to his face, and kissed him.

Vaguely, she heard Renard sigh, Taillefer chuckle, and the guards shift with discomfort. Only the kidnappers and Osana didn't react, unsurprised by her boldness.

When she pulled away, Amarande met Luca's eyes and leaned up and into his ear. "I love you. Tonight does not change that."

"I love you, too, Ama. Always, Princess."

Tears sparked in Amarande's eyes and she sucked down a shuddering breath before turning to Taillefer. "I expect to inspect his conditions as soon as possible."

"Of course, Princess." Taillefer half-bowed. It felt formal yet mocking, and if Amarande weren't so angry, she would've been annoyed.

She wheeled on Renard, who seemed to deflate in relief. "Remember, Prince, if he dies, you die."

If Renard was at all startled by Amarande tossing his own words back in his face, he didn't show it. Rather, he nodded. "I would be a fool to test you."

It was the first thing he'd ever said that actually pleased her.

RENARD'S chambers were not his own. That much was clear from the decor—oiled wood and leather, furs that seemed more a source of pride than comfort. Cobwebs, too, time collecting in a space that had once belonged to his father, King Louis-David, dead these four years.

Maids were already about, throwing open the blinds, tidying, trying very hard not to appear horrified about the thick layers of dust.

Amarande stood in the entryway of the receiving chamber, adding to the disaster as red dirt that had hitchhiked from the Torrent shed from her hair, tunic, breeches, and boots and onto the white marble flooring.

"The library and study are this way, followed by the bedroom," Renard was saying, like she might care about any of this. His voice crackled with an energy that didn't match the mundane words that came out of his mouth. "Of course, you'll have your own space. Follow me."

For once Amarande did as she was told, a young maid trailing along with a broom as the Torrent further left its mark behind both of them.

He led her to another sitting room, this one lush with aubergine satins and tapestries of mountain flowers and summer sun. A balcony extended off the side. Amarande aimlessly tried the knob, but the glass doors didn't so much as rattle. "We'll open those in the morning, Princess. Safety first, remember?"

Attached to the ladies' sitting room was a private bath and another bedroom, full of high windows and curtains that coughed dust, though not nearly as much as the main chamber. The maid was forced to leave them there as Renard closed the door to the suite behind them with a wooden slam. "Mother slept here most nights. But after Father passed she decided she wanted full chambers of her own. Actually, that's incorrect—she wanted to redecorate the entirety of these chambers, but the council told her no, so she moved out, into the next biggest set." Here, he laughed. Yes, he'd become giddy with proximity to his wildest dreams. "She will hate it when I'm allowed to redecorate."

The princess tilted her head. "I will not stop her if she aims to suffocate you with her preferred silk palette."

Again, he laughed. It was quickly becoming the worst sound she'd ever heard. "Do tell me, will you always be like this, Princess? Or will your tongue soften with pillow talk in the marriage bed?"

Amarande lunged at Renard. Both his hands blocked to cover the sword at his hip, leaving the rest of him wide open. She clamped her fingers tight around his neck, thumbs pressing together into his jugular.

"My bed is not your bed unless I deem it so, ring or not, title or not. Understood?"

His eyes flashed with what he wanted to say—*Do not forget, I have your stableboy.* But he kept those words to himself, nodding slowly instead.

She released her hold, purple splotches the shape of her fingers blooming across the width of his neck.

Renard swallowed. "I'll have the maids draw you a bath, Princess." He took a step backward, the majority of his giddiness drained, the remaining bits fighting to the surface. "The seamstresses will take it from there."

He placed his hand on the doorknob but paused for final instruction. "We shall wed in three hours' time."

Amarande's heart skidded to a stop, the blood freezing her veins, her breath still.

Three hours and her entire fight was lost.

CHAPTER
44

GUARDS breathing down his neck, Luca stood, bound and aching in every way imaginable—heart, head, body—as Amarande was marched up a set of stairs in preparation for the wedding.

The next time he saw her, she would be married and his love for her would endanger his life for the rest of his days. Where hope had been now was raw agony, a caustic burn at his heart.

As his princess disappeared around a balcony corner, Luca's chin dipped to his chest. His heart shuddered within.

"I've got him, boys." Prince Taillefer's voice broke through the pounding in Luca's ears. "Clean up. Rosewater soap and sparkling whites for tonight's festivities."

Luca's head shot up. He'd been sure Taillefer would prefer to deal with him later, that he would be eager to prepare for the wish he'd made plain that day in the meadow. Instead, the prince smiled, wide and self-satisfied with Luca's obvious shock, and Luca was struck that Amarande was right—Taillefer did look like a fox. From their limited interaction already, Luca very much expected the prince's cunning to match.

While Amarande was led into the winding depths of the Bellringe, Luca was marched through a close-set grouping of iron doors, one and then the other, until he entered another courtyard that sat beyond the main footprint of the castle but within the grounds.

"Are you taking me to the stable?" Luca asked the prince, because he suddenly realized that perhaps he wasn't simply to be kept, but put to work.

The prince's laugh was immediate and slippery. "And get you close to a mode of transportation that would let you sneak away? I think not."

"If my princess is here, I wouldn't leave."

"But if she made her way to you, you would."

This was true enough that Luca said nothing.

The stable was up an incline to the left—there was no mistaking the smell trailing to the stone-built structure atop the hill. Even without that clue, castle grooms were marching the Pyrenee party's horses in that direction in a dusty line of white stallions, the pirates' horses—Ferri, Laya, Boli—and the mishmash of Torrentian caravan steeds.

Meanwhile, Taillefer swerved them right, through a garden of close-cropped summer roses, somehow cultivated or dyed to bloom the colors of the kingdom—dark purple and shimmering gold.

"Do you like those? They're my creation," Taillefer asked when he noticed Luca's attention snagged on the flowers.

Again, Luca said nothing. The prince smiled coolly and plucked a gold one from the plant closest to him. He held it up in examination.

"They match your eyes," Taillefer mused just as he tossed it at the boy's face. Luca's reflexes, sharp from their time with Ama in the meadow, didn't fail him—he caught the flower just before its angry thorns could find their mark in the delicate skin of his sun-sore cheeks. Luca held the flower gently in his bound palms as the prince continued, sharpening his smile. "They'll be in your beloved's bouquet tonight. Don't fret; they'll hold their color until the very end."

Luca simply dropped the flower.

"My, you are a grumpy boy."

The prince grabbed Luca by the bindings and led him beyond the roses, through a maze of hedged walls, and then past a fountain, until they were at a small cottage with ivy-blanked windows. It looked like a gatehouse with no gate.

Taillefer unlocked it with a key around his neck, pulled the door open, and switched their positions. "In you go."

It wasn't a gatehouse at all, but an entryway. Two sconces weakly illuminated the space, which housed a spiral staircase that led only one direction—down. The prince lit a candlestick with the sconce flame. "I would suggest you not run, nor try to push me down. You will fall yourself and it will be the end of the both of us."

With each floor, Luca's heart dropped lower. Not even the dungeons of the Itspi nor the diamond mines of the Ardenian mountains went down so far. Nothing was this deep into the earth, not even the buried bones of those who came before.

They descended five dizzying flights, sconces blazing, and when the stairs ceased and they hit the final landing they entered a room that . . . Luca didn't know what to call it.

Shelves climbed to the rafters of the round room, neatly organized with tagged bottles of varying shapes and sizes. Cut plants of all kinds littered a long table pushed against one side, while seedlings sat too close to the fire. And displayed around the room were deadly species of all kinds—scorpions, snakes, spiders, jellyfish, embalmed in such a painstaking manner they looked as if they might escape out the open door.

There were beasts, too, ones no one would accuse of breathing—bodiless heads of great animals, mounted on plates of glass. Bear. Tiger. Shark. The symbols of the other kingdoms of the Sand and Sky. All literally cut off at the head. The mountain lion of Pyrenee was not to be found. But what was, interestingly enough, was the extinct black wolf of the equally extinct Otxoa.

Given the timeline of the Eradication of the Wolf, perhaps it was the dead king's and not something of Taillefer's making.

The prince caught him looking. "Yes, they're a metaphor." Taillefer marched Luca to an examination table in the middle of the room. "I spend much of my time down here studying and thinking, and I find that creatively it pays to remember who else is in the game." Taillefer tipped his chin to the black wolf and then to Luca, their correlation clear. "And who's lost it."

Taillefer drew the sword at his side; like his brother's it was as gaudy as full coffers could make it—gilded and bejeweled, a mountain lion's face peeking out from the hilt. He pressed the tip against Luca's jugular. "Remove your shirt or I will do it for you."

Luca did as he was told, awkwardly with his arms bound, and the blade barely moved from his skin. He got the tunic up and over his head, but it pooled awkwardly against the bindings at his wrists.

"Now, on the table. Lie down."

Again, Luca soundlessly followed orders. When he was situated, his bound arms and shirt across his chest, Taillefer advanced and clamped manacles around his ankles. Next came Luca's bound hands. The prince removed the binds and clamped Luca's arms at his sides with another set of iron manacles. The tunic and ropes were discarded beneath the table. The prince stood next to the table, heavy eyes appraising every inch of his guest while Luca stared at the shadows combing the dungeon ceiling. Luca had no need to guess as to why they were so far underground.

After a minute, the prince finally spoke.

"What happened to your leg?"

"Grazed by a Harea Asp."

Taillefer struck out for something on the shelves drilled into the bedrock above a worktable. He returned with a taxidermic Harea Asp, its jaws agape and ready to strike. "One of these?"

Luca nodded.

Taillefer moved the snake's head as if it were talking, his voice going high and hissy. "Then why are you not deceasssssssssed?"

As the prince laughed, Luca didn't dignify the impression with a reply.

The young prince was mad.

Taillefer shoved the snake right up against Luca's ear, its scales grazing his skin. "Answer me, boy."

Luca sighed. "The princess procured the anti-venom."

Taillefer and his snake made it a point to inspect the leg more closely. The prince prodded the blackened skin before saying to the snake, "Not your best work, asp."

The prince laid the snake right on top of Luca's leg, and when he flinched at its touch Taillefer grinned. "Now *that* is love. Or perhaps your princess thought you wouldn't be nearly as good-looking when overcome by rot."

Luca didn't answer.

"Is that *ink* on your chest? Does your princess know?" Taillefer asked as if it were a salacious secret and that she might be disappointed by a tattoo. When Luca stared at the ceiling, obviously not about to answer the question, Taillefer leaned over farther. "Don't make me put the snake on your head, boy."

Luca didn't look at him. "She knows. Everyone knows. I've had it since I was a baby. Before I left the Torrent on my mother's back, from what I'm told—my mother died soon after our arrival in Ardenia and never explained it to me myself."

The prince ran his cold fingers over the tattoo's five points. Luca held as still as possible. "Interesting. And right over your heart." Taillefer cocked a brow. "Who owns your heart other than your princess?"

"Nothing nor no one owns my heart beyond my princess."

"How very narrow-minded, your view of the world." The prince removed his hand. "Or perhaps your world is just that small. What is an orphan stableboy's world beyond his horses and his benefactor? And now she is your *sole* benefactor, isn't she? You are literally nothing without her. Homeless, jobless, alone."

"Or maybe my little world is all I need."

"Your world is no more." Taillefer smiled, but it wasn't friendly. "Your world is my world now."

Luca's lips snapped shut.

"And my world is most interested in curiosities. You, my boy, are definitely a curiosity. Not simply because you're handsome and kind, which is a rather rare combination, but because if you haven't noticed, there's nothing royalty loves more than his or her own power. And something about *you* made Princess Amarande forgo her power altogether, if just for a moment, to rescue you."

"True love. That's her motivation and it is mine. There's no mystery or curiosity in that."

"That's it, then? There hasn't been true love within these castle walls for centuries. Power and strategic alliance wins out every time. And before you tell me the Itspi is different, save your breath. It's the same there. Even your precious princess is the consequence of a relationship forged on power."

Luca met the prince's impudent expression with all the fierceness he had left. "All the more reason for her to hold on to the love that your brother cannot give her. I have loved Amarande in ways no one else could."

Taillefer rolled his eyes. "Being a stableboy has not diminished the confidence those looks of yours give you." The prince seemed satisfied when Luca frowned. He patted his captive on the hand. "Maybe one day I'll be clever enough to measure that, but for now I study curiosities I can quantify."

A new idea flared in the frigid blue of Taillefer's eyes.

"Perhaps you can define this love of yours in a way I can measure?" This time, the prince turned to the curve of the wall as far from the hearth as it could get. There sat hundreds of small vials, carefully aligned on ledges. He plucked something off the wall and then returned to his worktable and rummaged around.

Luca tried to watch him, but there were limits to his periphery in the shadowy space.

After finding what he wanted, the prince said, "It's likely to be extremely painful. Most things in the natural arts are, of course. My apologies."

Luca again stared at the rafters of the high ceiling. Somewhere, in the daylight above, Amarande was thinking of him. He was sure of it. "As long as I'm without my princess, my life is pain. Threaten me, torture me, starve me, but you will never see the worst of it."

"Our capacity for pain is endless; that's what makes us human," the prince answered, his tone almost academic. "Physically, mentally, emotionally—there is more than one way to make you wish you were already dead."

"A life without love is no life at all."

"Spoken like a boy lulled enough by false promises to think he had a chance to begin with."

Taillefer set whatever he'd taken on a small pedestal table, his body blocking it, before leaning down. He'd placed thick gloves on his hands, though they were cut in a way that left him dexterous enough to pull the straps across Luca's chest a notch tighter. Too tight. Much too tight. Luca's skin immediately blanched, circulation cut off at the edges.

"You, my friend, are under my care. Which means you don't have a chance now." Taillefer leaned in, flaxen hair falling upon his smooth brow. "But, trust me, you never did."

The prince reached behind him and pulled out a vial made from crystal-clear glass. Inside was a milky green liquid that stuck to the inner wall of the vial when sloshed. "This is something new I've designed, inspired by that charred homeland of yours. Dry, cracked, burning—the Torrent is a bout of infection about the earth, if you ask me. Pairs nicely with the Warlord's beloved fire pits, no?"

"Burn me. I don't care. Scars are nothing."

"Oh, I wouldn't dare disfigure that lovely face of yours." Taillefer smiled and reached behind him, holding up a second object. A plant. Fat clusters as big as a fist of small white flowers.

"Hemlock?" Luca asked, recognizing the flowers as those that had been around Taillefer's neck in the meadow. "I am to be poisoned, then."

"Brilliant guess, but no. This is an imposter for hemlock—giant hogweed's the name." Taillefer held it aloft. "It won't kill you, but it burns like a newborn star. Graze your hand on the sap and you'll look like you plunged it in a fire on purpose. Get it in your eye and you'll go temporarily blind. Oh, and the scars—black, with pain that stays as long as the color. Makes that asp wound of yours look like a paper cut."

Placing the plant away, he raised the vial again. This time, Luca watched more closely. "This is pure, distilled giant hogweed. A thousand times more powerful than the sap found within the plant's leaves."

A thousand times. That could eat right through skin. Reveal the muscles and sinew underneath. Bore through bones.

Yes, Taillefer was mad.

"Stupid name, though—giant hogweed. Perhaps I should coin something flashier? Fire sting? Fire flood?" Taillefer thoughtfully watched it roll and stick against the glass inches above Luca's face. "It's bright green—fire swamp, maybe? Get it?"

Luca said nothing.

"Perhaps you'll have a suggestion after you've experienced it?"

Taillefer flicked the bottle, and Luca's eyes automatically snapped shut, protective. This made the young prince snort. "I said I wouldn't maim that face and I won't. You're as good to me disfigured as you are dead."

The bottle went again to the pedestal table. "That said, I would like to get right to work—discovery waits for no man, least of all one who must prepare for a wedding in mere hours." The prince collected the plant and raised the green-and-purple stem, so that Luca could easily see where a cut had been made. The stem was hollow, oozing the poisonous sap. "We'll start with just the sap and work our way up from there, shall we?" Luca didn't respond. "Let's see. Because this is a matter of the heart, how about we just open you up right about here. . . ."

Squeezing the stem as he went, Taillefer dragged oozing sap in a line down Luca's sternum the same length as a grown man's hand. He pressed in, scratching his way across the flesh like he was heavy-handed with a quill on parchment.

Luca tensed against his binds, veins popping from his skin, tendons firing. The reaction was so swift, so intense, that the taxidermic snake flicked off his shin and plunked to the floor. His teeth ground shut, his eyes, too, the pain bald and bold, coursing through him as his skin melted and blistered. As promised, he was opened up. A gaping, raised line cleaving the skin of his chest in two.

Prince Taillefer watched it with reserved reaction.

"Interesting. That was much quicker than I expected."

Breathless yet heaving, Luca couldn't wedge his mouth open for a response. The prince turned again to his worktable and came back with a leather-bound journal and a pencil. Ready to document the next phase. "Let's see if your blood reacts the same as your skin, shall we?"

Luca tensed again, as much as he could, knowing it would not be enough. It couldn't be. Not if Taillefer decided to make ashes of him from the inside out.

The prince uncorked the vial and, with careful fingers, lowered it until the lip of glass hovered tight against the wound festering along Luca's sternum.

"Let's start with one drop, shall we?"

The sticky liquid took its time leaving the vial, long enough in fact that Luca's eyes sprang open, something about the pause giving him the courage to look. His vision cleared just in time for him to see a pale green drop roll across the lip and fall a hairsbreadth into his open flesh.

His jaw unclenched and he screamed then, so loud he thought it might shatter the whole of him. So loud he thought Amarande might hear. Or his mother in the heavens. Maybe the stars themselves if they weren't blind.

Prince Taillefer, though, wasn't moved, slowly and carefully resealing the bottle, placing it on the table behind, his eyes never leaving Luca's reaction. His hand began running in looping script across one page and then another.

In the space of a second that felt like a year, Luca knew without visual confirmation that the single drop had eroded the initial wound into something deep and gaping that pulsed with the full power of the Torrent's sun. "Pain" wasn't enough of a word for the way it felt, and in the twilight of his clouded thoughts Luca realized his whole body's suffering at that very moment matched his heart's ache for Amarande.

After a time, that feeling shifted, everything about Luca shaking as bile lurched toward his lips—it took all he had not to choke on his own stomach acid.

Taillefer paused his writing and waited to speak until Luca was strong enough to meet his eyes.

"On a scale of one to your princess marrying my brother, how does that feel?"

Luca began to cry.

CHAPTER 45

❧

THE pirates delivered their horses to the stable as they were told and lingered in the building's shadows as the guards and hired hands from the Torrent retired for refreshment and a good cleaning.

"If we don't hurry, there will be no food left for us. You know how mess halls go," Urtzi grumbled, his large shoulders tense with irritation and hunger.

"You're a big boy; just take what you want from filled plates and dare those spiders in purple not to scurry," Dunixi answered with a wave of his bejeweled hand. "Five minutes to regroup, that's all we need. Think of the bigger picture—we pull this off and you'll be eating the roast duck of your Myrcellian childhood in a sauce of passion fruit from Indu, accompanied by a dressing of chestnuts of Basilica, grapes of Pyrenee, and juniper berries plucked from the trees of Ardenia."

"I'd be fine with just the duck."

"Your tastes will improve with acquired riches," Dunixi spat. "Now shut up and listen."

Urtzi lowered himself to the ground at the base of a tree, grumbling. Ula leaned against the same tree, eyes reading the distance. From atop the stable's hill, they could see much, but nothing that was of help. Just giant swaths of castle stone hiding exactly what they wanted.

"They've separated our marks, but we can use that to our

advantage. We shall steal the princess first—this will throw them into chaos, because the wedding cannot go on without her. The first place they will check is wherever they've kept Luca, and when they find him there and then fall further into chaos, we snatch him up, put them both safely away, and then blackmail Renard for his crown."

Ula's head was already shaking. "No. That won't work. We can't get the princess first. She won't go anywhere without Luca. She would just as soon battle us again as go with us on the promise of her boy. We must capture him first. He's the carrot for all that she does."

"Did you have to say 'carrot'?" Urtzi whined. "I'd kill for some carrots right now. In fresh cream butter? Amazing."

Dunixi turned this over in his mind. The brains of the operation did not much like it when someone had a better idea.

"Okay. We'll get him first. But where will they have put him?"

"The dungeon," Ula answered immediately.

"Or the stable. He's a stableboy, after all."

She gestured, sour-faced and annoyed. "Do you see him here?"

"We're no longer inside. Let's go in and give them a look."

Ula rolled her eyes. "Dunixi, go ahead and inspect the stable, but did you learn nothing from our ride with the princes of Pyrenee? Taillefer was told to guard Luca, and that boy's wit is cruel. I saw him dropping beetles into the fire last night just to hear them pop. He's not going to release Luca into the stable to work and head to supper."

Urtzi's mouth dropped open and she rapped his chin with a quick tap from her knuckles. "We all know you want to eat, Urtzi; you've made that abundantly clear without admonishing my choice of descriptive suggestion."

Dunixi regrouped. "Okay, so we look around the stable, *just to check*, and then we find guard uniforms, slip into the castle, and head for the dungeon."

"We have supper in the middle of all that, yes?" Urtzi pressed. "Between the uniforms and the dungeon?"

Neither Dunixi nor Ula responded.

"Yes, good. Let's do it," Ula said to the leader, and started moving toward the stable entrance.

Prince Taillefer and Luca were not there, of course. Nobody but Pyrenee's approximation of Luca was there, spreading oats out for the hungry horses.

Urtzi took a fistful and ate them raw out of spite as Dunixi made one more pass, searching for the mark, and Ula located extra guard uniforms in prepacked saddlebags. She found some dried cherries and almonds in there, too, and slipped them in her pockets before pulling out one pouch and handing it to Urtzi as she gave him a guard vestment.

The three tugged the purple-and-gold numbers over their own clothes and headed down the hill. They were winding through ridiculously ornate gardens, arguing about where they should enter the castle, when they heard it.

A blood-curdling scream. One that seemed to come from the bowels of the earth itself.

Ula halted. "Luca. That's Luca."

"That's Luca *where?*" Dunixi sniped. "I see no dungeons here."

Ula held up a hand. "Listen."

The scream renewed. Heavy. Sharp. Pained.

She raised her second hand and gestured in the direction of where she thought the sound might be, beyond coming from below them. Around a hedge was what looked like a gatehouse. Ula ran up to it, and the door fell open—unlocked. She stuck her head in and then immediately ushered the boys inside. "Stairs," she whispered.

Dunixi plucked a candlestick from his pocket and lit it on a sconce, and then led the way as if he'd been the one who'd found the entrance in the first place.

Ula came next, curved sword unsheathed and hanging at her side.

Urtzi lingered at the top of the stairs, muttering, "Oh, now I'll never eat."

"Stop complaining and come on," Ula growled.

They ran down the steps, each stone curling into the next. After several turns, Dunixi slowed, holding up a bejeweled hand beside his sun-ravaged neck. Ula stopped on a dime. Urtzi was slower on the uptake, but it didn't matter with his lightning-quick reflexes, which allowed him to dodge Ula's back in favor of a catlike leap to Dunixi's step below.

When the pirates were still, they heard a voice, distinct and clear over the whimpering of a dying cry.

"Oh, very interesting. I'd say that was much less agonized than the last entry of the elixir. Are you getting used to it? Or are you simply losing your voice? Answer carefully. I have nearly two-hundred doses remaining in this vial and a hundred vials on top of that."

There was a pause, and Dunixi started moving again, slowly, quietly. This was one thing he was good at—moving like a ghost.

When Luca's voice came again, it was worn from screaming, and small. "Why?"

"Did the pain devour your memory? We've been over this."

"No," he said, before a pause as he seemed to gather strength. "Why do you have so many?"

From her spot, Ula watched as Taillefer smiled and turned his back, taking a moment to admire an entire curved wall of small glass vials. They ranged in color from cobalt to amethyst to crystal-clear and sparkling through with green liquid—this was the kind held in a gloved hand now. Dunixi made the smallest of movements with his hand and the pirates advanced forward, sneaking from the stair landing to an overflowing pile of dried wood beside a large hearth. A table was set there, too—a place for Taillefer to work as he reduced ingredients over the fire—adding to the weak coverage. The room was mostly round and held no real corners, no closets, no heavy furniture, or any other convenient places to hide. The prince's back was to the entrance, and his general orientation faced completely away. The pirates would have to rely on Taillefer's sense that nothing was amiss to avoid being detected. And yet they didn't retreat.

The prince turned back to Luca. "Ah, now that is a good question, boy, as half this vial would surely kill you on its own. And I don't have hundreds of you, now do I?"

Rather than prodding, Luca waited, tears streaming down his cheeks. He sniffed, his breath stiff and uneasy enough that they saw his chest stutter.

"Simple, my boy. When Pyrenee rules all of the Sand and Sky, it will need something to keep everyone in line. Swords and arrows can do much, fire pits and fear, too, but sometimes it's the smallest, least flashy things that can be the most terrifying." Taillefer raised the vial in his hand and smiled down on the boy, whose face had gone tight with all that the prince's words meant. War. Conquest of the continent, bought on pain delivered by whatever was in that vial that made Luca cry out so. "Consider yourself an early servant of the most powerful regime in the world. Thanks to you, I will perfect my dosages until I can use them on any man, woman, or child who dares to defy Pyrenee as sole ruler of the Sand and Sky. Now let's try for a fourth dose—will the fireworks be the same, or a little ho-hum?"

The prince held the cork stopper an inch from Luca's chest. The screaming started again, twenty times louder than what they'd heard before.

Raw. Aching. Piercing.

Tears immediately threatened to roll down Ula's cheeks. She tightened her grip on her sword. As if sensing exactly what she was thinking, Dunixi cuffed her wrist and gave the slightest shake to his head, white-blue eyes fierce. *Don't.*

Luca's scream seemed to last for eternity, though it must have only been a few minutes because, as it died into a whimper, the prince looked up from his journal, eyes lifted to the ceiling and the castle grounds above.

In the distance, a bell chimed. "Ah. Two hours until the wedding. I must be going. I want to look my best to watch history in the making."

The prince winked at Luca and then turned for the stairs. The pirates shrank back on instinct, drawing into themselves. Urtzi did so forcefully enough that a twig rolled off the top of the pile and down to the floor. On impact it dashed itself airborne . . . and landed on the prince's boot.

Taillefer bent to pick it up and the pirates held their collective breath. The prince snapped the twig in half and tossed it onto the hearth.

Then, humming to himself the dulcet tones of the wedding march so popular in the Sand and Sky, he made for the stairs.

But, as he exited, he paused on the landing, scrabbling in the half dark for something. The pirates exchanged glances, but not one of them knew what he was doing.

Then with a scrape and a loud clang, the prince swung a metal door shut and sealed his workshop. Next came the tinkle and turn of keys.

They were locked in.

"WHAT are we going to do now?" Urtzi asked with the quietest version of his voice Ula had ever heard in all the years she'd known him. Shock on this ogre of a boy was completely unsettling—and a complete indication of Taillefer's madness.

Dunixi opened his mouth, ready with his de facto leader's answer, but Ula cut him off, not bothering to wipe the wetness streaming down her cheeks.

"We're going to help him, that's what," Ula snapped, springing up and slipping past the two boys, out of their meager hiding spot.

She ran to the prisoner then, touching his arm. "Luca, it's Ula. I'm here. And I'm going to help—oh." Her breath caught as she saw the raised, festering wound up close. The women of the orphanage in Eritri had often told her stories of dragons, and this looked exactly like what might happen if a beast like that matched a claw with human skin. It ran straight down the middle of Luca's sternum, over his heart, and beneath it his chest struggled to rise, and his eyes blinked open.

But then something else caught her attention. A black mark, sitting just to the right of his newest scar. Her eyes pinned on it, all moisture leaving her mouth. Even her tears seemed to evaporate, time slowing, everything drying up into a pinprick of reality that only held that mark.

"Did . . . did Taillefer apply this ink to your skin?"

Luca hesitated, pain and surprise muddling together on his face as he took his time in answering the question. "No. It's my mother's work. Before I left the Torrent." Ula felt him trying to read her face through vision that was surely blurred from what he'd just been through. "Why? Ula, what is it?"

"Your mother gave it to you?" Even to her own ears, her voice sounded small. Meaning to her syllables barely attached. "Not your father?"

"It could've been him," Luca said. It appeared that every word was an effort. "All I know is I had it when I arrived in Ardenia. My mother was dead before I had the words to ask her."

Blindly, Ula nodded, her heart pounding at the shape—a stick triangle, but more. Five points. The snout and eyes were there, for sure. The ink satin despite its age. A chill grew on her spine, her eyes unable to tear themselves away.

"Ula, what is it?"

If it was what she thought it was, it was what she'd waited for her whole life.

She wasn't sure. But this boy must not die. That much she knew.

And so she said, "Urtzi, Dunixi, we need something for his wound. Do you see turmeric? Honey? Look!"

Urtzi did as she ordered, reading labels, but Dunixi laughed. "Turmeric? It'll turn yellow. Honey? Taillefer will be able to see that glaze from a mile away."

"I don't care how it looks, only that it works," Ula snapped.

"We won't escape without Taillefer coming back and letting us out," Dunixi sniped back, as if she were an idiot. "If we change how the boy looks, it'll be trouble. And I'm not sure why you're wasting time on this anyway—it's not as if he'll die of infection in a few days' time."

"Have a heart, Dunixi."

"We need him alive only enough to draw the princess out. But we can't get him out of here without Taillefer first seeing him. An obvious change to his appearance is an invitation for the prince's curiosity."

Ula turned to Urtzi. "Alcohol. We'll use that."

She began rummaging around, pulling off stoppers and smelling the contents, looking for anything that could count.

"Madiran," Urtzi crowed, holding up a cask; then, without caution, he took a swig.

Ula flew into action, leaping to snatch it away. "No, don't; the prince—"

"Yep, Madiran."

Of course he'd know wine on sight. Still, she was concerned. "Bring it here."

She took a sniff herself, waiting to see if Urtzi showed any sign of poisoning. It was indeed the powerful red wine of the mountains. Discarding sagardoa, it was the best disinfectant in the region.

When Urtzi didn't keel over, Ula rewarded him. "Perfect. And it'll blend in. He won't notice." Dunixi didn't argue, not that it mattered much to her. Ula's eyes shifted to Luca. "This might sting."

Carefully, she poured it along the serration of the cut.

"Not too much. If he's drunk and injured, he'll be hell to maintain," Dunixi chided, his back to the table as he read each and every label on Taillefer's carefully appointed wall.

"Stay away from there. None of that is ours to use."

"Come now, Ula. Torture serum could come in handy."

"I'm afraid for how much you think like *him*."

"It's not simply how one thinks; it's how one acts. I'm not *that* disturbed."

Ula rolled her eyes and caught Luca's expression—still pained, but his lips turned up at the corners, amused.

Next, she fished around the worktable for something to numb the pain. Anything.

An entire section of storage vessels was devoted to dried herbs, but there were a few vials there, too, with tags, much like the ones on the walls. She rummaged through.

Oils. Basil might work. Thyme too. But then her fingers shook as she came across a label that reminded her of one of her last memories of her father, crushing spices for a proper supper after finally finding work, in the months after their escape.

Clove oil.

Ula bent back over Luca. "For the sting."

"It's quaint to call it that." Despite the pain, he tried to smile, and so she did, too.

She dripped it over his ruined skin. Luca licked his lips and sucked in a deep breath. "Better. Thank you."

Ula nodded. Then she leaned in, lowering her voice until only Luca could hear it. "We're going to get you out of here. And we will get your princess. I'll think of something. I promise."

CHAPTER
46

❧

THE maids came in a bustle of warm water and rose petals of the darkest aubergine. They carried grapes and paper-thin cheese, too, arranged on an ornate silver platter suited for the wedding itself. They placed a pitcher of cool water, crushed ice clinking gently against the crystal, on a carved marble table between the tub and a velvet-lined golden chaise.

Like Amarande's maids at home, these girls expected to stay. To scrub. To dress. To gossip.

The princess was in no mood. She sent them away, not only for a chance at solitude but also because her own suspicions and Renard's words had sunk in—if Dowager Queen Inés wanted her dead, anyone could be motivated to make the mark. Being alone was best.

"Prepare the wedding dress in the sitting room, please. Use your best judgment as to my size to begin. I trust you will make it fit."

Honestly, Amarande didn't care if it did. All the better if they hacked apart too much of Inés's dress and made a mess of it. She'd proudly wear that to this disaster.

When they were gone, Amarande locked the door, and only then did she finally slip from her clothes. The tunic and breeches she'd stolen from Ula pooled in a cloud of grit on the floor. The pouch of diamonds hit with a thunk and she left them there, under the stinking clothes. However, her boots—and boot knife— she took care to shove far under the bed, not gambling with the safety of the only things of value she had left. If the knife were confiscated, she'd only have her hands to rely on. If the boots disappeared, so did her ability to run for it in something comfortable. Though she knew how to make do with bare feet as well as she did bare knuckles, she wanted to keep every advantage possible.

The princess lowered herself into the steaming water, her muscles softening on contact. Dirt and grime lifted from her skin, swirling on the surface with the rose petals.

Her stomach growled, and her eyes slid to the platter of plump grapes and delicately sliced cheese. Food only shared in the walls of a palace, not suitable for survival anywhere else in the Sand and Sky. Still, it called to her, hazardous as it could be.

With a similar thought in mind, the princess inspected the soap the maids had left, purple like the rose petals but this time made that way by lavender. It smelled fine, and when she wet it and ran the bar along a hardy patch of skin on her shin, it didn't burn.

Amarande scrubbed every inch of her body and hair, the stink of her days-long quest gone in mere minutes. But it would never leave her—there was no way to cleanse her heart of the journey. Or of Luca.

For the first time since she laid her father to rest, she was clean and somewhat relaxed, the warmth of the water soothing. The scent of the rose petals heady. Her muscles unwound themselves, knots unspooling, sinew stretching clear. Her heart slowing.

Amarande's eyelids began to pause with each blink, the mass of what she'd been through weighing them down like the gold pieces that her father had worn in his casket.

She forced them open just long enough to ensure the door was indeed locked. And, satisfied, she let them flutter closed.

WATER, cold and unforgiving, poured into Amarande's nostrils and mouth. The princess's eyes flung open, and blinking, she coughed. The immediate sensation of drowning was thick and pressing as water settled where air should be.

Dowager Queen Inés stood over her, pitcher in hand, chomping on grapes.

"Poppied lavender—that has Taillefer written all over it," she said, inspecting the soap and then tossing it in the chamber pot. "Up, girl. We need to talk."

The woman flung a towel at the princess and turned her back, waiting. Amarande's eyes again flew to the door. Still locked.

"How did you . . . did Renard . . . ?"

"I let myself in my own way." Inés allowed that statement to hang, full of what she didn't say—that she had a secret entrance and exit to the room and she was proud to spare Amarande the details. "He doesn't know I'm here, but before you scream for him and ruin his time in front of the mirror practicing kingly faces, listen to what I have to say."

The princess hesitated. She had no weapons and no clothes. Still, she had options. Amarande pictured herself bashing the Dowager Queen's skull against the unforgiving marble of the tub, or the table or the floor—the whole place was chiseled and diamond hard. Or holding the woman's face under the water until she drowned. Or maybe breaking the crystal pitcher into an assortment of deadly shivs.

"If you are thinking about killing me, I would remind you that I am queen for the next two hours and you and your stableboy would both join me in the afterlife shortly thereafter. Renard doesn't want your affections, Princess—he wants what you afford him. If your actions give him another way to win, he won't save you; he'll blame you. We don't see eye to eye, but he is my son and I know his heart." Then, "Out of the tub."

Amarande grabbed the towel and stood, taking a few delicate steps onto the marble tile. She tidied up and, with the woman's back still turned, pulled on the dressing gown left by the maids.

"What do you want, Dowager Queen Inés?"

The woman laughed hard enough it could be classified as a cackle. "What do I want? What *don't* I want?" When the noise died, her tone sharpened. "I want to not lose my crown in two hours, to start."

Amarande could match her expression and then some. "You aren't losing it; it was never yours. Blood to blood—the claim is not yours."

The Dowager Queen arched a brow. "Yet you have the right blood, and your claim is still worthless without you attaching yourself to another like a parasite."

Amarande pursed her lips. Water ran in rivulets down the back of the dressing gown, her hair a sopping mess, but she didn't dry it, not taking an inch of scrutiny off this woman.

The silence pushed the Dowager Queen into speaking again.

"Before others, I must be more reserved about my son's aspirations and sharing my feelings about *the rules*, but I need you to hear me plainly now."

Amarande stretched her patience, bringing it forth and stuffing down her desire to fight. She was in this woman's home, after all, as Inés had already taken pains to remind her. "Say your piece, please, Your Highness, and let me be."

The Dowager Queen wasted no time after that invitation.

"The moment your father died, Renard came to life. He saw his path in you, and he took it. You know this, do you not?"

The princess firmed her stance yet lowered her voice—Renard was somewhere beyond the door. "He is motivated because he believes *you* are scheming to marry another king and bear a stronger heir—born for two kingdoms, not one. And I must say, from my experience with your courtships of my father, he is likely not wrong."

Dowager Queen Inés didn't laugh or frown at this, her face placid as she skewered some cheese. Amarande's stomach audibly growled and the woman gestured to the plate. "Go ahead, I've already tested it. This particular food won't kill you."

Amarande did not take her invitation.

Inés reset. "I did pursue your father, but only because I believed him to be a good man. And when a good man turns a girl down, she so often fulfills those desires with something less than perfect."

"You wanted to talk to me plainly, but I do not need to hear of your desires."

"Oh, I wasn't alluding to carnal desires—girl, you will find plenty who will serve a queen of any sort in *that* way."

Amarande's cheeks went hot and she felt even more naked than when the Dowager Queen had found her in the bath.

"No, I mean power," Inés continued, lips in a tart smile at Amarande's blush. "Renard did not fall far from the tree. I married for this station, and, as you know, a woman has little rights in the Sand and Sky, title or not. I want to change that, but the crux is that I can't without a king by my side. You know a little something about that, do you not? I know it was part of Renard's pitch to you. He gives you the ring you need to rule, you give him early rights of his own, and together you've created the strongest alliance—no, *combination*—of kingdoms in the Sand and Sky. Domingu will rattle his dentures bowing so low to you, and Akil will wink and confide, smile sparkling, that he has always had a love of striking eyes like yours."

Amarande said nothing.

"I am here to help you. The moment you marry my son, I can no longer fight at your side. I'm rendered moot. But if you were to run away with your stableboy? I could retain power long enough to marry again and then use the influence of two kingdoms to change the rules. You could return, claim your kingdom with your stableboy at your side, and be done."

Again, Amarande said nothing. Like Taillefer's grinning offer in the meadow, this power grab relied far too much on her service and trust of someone who didn't deserve it.

The woman continued. "I proposed such a thing to your father after my husband died—that if he were to marry me and join our kingdoms, we'd have enough power to change the laws of succession. To give you a chance to rule in your own right. And any daughters after you."

This, Amarande had not known. As much as she'd learned in the yard, the meadow, and from her instructors, her father hadn't allowed her at Royal Council meetings until the last year. If this had been spoken of there, it was never in her presence. Of course, this woman had every reason to lie.

The Dowager Queen's eyes snapped to the princess. "As you are aware, he spurned my advances. The law didn't change. And now you've been all but kidnapped yourself to maintain the status quo."

Amarande swallowed, watching the queen as she laid a sliver of cheese on her tongue, chewed, and swallowed. The food was nearly gone.

"My son won't change the laws and you know it. He doesn't want to limit the power of men to the whims of women. He was born privileged and primed for the best life available—he has no interest in lifting up anyone else. Renard will only use a two-kingdom influence to win power for himself. Until every last dusty acre of this continent is under his control and the rest of us are in his shadow."

The Dowager Queen's eyes flashed and Amarande found enough certainty in them to stop her heart. War. Renard would put the whole continent at war to claim it for his own. With *her* army joined with his, he could very much achieve it. But so could Inés with the right husband. Koldo had said it herself—a prolonged, multi-front war was not something even Ardenia's great army could survive. If Inés had two armies at her disposal, Ardenia would struggle to stave off an extensive campaign.

"And then he will need heirs. Male heirs." The older woman's voice sharpened. "Renard will be your own personal hell until he gets a healthy heir and a spare."

Amarande cleared her throat.

"He knows I will not allow that," the princess said, though deep within, her confidence trembled.

"Ah, but it doesn't matter what you will allow. And that's the point, Princess. I've lived it—it's a grim life. And, in your case, one caused by an untimely death."

Inés watched Amarande now in a way that made the princess's eyes find great interest in the pattern on the marble floor. "I must say, it is very hard for me to believe that your tiger of a father just keeled over and died without foul play." Amarande grew stone still, a chill running the length of her spine. "And I think you don't believe that *story* either, do you?"

Amarande didn't confirm it verbally, but she knew the queen could read it all over her blank face.

"He was riding on the border shared by Ardenia, the Torrent, and Pyrenee, was he not? Touching the hands of strangers, hugging children, blessing the sick—all the solstice usual . . ." She raised a brow. "So many opportunities to push a new regime into motion with one forgettable, yet fatal, interaction."

The princess's words came out in a fevered rush, her mind swirling with the press of motivations from all sides, even those not within the glittering confines of the Bellringe. She no longer kept her voice down. "And you believe Renard would do that when you yourself have worked openly to steal his rightful claim with a well-timed marriage and sire?"

Here, Inés smiled tightly. The food beside her was gone, and she straightened from where she'd rested on the chaise that had once been hers.

"I did not kill your father, Amarande. Believe me, with the amount of maneuvering I must do as a woman to incite needed change in the laws of the Sand and Sky, the last thing I'd want to do is free up the girl who could bring my son early, uncontested rule and the world's strongest army. There is more than one reason I wish him not to be king, Princess."

"Mother, is that you?" The knob shook from the other side, and then the door flung wide and Renard stood there, key in hand.

The Dowager Queen's eyes swept from the key in his hand to Amarande's face. "See? Nothing is yours and yours alone, is it, Princess? It will never be."

The prince advanced, his jaw hardening, as he took in Amarande, standing there in her dressing gown, clearly not prepared for guests. The look he gave his mother could light any of the Warlord's fire pits. "What are you doing here? Get away from her. Now."

His mother smiled coolly. "We're just having a little girl time, Renard. Nothing to be afraid of."

His attention snapped to Amarande. "Whatever she told you is untrue."

Taillefer appeared at his brother's back, straightening a particularly flashy dinner jacket. Enough gold thread and sewn-in baubles to blend in with a fallen star.

"Is it untrue that you drugged her soap with poppy so that she might rest soundly until wedding time?" Inés asked, brow cocked. "A sleeping girl cannot escape."

At this, Taillefer gave a bashful smile, his talent recognized. Renard opened his mouth and then closed it, knowing his brother had inadvertently confirmed it.

"Is it untrue that you want to use her power to win *all* of the Sand and Sky?" his mother asked, smiling brilliantly.

Renard's ears reddened. He glanced away.

The Dowager Queen continued.

"Is it untrue that she would be happier with her stableboy?" Then the Dowager Queen's eyes shot to Taillefer—she hadn't been there for his orders, but she had no trouble proving that nothing happened in this castle without her notice. "Is he still in one piece?"

"Of course," the younger prince said too quickly. His brother said nothing.

Amarande saw Renard read her panic, color rising in his cheeks—his fury growing with each of his mother's words.

He couldn't deny any of those things.

Amarande's unease with her lot grew with each second his fury rose. How could she marry this boy? How was this the best option?

Renard seemed to sense exactly what she was thinking, watching her face with an edge that told her he wished to stop her thoughts in their tracks. He looked to his brother for aid, but Taillefer had nothing to offer. His mother smiled.

They're all mad. And each one thought her their pawn.

When the crown prince spoke again, it was nothing less than an undignified scream and spit—the edges of his blandness were fraying. "Mother, you mean to undermine me."

"Renard, if the truth undermines you, then your footing is nothing but quicksand."

"Leave. Now. Or I shall call the guards."

The Dowager Queen stood. "That will be most unnecessary." She turned to Amarande. "Don't forget what was said here, Princess. Power is sometimes not the kindest lens to reality." Her eyes skipped to her older son. "And some of us see more clearly than others."

"Out, Mother," Renard growled.

The Dowager Queen swept between her two sons, leaving in a very different way than she came.

Renard immediately advanced on Amarande. "Remember, Princess, if you do not marry me, you are dead, and your stableboy will suffer for it."

Her eyes shifted to Taillefer. "He suffers already. What's to stop me from taking him now and leaving this place?"

"My men will hunt you down."

"And my blood will be on their uniforms. You will have no claim to my army, and your mother will gladly feed you to the wolves to retain your crown." Her eyes shifted again to Taillefer. "And *you* will be blamed, too. That woman doesn't want any heir. She'd be better off without either one of you."

Taillefer didn't react, and Amarande wasn't surprised—he wasn't stupid. He needed his entire family in the ground for any meaningful chance to rule.

Renard's eyes were ice. He leaned in to her, his voice low and seeming to rumble into her lungs. "I will say this one final time—"

"Your Highness?" a small, feminine voice said from the door. "We have finished with the wedding gown."

Renard schooled his features and then turned to the maid at the door, who stepped back at the sight of him, his face still furious no matter how hard he worked to hide it. His voice, too, had an edge in it, though he tried very hard to soften it into the bland portrait he liked to project.

"Good. Get her dressed and downstairs within the hour."

CHAPTER
47

❧❧

RENARD pulled Taillefer into his study, fury lighting his features again as soon as he shut the door to Princess Amarande, across the way. Candles were lit, the dust gone. The marriage bed was piled in new sheets and linens, white and pristine. On a small aubergine pillow at the table, the crown of Pyrenee, striking gold and newly polished. The maids had lit lilac candles and placed vases of gilded roses around the room, preparing it for what was to come, though the new scents did nothing to mask the musty smell of disuse.

Renard flung himself into a pace. Taillefer settled onto a bearskin-wrapped bench at the foot of the four-poster bed. A painting of their sigil—the mountain lion—hung over the tufted headboard.

"There is too much time," Renard said. "She is too trained. This wedding will not happen if she decides it will not."

"Then go sit in there with her now until it's time to haul her down the aisle. Don't let go of her hand until you say the words uniting the kingdoms."

As usual, Taillefer sounded completely unbothered. This greatly annoyed Renard.

"I cannot," he spat. The crown prince sucked in a deep breath, his lungs seemingly failing to draw in air properly. "Everyone must believe she is here on her own volition. Ardenia may try to void the marriage and the coronation. We cannot give them any more fodder to do so."

Taillefer picked something off his boot heel. "Having seen that council in action, if they want to void your marriage contract, they will. The princess has nothing to do with that."

In anger, Renard knocked a vase of roses from a marble-topped table. It went down with a crash and he crunched across the crystal, his pace not slowed. "Where is the stableboy?"

Taillefer smirked. "Where do you think?"

Renard was not amused. "He cannot escape?"

"He's lashed to a table and barely conscious. He's not travel ready."

Renard shook his head, voice automatically lowering. "If she *can* carry him, she *will* carry him." He nodded and met Taillefer's eyes. "I must see him."

"As you wish, my brother."

THE two sons of Pyrenee entered Taillefer's workshop in a rush of boot heels across stone, Renard leading the way. They were so loud that there was movement on the table—a surprise and a relief to Renard.

The crown prince kept walking until he bumped into the table, jostling the stableboy. The boy's eyes opened, slit at first and then wide. Fearful. They were swollen at the edges—he'd been crying, recent and hard. *Good.*

"Are you here to kill me?" the boy asked, his voice bone-dry.

"No," Renard spat, taking in the prisoner's form.

He was lashed to the table as Taillefer had guaranteed, a festering wound longer than a man's hand running the length of his sternum. Fevered sweat sat heavy across his brow, capillaries broken at his bindings where he'd struggled. He'd already suffered. Again, *Good.* "I'm here to make sure you're still in one piece. Has my mother visited you? Or the princess?"

"Amarande? Does she know I'm here?" Ignoring the first question, Luca looked to Taillefer.

The younger prince answered, "She knows nothing, but she isn't the sort to let that stop her."

At this, the boy dared to smile. Renard slapped him.

"She won't be rescuing you. If she hasn't come yet, she won't come at all. I will make sure of it." Renard nodded, almost to himself. He turned to his brother, who fiddled with items of torture on the small pedestal table. "You are ready, are you not?"

Taillefer nodded, tugging on the golden jacket, the cut of it crisp along his shoulders. "I planned to spend an inordinate amount of time perfecting my hair in the mirror before the ceremony, but yes, otherwise, I'm prepared."

"Your hair is glorious, but no one will be looking at you anyway."

Taillefer feigned pain and Renard almost rolled his eyes.

"You will stay with the stableboy here—get him dressed and escort him to the wedding. She must see him in the audience. The threat must be clear."

"Am I not to stand with you at the altar?"

"Yes, fine. I will place him under guard. But you will oversee all of it. As long as this boy and his stupid dimples are alive, my hold over the princess is enough that she will marry me."

"Of course, Renard."

"Have him prepared by the time the bells toll again. And if you can do something to make him not nearly as handsome when she sees him, all the better."

Taillefer smiled and gave a nod.

And then the almost king returned to his castle to retrieve his bride.

CHAPTER
48

THE prince's footsteps disappeared up the stairs and Luca released a deep breath.

Renard had tried kidnapping and made no qualms about only having him around to keep Amarande in line, but love was something that he couldn't orchestrate, let alone break.

Luca would win. Love would always win.

And now he'd be in the chapel with his princess. Renard's paranoia actually played in his favor. Luca couldn't believe it. If the pirates could be there, too, there was so much they could do. The five of them, they could surely get out of there mostly alive. His princess had rescued him, but now he had the chance to return the favor.

It was enough that he almost smiled again.

But then Taillefer kicked into motion, turning to the large worktable and its cluttered contents. When he returned, the thick gloves were back on his hands and something new was hiding behind him. Gone were his playful smirk and laughing eyes. Rather than a fox, he suddenly looked every part a mountain lion.

Disfigurement, yes. That's what his brother had requested.

Luca's heartbeat sped, his lips parting. He kept his eyes as neutral as possible, though they nearly flicked to where the pirates hid again in the shadows.

"You heard my brother—as long as you and your dimples can smile at Amarande, she will marry Renard. That may still happen, but if it does, I may not be able to wait for the result that I desire."

The prince's voice was cold and calm. No audible madness in it, just abrupt determination.

"I've sworn to keep you safe—to keep you alive—but that no longer serves me."

THE prince rang a bell. and a guard visited. Taillefer barked orders. and the boy left in a rush. It was then that Luca drew in a breath, all hope he'd had five minutes ago gone. "You'd kill me so that my princess fulfills her promise. He will be dead at the altar and you will have his crown—you meant every word you said in the meadow, except that you'd let Amarande and me be."

"I did. But my mother's wishes mean we must speed up the timeline." Either Renard's convoluted theory was actually true or he'd convinced Taillefer it was—which meant both sons thought they were in danger of missing out on a rightful throne. Taillefer smiled. "And there's only one certain way to do that."

Luca began to struggle on the table. He didn't beg, preferring to fight.

"Don't worry, boy; I won't kill you. I'll simply *mostly* kill you. I can only murder you once, and I may need you again."

Then Taillefer revealed his newly procured items of torture. Yet another bottle of serum and a plant. This one very much like the giant hogweed, yet now Luca knew the difference.

Hemlock. This time there was no doubt.

Luca's eyes fell back to the prince, the pieces falling together in his mind. "Did you kill King Sendoa with that?"

The prince cocked a brow. "Did *you?* This very hemlock was culled from the stream beyond your stable at the Itspi. Did your king tell you to keep your dirty hands off his daughter? Did he puncture that soft heart of yours? Did you decide you were bigger than him and your ambitions were, too, and take it upon yourself to ready his horse with something deadly in his waterskin?"

Luca struggled against the restraints again now, anger mingling with the fear. This was another truth that could be twisted. They could kill Amarande and blame him—and then blame him for Sendoa's death as well. One tidy package. "I would never have hurt my king. We were as good as blood. As family."

Taillefer inspected the contents of the vial. "My mother would like both of her sons dead, and we *are* her blood. Blood and family mean nothing in the Sand and Sky."

"Please, don't. Don't. There must be another way. Take me to the chapel. I will talk to Amarande. I will tell her she must kill Renard. She can kill your mother, too."

"Your princess has yet to kill anyone. She needs the proper motivation. And you are it." Luca struggled harder against the restraints. Again, his eyes combed the shadows for Ula's face. She wouldn't just watch, would she? Taillefer opened the vial. "I wouldn't do that if I were you. The line between mostly dead and actually dead is a thin one. One drop and you live—two drops and you die."

Luca stiffened then, bracing, eyes open, watching the prince as he coated the stopper with a single drop of the liquid. A liquid that easily could've been slipped into King Sendoa's water, clear and innocent as it was.

Taillefer smiled. "Let us both get what we want when you wake."

The tincture made contact with the wound.

It didn't burn. Didn't sting. Didn't feel like anything much at all.

Taillefer returned the stopper. Removed his gloves. Pulled out his journal.

And then he simply watched.

Luca shut his eyes then, thinking of Amarande. Her smiling face. Her quick wit. Bumps and bruises and lemon cake in the meadow.

Then Luca's breathing slowed, chest rising every ten seconds, then once in a half minute. Then a minute. Then . . . not at all.

His eyes flew open, wide with panic. Taillefer watched, stoic and erudite, scribbling notes. No alarm, no worry, no empathy.

"Interesting," was all he said, and not even to Luca, but under his breath, as his pencil moved across the parchment.

Distantly, there was a clatter.

"Prince Taillefer, sir, you sent for assistance?" It was Ula's voice, projected over the shuffling of some feet. Taillefer, though, did not address her, every mad inch of him cataloging Luca's face and still chest.

And then the world started closing in, Luca's vision going from too much light to not enough. Black seeping in from the edges, until, like his breath, there was nothing at all.

CHAPTER
49

❧

THE wedding gown fit horribly.

The bodice drooped, the cut impossible to correct for a smaller frame. The three maids and castle seamstress frowned at this as Amarande stood upon an ottoman in the bedroom that would be hers, a floor-to-ceiling mirror hauled in before her.

They'd taken the right length off the hem, her shoes wouldn't show, and Amarande was relieved because she could wear her boots without a single person knowing.

Yet even with the hasty cut-and-tuck, the dress seemed too exhausted to go through with it.

You and me both, dress.

The fabric was dated and somehow tired, though it hadn't been worn in nearly twenty years. Gold—at least it was gold and not that blasted purple. Carrying that color was Renard's duty—aubergine and white with gold touches, just as he wore at their ill-fated dinner.

"Perhaps a sash? At the top? That will keep it from gaping," Amarande offered, though she wasn't sure the girls would go for it.

"Yes, yes, yes, Your Highness," muttered the seamstress through the pins in her mouth.

With the princess's guidance, they added one that was a red close to the garnet of Ardenia. They draped it over the top of the bodice, nearly to Amarande's clavicles, before letting it scoop around into a bow at her lower back.

"Yes, much better. Good work." The maids and seamstress appeared to enjoy this assertion from their newest royal, smiling to themselves.

Next, the maids went to work on her hair, brushing it until it flowed long down her back in silky ribbons instead of the wet tangle it had become after her sudden exit from the tub. It was still damp—the nature of her thick hair and little time—but they did what they could, twining together the topmost pieces into a braided crown that would be a lovely nest for a real one.

When they finished, Amarande tried very hard to produce a smile. "Thank you for your service. I'd like to cherish a few more minutes alone before the festivities begin. Please fetch me when it is time."

When they'd left, the princess took a deep breath and then threw herself back onto the bed.

"I can do this. I can do this. I can do this."

But the truth clawed at her heart and expressed itself in a frown she couldn't shake.

"I can't do this. I'm not here as a means to elevate men. To give up on my own dream. My own blood," she whispered to herself. "My chance at love . . . but I am."

Feeling the dizzy press of sadness and defeat, Amarande reached for the clasp locking the window—Renard hadn't touched it, and surely it would open. It cost her a straight minute and one of her nails, but she pried the thing open.

Amarande inhaled the evening air, warm and damply cool all the same—summer in the mountains winding from scorching dry to something almost like autumn as the sun set. Much like home. Though this would never be home.

No matter if she figured out these vipers long enough to survive them—this place, this title, this station, would never be home, nor hers.

Empty stomach curdling with the weight of it all, Amarande took another deep breath of fresh air and then bent to the puddle of clothes she'd asked the maids to leave on the floor. She reached into the stolen breeches and found the remaining diamonds from her necklace. A lot of good they'd done her.

The princess stood and again walked to the window. She held the diamonds in her palms, watching the facets shimmer in the sun's dying amber light, dozens of planes catching one after another, all shimmering in their own right. All vying to be the focal point.

Facets. So many facets.

Her father had often taken her to the diamond cutters' workshops. There was one in the Itspi, of course, for an official royal diamond cutter by the name of Wenta, weasel-faced from a life staring at minuscule things and producing the perfect shimmer. But there were sanctioned diamond cutters outside of the castle— ones who took care of gems purchased by faraway rich men who paid for the perfection of an Ardenian gem.

"Why do we go from stall to stall, Father? Aren't all diamonds the same?"

"No two diamonds are the same, Ama. No jewel, no cut." With the diamond cutter's permission, he held up the nearest stone. "Even one diamond can look completely different depending on the facet that catches the light in that moment. Just like in life—the facet in the shadow might have more beauty than the one in the light." He rolled the diamond in his hand over, exposing yet another glittering side. And maybe it was more beautiful. "Never underestimate what you don't see. In diamonds or in life."

There was no beauty to this situation, but Ama had the distinct feeling that the Dowager Queen had purposefully twisted the princess's situation to reveal another facet to the light.

Amarande rolled her own diamonds around in her hand, the stones swirling with captured luminosity.

What was a lie?

What was the truth?

What would be best for Ardenia?

For Luca?

For her?

As she tossed the questions over in her mind, something tossed *itself* through the window, striking her in the hand. The diamonds scattered, pinging across the marble.

A pebble.

She picked it up, and the diamonds, too. As she stood again, another small rock flew through the window, landing an inch from her foot.

Amarande stepped up to the window and leaned out to the night.

And there, walking in the garden, were Taillefer and his guards, who were carrying something large. None of them were looking up to her window two stories above, but a quick sweep of the court-yard provided no other suspects.

"Taillefer!" The prince turned, as if he did not expect to hear her voice. "Did you just throw two rocks at me?"

"What, me? No."

His fox smile slid into place with his denial and Amarande wound up to say more, but then the guards turned and the light shifted, and suddenly the shape of what they were carrying be-came not something but *someone*.

Even at the distance, even with the falling darkness, even with the angry slash across his chest beside his tattoo, Amarande knew.

"Luca."

His name was faint on her lips—almost nothing. Only she could hear it, pounding in her ears, over the churning of her breath. Her heaving stomach plummeted; her limbs immediately began shaking; a runaway chill raced across her skin.

Taillefer was prepared for her reaction. Every inch of this moment was orchestrated, she suspected.

"Don't do anything rash, Princess. He's only dreaming of you." The prince's eyes crinkled at the corners in a way that wasn't merry. "He will only ever dream of you for the rest of his days. But that was to be the case after the wedding anyway, am I right?"

The princess's body tensed with the whisper of battle. If the fall wouldn't kill her, she would've launched herself out of the window and onto the stone path before him, hands about his throat to squeeze the answer free.

"Will you speak plainly?" Amarande spat, color rising. From such a distance it appeared as if Luca had been cut open, his heart—the one that loved her dearly—removed. "Is he . . . ? You didn't . . . ?"

Taillefer's smile sharpened.

"My brother is a fool, after all."

And there she was, leaving Luca in the hands of Taillefer, throwing Renard's words back at him: *Remember, Prince, if he dies, you die.*

The prince had nodded and said, *I would be a fool to test you.*

Taillefer didn't state it clearly. He wouldn't. This boy loved to live in riddles—straight answers would never be his forte. But he had laid it bare.

Amarande's fingers clutched the windowsill as it hit her. Stealing her breath, her heartbeat, her everything. Every inch of her went numb as her world crumbled in. The unthinkable proved in the failing light of the worst day of her life.

Luca was dead.

And Taillefer wanted her to know.

Because he wanted to be king.

Because he wanted to see her suffer.

Because he wanted to demonstrate his handiwork—of his own volition or of an order, she didn't know.

But it didn't matter.

Renard was to blame. He'd sent Luca with Taillefer. He'd caused Luca's death.

Orders rose from the nothingness within her. To have the guards take him somewhere she could say good-bye. To make sure he was escorted to Ardenia for burial by his mother's grave on the grounds of the Itspi. His found family would need to say good-bye, too.

"Guards," she called, and when they looked up she would've been shocked if she'd had the capacity left for it—Luca's body was being transported by the three kidnapper pirates, all dressed in the colors of Pyrenee. They had always been the enemy, and now they wore the aubergine and gold to prove it. "Take care of him, please."

The other orders died unsaid. Mostly because they gave away what she knew now in her heart she must do.

The facets didn't matter. No matter what scenario she landed on, none was better than the next. None had a different path. All had the same conclusion.

She must kill Renard.

Taillefer too.

And maybe the Dowager Queen.

Eradicate them all and leave the throne of Pyrenee bare.

Amarande tore herself away from the window, tears welling in her eyes now, splashing down her face.

It was over. Her love. Her dream. Her motivation.

She bent and pulled the ransom note from the pool of her stained clothes and tucked it again into her bodice, right above her heart. Then she fished her boots out from under the bed. Pulled the knife out of the right one and held it in her hand.

She'd grown into the hilt under her father's direction. Under Koldo's guidance. With Luca in their meadow.

And now it would be her revenge. Most likely her death, too.

She slipped the boot knife blade point down in the front of her bodice, working it between the boning of her stays, tight against her sternum, and next to the ransom note that had started it all. A tuck of the sash across her minimal cleavage and it was completely hidden.

"Pyrenee will suffer," she whispered to herself, wiping at her eyes. She must not let on. She must be calm. She must wait until the right moment. She only had one chance to get this right.

She would make it so—and it would be the last thing she ever did.

CHAPTER
50

FIRST, Luca felt the pain. It came back to him as easily as breathing, though, in truth, it did constrict that. Next, he heard voices.

A boy's. Maybe two. And a girl. If he were dead, that voice would've been Amarande's, he was sure. Instead, it sounded very much like Ula.

Maybe he was alive.

"No," the girl said, voice twisted with anger.

"Why are you being so stubborn about this? The garden, your sword, the gold. End of story."

"No."

"No, what, woman? If you weren't so damn good with that sword, I swear I never would've been stupid enough to put you on this crew. You do not know your place."

"His eyelashes just fluttered." Urtzi's voice.

Immediately Luca felt a thump on his boot. That kicked his eyes from fluttering to open.

"Luca!" Ula screeched, crashing to his side.

His eyes adjusted until he could see her face. Then Urtzi and Dunixi. And finally their surroundings ... not Taillefer's workshop. The familiar mingling scents of lavender oil, oats, and more than a few horses.

"Are we in the stable?" Luca's voice was dry and cracking at the edges.

"Oh, here, have some water." Ula thrust a waterskin in his face. He tried to move his hands, but they wound around in sloppy form. She helped him sit up and, propping him, put the pouch to his lips. After a few great swallows, he looked again to their faces, and then to his clothes—they'd given him a new shirt, something of awful Pyrenee purple. Beneath the fabric, his chest burned, but he felt some sort of lashing around his ribs, covering his wound—dressed. "How did you . . . ?"

"Get you out?" Ula finished for him. When he nodded, her eyes lit up. "With Taillefer's permission."

Here, Dunixi chimed in, eager to explain. "You may not remember—the prince rang a bell, and a guard showed up and he ordered the boy to go grab others to help carry you. When he left, we appeared—thank the stars we were already in guard attire—and he laughed because it was our first day on the job but allowed it, and instructed us to carry you out under the princess's window."

"See?" Ula said. "I told you we'd get you out."

Luca met her smile, but then the reality of what had happened dawned on him. "*Stars.* Does she think that I'm . . . ?"

"Dead?" Dunixi answered. "Oh yes, I think she does."

Luca gripped Ula's wrist, his boots scrabbling against the hay-strewn stable floor as he tried to stand. "You were there. You heard Taillefer. And now Ama will do it. She'll attack at the wedding. And if she murders a single person in that chapel, they'll kill her and lie about what really happened. We have to get her out."

"Oh, we're not going to let her get *in*," Dunixi said, as Ula got Luca upright. His legs immediately buckled and he was back on his rear in the straw within a blink. Dunixi turned to the Myrcellian. "Urtzi, toss him over your back. We must kidnap the princess before she enters the chapel."

"Kidnap?" Luca whispered, his breath catching.

"Yes, *kidnap.* We are not your friends, stableboy. You're still blackmail, and your princess will be, too."

Luca's heartbeat filled his ears. "And then what? You'll give us back to Renard? To Taillefer?"

"Of course. Contrary to earlier events, we deliver goods as promised. And when we do, I expect Renard to shoot gold from his eyeballs."

"No," Ula spat, nostrils flaring. She stepped in front of Luca, stance wide, hands on her hips and her sword hanging sharp off her belt. "Enough about the gold, Dunixi. This is about much more than riches."

A sneer crossed the boy's face.

"Don't be silly, girl—there is nothing but riches. You agreed earlier, we need it to release the ship. Hell, we need it to simply live."

"Dunixi, I only agreed so that I didn't have to kill you right there. We need to save Amarande, not steal her. This continent will go to hell if Renard or *stars forbid* Taillefer get what they want. We have a chance to do the right thing for everyone in the Sand and Sky, and that is worth more than any gold piece."

Dunixi bared his teeth, eyes narrowing. "Urtzi, grab the stableboy."

Ula drew her sword, shielding Luca. "No."

Dunixi's jaw hardened and his face collapsed into a frown. "Urtzi, the stableboy. *Now.* If Ula swipes at you, swipe back."

The Myrcellian didn't budge. "You want me to fight Ula?"

"No, I want you to finally have the balls to kiss her." Spit flew from the Eritrian's mouth. "*Yes,* I want you to fight her! She's ready to fight you!"

"Urtzi," Ula called, and his gaze snapped to hers. "I will only fight you if you fight for him. Be on his side or mine, but if you choose wrong, I will cut you down. And then I will cut your master."

The Myrcellian boy stood there for a moment, fists out and ready, dark eyes shifting between them.

"Come on, Urtzi," Dunixi prodded, turning for the exit and the yawning night. "Our window to take the princess is closing."

Urtzi took a hesitant step toward Ula. She raised her sword out in a high guard, ready, her body low and angled in front of Luca. On the ground, Luca shifted up to his elbows, willing his legs to move and help him out of the way.

Ula and Urtzi locked eyes, and then something fell over the tall boy's face. With one powerful side step, he hammered one fist into the Eritrian's temple.

Dunixi's eyes grew wide with shock in the split second before they rolled back into his head and he slumped to the stable floor.

Out cold.

Ula's face broke into a smile and she lowered her sword enough to hug the tall boy's arm. "Urtzi, you big oaf, you finally realized you could take Dunixi, did you?"

"No, I always knew I could. I just didn't because you still followed him . . . and I want to follow you."

Ula bit her lip but didn't let go of his arm. Urtzi rubbed his neck and glanced down. After a beat, they broke apart and Ula sped back into action. "Do you think you can stand?" she asked Luca.

"With help."

Urtzi offered a meaty paw. With the Myrcellian as an anchor, Luca did indeed stand, swaying a little on his heels. "This will do. I'm sure I'll find my stride when I see Amarande."

Ula smiled and then bent to Dunixi's limp body. From it she pulled a handful of items—a slip of paper, a small vial, and a dagger. She stuffed the first two items into her pockets but handed the knife, the one that had been in the saddlebag he'd stolen, to Luca, eyes aflame. "Let's go save your princess."

CHAPTER
51

 (decorative flourish)

WITH every step, Amarande's tears dried. Her jaw tightened. Her resolve hardened. Her heartbeat pounded against the knife she'd carried with her for the majority of her life.

I will kill Renard.

I will kill Taillefer.

I will make Pyrenee suffer.

And, finally: *I will die in the process.*

That truth sat heavy in her heart. And yet it brought her peace.

Rather than giving up control to the vipers here, she would use her hands, her gifts, everything Father and Koldo had taught her, and end it all.

When it was over, the decision was hers, the action was hers, the fate was hers to choose.

That alone was worth it.

A stillness spread about Amarande, until it was no longer as if she was inside her body but out of it, looking down upon the queen's chambers. The maids finally summoned her at the latest chime of bells and brought her down the stairs.

The girls pressed a bouquet into her hands—a mixture of unnatural aubergine and gold roses—and vanished into the shadows. Her new escorts appeared at the landing, members of the Pyrenee council whose names she did not know, all dressed in yards of swirling purple fabric, sour looks upon their craggy faces.

She did not trust them.

If they laid hands on her, they would be sorry. Her knife could spill more than royal blood.

The councilors did not touch her, though. Rather, they surrounded her in a cushion, leading her through the same rose garden in which she'd seen Luca's body held aloft by the former pirates.

The sun had set, the cool sepia of twilight lighting the grounds. Lanterns lined both sides of their path, a sweet candlelit glow under the emerging stars.

Amarande squinted through the dim, attempting to read the shadows for a sign of where Luca had been laid to rest before the wedding. Not that it mattered. She wouldn't be able to find him. She wouldn't be able to say good-bye. She could only meet him in the afterworld.

There, at least, they could be together.

No laws. No rules. No expectations.

The princess quickened her stride. The chapel loomed ahead, torches blazing from the walls, guards stationed outside. Two on either side of the doors, decked out in their best uniforms, stoically reading the land before them. They let the princess's party cross the threshold without so much as a glance.

The beams and pillars of the foyer were hastily dressed in twists of golden roses and ribbon. Everyone was seated, and no one lingered beyond the main hall, save for a handful of guards—including Osana, in Pyrenee purple, Egia strapped to her side—standing sentry over morsels meant for after the affair. Perhaps in their haste of wedding preparation, Pyrenee had inadvertently admitted women to the castle guard—or possibly they didn't care who flaunted dead prisoners and guarded cheese. Silver trays of several stinking varieties lined tables along with shrimp culled from Pyrenee's single fjord port along the Divide and vats of the dark-red wine so beloved by those here.

She could hear music playing beyond the foyer—flute and harp, the instruments of romance. Already with the wedding march. Likely on repeat, with the princess meant to fall in at the beginning of the set.

There'd been no rehearsal. No care. Only the bare bones thrown together: the motions, the vows, the rings.

The crowns.

Amarande swallowed and stepped to the threshold of the chapel's main hall. Renard stood on a raised dais at the front, hands clasped politely before him, wearing his prince's crown for now. The one meant for a king had been placed on a pillow on a marble pedestal behind the minister. At Renard's shoulder was Taillefer, also cutting a prim figure, as if he didn't have blood on his hands. He was smiling, of course.

All but one of the councilmen abandoned Amarande to sit by the Dowager Queen in the front row. She, too, had a crown—clearly she was not eager to relinquish it before the proper coronation. Amarande wasn't sure the woman would give it away at all.

Not that it mattered.

Renard motioned to the musicians, who scrambled mid-song to reset.

In that moment, as everyone turned their gazes to the entrance, to admire her, a royal bride swaddled in gold, Amarande's heartbeat slowed. Her eyes were completely dry. Her lungs worked in a normal pattern.

She had no friends here. None. There was not a soul from Ardenia, with the council and Koldo given no notice.

Every single person was an enemy as much as a stranger.

After she pulled her knife, one of these people would take her from this world and join her with Luca and Father—maybe even her mother, if some of the tales were true.

As the music began, the princess lifted her chin, set her eyes upon Renard, and started down the aisle. The eyes of courtiers followed her as they murmured under the cover of music, narrating the show among themselves. These people had come to witness history.

The princess would not disappoint.

Renard smiled at her now, more genteel than his brother, again as pleasant as a painting. He did not wear his ridiculous sword at his side, maybe because he didn't trust her this close. Maybe he never planned on wearing it again so long as they were married. Maybe he'd have all the sharp things within the castle rounded up and stashed away and, for the rest of their days, the two of them would eat only with spoons like they had at their farce of a dinner at the Itspi. *Coward.*

It mattered not.

Pews creaked as she swept past, the councilor at her elbow trying to slow her procession into time with the music. After failing miserably, the prune-faced man peeled off to the side and sat with the woman who was his queen for a few more minutes.

The princess settled in beside her prince.

Renard looked to her, grinning as if he couldn't help himself, and whispered to her, a show of affection for the audience, "Smile, my love."

Amarande did not.

The music ended and the star-born priest began, looking not at the royals before him but over their heads, addressing the crowd.

"Today, we join the great kingdoms of Pyrenee and Ardenia, mountain neighbors for all eternity in the Sand and Sky, but after tonight, so much more." Then from his breast pocket, the priest pulled out two simple gold rings.

There was no disguising this wedding as more than a business exchange—that much was certain.

The priest handed a ring to each of them. Amarande knew she was supposed to pass off her bouquet, but she held fast to it and no one stopped her.

"Princess Amarande, repeat after me," the priest said as much to the crowd as to her.

"Do you, Prince Renard of Pyrenee, take me, Princess Amarande of Ardenia, to be your lawfully wedded wife, in sickness and in health, in peace and wartime, with love for both our kingdoms, until death do us part?"

Amarande repeated along with the priest, face placid as she enunciated every word.

Upon the vow's completion, Renard smiled at her and then to the crowd. "I do."

She slipped a ring onto his finger.

The priest turned to Renard, giving him no further instruction.

"And do you, Princess Amarande of Ardenia, take me, Prince Renard of Pyrenee, to be your lawfully wedded husband, in sickness and in health, in peace and wartime, with love for both our kingdoms, until death do us part?"

Renard finished his vow grinning hard, waiting. The whole room was waiting—the guards, lining the stage and exit in purple and gold, the Dowager Queen and her council, Taillefer and his laughing eyes.

One word, one ring, one kiss, and then the coronation would commence.

The corners of Amarande's lips quirked up. She imagined that from the audience it looked very much like the demure grin of a certain kind of princess.

But she was not *that* princess—the kind who would smile publicly and suffer privately, like the Dowager Queen, and likely her very own mother. No, that wasn't who she was. She wouldn't sit still, nor would she run away.

She was the princess who could do it, after all.

"I would rather die."

As the words left her mouth, Amarande tossed the bouquet at the line of royal guards standing nearest the dais and the ring at the priest. The distraction gave her just enough time to draw the knife from her bodice. Renard's features flashed in recognition and horror, but he was unarmed, too stunned to move, and had never been properly trained.

In the space of a breath, her blade sliced through the air, plunging into the soft spot under his ribs.

His heart and lungs, punctured in one fell swoop.

CHAPTER 52

❧

Renard's eyes widened as Amarande withdrew the knife. He stuttered forward a step, hands blindly reaching out in shock before his knees gave out.

Though the lifeblood was red and raw and immediate, the truth of it took a full second to register.

Then chaos.

Royal guards rushed forth as the prince fell to the dais.

The Dowager Queen's shrill voice smacked the rafters with all the right words: "Kill her! Kill her! My son!"

Amarande was immediately on the move, lunging after Taillefer, who'd spun for the crowd. She dove for his knees, tumbling off the raised dais and onto the fur-lined chapel floor, in the space between the platform and the first row of pews, where Inés and her men had been seconds before. The princess landed on top of Taillefer and tried to pin his arms, but they ran roughshod around his face and neck, doing all they could to avoid an assassin's smile.

Though he'd left his chest exposed.

Two hands wrapped around her knife hilt, Amarande plunged the blade straight into the meat of his chest, eager to mark Taillefer with the same sort of evil slash he'd given Luca before he'd died.

But as the tip made contact, instead of cleaving his flesh, her blade hit something solid with a massive clang.

Steel.

A chest plate. Beneath his suit coat and tunic, Taillefer had been prepared.

The failed blow jerked the weapon from her grip, the knife slipping from her hands and clattering under the first pew.

Taillefer simply smiled at her. "I knew you could do it," was all he said, and then he shoved her hard.

He rolled to freedom as she tried to right herself, at arm's length from her knife, her fingertips swiping blindly for it. And just as she touched the familiar curve of steel, a massive hand hauled her back.

The guards of Pyrenee.

It was over. This was it. At least she would die as if she were in battle. The Warrior King's daughter, ended in a way befitting her title.

That hand lifted her up, grasping the back of her bodice as if the guard were about to hang her on the wall. The stress of it all tightened the thing, and it became harder to breathe. She hastily swung bloodstained fingers over her shoulders and back, clawing at air, trying to make contact with the grip holding her. But the angle was all wrong.

The world turned before her, the torchlight bleeding into a halo. As she gulped in her final breaths, Amarande saw that the room had mostly emptied, the well-appointed crowd flooding through the exits. Behind her, motion, as men collected Renard.

"Kill her!" the Dowager Queen screeched as her guards pulled her through the foyer and into the safety of the night and her castle at large.

Amarande's vision was failing as she struggled to breathe, the periphery falling into blackness. Someone bent beneath the bench, collecting her knife for his own. To sell it, surely. These people were all about gold, and the knife that murdered Renard at his own wedding would fetch a tidy profit.

Sparkling white joined the black circling her vision as the princess's hands began to falter in their reach for the guard who held her. Her movements slowed with her breath.

A body appeared in the shadows at the edge of her vision.

A blade shimmered in her periphery. Basilican steel. There was a reason the metal was the gold standard for every serious swordsman—its quality was unmatched. Nothing was more effective when it came to doing the worst.

Death would be quick.

Luca, I shall see you soon.

The princess closed her eyes.

The blade scraped across the skin of her throat, but strangely, she felt no pain.

Death, as it turned out, did not hurt.

Amarande felt her body drop, and she hit the floor with a thud, her frame collapsing as the press of darkness closed in, surrounding her in a shield from the chaos of what remained in life.

The princess waited for a light to come. For something to pull her from this existence into the next one.

And then she heard the whisper of a familiar voice. Smelled a whiff of lavender—and something else. Cloves. Wine.

"Ama, open your eyes."

And there was a ghost.

Luca.

Clutching her boot knife in one hand, her father's sword in the other. His face split into a smile, dimples flashing, golden eyes alive. He was bent before her, a Bellringe guard's helmet squashed over his dark hair. Next to him was Ula, her golden eyes mirroring Luca's—and her blade point sitting gently across the princess's neck.

"Can you see him?" Amarande asked the girl, who to her knowledge was not a ghost.

"Yes. He's alive and he's yours."

"Am *I* alive?"

"For now," Ula answered, removing her sword tip from the princess's throat. Vaguely then, Amarande realized the giant boy from Myrcell—Urtzi, to use his name—was at her back, his grip lessening on her bodice. Air finally flowed into her lungs. "On the count of three, Princess, we run for the exit."

"Am I playing dead?"

"No, there's been enough of that," Luca whispered. "You're cutting down as many of these bastards as possible."

"One. Two. Three."

All at once, the Myrcellian unhanded Amarande, Luca thrust her father's sword into her hand, and the group rushed down the aisle.

"Wait! The princess is alive!"

"Get them! They're helping her!"

"To the exit! The exit!"

Before her, Ula dispatched one man and then another, her curved blade making quick work. Amarande batted away a guard who came lunging toward her left. Luca sank her boot knife into the eye of one who went for his helmet, trying to throw him off-balance. From behind, Urtzi grunted as he shook off man after man.

As they sprinted through the foyer, Amarande had an idea. "The tables. Toss the food!"

The four of them spread out, each grabbing the end of a table and flipping it, sending food tumbling over the marble, wine splashing and slick. They raced around the mess and into the night. The rose garden was quieter than expected, the guards stationed outside long gone, the guests and the Dowager Queen nearly to the Bellringe's inner wall. The party moved in a rowdy swarm, looking ahead but not back at what had just happened.

"This way. Our horses are ready," Ula whispered to the princess as they turned a hard left and ran toward a hill.

In the darkness, Amarande swiped for and then clutched Luca's hand. "How are you here? I saw you, your chest, and I thought you were . . ."

"Dead?" Luca asked, dimples winking in the moonlight. "I was. Mostly. But the pirates made sure I didn't take a turn all the way."

"Your chest, does it hurt?"

"It burns like a million suns," he admitted as they charged up the hill. His stride was falling apart now as he looked at her instead of his footing. No, it was more than that: His limp had returned, and a new unsteadiness seemed to jostle him, too—a remnant of Taillefer's handicraft. He'd worked hard to keep his new scars from the surface in the chapel. She held tight to his hand. "Can't believe I'm on my feet, actually, but I couldn't let them take you."

"Never let anyone take either of us again, promise?"

"Always, Princess."

She nearly lunged at him for a kiss, but she was aware that if she did it might blow their cover and cost her the chance to ever do it again. So, instead, she whispered, "I love you."

"I love you, too, Ama."

As the princess, her love, and the pirates crested the hill, the light of a torch met them.

"Dunixi," Ula spat under her breath. Amarande had assumed the Eritrian was waiting for them with the horses, but the way the girl said his name made it very clear she didn't want to see him. And next to Ula, Urtzi searched her profile for an order, his big hands curling into fists.

Ula held up a hand.

It wasn't the leader boy—it was a girl.

The moonlight caught the blue of her eyes and the dark fall of her hair. The sword at her side shone in perfect, deadly form.

Osana.

"I know an exit, and I have food," the girl said, holding up bulging burlap sacks. Amarande recalled she'd seen the girl stationed by the spread in the foyer. "Please let me come with you?"

All three pairs of eyes shifted to Amarande, looking for confirmation or an order.

The princess nodded and Ula ushered them along. "This way."

They'd only prepared three horses, but without a word, Amarande and Luca ran to the same horse. As they mounted, the princess looked to Ula. "Where is Dunixi?" The Eritrian's name was strange on her lips.

The girl smiled. "Sleeping off his greed."

"If that's the case, he may never wake," Amarande said. She looked to Osana. "Lead us."

The girl did indeed know the way. A mountain stream had eroded the wall surrounding the Bellringe deep behind the stable. The sliver of missing stone was just large enough for a fit horse to scoot through, and hidden by a weeping boulder. Through the wall and onto the other side and they were in a ravine that had clearly been used as a road. Koldo loomed in Amarande's mind as they crept out, telling her to catalog every inch under the waning light of the moon.

If Father's maps didn't hold this secret route out of the Bellringe and off King's Crest, she would see to it that it was added. And, if it came to it, used later.

Amarande settled in, Luca's arms about her waist. She wished for the warmth of his chest at her back, but he kept his distance; the press of any weight against his wound would be too much. Their return to the Itspi would be just as she'd pictured it before they'd been intercepted by Renard—Luca to Medikua Aritza's workshop first to disinfect and redress his wound. Then to the Royal Council to prepare for what was to come.

The ravine bled out into a mountain pass, where, if it were daytime, they could easily see for miles. But in the pressing dark, all they saw was the flicker of torches on the main road below—winding down from the Bellringe. It was the one they'd taken up to the castle and the one they would need to follow to return to Ardenia.

"The castle has sent a party out looking for us," Amarande said. The others nodded. "They will alert the camps at the border and no road we take will be safe."

"Good thing we have a ship," Urtzi answered.

True, not that it did them any good.

"I'm afraid it can't help us much if it's on the other side of the continent, Urtzi," Luca said in his kind way.

"Luca, did you really believe everything we told you?" Ula asked, her eyes alight.

"Well, I didn't really believe you had a ship at all, *land pirates*, but I'm giving Urtzi the benefit of the doubt at the moment."

In response, Ula held up a small slip of paper. "We have a ship. We have the harbor receipt for the Port of Pyrenee. Which happens to be this way." Ula pointed to a sliver of trail that went opposite the path that snaked through to the main road and the Pyrenee search party. Then she held out the slip so that Amarande and Luca could read the ink scratch in the moonlight.

It was truly a harbor receipt. Amarande smiled—yes, this was genius. "They can search every inch of these mountains, but they won't find us if we're on the water."

Pyrenee would exhaust itself searching the mountains in vain before regrouping and declaring war—considering the political complications of what Renard was trying to achieve with the wedding, the stakes with the other players in the Sand and Sky in all-out war would be a delicate thing.

The princess pointed her horse for the Port of Pyrenee. "The ship. The water. The Itspi. And then revenge."

CHAPTER 53

※❦※

But it wasn't that simple. Of course it wasn't.

Obtaining the ship wasn't the problem—Ula's slip and one diamond from Amarande's pouch did the trick.

No, it was after all that. By the time they'd loaded the horses, resupplied the food, water, and oats, and shoved out of the harbor, it was past midnight.

Under the stars, the ship, called *Gatzal*, angled toward the Divide—a waterway with sheer cliffs on either side. On one side, Pyrenee and the continent of the Sand and Sky. The other, Eritri and the mass of endless mountains beyond.

The waters here were so deep they seemed to well from the center of the earth itself, this gash drawn straight through a mountain range, doubly deep as it was tall. As if the stars in their wisdom had plucked up a dagger and carved straight through the face of the world, cleaving out an eye, blade dragging on bone.

Exhaustion hit Luca fast, the pain catching up as his adrenaline fled. The princess and Urtzi led him to the ship's captain's quarters. There, safely resting in an actual bed, Amarande undid his dressings and applied clove oil Ula had squirreled away, and he was out in five minutes, resting his head in the princess's lap as he had done in Naiara's carriage.

After a few minutes, Amarande gently propped him on a pillow and excused herself to the wash bucket, eager to finally remove Renard's blood from her dress.

Even when the blood was gone, she knew she'd feel it, the weight of her first kill sinking below the stain to the silk and her skin. If she blinked too long, she could still see the look on Renard's face when the knifepoint made contact—the shock, the recognition of what could not be undone.

Amarande had only made two passes with the rag, getting nowhere on the golden silk, when Ula appeared at her elbow. The girl's face was drawn and serious in a way it hadn't been even when she was fighting for her life. The joy of battle wasn't there, but instead another thing entirely. Apprehension? Worry? Or perhaps . . . hope?

"I have something you need to hear."

Amarande nodded and Ula didn't hesitate, leaning in, her voice low and flaring with her eyes.

"Princess, believe me when I tell you I do not say this lightly . . . the ink on Luca's chest? It's the sign of the black wolf—the Otxoa."

The princess stilled—movement, blood, breath.

The five points of ink bled into her vision. She'd always thought it a funny star, poorly drawn on a wiggly babe.

But now the face of the wolf she'd seen on the plateau pushed through, features lining up with the collapsed pentagram. Snout, jawline, ears.

Amarande's lips parted, but no words escaped.

"I do not share this to raise your hopes, as mine are already to the stars." Ula's voice rushed with barely a breath drawn between words. "But there have been rumors for a long while now that the Otxoa had one final son before it all fell apart. No one ever saw the child or could confirm it, but . . . ink like that has had the same meaning for a thousand years. I believe Luca to be the Otsakumea."

Something shot through Amarande at the word, her breath catching, as her mind scrabbled at Ula's words. *No.* It couldn't be.

Her lips barely formed the words, her eyes shooting from the dark windows of the captain's quarters back to Ula. This girl she now trusted with her life. "The wolf cub?"

"Yes. Torrence's rightful king."

From stillness, Amarande's body jolted back into working order. Her heart quickened its pace, her head suddenly light. Maybe this was why her father had never healed the Torrent. It wasn't that her mother was the Warlord—though the woman in the shadows of the Warlord's camp still stuck in Amarande's mind—it was that he'd been shielding the rightful ruler of Torrence all these years. Giving him lessons on reading, allowing him to learn to fight. Maybe this too was why he hadn't worried over changing the laws of succession. Because he believed by the time Amarande was ready to rule, someone she loved like family would be a ruler himself.

The princess felt this like a truth, as tangible as her pounding heart. Her father was wise and never shortsighted.

"Does he know?"

Ula shook her head. "I haven't told him. But there's an underground movement of those who want to reinstall the family. I could connect him and challenge the Warlord's rule."

The clarity of what this meant hit Amarande in that moment. It was a long road, but the change it could bring . . . King Sendoa came to her again: *Survive the battle, see the war.*

The princess was bone tired, but suddenly she was ready to run, to go, to fight.

"We could heal the Torrent," Amarande whispered, words gaining steam with each breath. "And give Ardenia a powerful ally against the wrath of the Pyrenee and the greed of the southern kingdoms."

And, no matter the law, she would have her prince and love in one.

EPILOGUE

THE Itspi without its king or princess was a quiet place. In the days following the funeral and all that came after, the visitors fled, the soldiers, too, leaving a skeleton crew of those who only circulated at the most intimate levels of the castle.

The maids. The cooks. The council.

Those left waiting for word, going about their duties in an anxious daze, every unexpected sound an imagined threat of war on the Itspi's doorstep. The Warrior King was still lying in state, rotting away and unable to defend what he built. Even his swords were gone and missing.

But one morning, the silence bent toward a low hum until the whispers rose to deafening.

At the gates, a rider swaddled in the copper exhale of the Torrent.

It wasn't the princess, or even Prince Renard or his minder, Captain Serville. No, it was someone else, surfaced from the abyss of absence.

Slight form. Dark hair. Blue eyes.

They knew her in an instant, though it had been fifteen years.

The Runaway Queen.

"I request to see the Royal Council. Now."

The north tower sprang to life, no hesitation. Satordi, Garbine, and Joseba were summoned from breakfast and straight to the council room. General Koldo, back to report from the front, was summoned as well, this visit more than falling under the duty of her regency.

The Runaway Queen was already in the room when the council entered, her riding gloves plucked off as she examined the scrolls left upon the council table—marriage contracts.

"It's no wonder my daughter ran off—these stipulations are ridiculous. A military state in Ardenia until a male heir is born? She's sixteen and she's been signed away as a broodmare with war on her shoulders."

The council scooted around the table. On gestured orders from Satordi, Joseba scooped up the scrolls and removed them. The Runaway Queen smiled. Satordi met her expression with something of his own, filled with brisk annoyance yet reverence— because the last time they were in the same room, this woman had worn a crown.

"Geneva, my lady, you forfeited your title long ago. Therefore, if you will excuse me, I will not address you as Queen."

She was Domingu's granddaughter by his third marriage and had been raised as a connection to be bought and sold. That upbringing sat heavy on her slim shoulders, and though she was as petite as her daughter, she had learned very early to hold a room as if it balanced on her palm. Her long absence hadn't diminished that talent.

"Fine. I did not come here to discuss such trifles."

"Yes, why are you here, my lady?" Satordi pounced. He liked to claim ownership of meetings in this room, even ones he did not call.

"I came to discuss succession. My daughter is missing, yes? You can confirm this news?"

"Princess Amarande is missing, it's true, my lady." Satordi bristled. They were teetering on the abyss of a dead line, and he didn't want this woman who'd abandoned her station and her kingdom to believe she stood a chance. If that was what she'd come for, she would be sorely disappointed. "Until the princess returns and marries for her crown, General Koldo is regent. The general is within the Itspi and is on her way here, though I'm not sure it's necessary to continue, as there is no need to discuss succession with you—"

"Permanent succession is indeed a discussion I wish to be a part of."

Satordi sucked in a stiff breath and launched into a more pointed statement.

"I apologize if you came all this way—from wherever you were—to discuss this, because there may be a misunderstanding on your part." Here, he stood, the implication clear—he was about to come around the table and escort her out. "My lady, a woman cannot rule on her own, as you know, and you have not the blood for this crown."

Geneva didn't move other than to grin again. "I don't, but he does."

The council room doors opened and in came General Koldo, donning fresh garnet and gold, and on her arm . . . a boy.

Sunset hair.

Green eyes.

A body built for battle though he'd yet to sprout a beard.

Satordi's breath died out and his eyes swung to Geneva, who stood much taller than she had right to, a little smirk about her lips. The other councilors stilled to stone in their seats, and Satordi's knees locked to keep him upright as he asked the necessary question: "Did you have a son with King Sendoa, my lady?"

"No, but she did."

Geneva gestured to Koldo.

"General?" was all the lead councilor could force himself to ask. Behind him, he heard Garbine mutter, "A bastard?" under her breath.

Koldo lifted her chin, as proud as ever. "This is Ferdinand, my child with Sendoa. Born more than fifteen years ago. I had him while on injury leave at the Itspi. The king was on the front, aiding Pyrenee as they fought an invasion by the Eritrians."

The Divide Conflict—where Sendoa was when his young queen vanished. The council knew what was coming next. The pieces were falling into place.

The Runaway Queen drew in a deep breath. "Upon learning of his birth, I worried about my daughter's place and future—mine, too. Sendoa loved Koldo in a way he could love no one else. His lack of marriage all these years is proof of that."

Satordi found his voice. "Did he want to marry you, General?"

"He asked, but I said no. More than once. I always rebuffed him—at first because I didn't want to be queen, and later because I worried my son would die if I did."

All eyes shifted to Geneva for confirmation of the last missing piece.

"I wanted to protect my daughter, who wasn't even a year old. I did not think of anything other than that. And, out of love, I did something horrible." She paused and not a soul breathed. "I stole away Koldo's child and fled from the castle. Blackmail literally in my arms, and my daughter's claim safe."

As Geneva spoke, the council shifted in their seats, eyes bouncing from her to Koldo to this boy who indeed was the spitting image of his father. His nose was like Koldo's, and the set of his stance, too—pin straight—but there was no denying who this boy's father was.

"I ran him to the stable, intent on stealing a horse. It was past midnight; the woman who kept the stable was awake, her toddler fussing. But I couldn't have her tell the castle where I'd gone and what I'd done." She lowered her eyes. "And so . . . I ensured she didn't."

The stableboy's mother long had been thought to have succumbed to sickness, her body found blue in the face, her son tucked away in their shared bed. She'd had a cough since the day she'd arrived in refuge at the castle. The boy was quickly adopted by the Itspi's other Torrentian refugees, and his mother's death wasn't interpreted as anything more than simply a tragedy, further speculation lost to the drama of the queen's disappearance. The Runaway Queen looked away as the truth became plain.

"After the frenzy of escaping with this tiny baby caught up with me and I realized what I'd done—to the baby, to Koldo, to the stable woman—I nearly came back. I was eighteen and terrified of my own decisions." Geneva's eyes shot up, ringed in dark blue. "But the truth was what the rumors have always whispered since—I wasn't happy in my arranged marriage. I wanted to find love. What I didn't know was that my heart would be filled while raising someone else's son."

Satordi's attention turned to Koldo. "Were you aware she had taken your child?"

The general nodded at once. "Yes. Not in the first moments, but when the queen was reported missing, it became obvious. Then the letters began to arrive."

Koldo reached into her cloak. Then she presented a scrap of parchment, yellowed and frayed. She held it out so that it could be read but didn't let go of it—or the boy's arm.

Keep the princess safe, teach her to rule, allow her to be fierce, and your son will live. Fail her and you fail him.

There was no signature, but it was not needed.

Satordi looked up from the parchment. "Are there more?"

"There were, in need of cipher usually—but I've burned all but this one." She paused. "Councilor, can I be frank?"

Satordi nodded.

"I—I'm not a sentimental woman. I can't be, with my path in life. But I am a human being, and though I knew it was dangerous to keep this letter, I did. I needed to remind myself that what happened wasn't just a dream."

Here, Koldo turned to Ferdinand. Her face, hard with the experience of seeing war so close and so often, softened in a way that none of the councilors had previously witnessed—and Koldo had been by Sendoa's side for more than twenty years. His favorite from her very first days in the yard.

After a moment, Garbine broke her silence. "General, you never showed your letters to the king? Or told him you'd birthed a son? Did he even know you were with child?"

"I didn't tell him, but we all know he was not stupid. And this castle has eyes."

That was true—and though Geneva hadn't gone into detail, even she had found out quickly about the bastard in the general's chambers.

"Those eyes did not inform this council." Satordi looked to both women now. "Who knows?"

Geneva's jaw stiffened. "It matters not—you're diving into long-dead weeds, Satordi. What matters now is that my daughter is missing, and though I am begging the stars for her safe return, Ardenia needs a ruler. A permanent one, or invasion isn't just possible, it's footsteps from happening—Koldo has seen it herself."

The general nodded, gravely. "Before returning to the Itspi, I personally dispatched soldiers attempting to poison the water source of our southern military encampment." Koldo pulled a small vial from her trousers and held it up. "Pure, distilled hemlock."

There was a sharp intake of breath from all three councilors at once. Koldo's description of Sendoa's last moments replayed just then—a sip of water, a cough, death.

"Though this specimen came from Basilica," Koldo explained, "the princess was correct when she characterized Myrcell as having the highest concentration of hemlock in the Sand and Sky." Satordi's jaw worked as the general continued, measured and clear—it wasn't the full investigation the princess had ordered, but it was damning nonetheless. "I have every reason to think either kingdom, or both, may poison our water sources as a way to circumvent all-out war with our superior army. I am honored to lead as regent, but without proper succession we are vulnerable to great danger."

Silence hung over the room, a shroud.

After a dark moment, the Runaway Queen turned and snatched the boy's hand. He was bracketed now by his two mothers: The one who birthed him and the one who raised him. On their guidance, the boy took a step forward, eyes trained carefully on the councilors before him—polite yet powerful, his shoulders back and straight.

Geneva lifted her chin and looked down at them like the queen she once was.

"I have brought you a king in everything but name. Make him one."

ACKNOWLEDGMENTS

First and foremost, this book would not have been possible without the undying support of my agent, Whitney Ross.

Whitney is not my first agent, and while we were still in the "getting to know you" period of our relationship, I sent her an email with the subject line "A question and an idea" in which I, a little *too* enthusiastically, vomited out the idea for what would eventually become *The Princess Will Save You*. We'd known each other less than a month, and I probably sounded a little *overwhelming* in that email, truth be told. But rather than run away from my "gender-swapped *Princess Bride*" thing, she simply replied, "I LOVE that idea," and we were off to the races. Whitney then proceeded to sell four books in six months, including this one and its sequel, and guide me through the steeplechase that is debut year, all without batting an eye. I am so grateful to have her steady presence, knowledge, and dedication in my corner.

Next, this book wouldn't be what it is without the thoughtful, loving, and sharp-eyed editing by Melissa Frain. At this point, I've had quite a few sets of editorial notes in my life, and Melissa's were the first to make me laugh out loud so hard that the cats woke up to take a look. She immediately got exactly what I was trying to do with the story, the characters, the world—*everything*—and supported my vision in every way possible while using humor and enthusiasm as tools to push me to make it all even better. Writers, get yourself an editor whose in-letter and in-manuscript reactions make you nearly spit out your coffee with glee.

Thank you to the other behind-the-scenes geniuses at Tor Teen and Macmillan, including: my copy editor, Barbara Wild, who taught me "daresay" is one word, among other things; Matthew Rusin for guiding the copy and graphics safely through the journey of production; and Lauren Levite for the publicity love. And, to the rest of the Tor Teen/Macmillan team, thank you for your hospitality and love—I appreciate every one of you.

Artist extraordinaire Charlie Bowater, thank you so very much for your gorgeous cover. I am flabbergasted at how you made Amarande and Luca come alive with all the fierceness and love they have for each other while managing to detail the unforgiving nature of the Torrent. You've hit upon something special, and I feel incredibly lucky to have had your imagination meet mine.

Thank you to those of you who held my hand and worked alongside me as this book went from idea to reality. Julie Tollefson, Megan Bannen, Rebecca Coffindaffer, Natalie Parker, Tessa Gratton, Amanda Sellet—all of you were there in my texts and at my side as I wrote this book in the spaces between working on two other projects. You were ready with chocolate, wine, and emoji-faced assurance (even at 5 a.m.), and I don't know what I'd do without you. And to the rest of our robust Kansas/Kansas City writer crew, thank you, too. We are so very lucky.

Many thanks to my running buddies, but most especially Nicole Green, Laurie Euler, and Sharah Davis, who listened to me across the miles as I wrote this. Your ears and wisdom mean everything.

And, to save the best for last: my family. Thank you to my parents, Craig and Mary Warren, who support me no matter what;

and to Em, who always makes me laugh. Thank you, Justin, who carries the weight of family obligations when projects become intense and doesn't complain a lick—and looks good while doing it. And thank you to Nate and Amalia for your patience and pride in Mommy's work. I love all of you, always.